D0400991

Ace Books by S. K. Dunstall

LINESMAN
ALLIANCE

ALLIANCE

S. K. DUNSTALL

ACE BOOKS, NEW YORK

ACE

An imprint of Penguin Random House LLC
375 Hudson Street, New York, New York 10014

ALLIANCE

An Ace Book / published by arrangement with the authors

ISBN: 978-0-425-27953-3

PUBLISHING HISTORY
Ace mass-market edition / March 2016

PRINTED IN THE UNITED STATES OF AMERICA

10 9 8 7 6 5 4 3 2 1

Cover art by Bruce Jensen.
Cover design by Diana Kolsky.
Interior text design by Kelly Lipovich.

Penguin
Random
House

ACKNOWLEDGMENTS

Once again, there are some wonderful people who helped to make this book what it is, and without them we would not have the book we have now.

Our agent, Caitlin Blasdell, who does not shy away from telling us when something doesn't work. We need this.

Anne Sowards, our editor, who once again turned our book into a better story than it would have been otherwise.

Sara Schwager, our copy editor, who did such a brilliant job of cleaning up our manuscript.

Bruce Jensen. We love your covers. May there be many more.

To everyone else toiling away in the background putting this book together and getting it out there. We know you are there doing all this work, and we appreciate it, even if we can't name you individually.

Mum, for sitting through the read-throughs again and for being there. Jenny, for being so enthusiastic when you read the story; and Leigh, who has supported us throughout, for understanding what these books mean to us, how much we put into them, and for celebrating our successes with us.

We can't not mention our beta readers, Arthur McMullen and Neil Martin. Your feedback is invaluable. And to Dawn McMullen, for being such a great friend and for arranging it all.

Helen Montgomery, for taking care of our garden and turning it from an overgrown weed patch back into a pleasant place to be. We couldn't weed and write; you gave us time to write.

Last but definitely not least, to all our readers. Your generous feedback for *Linesman* was unexpected and warming. You are amazing. We hope you enjoy this book just as much.

Thank you, each and every one of you.

NEW ALLIANCE DEPARTMENT OF ALIEN AFFAIRS— LIST OF LINES AND THEIR PURPOSES

LINE	REPRESENTS
1	Health of crew and lines
2	Small mechanics 1—air circulation, heating, cooling, power. Overall comfort and running of a ship.
3	Small mechanics 2—tools. Interact individually with other lines for repair, maintenance, management.
4	Gravity
5	Communications
6	Bose engines (engines with the capacity to take a ship through the void)
7	*Unknown*
8	Security
9	Takes ship into the void
10	Moves ship to a different location in space while in the void
11	Links ships together. Allows them to move/behave as a single unit.
12	Actual abilities unclear, but known to communicate across all lines and appears to have some control over other lines

ONE

SELMA KARI WANG

CAPTAIN SELMA KARI WANG didn't recognize the deep tone that cut across the ship comms. At least, not initially.

"I'll call you back," she said to her chief engineer, who had been explaining an issue with line five. He couldn't possibly have heard her over the loud tones, but he nodded anyway.

It was only when First Councilor—dressed in full council regalia—came on-screen that she realized what the sound was.

"Council announcement, people," Kari Wang said through her comms. "All hands, listen up."

They had never had a council announcement in all the years she'd been in the fleet.

"It must be serious," Will, her third-in-command, muttered sotto voce to Narelma, the comms officer. "I've never seen First Councilor in formal dress before."

Kari Wang had. Once. At First Councilor's swearing-in ceremony. She'd been young, straight out of academy, "honored" to stand guard beside the new councilor all day—in full dress uniform herself—on a day that sweltered at forty degrees Celsius in the shade. It had been the worst day of Kari Wang's life. She'd kept praying she wouldn't faint.

At the end of it all, the councilor had asked for iced water for them both. "I don't know who was going to collapse first out there," she'd said, fanning a thin piece of plastic to create a wind. "You or me."

Kari Wang had sipped iced water gratefully.

"Thank you, Spacer," and First Councilor had bowed to her, although she hadn't been First Councilor then, of course, only Tenth.

Kari Wang had spent the next three days in bed with sunstroke. She hadn't seen the woman again—except on the vids.

A long time had passed since then. Selma Kari Wang was a captain now, with her own ship, while Agda Ayemann was First Councilor.

"Citizens of Nova Tahiti," First Councilor said, and her voice was steady, if somber.

This same message was going out to millions of other people across the galaxy at the same time.

Had gone out, Kari Wang corrected herself, because they were in a different sector from Nova Tahiti, and the message would have been relayed.

"I am delighted to inform you," First Councilor said, "that Nova Tahiti has seceded from Gate Union to become a founding member of the New Alliance of Worlds."

Standing on the bridge, listening, Kari Wang didn't believe her to begin with. Yes, they'd had problems with Gate Union. Yes, the Nova Tahitian fleet had been irritated with Gate Union's tactics and the way Gate Union was trying to push them away from having any real power. But seceding from the most powerful political union in the galaxy didn't happen overnight.

Not until a coded, high-security message flashed on-screen. For her eyes only. She held her comms up to scan her irises, then read the message that came up.

Nova Tahiti Admiralty informs all ships that Nova Tahiti has seceded from Gate Union, effective immediately. All captains to implement immediate change of codes to Nova Tahiti native. There is to be no further exchange of classified information between Nova Tahitian ships and Gate Union. Personnel involved in Gate-Union-led initiatives are to return to their own ships immediately. Further information to follow. Repeat, all captains to implement immediate change of codes.

It was true.

Kari Wang looked up to the screen, where First Councilor smiled, although the exhaustion showed through, and the smile cracked at the end. What in the lines was going on?

"I am sure you will all join with me in looking forward to our new future," First Councilor said.

The ship rang with a final boong-boing-bong as the councilor signed off.

It was so silent on the bridge, Kari Wang could hear the air circulating. Will, intense and focused, turned to her. She held up a hand and turned on shipwide comms of her own.

"This is the captain speaking. I have had confirmation from Admiralty that Nova Tahiti has indeed seceded from Gate Union. I am about to commence a change of codes. Please note that as of now, there is to be no further exchange of classified information between Nova Tahiti and Gate Union. I repeat. No further exchange of classified information between Nova Tahiti and Gate Union. I will provide further information as it comes to hand."

She clicked off and started to implement the change of codes. This was something she'd never had to do before, outside of training. Luckily, the instructions had been drilled into her as soon as she became ship captain and redrilled every time she went back for training.

"We're not at war with them, are we?" Will asked. "I mean, what about the testing we're doing? Are we going to deliver the results?"

The GU *Kari Wang* was out near the rim, testing top secret warheads. Given the fragile relations between the factions in Gate Union, Kari Wang had been surprised a Nova Tahitian ship had been chosen to test them, but she'd been pleased, too. It was an acknowledgment that many of her crew were weapons experts—especially Will, who was a leader in the field of weapons used in space warfare. She hadn't realized how fragile those relations were.

"Nothing until we get further orders," she said.

Kelan McGill, her second-in-command, who'd been off duty, came in then, hair still tousled from sleep.

"Kelan, Will, you are in charge. I'm going to walk around the ship. Call me when something comes through." No one would call for a while. Who would bother with a ship out so far, with no one for parsecs, when half the Nova Tahitian fleet was actively working with other worlds in Gate Union?

Her crew were subdued and contemplative, not sure what was happening. Neither was she.

She was honest. "All I've got is official confirmation," she told them. "I wasn't expecting it, and I don't think Admiralty was either. As soon as I have more news, I'll tell you."

By the time she was done and back on the bridge, ship mood was a little brighter.

KARI Wang asked for further information and instructions and was told to wait. News dribbled in, mostly through the media, which you couldn't believe anyway. Not only that, the news that came was not often about the formation of the New Alliance. For an alien fleet had been discovered at the confluence, and the media ran with that.

Their rec screens were filled with images of alien ships, and speculation about the—presumed dead—aliens themselves. Who would have thought that a breakdown of the two main political entities in the galaxy could be second-run news.

"*I'm* more interested in the aliens," Will said, when they discussed it the next night at dinner. "Everyone is."

Kari Wang agreed, but as captain, the political situation was more important to her and the well-being of her crew. "I just wish they'd tell us something."

"Look at it this way," Will said. "We're New Alliance. We've got the alien ships." For the New Alliance had claimed them. "Maybe they'll assign us to them later on," and his deep-set brown eyes sparkled at the possibility.

New Alliance. The words left a nasty taste in Kari Wang's mouth. Two days ago, fifty of the seventy worlds that made up the New Alliance had been their enemy. What had caused such a cataclysmic shift in power? Surely, it couldn't just be access to alien ships. Or could it?

"It doesn't put us in any better position." Although she tried not to be pessimistic. She'd heard rumors of factions in Gate Union, but she'd thought her home world would come out on top. After all, they had First Councilor on Nova Tahiti, and Ahmed Gann on the Gate Union Council itself, both of whom were strong political negotiators. If any world could come out well, it was Nova Tahiti. It was said Gann could make or break Union worlds by casting his vote.

Yet here he was, on the news, smiling alongside First Councilor, and if Kari Wang was any judge of smiles, Gann's was a lot broader and happier than First Councilor's was.

WITH nothing else to do, she kept her crew busy setting up the warheads for the next round of testing, along with the regular drills and activities that always took place on ship.

Life settled back into some sort of normality. Eat, sleep, work, and wait for news.

She asked Will to organize a triball tournament to keep them busy. Six teams of thirty players. Each team played the other twice, and the winners would be decided in a playoff of the top two teams. If they didn't have time to think, they wouldn't have as much time to worry.

That was Kari Wang's job.

Sixty-two hours after the initial announcement, Medic Halliday called her up. "You're scheduled for some suit time. Do you want me to cancel it?"

In space, there were some things you did automatically, and some things you did over and over, so it became automatic. Every member of the GU *Kari Wang*—or the *Kari Wang* now, she supposed—had to spend time in a space suit, and in space. Including the captain.

"No." Normality was good. "I'll do it now."

In fact, she was looking forward to it.

It seemed to her the ship was looking forward to it as well.

Kari Wang laughed and patted the lockers, then looked around guiltily to be sure no one had seen her.

"Don't worry. It's normal for captains to show outward signs of affection to their ship," Medic Halliday said from behind her, half frightening the life out of her. "Touching, talking to it. They've done studies on it." He handed over his comms. "Thumbprint here, please. You have three hours out there. Come in when I call, or I'll send someone out for you."

Kari Wang pulled on her suit. "You're making that up. About the study."

"Not at all. A scientist called Abarca. One of those happy accidents they always talk about. Got himself a lover who was a ship captain. Found it annoying the way the captain used to talk to her ship, fondle it. Or so the story goes. They had a fight over it. Captain says something like, 'Don't come between me and my ship.' It split them up, but this scientist was quite turned on by captains." Halliday wiggled his eyebrows. "If you know what I mean."

She laughed at him, not sure if he was having her on. Captain groupies were a famous trope on the vids, but she'd never met one in real life.

"True story, this. Got himself another captain and shock, horror, what does this captain do but go around talking to her ship and patting it in odd places."

"What's wrong with patting a locker?"

"If you don't know, sir, I'm not the one to enlighten you. Anyway, by this time, the scientist in him was getting interested. He sought out another captain."

"What? Another partner?"

"I'm not sure. But this captain had the same predilections as the other two. A paper, as they say, was born. I'll send you the details."

Kari Wang was still laughing as she exited the air lock.

Outside was nothing but stars and the emptiness of space. All around her. It was grand and humbling at the same time. Up and behind the ship, the blue-and-green solar winds of the Edamon binaries flowed across space. She imagined she could hear it roar. She couldn't, of course. That was the air circulating in her suit.

"Suit's good," she said to Halliday. "Starting standard exercises now. Moving away from the ship. Going out thirty minutes."

Some spacers couldn't take space at all. Others could take it, provided they were close to the safety of their parent ship. Neither was useful to a spacer who one day might find him- or herself out in space with no ship in sight.

"Measuring heart, lungs, temperature," Halliday said. "Are you ready for maneuvers?"

Maneuvers was a set of acrobatic exercises they practiced both in the suit, in space, and on ship, in the gym. A spacer needed to be able to move accurately in a suit because a miniscule miss when you couldn't stop could mean the difference between safety and drifting forever in space.

Kari Wang was good at maneuvers, on ship and in space. She was accurate and agile.

The familiarity of the drill centered her. She felt calmer than she had since the announcement. No matter what happened, she still had her ship, she still had her crew.

In her helmet, she could hear the chatter from the bridge. There were two topics of conversation. Or one, rather, with passing references to the other.

"They called one of the ships the *Eleven*." Narelma was on comms. "They say that's because it's a new line. An eleven."

Kelan McGill was on bridge this shift. "That's just propaganda. If there was another line, why haven't we discovered it before?"

"Because we didn't know it existed."

A dark shape suddenly obscured the stars in front of Kari Wang. She pulled up midtumble, trying to work out what it was.

The chatter from the bridge continued. "There's no line eleven because it's a new line."

Then she realized. It was a ship.

Kari Wang opened her suit comms and cut across the chatter. "What in the lines are you doing on the bridge? Why hasn't someone said there's a ship out here yet?"

The talk stopped.

"No, ma'am," Kelan said after a two-second delay to check the boards. "There's no ship out there."

Another black patch appeared among the stars.

"There are two ships out here now," Kari Wang said. She gave the coordinates as she fired her jets to raise herself above the ship. Sure enough, there was a black patch on the other side. "Three. Find them."

She triggered the alarm herself and fired her jets on a long, wasteful spurt of fuel to get back to the air lock faster. "Coming back in," she told Halliday.

It would take ten minutes to get to the air lock. "Somebody find those damn ships."

"Looking, ma'am," Kelan said. "Still nothing."

What could hide a ship so well that only the naked eye could see it? "I don't like the way they're positioning themselves," Kari Wang said. It looked like an attack pattern to her. "Get our gunners ready." She gave coordinates of the third ship.

"Although I have no idea how far away from us they are." Visual references were almost useless in space when you had nothing to relate them to.

She heard the order go out, felt the ship mood change. Five minutes to get back, and she'd never felt so helpless in her life.

Four minutes.

"Still no—" Kelan said, then, "Shit. They've uncloaked." Alarms started clamoring. "That's some cloaking device. And it's four ships, not three." He opened the comms. "Gunners, you'd better be ready."

"Warn them," Kari Wang said. She didn't want to kill anyone by accident, especially not a former friend turned enemy. Or even a former enemy turned friend, if it came to that.

Kelan's voice came strong over the comms. "This is the GU . . . the *Kari Wang*. We are a working warship and armed. Please identify yourself."

Will said, out of breath, into Kari Wang's private comms. "They're equidistant from us and each other. It's too much of a coincidence to be natural." She guessed he had run to get to the bridge.

Three minutes back to ship.

She checked the positions on the screen in her suit helmet. Their symmetry made a perfect triangular pyramid, with the *Kari Wang* at the center.

"Identify yourself," Kelan repeated.

The four ships disappeared.

"They jumped," Kelan said.

Kari Wang didn't like it. They'd been too well positioned to be doing anything other than targeting her ship. She arrived at the air lock—at last—and waited impatiently while it cycled through.

"See if you can find out what they did." She didn't wait to remove her space suit, just released the helmet, so it dropped down her back, and ran for the bridge, clumsy as it was. "I want to move the ship out of the direct line of anything those four ships might have fired at us. Get me some coordinates." Just because they couldn't see it coming didn't mean there wasn't anything. It had been a deliberate attack pattern.

"New coordinates 230.113.144," her navigator said.

Everyone was calm. Even the ship seemed settled. They'd done this before, they were used to it. That was good.

She checked where the move would put them. Well away from any danger. "Move us now," and as she arrived on the bridge, she compensated automatically for the momentary change in gravity that accompanied the thrust of jets.

"We managed to identify the ships before they jumped," Will said. "GU *Byers*, GU *Haralampiev*, GU *van Andringa*, and the GU *Akaki*."

All combat class. Small ships, with crews of twenty or less. It smelled to Kari Wang like a quick hit-and-run.

The ship bucked. The board readings went crazy.

The presence that was the ship inside Kari Wang's mind disappeared.

"By its signature, they've surrounded us in a Masson field," Will said. "That's what it feels like. But it's too big."

The largest known Masson field was a meter in diameter. Large enough to chop any unwary body into pieces if you stepped into it. This was impossible magnitudes larger. Except . . . a Masson field did work around four equidistant points. If that was the case, then coming toward them was a massive flux capable of chopping the whole ship into pieces.

"Set the emergency jump," Kari Wang said. Every fleet ship had an emergency jump set. One that would get them out of trouble. "Jump as soon as you can." She pushed away the worry that the jump would be sabotaged. After all, they'd been Gate Union ships. Who knew what they'd meet at the other end?

How long did they have?

She felt the ship respond sluggishly to Kelan's request and knew, even before he said it, that they couldn't make the jump. "Lines aren't responding, ma'am."

It solved the question of what happened to the lines inside a Masson field, anyway. They were damaged. No one had ever made the field large enough to test that before. She didn't realize she'd placed her hand on the line chassis and whispered comfortingly to it—not until she saw Will's quick look.

A Masson field was made up of a network of force lines that undulated in long sine waves between the four nodes. The waves sliced through any matter in its way. That included metal and ceramics, which was the basic makeup of all ships.

Maybe the size of this one could help them. How far apart would the waves be?

"We'll skip between the force lines," she decided. "Jensen," to her navigator.

Jensen nodded, fingers dancing over the board.

But they were out of time. The wave sliced through the bridge like a hot wire through wax, chopping the ship into neat-edged pieces. Kari Wang's second-last conscious thought, as the wave caught her at the knees, was that they would never have been able to dodge the field. The sections were too small.

Her last conscious thought was that her space suit had automatically sealed itself.

TWO

EAN LAMBERT

EAN LAMBERT WAS on the *Lancastrian Princess*, halfway through his voice lesson with Messire Gospetto—self-proclaimed vocal trainer to the famous—when Captain Helmo announced through the speakers, "All staff. Parade assembly on the shuttle deck."

Ship lines had been melancholy all day, but at that they dipped to a cold, bitter low Ean could taste. He checked the lines. Michelle was in the workroom she and Admiral Abram Galenos shared, knuckles pressed against her mouth in an uncharacteristic display of uncertainty. She glanced toward the speaker, took a deep breath, and exited the room.

Gospetto threw up his hands. "How am I supposed to work with this going on?" Ean knew by now that the theatrics were all for effect.

"That's us," Radko said. "I'm sorry, Messire Gospetto. We'll have to cut this session short. I'll escort you back to your shuttle."

Which was, of course, bound to get him moving fast because all the action was on the shuttle deck. Ean wondered if Radko had done that deliberately.

They made good time, but when they got there, Radko had to subtly coerce Gospetto into his own shuttle, and he resisted. It was only when Ean moved toward him that he backed away hurriedly. Ean had once accidentally used the lines to throw Gospetto across the room, and the voice coach had never forgotten it.

"We'll have to remember that trick next time we want him to leave," Radko said, as they hurried down to shuttle bay six, where the soldiers were lined up with parade-ground precision outside the air lock.

It was bad enough people's thinking Ean was strange. He didn't want them scared of him, too. Although Gospetto had spent days in the hospital because of it.

They were last into line.

Captain Helmo and his senior staff stood to one side. Michelle stood with them, any uncertainty hidden behind what Ean thought of as her politician's face.

Ship mood was somber.

"Linesman Lambert." It took a moment for Ean to realize the words were coming through line one, that Helmo was speaking to him. Could a captain do that?

He turned to look at Helmo.

"With us, please," and Helmo inclined his head.

Ean slipped out of line.

The air lock opened. Two hundred soldiers snapped to attention.

Ean slid in behind Helmo as Abram walked out with a woman who wore commodore's pips. Two hundred soldiers saluted.

The woman's gaze stopped at Ean—the only one who hadn't saluted—before moving on to the captain. "Commodore Jiang Vega, Chief of Security for Crown Princess Michelle of Lancia, requesting permission to come aboard."

They'd known it was coming. Abram's promotion to admiral had been ratified weeks ago—even before the official formation of the New Alliance—but the ripple of unease that spread through the ship was so strong, it was a wonder the assembled soldiers didn't sway under the force of it. It forced Ean back two steps.

"Permission granted," Helmo said.

Vega outranked Helmo, but everyone seemed to expect that he had to grant her permission. Abram had never asked permission to board. After this, Vega wouldn't either.

No one, not even Abram, went onto the bridge without requesting permission first, though.

Michelle's personal assistant—Lin Anders—followed Abram and Vega over to the captain's party. Before Ean had been able to listen in to the lines, he hadn't even realized Michelle had an assistant on board. He'd thought Lin was another of the many dignitaries who crowded around Michelle at every opportunity.

Abram smiled at Ean. Lin scowled.

Ean wasn't sure what he thought about Lin. He thought Lin was a little scared of him, worried that he'd snoop through the lines and spy on him.

"If he doesn't have anything to hide, why would he worry?" Ean had asked Radko once. Besides, why would he even want to spy on him?

"It's the thought of what you can do, Ean."

"I don't go out of my way to spy on people." Did Radko think he spied on her? "Are you worried I will—" How did you ask? Spacer Radko had been his constant companion since he'd been on board the *Lancastrian Princess*. Ean wasn't sure if she was watching him, or was there to be sure he didn't get into trouble. Probably both. After all, he was a civilian on a military ship.

Radko had laughed, a comforting sound. "No, Ean."

Radko wasn't scared of him. Michelle wasn't either.

"Her Royal Highness, Crown Princess Michelle," Abram said to Vega.

Vega saluted, then took out her weapon and held it out, palms upward, toward Michelle. "Your word is my law. By the oath of all who serve, I pledge to protect you. I will lay down my life for yours. If you find me lacking, or in any way unsuitable, end this pitiful life now, for I have sworn, by my honor, to serve you. "

Michelle could have taken the weapon and killed Vega right there. It wouldn't have been murder, for it was written into the law of Lancia that a member of the Emperor's family had the right to refuse the oath of a guard, and the right of refusal was to take the weapon and use it on the person declaring allegiance. Michelle wouldn't even have been the first to do it.

Michelle hesitated—which must have made Vega sweat, for it made Ean sweat—then pressed her own palms together under her chin. "As heir to the House of Yu, I accept your sacrifice."

Vega relaxed fractionally. Ean knew if Michelle wasn't happy with Vega, she could easily reverse the decision with a single blast at any time. Vega had to be aware of that.

"Captain Helmo," Abram said.

Helmo nodded his thanks. "Dismissed," he said to the crew,

and they marched out, one synchronized unit. All except the last team, who moved over to the shuttle and started unloading crates of Vega's luggage. She had a lot of it.

"You're with us, Ean," Abram said, as Ean wondered if he should go, too.

Michelle and Abram stood apart as Helmo introduced the officers. "Ship second, Vanje Solberg. Navigator, Ming Ju. Ship third, Chang Damodar. Senior linesman for the New Alliance, Ean Lambert."

Vega's gaze dropped to Ean's shirt. He thought she was looking at the ten bars on the pocket, but she said, "I thought he was part of Her Royal Highness's personal staff. Why does he wear a fleet uniform?"

They were the only clothes he had.

And if Vega knew that Michelle owned Ean's contract, then she knew Ean's history and the history of everyone else on Michelle's staff. Lin Anders should worry more about that.

"The uniform affords him some protection," Abram said.

Vega gazed sharply at Abram. "I fail to see why a high-level linesman needs protection." Not challenging him—no one challenged Abram—but subtly exerting her right as the new head of Michelle's security to question potential security issues. "They are the most protected species in the galaxy."

Species. She made it sound like they were aliens instead of humans. They weren't even a different race. Some humans were born with line ability, others weren't.

"I also fail to see why a level-ten linesman is contracted outside of a cartel house."

If you listened to Jita Orsaya, the cartel houses wouldn't retain their dominance for long. The military would purchase every high-level contract they could. Ean knew a lot of New Alliance fleets were trying to do so. Many of their admirals had asked him for advice. Some had asked for recommendations. As if Ean would know. Until Michelle had bought his contract, he'd never met another level-ten linesman.

"He's actually a level twelve," Abram said. "The only known twelve in the galaxy, and that's the best-kept secret in the New Alliance right now. We also have a ten. Jordan Rossi is contracted to Yaolin and answers to Admiral Orsaya."

"I have heard of him, at least."

Abram smiled faintly. "Ean is a well-kept secret," he said. "We like to keep it that way."

Michelle's comms chimed a reminder. She glanced at it. "You must excuse me," she said. "I have a subcommittee meeting I must attend on Confluence Station."

They watched in silence as she made her way down to shuttle bay one.

"Bay one holds a four-seater?" Vega asked.

"Her Royal Highness's personal shuttle," Helmo confirmed.

"And her bodyguard?"

"We have a team on Confluence Station."

"No protection on the way?"

"It's a considered risk," Abram said. "Her Royal Highness needs some time to herself. This is New Alliance territory, protected by warships," while the *Lancastrian Princess* smugly showed Ean the forty-millimeter laser cannon, the Pandora field diffuser, the expensive shielding on the shuttle, and three lockers primed to open at Michelle's touch. One locker contained a blaster, one a Taser, and the third a knife. Ship thought Michelle was safe even if Vega didn't.

"We are at war," Vega pointed out. "She would be a valuable hit. The mothership deployed twice to incidents as I came in."

There were always ships trying to get closer to the alien fleet. Most of them were journalists and thrill-seekers, who thought a military no-go zone didn't apply to them although there had been three actual enemy attacks. None of them had gotten closer than the outer perimeter.

Those ships were small problems in the scheme of things. Manageable.

No one talked about the bigger worry. That a ship would jump right into the middle of the fleet and destroy it. Jumping one ship into another ship's space caused an explosion that could destroy a world. Admiral Katida of Balian had told Ean that half their resources right now were occupied with calculations that randomly moved the ships in the fleet, to make it harder for the enemy to work out where a ship would be at any given moment in time, theoretically making it harder to jump into one of them.

Ean had heard her lines, vibrating with a worry she didn't

articulate. That same worry was a constant hum from the *Lancastrian Princess* and the *Wendell*.

"It's a considered risk," Abram said again of Michelle's shuttle.

After the shuttle had cleared, Vega got a guided tour of the *Lancastrian Princess*. There were places Ean hadn't seen before. Vega looked at him once or twice, as if wondering what a linesman was doing tagging along. Ean wondered, too. He wasn't senior staff on the *Lancastrian Princess*.

The ship lines were subdued.

That made him remember that Helmo had used the lines to call him over earlier. While Abram was describing the refresher training each crew member undertook every six months, Ean moved up beside Helmo. "How did you know I would hear you earlier?"

"I didn't," Helmo said. "I hoped you would. Ship response is changing the longer you remain on board."

He made it sound like Ean was subverting the *Lancastrian Princess*.

Helmo smiled. "I foresee some interesting things we may be able to do with the lines in the future."

The *Lancastrian Princess* was only the second ship Ean had ever spent time on other than when he was mending the lines. The first was the one he'd traveled on to Ashery to begin line training, and he'd only been on that ship a day. He'd done line repairs that had taken longer. If Ean was subverting any ship, this was the one he was doing it on.

"Not subverting," the lines said into Ean's head. *"Fixing."*

Sometimes Ean and the lines didn't understand each other. The ship had taken his thoughts and changed "subverting" to mean a broken line. At least, that's what it sounded like.

"And Captain Helmo doesn't mind?" The first time Ean had fixed a line, Helmo had told him to stay away from the ship lines.

"Ship is content."

Ean hadn't yet found a way to differentiate when the lines talked about the ship or when they talked about its captain. When he was on other ships, talking about Helmo, he used the same song that he did to talk about the *Lancastrian Princess*.

Vega turned, with a frown, at Ean's singing.

"Lambert singing is normal, Commodore." Lin's voice was caustic. "It's how he communicates."

Ean hadn't meant to start singing.

They arrived on level five. "One of Her Royal Highness's offices," Abram said, of the workroom he and Michelle had shared. "This is where she does most of her work."

Ean looked around the workroom with fresh eyes. He'd spent a lot of time here, and Abram and Michelle practically lived here when they were on ship. Large screens on the wall, two workstations at one end. Three couches at the other. Ean's couch—or the one he used—was actually the interview couch, where Michelle did all her interviews. It was unsettling to think that Vega would come here to work.

They moved on. "Her Highness's other office." This was more formal, with a desk and chairs locked into the floor, and an outer office with screens on the wall and a workstation built into the desktop. Ean had never seen it before.

"When I'm on ship, this is where you will find me," Lin said.

Ean had never seen Lin in Abram and Michelle's workroom.

They moved on to the sleeping quarters. Lin's apartment was at the far end, close to the office he worked in. Michelle's at the other side of the floor.

"Her Royal Highness's suite."

Did Abram find it as strange as Ean did to keep referring to Michelle as Her Royal Highness? Abram normally called her Michelle and, on occasion, Misha.

Ean's rooms were down from Michelle's. "Linesman Lambert's quarters."

Vega gave Ean a sharp look. "Are they sleeping together?"

"No," Abram said.

"So why is he—?"

"He *is* here," Ean said. If Vega wanted to ask questions like that, why didn't she direct them to him?

"Linesman Lambert is a member of Michelle's personal staff," Abram said. "This is the logical floor to house him on."

"Crown Princess Michelle has a personal staff of twenty on ship." Did Ean imagine the emphasis on the title? "No one else sleeps on this floor. They have their own quarters."

Something in her tone made Ean determined to dig in. "Lin does." Not that he'd known that until today.

"Lin is the Crown Princess's personal assistant. He needs to be close."

"Lambert is our top-level linesman," Abram said.

Vega didn't say anything else, but Ean knew his days on level five were numbered. Lin looked happy, at least. Abram looked . . . like Abram normally looked, which was inscrutable, except his eyes creased slightly at the corners. That normally indicated a smile, not a frown. "I will leave you to sort that out with Her Royal Highness."

Abram's cabin—now Vega's—was on level four. Ean hadn't known that. Or that Abram had a two-room office on that level, too, down from Helmo's. The crates the crew had unloaded from the shuttle were stacked on the floor.

The tour went on. There were cargo holds and weapons bays on every level. Ean knew the ship had weapons—after all, he'd been there when they'd been fired—but so many.

"We could fight a war with this ship alone," he said, to no one in particular.

"With you on board or off?" Helmo asked.

Michelle had always referred to Ean as a weapon. Katida did, too. Maybe Helmo was picking that up from the ship.

"On." For after all, wasn't he part of the crew, and he would be more so when Vega moved him up to crew quarters on levels eight and nine.

"Well then, of course we could."

This time it was Helmo who got the look.

He was as straight-faced as Abram, but Helmo was easy to read through line one, which held a touch of amusement right now.

When Ean had first come on ship, he'd never have believed Helmo had a sense of humor, and he definitely wouldn't have shown it in Ean's presence. They were long past the "Don't touch my ship," of those early days.

The VIPs were housed on levels six and seven. "We have forty guests at present," Abram said. "At its busiest, we had 186." The guests had come to observe the *Eleven*. "Many of them moved over to Confluence Station when it became available, but space is at a premium there."

It was rumored Governor Jade, of Aratoga, had ordered a new station and that those who stayed were hoping for space on that when it arrived. It was a good time to be in favor with Aratoga.

"Thirty of those remaining are military." Vega had done her homework. "Each world has to provide one warship for the New Alliance. Some of those ships are already here. Why haven't the guests moved out to their own warships?"

She could only be talking about Admiral Katida, of Balian, whose warship had arrived even before the New Alliance had been ratified. Ean might warn Katida that her time on the *Lancastrian Princess* was limited.

Abram smiled faintly. "Admiral Katida likes to be where the action is," so he hadn't missed the reference either. "I'd be worried if she did want to move off ship. It would mean we're in trouble."

The grand tour finished in one of the smaller meeting rooms. "Captain Helmo can answer most of your questions," Abram said. "Of course, you are welcome to call me at any time. I will be on Confluence Station until we determine the New Alliance headquarters, then on whatever world that is."

"Are they close to deciding on a world?" Vega asked now. "The escalation of the war makes us vulnerable on the edges of space like this, with no planets close by."

"We're making progress," Abram said.

The council was moving about as fast as a generation ship seeking new worlds. Based on the parliamentary sittings Ean had attended, Abram would be ready to retire before they decided. There was only one thing sixty-nine of the worlds agreed on. Headquarters couldn't be on Lancia. Lancia had too much power already.

"It's unfair really," Ean had said to Katida over a breakfast earlier in the week. "Michelle and Abram have done so much of the work getting the New Alliance together. People should at least acknowledge that." Not that he, personally, wanted headquarters on Lancia. Lancastrian himself, he'd sworn when he left Lancia he was never going to return. He still had no plans to do so. But Michelle and Abram had been instrumental in the creation of the new political entity.

"Lancia scares people," Katida said. "And Emperor Yu and

Lancia without Lady Lyan as the intermediary is a scary thing."

Katida was Balian. Sometimes she came across as pro-Lancian, sometimes she warned him against them.

"The luckiest thing Emperor Yu ever did for Lancia was place Abram Galenos in charge of Lady Lyan's safety," Katida said. "Galenos has been a tempering influence and can take more credit for Michelle's being the way she is than Yu ever could."

"Like a father figure?" Ean had asked. Michelle and Abram were friends. He didn't act like a father. Surely, he'd be more protective if he was. Then, who was Ean to say how a father should or shouldn't act. His own father had beaten him. They'd never be friends, not like Michelle and Abram were.

"Ean, no one would dare suggest that Crown Princess Michelle had any parent except Yu. I'd never mention that aloud again if I were you."

"What about her mother?" He tried to remember what he knew about Michelle's mother. Not much. The media on Lancia had been full of tales of Emperor Yu and Michelle's grandmother, Empress Jai. No one had ever talked about Yu's wife. "Is she still alive?"

She'd had six children, one of whom was dead. He remembered that from when he was a child. The oldest boy, who'd had a penchant for racing Girraween Storm lizards, had broken his neck. Yu had executed everyone in the stable for allowing him to race in the first place.

"Empress Ning is alive," Katida had said. "She lives in the hills behind Baoshan," the capital of Lancia. "With a staff of a thousand servants, or so the rumor goes. Personally, I think it's more like a hundred. She's never seen in public."

Ean forced his thoughts back to the present, to the deck where Abram and Vega were still discussing the new headquarters.

Abram looked at him and raised a brow slightly, almost as if he could tell what Ean was thinking. "No progress on a permanent home," he said. "But we have made progress elsewhere. The line committee has agreed to allow a small group of linesmen to begin training with you, Ean. You are to start tomorrow."

At last.

"Her Royal Highness has made a team available to work with Linesman Lambert," Abram told Vega. "Bhaksir's team will accompany you, Ean. I'm sure you have things to prepare."

Which was a dismissal. Ean bowed and left.

VEGA waited until Ean was out of earshot to ask, but Ean heard her through the lines anyway. "Do you mean he will be escorted by royal guards from this ship?"

"Yes."

"He is a linesman working with the alien ships. Surely your department would supply an escort *if* he needs one."

"Linesman Lambert goes nowhere without a bodyguard," Helmo said, while Abram added, "Lambert is a member of the Crown Princess's personal staff and is accorded the same privileges and protection as her other staff."

Was that why Ean had to tag along on the tour? So Vega knew he was part of Michelle's staff? Because Ean couldn't see a single other reason for Abram's inviting him. His contract was with Michelle, not with Lancia, and even Ean understood his contract would never be handed over to the Lancastrian military, let alone the New Alliance.

Owning Ean's contract gave Michelle a powerful lever in negotiations with other worlds. They needed linesmen—Ean especially—to communicate with the lines on the alien ships. If Michelle had had more time that first day, when she had come to House of Rigel to avenge her dead linesman, she would have signed Ean up on a generic Imperial contract rather than a personal Imperial contract, and all those people who trusted him now because he did work for Michelle would have mistrusted him because he'd be working for Yu instead.

ON the days when they were both on ship, Ean had a personal training session with Fergus Burns after Gospetto's lesson. He found Fergus in the VIP lounge, the large public area that doubled as a function center and meeting room for the politicians and high-level military who currently resided on the *Lancastrian Princess*. He and Katida were watching the news.

Lancia owned Fergus's contract. Officially, he worked out of Abram Galenos's office. In reality, he worked with Ean and was stationed on the *Lancastrian Princess*. He had a cabin in the VIP area. No doubt Commodore Vega would have something to say about that as well.

They'd been working for months on the line-training plan.

"I take it the grand tour is over," Katida said.

"Grand tour?" Should she even know about it?

"Big shoes to fill, Ean. She'll be trying hard."

She probably had been trying hard; it wasn't Ean's place to say if she was or wasn't. He looked at the screens on the wall, so he didn't have to answer. Today, the sound was turned up on the Galactic News feed. Reporter Coral Zabi had the *Confluence* fleet on-screen behind her.

"As the war between Gate Union and the New Alliance drags on," Zabi said, "the New Alliance refuses to use the one weapon at its disposal that would give it the edge in this war. The alien ships."

"How can they say that?" The ships didn't have crew; many of them needed repair. Zabi knew that. She'd had her own guided tour of some of the ships.

Katida glanced at the screen. "No news," she said. "So they're making their own."

"They're supposed to be our official reporters." Blue Sky Media and Galactic News had signed contracts ensuring their ships could stay with the New Alliance as official media.

"That doesn't mean they're pro–New Alliance," Katida said. "And Zabi wants out. I suspect she's hoping that if she favors Gate Union, we'll kick her out eventually."

That wasn't going to happen, for the two media ships were accidental additions to the *Eleven*'s fleet. Not that either media group knew that.

"More likely," Katida said, "their lawyers will finally realize the contract is worded so only the ship has to stay, not the reporter. They're taking their time about it. Sometimes I feel like giving them a helpful push."

The fact she hadn't done so meant that Zabi wasn't a problem yet. People like Katida—and Abram and Michelle—didn't let problems sit. They dealt with them.

Ean looked away from the screen. It was time for some good news. "We start training tomorrow," he told Fergus.

Katida would already know, for she was on the committee that had chosen the trainees. Ean had overheard most of the debate around who would participate, for the debate had been held on the *Lancastrian Princess*. Twenty linesmen had been chosen; a careful maneuvering of alliances and favors owed. Ean would have preferred people who wanted to train.

"Finally," Fergus said.

The linesmen came under stringent conditions. They had to be part of, and known to be loyal to, the military of their world. They had to sign and abide by a strict secrecy agreement. They also had to be open to new ideas and be willing to work outside accepted line practices.

He'd already begun teaching the linesmen on the *Lancastrian Princess*, along with Jordan Rossi and single-line Fergus. That was going well, even with Rossi, who claimed that his lines were, "Just fine, thank you," but hadn't missed a day's training yet.

Starting tomorrow, Ean would be teaching strangers.

"Speaking of training," Fergus said. "We have a lesson." He stood up and nodded to Katida. "Admiral."

Katida nodded at him and smiled at Ean as he turned to follow. "You'll be fine tomorrow," she said. "I've a nice, strong linesman for you. You'll like her."

"Thank you." He could feel all eight of her lines reassuring him. As he followed Fergus out, he wondered how deliberate that had been. Normally, he picked up her lines when she was worried or anxious, but this—it felt deliberate. Maybe Helmo wasn't the only one learning to use lines differently.

SINCE Fergus had never worked as a linesman, he'd learned, but never used, the push method of working with the lines. Ean didn't have to teach him to unlearn old ways. All he had to do was teach him how to listen to lines and how to sing them true when they were off tone.

Fergus had learned the basics already and was now singing to the lines as if he'd been born doing it. He practiced all the time, even when Ean wasn't there. Their "training" nowadays consisted of Ean's checking to ensure Fergus was still singing the lines true, then the two of them singing together, communicating with the lines.

When Ean found his mind wandering—again—to the next day's training, he tried to pull himself together. Fergus always gave 100 percent. So should he. "Let's have another go to see if we can discover what line seven does."

So far, the alien lines and the humans hadn't come to a common understanding on what it was that seven did. When Ean asked, he got a vivid impression of the void and the communality of the lines. When Fergus asked, he got completeness.

They started by greeting the sevens. They greeted them together, every line on every ship. When they had first begun doing this exercise, Ean had tried to greet each line individually, starting with the seven on the ship they were on. He had found that Fergus couldn't sing to a single seven. He always sang to them all.

All the sevens answered back to him, too.

Ean wasn't sure if it was a function of single-level linesmen that they couldn't differentiate between individual lines, if it was specifically line seven, or if it was Fergus. He hoped it wasn't just Fergus. He knew the other man worried about it as much as he did.

He listened while Fergus sang.

It wasn't that Fergus couldn't pick out single lines. Today, he picked up that line seven on the Galactic News ship was slightly off and sang it into true. Yet even when he sang the line straight, it was more a communal effort than directed solely at the line that needed fixing.

If Ean was honest, he addressed the lines in a similar way sometimes, but he could single out a line to talk specifically to if he wanted without talking to all the others. Was it simply the way linesmen were taught? After all, lines were social, more like a hive mind than individuals.

"You try by yourself." It was the last thing they did every session. Get Fergus alone to ask line seven what it did while Ean listened. It was a forlorn hope, but they kept asking, hoping that one day the answer might make sense. The lines were patient, always answering, no matter how many times they were asked.

Fergus asked, and was answered. *"Completeness? That's us?"* and Ean heard strong agreement and an equally strong sense of the void.

"Completing the void," a dispirited Fergus said when they gave up half an hour later. "How?" He sat down and rested his chin on his hands. "Maybe there's no human equivalent for line seven. I mean, they *are* alien, and the aliens have two brains."

That was theory only, for no one had been able to dissect an alien yet. The ship crew were in stasis, like those of the crazy ship *Balao*. No one knew if the humans on the *Balao* were dead yet, so how could they know if the aliens were?

Ean shivered, trying not to think about crazy ships.

"Or some other part of their body," Fergus said. "Something humans don't have an equivalent of."

Fergus didn't normally get depressed.

"We didn't think line eight had a human use either," Ean said. "We know now. Seven will come, Fergus."

"Do we even know what line eight does, really? Sure, it protects the ship, but define protection. You say it's security, but security for what? Are we misinterpreting that, too?"

"When I talk to the eights, I get a feeling of—" How did Ean say this in words? It was easy in his mind, where words and thoughts jumbled with the other senses. "I get a feeling of protection. As if that's what the line's job is. To protect."

Was Fergus right? Was Ean assuming it was security because the eights protected their ships? After all, humans had spent five hundred years pushing the lines straight when they could have been communicating with them. "Who knows?" he said. "We could be wrong."

"That's comforting, at least," Fergus said, and Ean could hear through the lines that he did find it comforting.

"We'll work it out one day," Ean said. "Completing the void, and when we do, it will be so obvious, we'll wonder why we didn't understand it."

WHEN Ean arrived in the workroom-cum-office after dinner that night, Michelle was standing at Abram's desk, staring at the main screen. Admiral Orsaya and Abram—both currently on Confluence Station—were on the comms.

"The debris has the same characteristic pattern of the weapon that took out the *Kari Wang* two months ago," Orsaya said. "Chopped into pieces, as if multiple shearing forces at right angles had acted on the ship."

The attack on the *Kari Wang* had tipped the temporary uneasy peace into outright war.

Katida and Orsaya and a dozen other military personnel had discussed it in gruesome detail the day after it had happened. How cleanly the edges had been cut, how the two-meter intervals were smaller than any known ship compartment, so no matter where the field cut, it would always kill everyone on ship. If not from the initial shear, then from the immediate loss of air afterward.

"Impressive," everyone had agreed.

"The problem is," Orsaya had said, "Gate Union doesn't have a weapon like that. At least, they didn't nine weeks ago."

Orsaya was Yaolin, one of the twenty worlds in the New Alliance that had come from Gate Union.

"What about the weapons the *Kari Wang* was testing?" Katida had asked.

Orsaya hadn't said an outright no, but she'd shaken her head doubtfully.

After that, they'd gotten on to the detail of the space suit Captain Kari Wang had been wearing at the time. The captain's legs had been sheared off in the wave, but the design of the suit had allowed it to seal and stop the bleeding. It was Nova Tahitian built, and had kept her alive for two days until the medship arrived.

That discussion had been even more gruesome than the one about the weapon itself. Ean had tuned out, but everyone was well pleased with the design of the suit. Some of the admirals had said they might look into that brand for their own fleets. Anything that kept someone with such catastrophic damage alive long enough to be rescued was good, in their opinion.

"This ship, the *Buttress Flyer*, carried a research crew of twenty—headed by one Professor Gerrard—from the University of Ruon," Orsaya said now to Michelle and Abram. "They were investigating dark matter on the edge of intergalactic space, running experiments and beaming the data back, which is how we come to have this feed."

On-screen, Ean could see the black of space with a thin sprinkling of stars.

There were two feeds. The first from the bridge, where the captain was saying to his navigator, "I swear I will never work with university people again. You know what that idiot wanted today. Fresh fruit. Out here in the middle of nowhere. When he won't let us jump anywhere because it might ruin his experiment."

"More likely because he's too tight to pay the jump fee," the navigator said.

"I told them. They're Ruon citizens. They'll have to book weeks ahead if they want to jump anywhere. You know what he said?"

"That science is above politics?"

"No." The captain put on a lecturing tone. "You don't need to worry about that, Captain James." He tapped the side of his nose. "*I* have people I can call on."

On the other feed, the owner of the pompous voice—it was an uncanny likeness—was saying, "Are you questioning my methods, Hannah?"

"No, Professor. I just wonder if the background radiation is interfering with our readings."

On-screen, on the bridge, a ship appeared out of the void.

A proximity alarm sounded. Six months ago, Ean hadn't even known there was such a thing.

The voices on the bridge changed, suddenly alert.

"Ship at 124.6438.278," said the captain. "Check on those idiots," he said to the navigator. "Tell them to get into their emergency suits."

"If they're too stupid to work out what to do," the navigator said, but he stood up. "I bet they haven't done a thing. I'll be as quick as I can." He stopped as he looked at the screen. "There's a second ship at 124.6438.281. And a third at 137.6438.278."

"And a fourth." The captain was grim. He ran his hand across the boards, presumably to open line five, for he said, "This is the *Buttress Flyer*. Ships who have just arrived in this sector please identify yourselves. And get the hell away from our space." Ean knew if this hadn't been a recording, he would have heard it through line five and felt the wash of panic that came with it.

"I repeat," the captain said. "You are in occupied space. Get the hell out of here." There was the noise of someone's thumping something hard—probably a panel. "Why in the lines won't one of you answer me?"

He kept talking until the ships disappeared offscreen.

"They jumped," the navigator said.

On the second feed, Gerrard continued lecturing Hannah. "I spent years on these calculations. I wouldn't forget such a vital thing as radiation."

"Shouldn't we find out what the alarm is about, Professor?"

"In a moment, Hannah."

On the bridge, the navigator said, "I'm just glad they didn't jump into us." He made for the door. "I'll go check on our paying customers. Placate them if need be."

"Wait," the captain said sharply. "Something's not right. Let's do a systems check fir . . ." His voice slowed, and kept slowing, so the rest of the words were dragged out to a tenth of their normal speed. The few stars on-screen undulated, as if the ship had been pushed up, then down again, then disappeared altogether.

Orsaya's face reappeared on Michelle's screen. "That's all we have."

"How long ago did this happen?"

"Sixty days," Orsaya said.

"The same day as the attack on the *Kari Wang*?" Michelle asked.

"We think it may have been a practice run."

"Four ships." Abram said. "Equidistant?"

"Unconfirmed. Given the coordinates for the second and third ships, and the approximate location of the first, we can extrapolate the likelihood. There's a ninety percent probability of that being the case."

Abram's face was unreadable. Ean wished Abram was on the *Lancastrian Princess*. That way he'd have a better idea of what he was thinking

"Studying dark matter, you said?"

"Affirmative."

Abram paused, and Ean got the impression that he was considering whether to ask his next question. "Snooping into a Ruon ship," Abram said. "What's so important about dark matter, Orsaya?"

"Nothing that I know of." Orsaya's gaze was serene, but the undecipherable glance she sent Ean's way was scarily sharp. He had to remind himself they were on the same side now. "It's how he got the money to finance the expedition that interests me."

Abram raised a brow.

"Gerrard had two passions. Dark matter and line ships."

Ean didn't even know what dark matter was.

"An odd pairing," Abram said.

"Everyone has hobbies," Orsaya said.

Orsaya's own hobby—linesmen—was more of an obsession. It was easy to see why she'd follow someone who was interested in line ships.

"He could tell you more about the *Havortian* than I could. Back when he was still talking about it, that was. Then he got the money for this trip to investigate dark matter, and suddenly the *Havortian* might as well have not existed."

"You think he was paid off?"

Sometimes, the jumps in logic made Ean dizzy. How did you get from someone's not talking about the *Havortian* to being paid off?

"Dark matter is an unfashionable study. Gerrard had been trying for years to get funding. This experiment he's doing is very expensive. Yaolin investigated funding for it."

Ean could translate that one. Orsaya had wanted Gerrard's information about the *Havortian*, and if she could have gotten it by paying for his experiment, she would have.

"It was too expensive for us. And that trip there"—Orsaya indicated the screen, which had earlier shown the destruction of the *Buttress Flyer*—"that was the culmination of five years' planning."

Abram nodded slowly. "He learned something about the *Havortian* that someone was prepared to pay for."

"We've spent five years trying to trace the source of his funding. Every time we think we're close, the game changes on us. That comment there"—Orsaya indicated the screen again—"about his having no problem getting jumps, is the best hint we've had in years. Gerrard's from Ruon, which is an Alliance world and always has been. Thus the funding isn't from a New Alliance world."

Ean could see Abram, frowning as he did when he thought.

"Professor Gerrard's work wasn't important enough to warrant silencing him," Orsaya said. "He might simply have been unlucky. After all, you can't test a weapon like that on an armed warship. The ship might fight back."

The *Kari Wang* hadn't fought back. It hadn't had time.

Ean shivered at the casual way Orsaya assumed someone might pick on an unarmed ship. Imagine if that truly was the case and some top secret military experiment decided to try out its deadly weapon on you because you were isolated and no one would notice that you were gone.

"Surely, that's risky," Abram said. Ean noticed he didn't say "unlikely." "The chances of being caught."

"Out on the rim. You'd have to be unlucky. We only found it because I had a watch on anything Gerrard did, and there hadn't been any comms from him for weeks. He was regular about sending data home. Paranoid about losing it."

Abram blew out his breath and inclined his head. "I'll check for other ships that haven't reported in. Especially those out on the rim."

From the face Michelle made, Ean thought that might be a big job.

THREE

EAN LAMBERT

THERE WASN'T MUCH preparation required for the first day of training. Ean and Fergus had planned it—right down to the number of paramedics, how many oxygen cylinders were required, and where they should be placed.

Their first lesson would be on the *Gruen*, a Gate Union ship that had been captured by the Alliance—along with the *Wendell*—when Ean had inadvertently joined them to the *Eleven*'s fleet. Captains Piers Wendell and Hilda Gruen had been returned to Gate Union afterward, but Wendell and his crew had come back to take their ship. They were now irretrievably part of the fleet because of it. The *Gruen* had a new captain and a skeleton crew but was otherwise empty.

Ean had plenty of time to be nervous. These were linesmen—his peers—and he already knew what the higher-level linesmen thought of him. His methods of singing to the lines were not widely accepted. Now he was to teach other linesmen his method.

"Don't worry about it," Radko said, as she, Ean, and Fergus walked together to the shuttle. "You're a twelve."

It was his methods that were in question, not his line level.

"The highest linesmen outside a cartel is a six, so you'll get sixes. They'll be fine."

There were at least three higher-level linesmen outside the cartels. Himself, contracted to Michelle; Jordan Rossi, the ten contracted to the Yaolin fleet; and Admiral Katida, who was an eight. Four if you counted single-level linesmen, for Fergus was a seven.

At the shuttle bay, Bhaksir's team waited with Craik's team. Sale was there, too. She had recently been promoted to group leader and was in charge of the teams that went out to the alien ships. Bhaksir now reported to Sale. Ean wasn't sure if they were all going out to the *Gruen* or if Sale and Craik were going farther on. He would have asked, but his mouth was dry from nerves, so he sat back and listened to them talk about Vega's weapons collection and tried to relax.

"All those crates," Craik—now the leader of Sale's old team—said. "Every single one of them filled with weapons. She's put them on the wall of her office. She even has an Akermanis rifle. It fires real projectiles. Little pieces of metal. Have you seen it, Ean?"

Why would Ean have been in Vega's office? He hadn't even been in it when it had been Abram's. He shook his head.

"Pity."

"I hear she's got a Pandora field diffuser," Bhaksir said. "Imagine that as a weapon."

"That's not a weapon," Craik said. "It's a diffuser."

"Haven't you ever narrowed a diffuser beam down to a single point? It's deadly."

The discussion lasted until they arrived at Confluence Station to pick up Jordan Rossi.

Rossi was everything a level-ten linesman should be. Tall, broad-shouldered, muscled, confident, sure of himself and his ability to manipulate the lines. He'd been a powerful man. He still was, although right now he was on the wrong side of a war—for a linesman—behind a layer of military secrecy so deep he didn't get to use much of that power.

Rossi buckled himself into his seat. "It takes twenty soldiers to hold a linesman's hand?"

Eighteen, actually, for a New Alliance team consisted of eight soldiers and their team leader.

"Three linesmen, Rossi," Sale said. "Orsaya made us responsible for your safety as well."

Ru Li, one of Bhaksir's team, said, "That's why there are only two teams. We couldn't fit another team in the shuttle along with your ego."

"Ahem," Bhaksir said.

"Sorry, ma'am," although he didn't sound the least bit penitent.

Rossi grunted. "Don't expect any support from me," to Ean. Which was honest, and very Rossi.

"How do you want to do this, Ean?" Sale asked.

Until now, the only people he'd trained had been Fergus and Rossi and the linesmen on the *Lancastrian Princess*. Fergus had taken to singing to line seven as if he'd been born doing it. Rossi? He thought Rossi was coming along better than Rossi wanted to admit, but it was asking a lot, going against a method Jordan Rossi had spent his whole life using.

"I'll start by introducing them to the lines," he said. "Like we did with Fergus."

"Singing to the lines," Rossi muttered. "Who'd ever have thought it would come to this?"

Sale nodded. "Good," she said to Ean. "We've emptied a cargo hold. There are oxygen stations all around, and plenty of paramedics." Line eleven was a slow, regular thump-kerthump beat that tended to give strong human linesmen heart attacks as their own heart tried to beat the same line time. The stronger the linesman, the worse they succumbed to it. Ean, luckily, was starting to get used to it.

"I want ten minutes at the start to make sure everyone knows what to do when someone has an attack." She wasn't asking, she was telling him.

"Okay."

These linesmen were going to think they were all crazy.

ON the *Gruen*, they were greeted by Team Leader Perry, who was nominally in charge at the moment, for the *Gruen* captain wasn't on board. Captain Edie Song was seldom on board.

"The trainees haven't arrived yet," Perry said. "The paramedics have. They've set up in the large cargo hold."

"Thank you." Sale led the way down.

Ean paced the large expanse nervously as he sang to the lines, explaining what he was going to do.

The *Gruen* was one of the *Eleven*'s fleet ships, so he expanded his song to include them all.

"We're here. We're with you. You are of our line." The underlying tone was supportive. Even line eleven, a subdued beat behind them.

Ean relaxed. *"Thank you."*

He looked around the training area. It was an ordinary cargo bay, larger than he was used to. Nets hung around the walls like great wall hangings or some crazy playground for adults. On the *Lancastrian Princess*, Captain Helmo had recently emptied a storeroom and opened it to the crew, who spent half their rec time clambering over the nets. Even Radko spent her spare time there. It was the most popular place on ship.

The floor was crisscrossed with covered channels. When the cargo holds were in use, the cover folded back to allow the nets to be hooked into fastenings built into the channels.

The main difference between this cargo hold and the one on the *Lancastrian Princess* was the temporary oxygen stations built into the netting on the walls, spaced two meters apart. A pair of paramedics manned every third station, with an extra pair either side of the dais set at the end.

"Incoming," Bhaksir said, glancing at something on her comms.

Twenty soldiers in different uniforms flooded in. They looked around as if wondering what was going on.

Both elevens were quiet. Ean hoped they'd remain quiet. He rubbed his hands down the side of his gray uniform. There was one familiar face. Engineer Tai, from the *Lancastrian Princess*. He didn't need to be here, for Ean was training all the *Lancastrian Princess* linesmen, but as Michelle had pointed out, "They'll expect us to send someone from my ship. They'll be worried if we don't."

"Shouldn't they expect you to train your own linesmen," Ean had asked. "After all, I work for you."

"Logically, yes. Emotionally, no. If we don't send Tai, people will think I'm getting favors."

Tai smiled at Ean briefly as he swept past.

Fergus made a soft sound of surprise. "They're not all sixes." He nodded at a woman in the blue of Balian. "Look at that."

Ean and Rossi looked. Then they looked again, and all three of them moved closer—almost synchronized—to see if they had miscounted. Seven bars under the name.

Another high-level linesman from Balian. How many more was Admiral Katida hiding? And was Katida—a level eight— the highest, or did she have some nines and tens tucked away, too?

The name above the Balian's pocket was *Hernandez*.

"What's your problem?" Hernandez demanded.

Rossi shook his head slowly.

"Where does Balian get you people from?" Fergus asked.

She bristled visibly. "If you have a problem, say so now."

"No problem," Ean said hurriedly. "We're surprised to see a seven outside the cartel houses, that's all."

"Says a man who wears the uniform of Lancia and has ten bars on his pocket." She looked at Rossi. "Or a Yaolin uniform."

"I didn't say anything," Rossi said.

Ean was glad Sale called for their attention then. "Every single one of you," she said, glaring at someone who'd succumbed to the ecstasy of line eleven and wasn't listening to her. Ean looked around. There were more of them not listening than he realized.

Sale sighed, and the irritation in her voice increased noticeably. "All of you, look around at your companions."

Most of them did.

"If they're not looking back at you, nudge them. Jab them hard if they need it."

Ean moved over to a six nearby who was smiling. He waved a hand in her face, while the linesman next to her jabbed her in the ribs. She turned to them both, still smiling. "It's . . . incredible."

"You get used to it."

"Look around you, check where the oxygen stations are," Sale said.

They looked around. A couple of them sniggered at the excess.

"You're linesmen. Prone to heart problems when the lines get too much. Yes, all of you," to one man who protested at that. "I don't care how fit you think you are. I don't care that the medics tested your heart for every condition known to man before you came here. You'll have problems. Does everyone know where the oxygen stations are?"

A few rolled their eyes.

"You're an ungrateful lot, but you'll thank me for this later. I'm going to show you what to do in the case of line-induced heart problems."

"Line-induced?" Hernandez asked.

"That's what I said." Sale looked around. "I need a volunteer."

Ru Li waved and indicated himself.

Sale scowled at him. "You're so short, no one will see you." He was also an exhibitionist and kept the whole team entertained with his mimicry. "All right then. Come up. You can do it on the dais."

Ru Li leaped onto the low platform from standing.

"Show-off," muttered Tai, who was standing near Ean.

Sale beckoned to one of the paramedics, who came forward with an oxygen tank and mask. "Do your thing, Ru Li."

Ru Li started gasping for breath.

"Oxygen."

The paramedic held up the oxygen tank.

"Mask."

The paramedic held up the mask.

Ru Li was acting his heart out. Choking, gasping, and looking as if he couldn't breathe. Ean wished the paramedic would give him oxygen. "What if he's not acting?"

A linesman snatched the oxygen tank out of the paramedic's hand and pushed the mask over Ru Li's face, turning the valve high.

"Well done," Sale said. "What's your name?"

The name above his pocket was *Chantsmith*. Chantsmith started CPR.

Ru Li pushed him—and the oxygen—away. "Enough. I'm choking."

Sale looked back at the trainees. "Remember where the oxygen is. Remember what to do. You've all done CPR training. In fact, you did a refresher this last tenday. You know what to do next. Most of all, don't panic. Be like our collected friend here." She nodded at Chantsmith. "Don't panic." She paused, long enough to be sure she had their undivided attention. "Now, meet Linesman Ean Lambert. Ean."

She stepped down.

Ean stepped onto the dais.

The faces that stared up at him were a mix of antagonism and skepticism. Some—like Hernandez—were openly hostile although Ean wasn't sure if the hostility was directed at him or just Hernandez's natural expression. Behind them were

familiar faces. People he knew. People he trusted. And underneath it all, the music and support of the lines.

"We're going to greet the lines," he said, and was glad his
voice remained steady. They'd greet the whole fleet, for all of the
Eleven's ships were listening in. After all, the *Gruen* was one of
theirs. "One line at a time. I will sing. Then you sing. Match my
song exactly. After that, the line will answer. If you don't hear
the line answer, don't worry. For some, it takes practice."

Some of them started to look doubtful. Others looked as if
they had no idea what he meant. A few had been primed and
knew what was coming. Interestingly, Hernandez wasn't one
of those who'd been primed.

"We're on the *Gruen*." He sang the sound that other lines
used to identify the ship. "This is line one. I'm saying hello to
it. He sang the greeting. "Now it's your turn. Sing. Exactly
what I sang."

Three voices raised above the rest. Fergus, who could
always be relied on, Engineer Tai, who'd done this almost as
often as Fergus and Rossi had, and Jordan Rossi, who'd never
admit that he sang to the lines, but he did.

"Wait," Ean said when they were done, and waited for the
line to answer. Then, "Line one, Helmo's ship."

Tai sang this particular line with gusto, and the line
answered him back in kind.

They went through the other line ones in the *Eleven*'s oddly
assorted fleet. After the *Gruen* and the *Lancastrian Princess*,
they greeted the *Wendell*, Confluence Station, the two media
ships, and, finally, the *Eleven* itself.

"Line two," Ean said, and started on the line twos in the
same order as he'd done with the ones.

He didn't watch the people in front of him. He closed his
eyes and listened for their lines. Some of them were openly
skeptical, not hearing when the lines answered back. There
were a couple who might have heard something.

"Line three."

He went through the lines, all the way up to ten.

He opened his eyes and looked at the trainees. He could
feel line eleven waiting. "Line eleven," he said, and sang the
greeting.

Line eleven greeted him back. A strong heartbeat of sound

that sent him to his knees. He normally coped better nowadays, but here, in this cargo hold, he picked up some of the raw newness of the trainees. "Sing," he urged them with what voice he had left. A paramedic pushed an oxygen mask over his face

Sale stepped up to the dais again. "It's important to know when oxygen is enough and when you need to kick-start the heart. For the heart is still beating. Or trying to, anyway. It's—"

Line eleven surged again.

Line ten shuddered sideways. Line ten! Whose sole job was to move them from one place in the void to another.

"—that your brain is telling it to beat nonhuman time."

No one was listening.

Ean struggled to stand up. "Something happened," he told Sale.

"Line-related?" Her gaze swept the trainees, who were all on the floor, lying on their side, lower arm supporting their head, oxygen masks over their face in the classic heart-attack pose Ean had come to know well. Paramedics attended the worst of them.

The Balian, Hernandez, was almost as bad as Rossi.

Ean shook his head.

An alarm sounded—the long whoop, whoop that signified an enemy attack. A mechanized voice said underneath it, "Proximity alert."

That was followed by Team Leader Perry. "Ship at position 3467.3418.2467. It's trying to jump into our space."

Through the lines, Ean could hear crew on the *Lancastrian Princess* and *Wendell* say almost in unison, "The *Gruen* has shifted position."

Had the *Gruen* gone into the void to do it?

It looked as if Gate Union had finally tried to jump a ship into the middle of the fleet. If line ten hadn't moved the ship, they'd be dead now and wouldn't even know it.

How had the ten moved them?

Some of the lesser-affected linesmen struggled to get up.

Sale was already moving, as was Craik and the rest of her team. "How many, how close?"

Ean glanced back at the trainees. They had plenty of support and wouldn't be doing much for a while. Fergus was competently handling things.

He followed Sale.

"One ship, but they're too damn close." Perry's voice shook. "They jumped in."

"Shit."

A set of lines Ean hadn't even realized was close disappeared. The relief through line one was so strong, he could taste it.

The attack alarm stopped.

"It jumped," Perry said. "For a moment there, I thought we were toast."

Sale slowed. "Probably some crack-brained tourist trying to get close to the alien ships." Ean could hear she didn't believe that.

Line ten rippled again. Another funny, sideways ripple like the first.

"I think it's back," Ean said.

The attack alarm sounded again, and the proximity alert under it.

Perry's voice was shriller this time. "The crazy bastard. He's jumped back in."

Sale started running again. "Just shoot him. Who's on the weapons?"

Ean saw the scramble on the bridge through the lines as Perry gestured to one of his team to get to the weapons panel. "Beyer, sir, but we're not primed. It will take a couple of minutes to bring the guns online."

Sale burst onto the bridge. "The guns should always be primed." She moved alongside Beyer and started bringing up panels.

"I've got it." Craik took over. "Answer your comms," for Sale's comms had been sounding since the first ship had appeared. She had two calls. Helmo and Wendell.

The ship disappeared again.

The alarms stopped.

"If he jumps back," Sale said, "he's doing it deliberately." She opened her comms to both captains at the same time. "Sale."

"We're preparing for an emergency jump," Helmo said. "Have Ean ready to call both fleets in."

Sale looked at Ean. He nodded. He could hear the preparations on both ships.

He sang in a soft undertone to all the ships in the *Eleven* and *Confluence* fleets, trying to keep the panic out of his own lines. *"We have to jump."*

"Now?"

Ships liked to jump. Sometimes Ean forgot that. Sometimes he wondered if their natural habitat actually was the void.

He was about to confirm, when line ten shuddered sideways again. "The ship's back." He could hear the new set of lines, close to the *Gruen*.

"Gruen's moved again," Wendell said.

"Ship's back." Perry had gone beyond panicked; his voice was high enough to make Ean's ears hurt.

"God," said Helmo, which was the strongest word Ean had ever heard him use. "We can't keep being this lucky."

"It's not luck," Ean said. "It's—"

A chorus of lines overwhelmed him. *"Fix broken lines,"* the *Gruen* said, urgently, backed by 135 other sets of lines.

It wasn't hard to guess what they meant by broken. A ship that kept coming back into the same space, over and over, when other ships would logically stay away. Except, how did you fix it?

Ean could only think of one thing to do. He sang—to all the line eights—for they controlled security. *"Hold him here. Don't let him jump again."* And he pulled as hard as he could on his own line eight.

The other eights joined his line, and the intruding ship was locked into a stationary web.

"Ready to jump," Helmo said. "Ean."

"No." It came out in song, on the comms, for Ean hadn't yet learned how to hold lines and communicate at the same time. He shook his head frantically at Sale. There was no need to jump anymore.

"Not ready, Captain," Sale said.

The only reaction from Helmo was a blink. Wendell threw up his hands and started a fast pace around his own bridge.

People on the other fleet ships wouldn't even know this was happening.

Rossi did, for Rossi had dragged himself out of his eleven-induced stupor and was weaving his way toward the bridge—following the sound of Ean's lines.

"The ship can't move now." It came out in song, too, on all three ships, and over the ship's speakers because he couldn't let go of the lines to take them off.

The *Gruen* crew looked at him strangely, but he'd worked with Sale before. She understood. "How long?"

He shrugged.

Sale turned to Craik. "Is that gun ready yet?"

"Another minute," Craik said. "It wasn't in standby mode, it was off."

"What's happening on that ship, Ean?" Sale asked.

The eights seemed to be holding the ship on their own. He loosened his own hold. The other eights kept tight hold of the rogue ship. He sang a quick thank-you to the lines, then used line five to put the security feed from the intruder's ship onto Sale's comms. And into Helmo's and Wendell's. All three promptly pushed the feed onto larger screens on the bridge. He wished he'd thought of doing that himself.

"If I sang the ship into the fleet, I could see everything."

"No." Explosively from Helmo and Sale, but Wendell stopped pacing and was considering it.

Sale looked at the screen, where a lone man—dressed from head to toe in black—was trying to get control back. He looked up at the camera, as if he could sense they were watching him, and snarled.

"Friendly soul," Sale said. "How many weapons do we think he has? Can you give us different views, Ean?"

There were four cameras on the bridge. Ean showed them all, one in each quarter of the screen.

"Doesn't tell us much," Sale said. "Keep them up there so we can see what he's doing. She looked at Bhaksir. "Prepare a boarding party."

Bhaksir nodded.

"Not you," Sale said, as Radko hesitated. She was, after all, part of Bhaksir's team. "You have your job."

That made it official, Ean supposed. Radko *was* his bodyguard.

"We'll cover you from the third quadrant," Helmo said.

The intruder had two weapons, but the crews on the *Gruen*, *Lancastrian Princess*, and the *Wendell* watched the screens so closely they knew the exact moment he was about to fire. Bhaksir was taking evasive action before each shot had left the ship.

Boarding the ship was anticlimactic. The stranger didn't fight. He held up his hands when Bhaksir stormed on and allowed himself to be arrested. Hana and Gossamer led him back to the shuttle.

"That was too easy," Sale said. "What are we missing?"

"He was outnumbered," Ean pointed out.

"Ean, if you're going in as a suicide ship, you don't give up without a fight. You try to take some of your enemy with you."

Ru Li was checking the boards. "Bhaksir, you need to see this."

Bhaksir took one look and waved Ru Li away. "Let's get off this ship, people. He's rigged it to blow."

They ran back to the shuttle so fast Ean had difficulty switching the feeds to follow their progress. Bhaksir counted down as she ran. In five-second intervals.

"Fifty-five. Fifty."

Beside Ean, Radko clenched her fists and took up the count, stopping between to whisper under her breath, "Hurry, hurry."

"Go," Bhaksir said, when they were back on board. No one strapped in before Hana took off.

Ean held his breath until the shuttle pulled away.

"Ten seconds. Hurry," Radko said, more a plea than anything.

An alarm on the intruder's ship beeped. Recorded laughter poured out from the speakers.

Sale scowled at the screen. "This guy's got a real sense of humor. Crash positions, everyone."

Radko pushed Ean onto the floor.

If Radko thought it bad enough to make him take cover here, on the *Gruen*, then Bhaksir and her team would never survive.

"Five."

"Let go of the ship," Ean sang. Urgently. *"Let it jump. Now."* For he could feel that the only thing preventing the ship from jumping was the line eights' hold.

The eights let go. The ship disappeared.

The alarms stopped.

"Is the ship still there?" he asked Radko, braced above him.

She didn't hear him. She was watching the shuttle on the screen, whispering under her breath, "Hurry, hurry."

"Where's the ship?" Sale demanded. "It should have blown by now."

Ean pushed Radko away and climbed to his feet. "It probably did."

"So where's the explosion?"

"I think somewhere else. The place it was trying to jump back to before."

"Nice," Helmo said. Ean could feel his relief pouring in through the lines on the *Lancastrian Princess*. And from the *Wendell*. And here, from Sale and Radko. "Poetic justice and a message, all in one neat package."

"Let's hope he had some companions back there," Wendell said. "I'd like to think this guy's antics scared them as much as it scared us."

"What happened, Ean?" Sale asked.

How did he describe it?

"Linesman's view," Radko prompted.

That was easy. "The lines didn't like the ship's jumping so close to their lines, so line ten kept stopping him by moving sideways a bit. I think. Afterward, when he kept coming back, line eight—all the line eights—held the ship here while Bhaksir went out to his ship. The bomb triggered—was it a bomb?"

Sale and Radko both nodded.

"Then we let go, and the ship jumped, because that's what it was trying to do."

"Nice," Sale said. "Well done. It's handy having you around." She turned to Craik. "Take your team down to the shuttle bay to greet Bhaksir. I want this maniac locked up tight. Search him thoroughly."

"You'd better search the trainees," Helmo said. "The timing is too coincidental to be anything but deliberate. They waited until they could accurately pinpoint where a ship was. One of them will have a trace."

On the *Wendell*, Captain Wendell nodded, as if he'd come to the same conclusion.

"Sh—" Sale bit off what she'd been going to say. "We're unlikely to have another ship jump into our space in the short term," she decided. "Surely it would take time to set up. The trace can wait."

Helmo nodded.

Ean looked at Radko. "We'd better get back to the trainees, I suppose."

"SHOULD we start hunting for traces?" he asked, as they started back. It felt as if they'd been gone hours, but it couldn't have been long. He could see through the lines that some linesmen were still out, Hernandez—Balian's seven—being one of them. Fergus and Chantsmith were organizing the more alert linesmen into helping load those still comatose onto stretchers.

"No," Radko said. "Wait until we have more people.

"What if Gate Union uses it to send another ship in?"

Sale thought they wouldn't, but what if she was wrong?

"They won't have one ready."

How could everyone be so sure? Yet the mood on all fleet ships had definitely lightened. As if everyone thought they were out of danger.

"Not many people volunteer for suicide missions," Radko said.

They collected Rossi—still not quite at the bridge—on their way back.

THE cargo hold was empty.

Ean hadn't been paying any attention; he'd been watching Bhaksir's shuttle arrive back safely. He looked around the empty cargo hold, then checked the lines.

The first of the paramedics, with her stretcher, entered the shuttle bay.

"Radko." He brought up the image on his comms.

"I see it," Radko said, and pulled out her own comms. "Bhaksir, Craik. You might want to wait until we get the linesmen out of there."

There was a shout from the shuttle bay and the crackle of blaster fire. Then more shouts and the pounding of feet, followed by a shouted, "Don't hit the linesman."

"You're a little late," Bhaksir said tersely. "The prisoner escaped. He took a hostage. Who in the lines let them in here?"

FOUR

EAN LAMBERT

CHANTSMITH WAS DOWN, being attended by paramedics. He was alive, at least, for he moved, although his left side was burned.

"The suicide pilot escaped," Bhaksir said into her comms to Sale. "He's got a blaster. And a hostage. Fergus Burns."

Ean sang the corridor line feed up onto a screen on the bridge, and another in the shuttle bay. *"Follow them,"* he told the lines. *"Keep showing where they are."*

Sale said, "Craik, take a team after him. Bhaksir, your responsibility is the linesmen."

Through the lines—and on-screen—Ean saw the escapee prod Fergus with the stolen blaster and motion him over to a panel. He opened the panel and felt around inside. The song of lines three and five changed. An acrid smell made Ean sneeze.

The image disappeared offscreen.

"We've lost the images of that sector," Sale said.

The pilot had destroyed the link between the camera and the comms. But though the image might have gone, Ean could still see through the lines, and Fergus's line seven was clear. "They're near the jumps. Come on," to Radko. "I can tell where he's going."

"Let me know when we're getting close," Radko said. She opened her comms. "Ean and I are in pursuit. He says they're at the jumps."

Ean made for the lifts. He'd used the jumps once. He hadn't liked it then, didn't want to always practice them in emergency situations.

Their escapee exited at level three, and from the surge in Fergus's line and his stumble as they exited, Fergus hadn't used jumps much either. It wasn't an experience for the faint-hearted.

"Level three," Ean said.

"Bastard's heading for Engineering," Craik said. "He can do a lot of damage in there."

"Wait," Ean said. "Come around from the other side. I'll lock the doors so that instead of your chasing him, he runs into you."

Craik's team ran past the first set of jumps and kept running toward the next set, nearer the crew quarters.

On the bridge, Perry said, "He'll be in Engineering before they can stop him."

"They know what they're doing," Sale said.

Ean sang the doors on level three locked. All the doors except those in the corridor that led to the jumps Craik was leading her team to.

The escapee tried the first door. Found it locked. Moved on to the next. He stopped at the third door and took something from his pocket. The melody of line three changed. Ean changed it back. The melody changed again. Ean changed it back.

On the third attempt, line eight joined in. A surge of sound that crackled and spat. The escapee swore and dropped his tool.

"You can do that?"

"He should not have been harming the ship." Another of the lines might have sounded smug. Line eight was serious.

"Thank you."

A pleased hum followed. Lines liked to be acknowledged.

The escapee snatched up his tool and prodded Fergus on.

Craik and her team had reached the jumps. "Still level three?" They were already jumping.

"Yes." The lift arrived on level three. Ean started toward the escapee and Fergus.

Radko stopped him. "Are we following him, or are we going the same way Craik is?"

"Same way as Craik."

"I want to follow."

Ean turned and ran the other way.

"How close, Ean?" Craik asked.

He had to stop to answer. "Two corridors."

"And us?" Radko asked.

Fergus's line was strong. "Maybe the same." He sang to line seven. *"Be ready."*

Fergus's line surged. *"Okay."* He sounded as out of breath as Ean.

"Keep moving," his captor snarled. "You hold me back, I'll kill you."

If he'd been going to kill Fergus, he would have done so by now. He must see some value in having a hostage.

Through the lines, Ean saw Craik and her team thunder round the corridor in front of the captor, who turned. He dragged Fergus back the other way, toward Ean and Radko, using Fergus as a shield between him and the approaching soldiers.

"We're close," Ean said. "Around the next corner."

Radko stopped. Ean leaned against the wall, trying to get his breath back.

"Can you get Fergus to drop as he comes around the corner?"

"I'll try," and he sang careful—somewhat winded— instructions to the line seven that he knew was Fergus. *"Drop fast as you come around the corner."*

He hoped that was a nod from Fergus, for there was no other reaction.

He could hear their footsteps now, not just through the lines. Hear Craik, behind them, shouting, "Stop, or I'll shoot."

Fergus's drop was more fall than drop, and he nearly took his captor down with him. Luckily—for Fergus—the other man caught himself in time. He straightened. Into a faceful of blaster fire from Radko.

Craik and her team arrived then and held their weapons while Radko checked the downed man.

"He's dead."

Ean helped Fergus up. "Katida once said no one ever used blasters on a ship because you could damage the ship."

"Someone lied then," Fergus said. "All I've seen used are blasters."

"That," said Craik, "is because the people we fight use blasters. We don't always have them on the heat setting, mind. Sometimes we put them onto stun."

"I haven't seen them on stun," Ean said. "Are you okay, Fergus?"

"I am." Fergus was shaking. Ean could feel his relief

through line seven. He could hear the lines reassuring Fergus although Fergus wasn't listening right now. "I was so relieved when you contacted me through line seven. I thought I was dead. I know I should have tried to stop him. But I couldn't. I just wanted to stay alive."

Ean patted him on the shoulder. Awkwardly, like Sale might.

Craik called for a stretcher. "Not going to lug a maniac through the ship if we don't have to."

Ean looked at them crowded around the body, then looked at Radko and Fergus. "We should get back." The linesmen were his responsibility.

THE trainees were on the shuttle, waiting—they thought—for Sale to give the okay to take off. They didn't know it, but even now, Sale was instructing Craik and her team to search them.

Most of them had recovered although two paramedics hovered close to Hernandez in case line eleven grew strong again. Another two attended Chantsmith.

"What was that?" one of the trainees demanded. "An alien attack?"

"No. He was human," Ean said, then he realized what attack they meant. "Oh, you mean that. It was just a strong line." Line training felt like hours ago now although according to his comms, only twenty minutes had passed.

He moved among them, singing softly to the lines, trying to gauge how they were from a combination of line one on the *Gruen* and the trainees' own lines. Fergus and Radko followed, doing their own human version of the same thing by talking to each of them. Craik and her team followed them, scanning for transmitters.

Sale joined them there. "Any problems?"

"Not so far." Or none more than people irate at the thought they were being accused of siding with the enemy.

He had two people left to check. Chantsmith and Hernandez.

Sale tapped her comms to get the linesmen's attention. "The shuttle will take you back to Confluence Station, where you're all scheduled for medicals. Make sure you have them before you return to your home ship or station. Watch out for each other. If you think someone is in difficulty, push them to the head of the queue. The medic assigned to you is experienced in line-related difficulties. Tell him about any problems you might have."

That might be the medic from the *Lancastrian Princess*, or—more likely—one of the doctors in Orsaya's team who looked after Rossi.

Craik found a transmitter on Chantsmith's back. Ean thought that he might be mortified if he hadn't been doped up with painkillers. Ean couldn't tell much from his lines at all.

One more. Hernandez?

"What are you looking at?"

That sounded normal.

"Everyone's fine," Ean told Sale.

"Good." She shepherded him, Fergus, and Radko off the shuttle. "All clear," she told the shuttle pilot.

They watched the lights on the air lock cycle from green to red and eventually back to green again.

"Hernandez is strong," Ean said. Initially, she had been as bad as he and Rossi had been when they'd first come across the full strength of line eleven.

Fergus nodded. "She doesn't respond like a seven, that's for sure."

Sale looked at them both sharply.

"Can't you tell?" Radko asked. "Isn't that how you discovered what line Admiral Katida was?"

He had, but, "I need her alone and somewhere quiet for that." Line quiet, he meant, without being surrounded by other human lines all learning to communicate as lines did. "And she's prickly enough that if she knows what I'm doing, she'll try to block me."

"That strong?"

"I think so, yes."

"SO," Katida said at breakfast. "I hear the alien lines won't allow two ships to jump into each other's space." Her smile was ferocious. "That must be worrying Gate Union right now. How soon before we get the human ships to do the same?"

They had been on a human ship, the *Gruen*. "I think line eleven did something first." But after that, the *Gruen* line ten had moved the ship away from the suicide ship without any further help. And because he knew she was going to ask, "I don't know if they can do it without line eleven."

"Pity."

Had all alien ships been part of an eleven fleet? Surely, they would have had lone ships. How did they deal with potential collisions? It wasn't something you could practice without being sure of the result.

"Is it line seven, do you think?" Katida asked.

"No." That was one thing he was certain about. Line seven had done nothing at the time.

Right now, everyone seemed convinced Gate Union wouldn't try again. So much so that Fleet Control had stopped the constant random moving of ships. "What if they do send another suicide ship?"

"Will they succeed?"

"No . . ." The lines would call on him to fix the "broken" lines. He'd talk to them anyway, to make sure they did.

"It's a pity we can't get non-eleven-linked human ships to do the same. Then this war would be a battle of equals rather than one side with a massive hold over the other."

"We'll work out how they do it, eventually." The ships had proven yesterday they could avoid each other. Unfortunately, no one wanted to try it without more testing. And you couldn't test if you didn't jump.

"I know we will, Ean. But will it come in time for us to force Gate Union into giving us jump slots?"

"You wouldn't need slots then."

"We'd still use jump slots," Katida said. "We can't train everyone in the new process. It would take years. We still need to regulate traffic. The gate system is the best way to do that. We don't want to destroy it."

"They're trying to destroy us."

"We simply need to show them that we can destroy them if we want to. Scare them into dropping their sanctions."

Ean had always expected that if the New Alliance won the war, then Gate Union would be reduced to secondary citizens. "That means things won't have changed at all."

"Oh, they'll have changed," Katida said grimly. "Not all for the better, I grant you, but definitely changed." She dismissed the subject with a wave of her hand. "Enough about politics. How did you like the linesman I sent you?"

"She's strong," Ean said.

Katida's line eight exuded satisfaction.

"You should be training as well," Ean said. Her eight was stronger than her lower lines. "And you should be exercising all your lines, not just eight."

"I would love to learn your method," Katida said. "But let's not forget it's only the people on this ship who know I am a linesman."

"Why do you hide it? You should be in a cartel house. So should Hernandez."

"The problem with the cartels, Ean, is that they demand a loyalty some Balians can't give."

"To Gate Union?" For the cartel houses were allied to Gate Union.

"And to the line cartels."

"Someone trained you." Hernandez and Katida were both trained in the lines. Someone must have known about them. "I mean, who certified Hernandez? Because we think they got it wrong." Hernandez's reaction to line eleven had been too strong for a seven.

"Wrong?"

He didn't want to raise her hopes. "Ask me after we've done more tests." If they were right, and Hernandez was a higher level than her bars signified, then whoever had certified her had done a terrible job. If Hernandez had been miscertified, how many other linesmen had? Ean himself would have failed certification if Rigel had taken him to the Grand Master to be certified. If then–Grand Master Morton Paretsky could deliberately fail one person, he could do it to others.

"She trained at House of Sandhurst," Katida said. "I'll find who certified her."

"Thank you."

A ship arrived then, another set of lines among all those that came and went with regularity. Human line ships all had a similar sound. A base identifying beat, overlaid with the ship sounds.

Except this one didn't have an overlay.

Ean lost the thread of what Katida was saying as he listened. "A new ship arrived," he told Katida. "Brand-new. Fresh lines. They're still—"

She looked at him, then pulled out her comms. She called up the Balian warship. "Captain Seafra. Which ships have arrived in the last ten minutes?"

Ean knew Captain Seafra almost as well as he knew the fleet ships now. Katida called her often.

"No ships, Admiral," Seafra said. "Not for the last twenty minutes. Everything was cleared for the arrival of Aratoga Station. That arrived two minutes and twenty-seven seconds ago."

"How new is it?"

"New?" Seafra scratched the back of her head and looked away from the comms a moment. "Fairly new, I'd say. It's just been commissioned."

"Thank you." Katida clicked off. "Define 'new,'" she said.

He was lucky Orsaya wasn't there, Ean reflected, as he finally escaped with the valid excuse, "I've got line training," or they'd still be talking about it. He jogged down the corridor to where Radko was coming to see what was keeping him.

"Do you think that because human ships are all cloned from the same set of lines, they have the base personality of the *Havortian*?"

"I think," Radko said, "that we're late, and we have a timetable." Radko, Bhaksir, and Sale were all particular about timetables. She jogged beside him and increased the pace. "It's an interesting theory. Do you believe it?"

What did he think? "I think—" That he still couldn't run and talk at the same time.

He sank into his seat in the shuttle and gained his breath. "I think the ships have all been cloned from the *Havortian*, and when they're first built, they are all basically the same." He thought about Helmo and Wendell. "They develop unique personalities from their captain, and from their crew."

FIVE

SELMA KARI WANG

KARI WANG WOKE in a military hospital.

She stared at the walls, wondering if she was still in the last throes of death. She'd heard those final seconds elongated out forever. If she could choose her final seconds, she'd choose to be with her ship.

"Drink this." An orderly pushed a straw into her mouth. She sucked obediently. Water. She pushed it away.

"My crew?"

The orderly didn't answer, which was answer enough in itself.

"My ship?"

The orderly moved away.

She couldn't feel her legs.

She went over and over the last three minutes of ship time. What if she had moved the *Kari Wang* the other way? What if she'd moved five seconds earlier? What if she'd jumped as soon as the other ships had?

The medical staff came and went. Drink this, move that. How does it feel?

She still couldn't feel her legs. She used her elbows to raise the top half of her body, already knowing what she'd see. The hump of a cage over her thighs that went down to almost where her knees might have been. Below that, the bed was flat.

A commodore in a shiny dress uniform came to sit by her bed one day and debrief her. He brought with him two aides, as smartly dressed as their boss, and a long-nosed soldier with a deep red face who wore the seal of a psychiatrist to the right of his name—*Ofir*. He looked as if he should be in the bed, not her.

"Tell us what happened?" the commodore said.

She wished he'd go away, but she was a soldier, so she reported to the best of her ability. Not that she was very clear, not with the drugs they were sending through her system.

"Four ships. Cloaked." She had to enunciate carefully. "GU *Byers*, GU *Haralampiev*, GU *van Andringa*, and the GU *Akaki*." Bless Will, with his attention to detail. She blinked hard at the memory.

"Are you sure?" one of the aides asked.

She nodded. Once.

"Are you absolutely sure?"

"Yes." She made it as clear as she could.

"Captain Kari Wang is a decorated officer," Ofir said. "She ran a ship with two hundred crew."

That ship was gone now. As dead as her crew.

He added gently, "I don't think you should be questioning her observations." He winked at Kari Wang.

She couldn't even smile.

The aide nodded but said stiffly, "Those ships were accounted for. None of them was anywhere near that sector at the time of the accident."

Accident. The surge of anger was the first real emotion she'd felt. "It wasn't an accident. It was the deliberate destruction of my ship. An act of war."

"Maybe you didn't have time to identify the ships properly," the commodore said.

Will had identified them. He didn't make mistakes like that. "No." All Kari Wang wanted to do was get rid of them. "Four ships. Cloaked. They uncloaked." The adrenaline rush from the anger subsided and left her head as muzzy as her mouth. "They jumped. They left a Masson field. As big as—" She couldn't move her hands wide enough to encompass the enormity of it. Couldn't control her hands either. One knocked into the other aide, who jumped back, startled.

"A Masson field?" the first aide said. "Do you know how big they can make them?"

A lot bigger than people realized.

"Cut. My. Ship. To. Pieces."

The commodore and his aides looked at each other, as if wondering if she was lucid enough to report. The commodore stood up. "Thank you, Captain. You have been most helpful."

The psychiatrist stayed behind. "My name's Jon Ofir," he said. "Call me Jon. I'll be around. If you need me, ask. Everyone here knows me."

She moved her head in acknowledgment, almost too tired to nod, and didn't even notice him go. What could she have done differently in those last three minutes?

ONE day, she woke to realize she could feel her legs again. Which was impossible because she didn't have legs anymore. But feel them she could, and the doctors who crowded around that day all looked pleased with themselves.

"Move your right leg," a bearded doctor ordered her.

She ignored him. Beards were an affectation she'd had little to do with. It was inconvenient to shave in space because the tiny pieces of hair got into the water supply, then could get into the wrong places and had to be broken down. Most spacers depilated rather than kept beards or shaved. Then they never had to worry about things like stray hair causing the water purifier to clog up.

"Captain Kari Wang." This was the earnest young doctor, Fitch, who'd been there since the beginning. He reminded her of Will when Will had first come on board as her third-in-command. Serious and focused. Yet underneath Will's serious exterior had lurked a wicked sense of humor and an instinct you could trust.

Will was dead now. She should have died, too.

"Can you move your right leg, please?"

He sounded like Will, too. He even looked young the way Will had. Far too young to have earned the array of purple ribbons that sat under his name.

She moved her body like she would have if she'd still had legs. Her leg felt heavy, which was impossible, of course, and hard to lift.

There was a pleased murmur from the watchers above her bed.

What had they done to her?

"Now the left leg," the bearded doctor said.

"Captain Kari Wang. Can you move your left leg please?" Fitch asked.

She moved her left leg, too, because they'd hang over her forever, demanding she do things if she didn't.

The watching doctors broke into spontaneous applause. Fitch's grin stretched almost ear to ear. "Congratulations, Captain. You have a new pair of legs."

She stared at the bright white ceiling and ignored them.

The light dimmed with the night. Brightened again with the new day. Over and over.

They should have let her die along with the rest of her crew.

SIX

EAN LAMBERT

LINE TRAINING WAS coming along well. Or parts of it, anyway.

Ami Hernandez was as strong as any linesman Ean had known. She was prickly with it, and as soon as she heard Ean in her mind, she rammed up a wall. Ean could have forced his way past, but it wouldn't have been polite.

"I just want to test you," he said, exasperated.

"I've been tested." A strong blast of defiance came with it.

Ean looked at her with interest. There was a story there, that was obvious.

Rossi snickered. "Finding training a little difficult?" he said to Ean.

"You can't talk," Hernandez said. "With your secret singing and your experiments."

Rossi narrowed his eyes.

"We're all linesmen here," Ean said hastily. "We work together." They were going to spend a lot of time in each other's company, and it was hard to keep things private with lines. Not only that, if Hernandez was as strong as he thought she was, she'd be sharing some of the line-repair load soon. He turned to Fergus.

"Maybe we should ask Hernandez to work with you on line seven."

"Sure," said Fergus, although Ean detected some disappointment through the lines, almost jealousy.

What was wrong with everyone today?

He looked back at Hernandez. If she wouldn't show him her level, maybe she would show the lines. "Hernandez. I want you to lead the next round." They'd already greeted the lines, so they needed something else to sing about. "Ask each line on the *Gruen* how it is. One at a time."

"How it is?"

"That's what he said, sweetheart. Or don't you understand Standard?"

Ean was going to have to do something about Rossi's sniping.

"I understand Standard, all right. What I don't understand are the strange requests I'm getting from high-level linesmen that are making me question their sanity."

Maybe Hernandez could take care of herself.

He listened as Hernandez asked line one how it was. There was a hint of martyrdom in her greeting, as if she was tired of the exercises.

Line one heard her and grew sad.

"No, no," Hernandez hurried to assure it. *"I'm not annoyed at you. I'm annoyed at him."*

Annoyance didn't seem to be a concept the lines understood.

"You know she trained at House of Sandhurst," Rossi said. "Two Hurst kicked her out before she was certified. It was the day of the certification ceremony, so she went along anyway. Forced herself in—because no one knew she wasn't part of the house anymore, and Hurst was busy with the private certification for Tomas Teng."

One mystery solved.

"Of course." Rossi's lines were maliciously gleeful. "He didn't realize she was a ten. Even a cartel master will put up with a lot from a ten."

The lines of the ship picked up Rossi's glee and echoed it.

Hernandez stopped. "Do you mind?"

"Sorry, keep going," Ean said. He considered Rossi's words, spoken and unspoken, as he listened to Hernandez lead the other trainees. Rossi thought Hernandez was a ten, no question.

So did he.

The song of line eight soared in response to her query. *"Secure, safe."*

The other trainees didn't respond, but Hernandez nodded, and nodded again to nine's *"Waiting"* and ten's *"Ready."*

Hernandez stopped. "The lines are fine."

She was correct. The *Gruen* was always lonely and melancholy when they first came onto the ship, and no wonder, given its skeleton crew. But they'd been working two hours already.

It had brightened up with people around it. And because they used it as a training ship, the lines were strong and straight, with line one the only weak line.

It was time Ean let Admiral Katida know she had a ten in her fleet.

THEY left the lines on the *Gruen* singing with that peculiar kind of line pleasure that came from having people around them, but Ean knew it wouldn't last. And the *Gruen* wasn't even the loneliest ship.

"People for us, too," was a tiny whisper in the back of his mind, and he wasn't sure if it came from the *Eleven*, or the *Confluence*, or both. Along with the whisper came views of empty corridors, and the loneliness was an ache that made him clench his teeth together.

"What's wrong?" Radko asked.

Ean shook his head.

"I'm doing what I can." Maybe he could hurry it up. He'd talk to Abram and somehow make it happen.

It was almost as if Abram had heard his determination, for he was on ship with Michelle when Ean arrived back from training. Ean stopped at the door of the workroom, unsure if he should disturb them. They didn't get much time to talk anymore. He went down and used the fresher instead.

He'd give them a bit of time alone before he inundated Abram with demands.

Michelle was waiting in his sitting area when he came out. She looked more relaxed than she had in a long time. "I found the perfect fresher for you, you know. This big." She stretched her arms wide. "Helmo said it wouldn't fit."

He hurriedly pulled on clean trousers and shirt. "I don't need a new fresher." He knew his cheeks were pink.

"I'll have it installed in your apartment when you get one."

Ean had never had an apartment in his life. A one-room walk-up with his father. A room at Rigel's cartel house, and some squats in between. And now a cabin. He was never likely to have an apartment to put a new fresher in.

Michelle smiled her dimple smile and stood up. "Abram wants to talk to you."

Abram hadn't changed. There was more braid on his collar; he was a little more tired if that was possible. He held out a glass of tea.

"Thank you." Ean took it and went to sit on the couch he considered his.

"I see line training is going well," Abram said, taking his own tea over to his couch.

With Michelle settled on her couch, it might almost have been like old times. Ean knew it wouldn't last but relaxed anyway.

"It is," he said. "And I'm glad you're here because I want to talk about crew for the *Eleven* and the *Confluence*. They need crews. They need linesmen around all the time." He'd even take nonlinesmen.

Abram grimaced. "A lot of people want to talk about crew for the alien ships. Especially the *Eleven*. Everyone thinks they should crew it."

"Someone has to," Ean said. "These ships are atrophying from lack of crew."

"Atrophying?"

"The lines. Line one particularly. Line one on the *Eleven* hasn't been this bad since we discovered it."

"Which wasn't that long ago," Michelle said.

Ean turned to include her in his plea. "The lines don't understand why we're not doing something. We've had plenty of time."

"I wouldn't call it plenty," Abram said.

"But—"

He held up a hand to stop anything else Ean might say. "It so happens, everyone wants these ships crewed. They're no use as a military fleet if they're not."

"Thank you." It couldn't be that easy.

"The consensus is that we'll give the *Eleven* a multiworld crew, under the auspices of a combined New Alliance military unit. Each fleet is searching for crew now."

"Linesmen?"

"Linesmen," Abram confirmed. "Two from each world. One a known, certified linesman from within the world fleets, the other a failed linesman from the same."

Ean couldn't speak. When he could, all he said was, "I'll

be back," and went out, back to his room, where he caroled the news joyfully to every line in *Eleven*'s fleet.

He could hear/see Michelle and Abram in their workroom.

"Do you hear that?" Michelle said, smiling. "He's telling the ships."

Abram's voice was dry. "I live for the day when none of us need mechanical helpers to communicate ship to ship." But he smiled with it.

Even Helmo, talking with Vega in Vega's office, smiled.

"And then us?" the *Confluence* asked.

"And then you," Ean promised.

He came back to the workroom smiling. "Thank you," he said to Abram.

Abram smiled. "I'd like to say I did it all myself, but everyone wants it. Getting a captain will be our first order of business once we move into a permanent parliament. I suspect our biggest problem will be agreeing who that captain should be. But." He held up his hand again. "That's not what I'm here for. I'm here to talk about moving the ships."

"Are you worried about another attack?" Ean had worried for weeks afterward, until Radko asked if he trusted the ships.

"Of course I do."

"Then trust that they will let you know. They did last time." He'd stopped worrying after that.

"Not an attack," Abram said. "We want to move them to their permanent home."

Each fleet of ships was tied together. The *Eleven*'s fleet— the *Lancastrian Princess*, the *Wendell*, the *Gruen*, the two media ships, Confluence Station, and the *Eleven* itself—were linked and moved as a single unit. Likewise, the *Confluence* and its fleet of 128 ships moved as a single unit, too.

Not many people knew that.

Ean took a mouthful of tea. And another one.

"Tomorrow we vote on the permanent headquarters for the New Alliance," Abram said. "We would have voted a week ago except we were waiting for jumps. It will be too dangerous to let Gate Union control the jumps after they know where the new headquarters are."

"So you'll move the ships first? What if they don't vote for the place you want them to?"

"They will."

Ean hoped Abram was as sure as he sounded.

"We're not going to move them until the vote. That would be presumptuous of us." Abram and Michelle shared a smile.

"We want you to move the ships as soon as the vote is passed," Michelle said.

They didn't ask if he could do it. He'd have to.

The glass was slick in Ean's hands. It would be easy, wouldn't it? They had done it before. So why was he nervous? "Both fleets at the same time?"

"Yes, although we have two jumps if you need them," Abram said. "Helmo has the jumps set. All you have to do is tell him when you are ready."

There was no word for "can't" in either Michelle or Abram's vocabulary. You did what you had to do or died trying.

Ean wiped his hands down his trousers and picked up his glass again. "What time?"

"At 15:00 hours," Abram said.

EAN canceled line training for the following day since it was scheduled for early afternoon and wasn't slated to finish until 16:00 hours.

The Balian trainee, Ami Hernandez, called him up to complain. "You can't force us to go out there every day and sing songs because *you* want us to, then cancel when you feel like it."

"You are allowed occasional days off," Ean said.

"It's not acceptable. You drag us out here. You force us to sing. You make us do things that no linesman has ever had to do. Then you interrupt our training in the middle of it."

Ean held his comms out in front of him and let her rant. She was strong. He could have sworn that some of her feelings were coming directly through line five, not through the comms.

He became aware she had stopped.

"You're not even listening," Hernandez accused.

"Oh, I was," Ean said. Listening harder than she could have imagined. "Keep talking. It was very interesting."

"Don't patronize me." She clicked off.

AT 14:00 hours, Ean made his way to the bridge. "Permission to come onto the bridge."

"Granted," Helmo said.

The bridge was quiet. Ean rubbed his palms down the sides of his trousers. The jump had been timed for 15:00 hours exactly. They had a window of fifteen minutes.

What if he couldn't do it?

"Nervous?" Helmo asked.

"Is it that obvious?"

"I'm nervous," Helmo said. "I don't know about you. So much can go wrong. Do you know how many modules they've added to Confluence Station between the last time you moved us and now? And if Gate Union knows what we're doing, they could always do the ultimate and have us jump into another ship. It would wipe out the New Alliance."

He wasn't inspiring confidence. He wasn't even worrying about the things Ean was worrying about. Like could he move all the ships together? What if he accidentally melded the two fleets, so that forever more the whole lot had to travel together? What if he couldn't move them at all?

The council meeting was on Confluence Station. They watched it on the screen on the bridge. Council resumed at 14:45. There was the usual settling in and official detail—declaration of council session open, evidence of recording—that always happened. At 14:57, Governor Jade of Aratoga proposed Haladea III as the headquarters of the New Alliance. The speaker gave time for dissent. There was no dissent.

At 15:01, it was agreed by a majority of 76 percent that the New Alliance headquarters would be on Haladea III.

On-screen, Governor Jade of Aratoga proposed they move to Haladea III at the earliest opportunity.

"This is us," Helmo said.

Ean sang to the lines.

He was aware of the ships. The *Wendell*, the *Gruen*, the media ships. Confluence Station. The *Eleven*. All of the *Confluence* fleet. Please let them keep their fleets separate. All ships answering his call, preparing to jump with him.

He didn't think about how he had no idea what he was doing. That would be disastrous.

Helmo's voice, beside him, was calm, with none of the

professed nervousness he'd spoken about. "Jump ship." Yet Ean could see through line one that he was nervous.

One hundred and thirty six line nines made a chorus as big as infinity as the ship entered the void.

He had forever in the void. Enough time to check each of the lines individually—1,362 ship lines. He could feel his own lines expanding, changing.

Then the crystal notes of line ten joined the chorus, and space moved.

He sang a special thank-you to the two elevens, who had kept their ships together, and safe.

Then he came back to the real world, where Helmo was getting stats from his crew. Line one was calm. Relieved. Satisfied even.

"Nicely done," Helmo said to Ean.

SEVEN

STELLAN VILHJALMSSON

STELLAN VILHJALMSSON FORCED himself to ignore the acid in his stomach by watching the news on the wall screen. Right now it was showing Haladea II and Haladea III. So the New Alliance had a permanent home now. The image panned to show the alien ships against the blackness of space, turning so that the ships were then reflected with the dual worlds behind them.

And Haladea III had 130 new satellites in temporary orbit above.

It had been five months since the discovery of the alien fleet, three and a half months since the signing of the documents that formalized the New Alliance. Three and a half months since the formal declaration of war. How long before they used the ships in battle?

Stellan had seen the damage the *Eleven* could do. If Gate Union didn't manage that threat quickly, it would lose any advantage it had.

On-screen, Admiral Markan ponderously explained how the New Alliance was undermining the line cartels and what a threat that was to line ships. And how underhand the New Alliance was, with its unfounded accusations of Gate Union destruction of ships, which was nothing more than an excuse to go to war.

Stellan said to the screen in return, "And the fact that we deliberately destroyed one of their ships that had our top secret research on it doesn't have anything to do with that, does it?"

"If you're talking about the *Kari Wang*," Markan said from the doorway, "you need to snoop into top secret files more."

Stellan wasn't a spy, he was an assassin. He pushed down the reflux admitting it gave him. "I leave the underhand stuff for others."

Markan came in and sat heavily across from Stellan at the table. "But since you mentioned it, we have a standing order for all our operatives to listen for anything they can find out about the destruction of the GU *Kari Wang*."

"Because Captain Kari Wang named the four ships who attacked her?"

The media had gotten hold of the names early on. Since then there had been accusations and counteraccusations from both sides.

"Because we know where each of those ships was the night the *Kari Wang* was destroyed. And none of them was anywhere near the sector she was in."

"It's not something a captain like Selma Kari Wang gets wrong." Or her crew.

"Exactly. She positively identified those ships."

Which meant that someone had framed Gate Union. The New Alliance, forcing a start to the war they had avoided for so long? Did they believe they would win because they had the alien ships?

"The *Kari Wang* is old news, Stellan. We've bigger problems to worry about."

"Like a war we're not even fighting yet? Where are the battles, Markan? Are we so scared of what those ships can do that we won't attack?"

"There are battles aplenty, Stellan. You're just nowhere near them."

"Yet you've failed in the most obvious target." Stellan waved a hand at the screen, where the 130 alien ships were on-screen again. "They were sitting in the middle of nowhere for months. Why didn't you jump a ship into them? You knew the coordinates. This whole war would have been over by now."

They couldn't do it now that the ships had moved. Destroying a whole planet, even as an act of war, would turn everyone against them, including their own side.

"Teach your ancestor to hunt worms, Stellan. Of course we tried that." Markan scowled. "The New Alliance sent our ship back and blew it up in our own damned space. Scared the lines out of the two ships accompanying our pilot, too, because they sent it back three times before they blew it."

"What? Three jumps? Cold jumps?" Stellan shivered. Even Galenos wasn't that stupid. Or was he?

"Three cold jumps. And you wonder why I'm so hesitant to go up against them." Markan rubbed his hands as if he were cold. "This was never a war we planned to win on battles, Stellan. It was supposed to be won on economic sanctions. We stop them jumping for six months, they come begging us to end hostilities."

The union of gate worlds had been created to control jumps, for ships jumping through the void and coming out on top of another ship caused an explosion that could destroy a world. Space was big, and ships small in comparison, but ships jumped close to worlds, and they liked to jump close to space-ports. The more populous the world, the more probability another ship would be close by. Roscracia, for example, had thousands of ships arrive daily.

Hence the gate controllers.

Six months of preventing ships from jumping wouldn't destroy the New Alliance, but it would show that Gate Union *could* destroy it and would lose the worlds of the New Alliance a lot of money. Markan's logic was sound. Yet if the New Alliance could prevent ships jumping into each other, it didn't need Gate Union to monitor the jumps for them. The war would be fought on battles alone. One hundred and thirty alien ships could do a lot of damage.

"You've got a problem," Stellan said.

"Don't I know it."

Markan looked tired and worried. For a fanatic who lived by the mantra "healthy body, healthy mind," he was the worst Stellan had seen him, and they'd known each other since they were both fresh-faced spacers on their first day at Roscracian Fleet Training.

"Which is why I called you in."

This was it. They were about to get down to business. The reflux in Stellan's stomach started rising into his throat. "Who am I to kill this time?"

"You haven't got the stomach for it anymore, Stellan. Next person you try to kill will end up killing you."

"So I'm out?" He was a career soldier, albeit in a specialized field. People like him, booted out of the fleet, were dead in five years. They couldn't take civilian life. He realized he was rubbing his hand—the hand that had murdered 157 people so far—and forced himself to stop. He couldn't wipe away the blood of the past, but nowadays it haunted him.

"Change of career, Stellan. If you can't kill people, you're useless as an assassin." Then Markan smiled. "This time your job is to *not* kill someone. Do you think you could do that?"

Stellan glanced up at the screen again, so he didn't have to look at Markan. "This isn't like you." He said it slowly.

"It's not a charity job, Stellan. You might find it harder than you think. We have to know how the ships avoided each other. We have to know if it was a fluke or deliberate. And if it was deliberate, how long it will take to pass that on to other New Alliance ships." Markan tapped his comms to bring up two images, side by side. "These are the two people who will know."

Stellan recognized the man on the left, although it took a moment, for he looked strange in beige rather than in the midnight blue he normally wore. It was interesting how much the clothes defined a person. "What is Jordan Rossi doing in a Yaolin fleet uniform?"

"Yaolin bought his contract."

"You're joking, right?" Level-ten linesmen didn't contract outside the cartel houses.

"I would love to say I was. Unfortunately, it was part of Jita Orsaya's legacy. She had to have planned it."

Stellan had met Markan in the officer's bar at Roscracia Barracks two weeks after the surprise formation of the New Alliance. It was the first time Stellan had come across the giveaway twitch that came with the mention of Admiral Jita Orsaya. It told him there was more to the Orsaya debacle than Markan was admitting.

"Getting a ten, or taking the ten over to the New Alliance with them?"

"She was working with Lancia," Markan said. He indicated the other man on the screen, who wore the gray of Lancia and the braid of Lady Lyan's personal staff. "Lancia knew we would control the lines, so they took steps to ensure they had their own linesman."

The Lancastrian linesman's light brown hair was longer than regulation. Typical linesman. He couldn't even dress in uniform properly. The gray of his uniform highlighted the gray of his eyes, and the whole was accentuated by the long, dark lashes that framed them. Had the linesman chosen Lancia because he knew the color looked good on him? Linesmen could be like that.

"I don't know him at all." Level-ten linesmen were rare. He should have at least been familiar with the image.

"That is Linesman Ean Lambert. Formerly of House of Rigel, now part of Lady Lyan's personal staff." Markan stabbed a finger in the direction of the screen. "That is the man you're going to get answers from."

House of Rigel was a nothing house. Tucked away on the lesser gate world of Ashery, and only there, no doubt, because there were three other slightly more prestigious houses on the same world. Stellan looked between the two images. "Why not Rossi?"

"That, my friend, is as complicated as this whole war. Where do I start? First up, Lancia owns Lambert's contract. As you can imagine, they're pushing him as *the* eminent linesman and the old Alliance supports Lancia's expert rather than Yaolin's."

How did Jordan Rossi feel about that? He was, by all accounts, a man used to people's knowing how important he was.

"Lambert's the one they call into parliament when they want line questions answered. He's gone from nothing to line expert in a few months. He advises people like Galenos. If anyone knows what's going on, it will be Lambert."

"That doesn't sound like Galenos. Taking advice from a neophyte."

"It doesn't sound like Jita Orsaya, either, but she risked everything to get him out to the confluence."

That could be explained if Orsaya and her world had been planning to defect. It was a way to get the *Eleven* close, so the Alliance could attack Gate Union.

"We can separate Lambert from the Lancastrian security that protects him," Markan said. "We don't have anything similar for Rossi."

In this new order, Admiral Jita Orsaya was responsible for Yaolin fleet security where it interacted with the New Alliance. Stellan had worked with her before. He could well believe they couldn't get past Yaolin's security. Even so, her security paled beside Lady Lyan's. "Yet you think we can get to Lambert from behind Galenos?"

"It's not Galenos anymore, remember. The security of Lady Lyan's personal staff now falls to Commodore Jiang Vega. She's still settling in."

Galenos had been with Lady Lyan for years. The changeover was bound to be unsettling for everyone. It was unsettling enough for Stellan. The Galenos/Lyan combination had been a known factor. The Vega/Lyan combination was an unknown.

What sort of security would you give a high-level linesman anyway? The very fact they were essential to the functioning of ships that passed through the void gave them automatic protection. No one would deliberately kill one.

Although, if the rumors were true, Abram Galenos had executed Rebekah Grimes for war crimes. In which case Stellan wouldn't want to be either of those linesmen on the New Alliance side.

In a war like this, where Gate Union was doing everything it could to restrict New Alliance access to lines, the New Alliance would do everything it could to ensure the safety of the only two high-level linesmen they had access to.

"How do I get to Lambert?"

Markan got them both tea. Stellan hoped it was coincidence that he'd waited until Stellan's stomach had settled before he served it.

"Line politics. Delivered to us courtesy of Jita Orsaya," followed by the obligatory teeth grind and twitch. "How much do you know about the Grand Master of the line cartels?"

His—or her—job was to look after the welfare of the linesmen. If a linesman had problems with his cartel house, for example, he'd ask the Grand Master to sort it out. That was the theory. In practice, it depended how powerful the house and what level the linesman was. It was a prestigious job, equivalent to a head of state. "Let me see," Stellan said. "Leo Rickenback is currently Grand Master." He hadn't met Rickenback himself, but in the months Rickenback had been in the position, Stellan had spoken to two cartel masters, both of whom had been positive about the appointment. "The cartels seem happy with him." Not Markan, of course, because he openly supported Iwo Hurst, of House of Sandhurst, for the role.

"They chose Rickenback because Orsaya pushed them into it."

"Because she wanted Rossi?"

"Because we were allying with Hurst. That woman." Markan finished his tea in a long gulp and poured more. "She chose the only person the other houses would have been happy with. Sometimes, I think obtaining Rossi was pure luck on her behalf."

Jita Orsaya made her own luck.

"Enough about her," Markan said. "We've been slowly undermining Rickenback's position." Stellan wasn't sure if the "we" was Gate Union—for why would they bother—or simply Iwo Hurst and his cartel house.

"So how does this get me access to Lambert?"

"Morton Paretsky wants his old job back. He wants to force a revote. It will be a three-way vote, but Paretsky has been out of it for six months. He doesn't realize how close Hurst is to the numbers."

Stellan nodded.

"Paretsky's looking for a cause, and he thinks he's found it. Apparently, there was some irregularity with the way Cartel Master Rigel signed Lambert over to Lancia."

With Lancia involved, Stellan wasn't surprised.

"Lady Lyan threatened Rigel," Markan said.

"That's really going to stick."

"We've convinced Paretsky it will. Rigel will play along. He'll do anything if the price is right, and we've paid him enough."

"How will open warfare between the cartels help me get close to Lambert?" They were at war and everyone knew the cartels were biased toward Gate Union. Lancia could tell the cartel masters to go away, and no one could do anything about it.

"It won't, but we paid Rigel to ensure Lambert meets with him. Rigel thinks Lambert's misplaced sense of loyalty will do that much. The cartel business is an excuse to get Rigel onto Haladea III."

Misplaced sense of loyalty was an odd phrase to use in relation to level-ten linesmen, who had no loyalty to anyone except themselves.

"Does Rigel know what you plan?"

"He thinks we're going to offer Lambert a job."

With Lady Lyan owning the contract. Rigel couldn't be that naïve.

"So Rigel gets me access to Lambert. What then?"

Markan took out a phial. "Dromalan truth serum."

Stellan pulled the sleeve of his uniform down over his fingers before he picked up the little bottle. Markan may be blasé about handling it, but once it got into your bloodstream you couldn't stop it working. He didn't want to start blabbing his personal secrets out to anyone who was around to listen.

He realized he was rubbing his killing hand down the side of his leg. He forced himself to stop.

If Markan noticed, he ignored it. "I've sent you through a list of questions. Record everything."

"And afterward?"

"Let him go."

"The logical thing would be to kill him."

"You haven't the stomach for it anymore, Stellan. We're not using you here because you were once a good assassin. We're using you because of your ability to get into an enemy territory and get close to a subject."

"What's my code?" Stellan was looking forward to the assignment in a way he hadn't looked forward to one in years.

Markan held out his hand for Stellan's comms. He tapped in a code. Stellan checked it. He'd been caught once with an invalid code. He wasn't going to be caught again. He managed—just—not to raise his eyebrows at the permissions on the screen. Markan really wanted information from this linesman.

EIGHT

✦

SELMA KARI WANG

THEY DIDN'T LET Kari Wang rest with her brand-new pair of legs. They made her learn to walk again.

Kari Wang didn't see the point of it. She missed her ship. She'd betrayed her crew by staying alive when they hadn't. They should have let her die. Instead, she had to do endless exercise, all of it in a long, narrow room while medical staff watched her.

She felt like a Twicket lizard, a pet that had been all the rage when she'd been a girl. Her best friend had one. Mottled pink-and-gray creatures. And she was mottled, all right, the scarring was intense—and that was from the operations she'd had—not the catastrophe. You kept the lizards in a glass cage with a treadmill and gave them nothing else to do. The lizard would run on the treadmill. Probably out of boredom, Kari Wang decided. As it ran, it converted energy from its body fat, and the reaction made it change color, the pink deepening to a rich mahogany-violet eventually.

Her friend's lizard had run itself to death.

Maybe she could run herself to death.

She couldn't even walk a straight line.

"You're doing well today, Selma," Fitch said. "Your balance is much better."

He called this balance. Once she'd been able to hold her balance during a gravity change on her ship and maintain the same position from null gee to two gee.

Fitch showed her the balance chart. "Five days ago, you listed off after the third step. Now it's only after the sixth or seventh. That's quite an improvement."

Three steps in five days. "Quite."

"It is," Fitch agreed, his earnest expression so like Will's,

Kari Wang had to look away. So many things reminded her of what she had lost. It was best if she didn't think at all.

Today's audience was larger than usual. Sometimes that happened. Jurgen Arnoud, the bearded doctor, loved explaining the groundbreaking medical advancements that had gone into rebuilding her legs. How important it was, how valuable it was.

They should have tried it on someone else. A captain always went down with her ship.

The visitors watched her unsteady progress. She ignored them.

One of them wore an admiral's uniform. Admiral Marsh MacClennan.

MacClennan was frowning although not at her.

Military psychiatrist Jon Ofir was there as well. He dropped by every day even though she'd made it plain she didn't want to talk to him. Jon was frowning, too, but he *was* looking at her.

As for the two people with them, Kari Wang wondered if she had died after all, and this was some cruel afterlife. Ahmed Gann, who, until their sudden, unexpected secession from Gate Union, had been the Nova Tahitian representative on the Gate Union Council. He was now the equivalent for the New Alliance.

Beside him stood the First Councilor.

Maybe the whole thing was a horrible dream she couldn't escape from, and when she woke up, she'd find Nova Tahiti was still part of Gate Union, her ship was whole, and there was no such political entity as the New Alliance. Lines, she hoped so.

Gann was talking rapidly to the others.

She had no balance, nearly fell. First Councilor stepped forward to help her, then stepped back as Jon Ofir shook his head slightly.

"She's lost her ship," Admiral MacClennan said. The words were flat. "Have you read any of the studies on the relationship between captains and their ships?"

Maybe he'd read the same paper Medic Halliday had.

Jon said cautiously into the silence that followed MacClennan's words, "One does have to question her mental fitness at this moment. She *has* just lost her ship."

"And her crew," MacClennan added.

"Not to mention her physical fitness," Dr. Arnoud added. "She can't even walk a straight line."

They must have known she was listening though none of them showed it.

"Put her in another ship, and who knows what she'll do," MacClennan said.

She was never going into another ship.

Ahmed Gann put his palms together. It looked like praying although Kari Wang was sure he wasn't. "We will never get another opportunity like this. If you want Nova Tahiti to have any power in the New Alliance, this is the surest way to get it."

"Provided she's mentally up to it," MacClennan said. He looked at Jon. "Will she recover?"

"Maybe. Her psych profile is good. We won't know for months, maybe years, whether she'll ever get over the loss of her ship. I've never heard of a captain's going on to a new ship."

Neither had Kari Wang, and she didn't plan on being the first.

"Do we have any choice?" First Councilor asked. "As Ahmed says, we'll never get this opportunity again."

"One crazy ship in the making," MacClennan muttered.

"Look at it this way," Gann said. "Everyone will be watching her. We'll have plenty of warning."

"And if she fails?"

"Are we any worse off than we are now? Lancia and those close to her will control the council while the rest of us scrabble for what power we can. If we *succeed*," and Gann paused for a moment. "If we succeed," he said again, softly.

Kari Wang's legs were starting to shake. She kept walking.

MacClennan finally turned away. "She'll need medical staff to accompany her."

"I am her senior specialist," Dr. Arnoud said.

"Fine. And a psychiatrist." He looked at Jon, who nodded.

"We'll need to get you special clearance. This is highly classified." Everyone with him nodded this time. "And you'll all be taking thorough Havortian tests. If I see even a hint of line capability in those tests, you're out of the program." He paused. "In fact, all of you take the tests. I'd hate to see something go wrong because we missed a linesman."

Then he glanced back at Kari Wang. "Good night, Captain," and marched out of the room ahead of the others.

Kari Wang kept walking. They could plan all they liked. She was not going to captain another ship. Ever.

THE following week was filled with two hours of walking in the morning and evening, and in between Kari Wang sat the most rigid Havortian tests she'd ever undergone. They were a waste. She'd been tested before she took her ship because the one, unalterable condition in most fleets was that a linesman couldn't become captain of a ship. The reasons behind that were lost in antiquity. Or behind a veil of secrecy so deep, the people who were guarding the secret probably didn't even know why.

Admiral MacClennan came back every day for the next week and watched Kari Wang's exercises with a brooding intensity that bordered on stalking. On day seven, Kari Wang stopped in front of him, close enough to be rude. "Surely you have better things to do with your time than sit around watching patients in a military hospital." She'd never seen an admiral who wasn't busy. She'd never talked to an admiral that way before either, but what did that matter now.

"I do," he admitted, but he nodded to himself as if he was pleased she had finally called him out on it. Maybe she imagined that, for no superior officer liked being told off by his or her juniors.

"Why don't you go and do it then?"

Dr. Arnoud put up a hand as if he wanted to shut her up. "She's on a lot of medication, sir," he said apologetically to the admiral.

Sometimes, Kari Wang forgot the doctors were fleet personnel. This was a military hospital, and given the size and the equipment, it was probably the base hospital at Goed Lutchen, fleet headquarters on Nova Tahiti.

She'd never thought to ask. In fact, she'd asked nothing so far. Any of her own crew would have tried to find out as much as they could. If she ever woke from this nightmare, she was going to be very disappointed in herself.

MacClennan grunted. He looked at Arnoud, and at Jon, who had just arrived. "Has she done the Havortian tests yet?"

Kari Wang thought the doctor might have been glad for Jon's timely arrival. It gave MacClennan someone else to glare at and someone to answer his questions.

"She has," Jon said. "Results are mostly negative." He hesitated, as if he didn't want to say it, then looked apologetically at Kari Wang. "Her responses on the right auditory cortex showed no line ability, but they have changed since the tests from before she became captain."

"Of course they have," MacClennan said. "She's had her own ship." He looked her over. "It will be interesting to see how it changes after this. I want you to run tests every week from now on."

Nothing was going to change.

"Everything we could test, we did," Jon said.

"Perfect pitch?"

In fact, Kari Wang couldn't hold a tune. This nosy admiral didn't need to know that.

"Nothing else tested positive on the Havortian scale, sir."

Kari Wang turned away to resume her unsteady progress up and down the room. They could talk about line tests as much as they wanted. She wasn't interested, and she had no plans to take on a new ship. She'd told both doctors that, and the psychiatrist. No one listened.

She concentrated on the line on the floor. She was getting used to her new legs. They said they'd made them exactly the same length as the old ones, but for some insane reason her feet kept hitting the floor before she expected them to. She thought they might have miscalculated on the height.

When she couldn't take that anymore, she went onto the bars. It felt good to be on something she could control. Initially, her arms had been almost as weak as her legs due to lost muscle tone. That hadn't taken long to fix. Off the ground, she was now as agile as she had been on ship.

That was the thing, wasn't it? In space, one didn't need legs.

NINE

EAN LAMBERT

THE MESSAGE WAITING on Ean's comms after line training was a reminder of a life so long ago it felt like a dream. How long had it been? Nearly six months.

Cartel Master Rigel. Ean's former boss.

Returning on the shuttle with Fergus and Rossi, fresh from a session teaching other linesmen to open their lines, he knew that his own were wide open. Anything he said or did would go out to receptive lines nearby, including human lines like Fergus and Rossi.

"I thought training went well today," Fergus said.

Their twenty linesmen were coming along. The training was counterintuitive to how the linesmen had been taught to communicate with the lines all their life. Today there hadn't been as much resistance as there had been in earlier sessions.

Jordan Rossi snickered. "He's corrupting their lines. Naturally, they will resist it."

"You have to unlearn bad habits," Fergus said.

"That's fine for you to say. You don't have any habits to unlearn. And I was doing quite well in my 'bad' habits, thank you."

Despite what Rossi said, Ean could feel through the lines that Rossi had been happy with training today. Or his component of it. Rossi leaked lines like a breached ship leaked air.

A bad analogy, he decided, thinking on Radko's space-survival lessons. Air didn't leak from a breached ship, it exited fast, freezing into a cloud of vapor as it went. He needed a better analogy. Like a sun leaking radiation? He glanced at Radko, who was sitting back in her shuttle seat, her eyes closed. She was particular about her lessons.

Like a sun giving off radiation then.

Jordan Rossi gave him a strange look.

The problem was, Rossi might leak lines, but Ean was closer to the alien lines in that respect. They shared everything, and the better Rossi got at working the aliens' way, the easier he'd be able to read Ean back.

Ean decided to ignore the message from Rigel for the moment. He didn't want to share it.

Instead, he thought about the training and what they could do to bring the linesmen onside. It would help if Jordan Rossi, respected line ten that he was, endorsed the training. But Rossi was never going to destroy his own reputation by doing that. Not unless there was some advantage in it for Rossi.

Yet Rossi was—happy wasn't a word one ever ascribed to him—but his lines were singing with what other people might describe as contentment.

He wasn't aware he was snooping until the line sound changed, and Rossi said, "Get out of my lines, bastard."

"Sorry."

Radko opened her eyes.

Rossi held up his hands in mock surrender.

Radko closed her eyes again.

Ean looked away guiltily. He had been snooping, even if he hadn't realized it.

He could have spoken to Fergus, yet around this time on every shuttle trip, Fergus started to grip the armrests. Ean hadn't noticed it on the first trips he'd taken with Fergus—he'd had other things on his mind, hadn't he—but it was always noticeable after line training.

"He's lost his line," Rossi said.

"Who? Fergus?"

"This is around where the lines drop out. You and I don't care because there are still twos, threes, fours, and fives on the shuttle, but there's no seven."

And he accused Ean of snooping.

"You'll see," Rossi said. "He comes good again around the same distance from a full line set."

Even Radko opened her eyes to look at him.

"When were you thinking of sharing this?" Ean asked.

Rossi shrugged.

The problem with Rossi was that you couldn't tell if it was

something he'd just worked out or if it was something he'd known for ages.

Fergus tried to smile. "I'll get used to it eventually. It's more noticeable after training."

"You should have told us about it," Radko said.

"I'm never sure what's normal and what's not."

"Nothing's normal about a single-level linesman," Rossi said.

"We don't know what's normal and what's not," Ean said. "Right now, Fergus, you're the standard, and whatever happens to you *is* the norm."

There would be more single-level linesmen soon, when the crew Abram had promised for the *Eleven* was finally assembled. To date, seventy full linesmen and fifty single levels—it was harder to find failed linesmen within the fleet system—had been chosen. Right now, those people were all being vetted by the security of the other worlds.

After that, a captain, and, finally, they'd have a crew for the *Eleven*.

Then they'd start all over again looking for a crew for the *Confluence*. And then for the *Confluence* fleet ships.

Abram, Michelle, and Katida had all warned Ean privately that while the crew would be available as soon as they all passed security, the captain was a different matter. It would take as long to agree on a captain as it had to agree on a world for the New Alliance headquarters. Ean hoped not. He was looking forward to working with the single-level linesmen.

Fergus was a strong line. From the data Abram Galenos had on the linesmen who'd failed certification, most of them had done well on the Havortian tests. Ean suspected many of the singles would be stronger on their single line than the linesmen who had multiple lines.

He watched Fergus try to relax. What was the range of a human linesman anyway?

"Did you lose your higher lines before or after Fergus did?" he asked Rossi, but of course the other linesman didn't answer that.

It wasn't a long trip. Ean could still feel line eleven, and through eleven knew he could contact the other lines if he needed to even if he couldn't hear them right now. He watched Fergus to see when he relaxed.

Had Fergus always missed the lines when they went out of range? Or was it only since he'd learned to listen to line seven? And now that he'd learned that, did passing through the void strengthen the effect? Every time Ean entered the void, he came out more attuned to the lines. Was that the same for Fergus?

Fergus tried to laugh. "I feel such a fraud."

"Fraud?" Rossi raised an eyebrow. "It's an interesting word."

Fergus had been Rossi's personal assistant for twenty years. How anyone could put up with Jordan Rossi for twenty years was a big question in itself, but in a weird sort of way the two were friends. Not that Rossi would have called it that. And in a weird sort of way, Ean could tell Rossi was trying to help right now.

Not that Rossi would have admitted that, either.

Ean's comms buzzed. Rigel again. He frowned down at the message. When he looked up, Fergus's grip had relaxed a little.

"I think we're coming back into range," Fergus said.

Sure enough, the higher lines were coming back faintly.

EAN waited until he was in the privacy of his own cabin before he called his former cartel master.

Rigel had changed his hairstyle. He had blond, spiky tips under an aqua base that made the Rigel-cartel greens look washed-out. Ean made a mental note to tell Gospetto that plaits were out of fashion. Voice coach Gospetto had been complaining lately about how isolated Confluence Station and Haladea III were from the fashionable worlds. No one could see him here. No one even knew what work he did.

"Ean." Rigel's tones were as oily as ever. "You're looking well."

There was no lag, which meant Rigel was in this sector. The Rigel cartel house was on Ashery, which was half a galaxy and four communication sectors away.

"Thank you. So are you." It was meaningless small talk,

which he'd learned from Rigel himself. Why would the cartel master come all the way out to the Haladean worlds? There was only one reason Ean could see. To talk to him.

Sure enough. "I'm visiting Haladea III on business," Rigel said. "Why don't we meet for dinner, see how you're going?"

A cartel master didn't need to travel on business. Business came to him, and Ean couldn't remember the last time Rigel had traveled off-world when it wasn't a holiday.

He had a bad feeling about this. "I'll need to check what work they have lined up for me."

"Of course, of course," Rigel said heartily.

"How long are you here for, Rigel?"

"Awhile."

Ean interpreted that as being at least until he saw Ean.

He clicked off. Rigel was here for a reason. Ean just had to work out what that reason was.

WHEN Ean had first boarded the *Lancastrian Princess*, its lines had been perfect—minus a slight off tone in line six, which had only taken minutes to fix. Lines two to ten were still perfect, but line one was—not off, but unbalanced—unsettled.

According to Radko, Abram Galenos had become Michelle's head of security as soon as her father deemed her old enough to take on political roles, and Marcus Helmo had been their captain for ten years. The crew was stable. Radko herself was one of the later arrivals, and she had been on ship five years.

Until now, when Abram had moved on to become Admiral and Vega had moved in to take his place.

It wasn't just the settling in of the new head of security. Michelle was lonely, and the lines of the ship echoed some of that loneliness.

All the ships were lonely. It was his job to fix it.

He got himself a glass of tea and sat on the couch in the workroom. It had been a ghost room since Abram had left. Michelle spent a lot of time on Haladea III, but Ean thought she avoided the room. She spent more time in her quarters now, whereas once she had only used them to sleep and dress.

Empty corridors in the alien line ships. On the *Gruen*, the second skeleton shift was replacing Perry's team. Melancholy on the *Lancastrian Princess*.

He was on his second glass of tea when Michelle arrived back from her latest subcommittee meeting. She arrived in shuttle bay three because Vega insisted on a full team of bodyguards traveling with her. Sometimes, Ean chafed at his own restrictions. It must be a hundred times worse for Michelle.

Michelle was dressed in blue again today. A formal dark blue silk dress that came down to her knees and showed elegant legs through the slits up the sides. Everything looked good on Michelle. She smelled of fizzy citrus with a hint of Haladean moonlight orchid.

Ean's mood brightened. He poured her a glass of tea.

"Thank you." She looked exhausted as she sank onto her couch but smiled at him. Her dimpled smile. The one where he couldn't help smiling back. Her own smile grew wider. She drank most of the tea before she said, "The council sits tomorrow. The first item on the agenda is a captain for the *Eleven*."

He'd been waiting so long, it was almost anticlimactic.

"I want you to attend the council sessions," Michelle said. "You need to direct them."

What did she think he could do?

"They'll take days to come to a decision. Possibly weeks. I want you to attend every day. You'll be invited to functions. Lin will tell you which ones to attend."

Lin was going to love that.

"Talk to people. They will ask who you would like to see in the position. When it's appropriate, you'll mention names of people who will make suitable captains."

Ean could give her a list of candidates right now. Every single military member on the council had spoken to him about suitable captains for the alien ships. A lot of the nonmilitary had, too.

"We've organized a reception so everyone can meet the potential captains. Three nights hence. We'll make sure you meet the people you need to meet."

"Send me the names of who you want me to choose." Once, he wouldn't have understood what she was asking without its being spelled out. He'd come a long way from the simple linesman from Rigel's cartel.

*   *   *

LATER, Ean called Rigel. Rigel answered promptly, a lot more promptly than he'd answered Ean's calls when Ean had worked for him.

"I'm on planet tomorrow. Why don't I meet you after I finish," Ean said. That way he wouldn't have to ask Vega or Helmo for a shuttle. "We could go for a drink."

Rigel's face creased into a smile. "I look forward to that. Where shall I meet you?"

Ean didn't know Haladea III at all. But half Bhaksir's team had taken leave recently. They'd spent time at a bar called the Night Owl. "The Night Owl. I'll call you when I finish."

TEN

EAN LAMBERT

WHEN EAN AND Radko arrived at the shuttle bay the following morning, Commodore Vega was waiting.

"Linesman Lambert. A *private* word with you."

Radko opened her mouth to speak.

Vega glared at her. "Spacer Radko, do you honestly believe anything will happen to him on board the *Lancastrian Princess*?"

"No, ma'am, but—"

Vega indicated the shuttle air lock. After a momentary hesitation, Radko moved on past them.

Alone, Ean felt vulnerable. Which was silly because he was safe here. At least, he had been until now.

"Safe," the ship agreed, and Helmo looked up from his console on the bridge as if the ship were saying it to him.

Ean waited.

"You might have the courtesy to notify me next time *before* you make plans of your own. Or even *after.*"

Were they talking about Rigel? He'd told Radko he'd agreed to meet with Rigel after the parliamentary session. Had he gotten Radko into trouble? "It was my idea."

"I am well aware it was your idea." Vega paused. "It's bad enough having to divert crew to guard you anyway when it's not their job. But to find that you're making your own plans—without consulting me—is not acceptable. Suddenly, I have to divert extra crew to watch you when they should be doing their own jobs."

"Oh." He should have talked to Radko first. She'd probably had other plans. But wouldn't she have told him? She was honest about things like that. "I'm sorry for the inconvenience."

"Next time let me know *before* you make plans." Vega turned on her heel and marched away.

Ean waited till she was out of sight before he entered the shuttle.

He was surprised to see Fergus Burns sitting next to Radko. Fergus was wearing the midnight blue uniform of House of Rickenback. The colors he'd been wearing when Ean had first met him.

Fergus grimaced at Ean's questioning look. "I know. I feel bad, but I cleared it with Leo. Apparently, there are some linesmen on planet. Admiral Galenos feels they'll talk more readily if they think I'm one of them."

"Doesn't Rickenback mind?" Effectively, Fergus was using the uniform to infiltrate the enemy. Ean could hear a trace of guilt in Fergus's line. He minded.

"Galenos and Lady Lyan are convincing talkers."

They were. But wearing a cartel uniform might not be the smartest move on a New Alliance world, considering all the cartel houses were allied with Gate Union. They were asking a lot of Fergus.

Fergus was a linesman. Technically, that placed him under Ean's care. Ean should talk to Abram about deliberately endangering him.

Radko said into the silence that followed, "Ean. Don't let Vega upset you. She's not used to linesmen, she's used to soldiers. She likes to be in control."

"*Did* you have something to do after this?"

"Other than follow you around? No."

He blew out his breath. "Thank you."

The shuttle took them to Confluence Station, where they met up with some of Bhaksir's team. Ean wasn't sure if they were off duty, if Vega had pulled them off to escort him later, or if they were there for Fergus. He didn't ask.

They caught a regular troop shuttle down to the planet with some off-duty crew. One advantage of having a world close by was that crew got rec leave. Everyone was in high spirits.

The last time Ean had landed on a planet had been after repairing the *Scion*. He'd been returning to Ashery, to Cartel Master Rigel's house. Back then, he'd been the only passenger in a luxury shuttle where he'd been too tired to appreciate the Naugahyde seats and the fine alcohol on hand. It had been his last job for House of Rigel. He'd arrived home, dropped into bed, and woken to find Michelle trying to kill him.

Ean smiled at the memory. It was only five months ago, but it felt like a lifetime.

This shuttle was a world away from that one. Four long bench seats facing each other. Two sets of two, ten soldiers to a bench. It was full. Ean was in the middle of the second row, Radko on his left, Fergus on his right. Radko's team leader, Bhaksir, and three more of the team—Ru Li, Hana, and Gossamer—were there as well.

Fergus didn't have an armrest to hang on to. Ean watched the other linesman's knuckles go white where he gripped his seat belt and wondered if he should sing.

Radko caught his eye and shook her head. She leaned close. "You can't spend all your time on planet providing a line for him. Let him get used to it now. Otherwise, you're simply making it worse."

The spacer opposite Fergus said, "Don't take space travel well?" He wore a Nova Tahitian uniform. The whole carrier could have been an advertisement for the united worlds of the New Alliance.

Fergus shook his head although in truth he traveled much better and was far more experienced than Ean. Tiny beads of sweat stood out on his forehead.

What would it be like to lose your lines altogether?

The spacer pulled down a sick bag. "You know how to use one of these?"

Fergus nodded and even managed to smile. "Thanks."

The lines were strong in Ean's mind at present. Lines two, three, four, and five on the shuttle, and through them he could hear the lines of the ship he'd left although they were faint. Ship lines were good. Shuttle lines were good.

They landed. The pilot cut the engine.

"Welcome to the headquarters of the New Alliance," Radko said, and made Ean and Fergus wait while the other occupants exited. She let them leave when only Ru Li and Bhaksir were left.

Ean exited, blinking in the strong sunlight, to where Hana and Gossamer waited for them. Ru Li and Bhaksir followed them out.

"There's something about the smell of a world," Bhaksir said.

For Ean, who often received information from the lines as scents, the smell of the world was quite mild.

"Yes, especially when we're about to go clubbing," Ru Li said. He spun a graceful pirouette. "Let's deliver our linesmen and go, people."

Ean didn't need four guards, plus Radko, to get himself to a meeting. Fergus might, because he was supposed to be making people believe he was sympathetic to the line cartels.

"We're not packages," he said. "We can deliver ourselves."

"Hoo, man. That's more than our job is worth. Do you want to get us the sack?"

Bhaksir looked at Ru Li. "Do you want to take first guard duty?"

"No, ma'am." Ru Li bowed apologetically. "I didn't mean anything by it, ma'am." He bowed to Ean. "Sir."

Ean wasn't sure if he was joking or not.

"Don't push it," Bhaksir warned. "Or you will be doing guard duty."

Ru Li danced another apologetic pirouette. "Sorry, ma'am."

"You'd better be."

They gathered in a group around Ean and Fergus and escorted them across to the barracks proper.

Bhaksir said to Fergus, "We'll deliver Ean first, then you."

Fergus nodded. At least he'd gotten over his initial lack-of-line sweats.

"We'll be at the Night Owl, waiting for you," Bhaksir told Ean.

"I thought you were going clubbing," Ean said.

"We are," Ru Li said. "After we've dumped you. After all, no one wants to sit in a stuffy parliament if they don't have to."

"Ru Li."

"Sorry, ma'am. But I haven't been on planet for ages."

Bhaksir actually smiled. "Contain your enthusiasm for another five minutes."

"What about you?" Ean asked Radko. Ru Li was right. Council meetings could be boring. Ean had been to plenty of them when they'd been held on Confluence Station.

Radko shook her head. "I'm coming with you."

"You shouldn't need to guard me in parliament." Half the people in the chamber were soldiers.

The New Alliance Council was modeled more on the quasi-military structure of Gate Union than it was on the regencies of the old Alliance. Seventy politicians, one from each world, plus seventy admirals, also one from each world. That made 140 seats, 140 votes. Unlike the old Alliance system—where each world provided a single political representative when council sat, and it didn't have to be the same one every time— these representatives were permanent members of the governing body.

"A new structure for a new future" was the common mantra, and while the sessions had been held on Confluence Station, Ean had picked up from most of them the satisfaction that their two votes were equal to Lancia's two votes.

Sometimes, their fear of Lancia seemed to be the one thing that united them.

"I'll be safe," Ean told Radko.

"You don't assign her work, Ean," Bhaksir said. "I do."

"But—"

"Are you questioning my decision?"

"No, but—"

"Really not questioning?"

"Ean," Radko said. "We've a sitting to attend. We'll be late."

AS a child growing up in the slums, politics had been something that affected Ean mostly in the fallout from political decisions. Bad decisions generally meant a flood of new poor into the slums. More people in an already overcrowded area, which led to turf wars.

Once Ean had become a linesman, Cartel Master Rigel incorporated the study of politics in his training. Along with fixing his teeth, fixing the crooked finger he'd broken as a boy, teaching him how to dress, to read, and how to speak flawless Standard. As he'd said, "Level-ten linesmen rate high on the social scale. People expect a standard of dress, speech, and knowledge. You may even occasionally mix with heads of state."

Occasionally! Ean had spent the last five months mixing with heads of state.

He knew everyone in the chamber. He'd spoken to each of them, individually and in groups.

Admiral Carrell of Eridanus was speaking. Eridanus was one of the twenty worlds that had come across to the New Alliance from Gate Union as part of the deal brokered by Nova Tahiti and Yaolin. Carrell was paranoid about the power of Lancia.

Carrell stopped speaking and nodded to Ean as he slid into one of the visitor's seats. "Linesman," he said.

Five months ago, most people wouldn't have even recognized him as a ten, let alone stop talking when he walked into the room. Ean nodded back.

Carrell resumed. "The fact remains. Haladea found this ship, but Lancia controls it, the way Lancia controls all of the alien ships. If we let them choose the captain, aren't we effectively giving them the ships?"

Lancia's biggest concern was that the captain would be anti-Lancia. Ean was more worried the captain wouldn't be suitable for the ship. Or that the two factions would reach a stalemate and not choose a captain.

Governor Jade, from Aratoga, said, "But Admiral, so far Lancia has had more success with the ships than the rest of us combined." Jade was pro-Lancia. She would support Lancia's choice.

"That's because they have a level-ten linesman," Almasett from New Viking interjected.

"So does Yaolin," Carrell said. "Why doesn't Yaolin control *one* of the ships?"

Even though there were 130 alien ships out there, when they said "one" like that, they meant one of the two ships with an eleventh line. The *Eleven* or the *Confluence*.

That was a tricky one to answer without giving away secrets that those who knew them didn't want known. Everyone looked at the Yaolins, most specifically to Admiral Orsaya, whose tone was frosty as she said, "Lambert didn't spend six months at Confluence Station. Linesman Rossi did."

It got nods all round. Ean hoped that didn't get back to Jordan Rossi.

"Even with only Lambert and Rossi," Admiral Galenos said, "we have as much capacity to mend ships' higher lines as Gate Union has at the moment."

There were more nods at that.

Galenos didn't stop there. "With the problems the stronger lines had at Confluence Station, we'd like to be certain the problem has gone away before we hand any ship over to another linesman."

"Quite," Carrell said, and there was a long pause, which Governor Jade was about to break, when Carrell said, "But we are here to talk about a captain for one of the line-eleven ships." His intense gaze swept the entire chamber. "This captain should be from a world other than Lancia."

"So who do you suggest?" Ahmed Gann asked.

Carrell stopped, almost as if he hadn't expected to get far enough to answer that question. "Someone from another world," he said, finally.

"And how do you plan on that?" Orsaya asked. "We're looking for a captain, Admiral. Someone with experience. And we all know how likely that is. Do you want us to put in an inexperienced Eridanus captain?"

"I don't want an inexperienced captain. None of us do."

Orsaya's voice rose over the babble that resulted. "You want us to put an experienced captain on the *Eleven* instead?"

That was never going to happen. They'd been talking about it for months. Captains and ships bonded. Michelle could have asked Helmo to captain the *Eleven*, but he would have refused, and it would have been the last time they spoke civilly to each other. The *Lancastrian Princess* was Helmo's, and Helmo was the *Lancastrian Princess*'s. Nothing would change that.

No, Abram and Katida had both said the only way they would get an experienced captain on the *Eleven* was to take a second-in-command from one of the ships. Maybe Helmo's second, Vanje Solberg. Except few worlds wanted a Lancastrian on the *Eleven*.

Ean lost track of the conversation. So had everyone else, it seemed, for half of them seemed to be holding their own animated conversations.

Admiral Katida called for silence and got it.

Her voice was clear above the last few passionate speakers. "No one denies that we would all like an experienced captain on the *Eleven*. Given we can't have that, we must—"

Admiral MacClennan from Nova Tahiti raised his hand.

"Admiral?" Katida sounded wary.

MacClennan never spoke. Why should he? Ahmed Gann was the most persuasive speaker on the council, according to Abram and Katida. Katida had also warned Ean, "Don't underestimate MacClennan, Ean. He knows how to get what he wants, and you don't get to be where Ahmed Gann is alone."

"What if we could have it?" MacClennan asked. "An experienced captain, I mean."

"And how are we likely to get that?"

"Permit me, if I may?" and MacClennan looked around the chamber for permission to continue.

"Go ahead," Michelle said, for the politicians, and Katida nodded for the military.

MacClennan brought up an image on the large screen on the podium. A woman, around forty years old. She wore a Nova Tahitian uniform. Behind her face, the background was that of a warship.

"Selma Kari Wang," MacClennan said.

The name caused an animated buzz of conversation among the seated parliamentarians.

The woman whose ship had been chopped to pieces. Like Professor Gerrard's had. Ean could see the name of the ship behind the woman. GU *Kari Wang*. The registry was Nova Tahiti. Radko could have told him how many people the ship carried. Ean based his guesstimate on the fact that the shuttlebay doors he could see were numbered 6–10. It was a big ship.

"The *Kari Wang* was testing new weapons out near the Edamon binaries," MacClennan said. "It was a combined Gate Union/Redmond interworld exercise."

Ean knew about combined exercises. The alien ships and the line elevens were a combined exercise, full of red tape that slowed everything down.

"Her ship was chosen because of its exemplary record."

MacClennan had to stop for a moment. Ean couldn't work out if it was staged, but if it was, it was cleverly done.

"Less than three days after Nova Tahiti joined the New Alliance, four Gate Union ships used a Masson field to destroy the *Kari Wang*. The crew were killed, all except the captain, who was in the middle of her prescribed regular space training and happened to be in a suit at the time."

"That was lucky," Speaker Rhodes from Al Fawaris remarked.

There was a wave of awkwardness that Ean could taste—even without lines—from the military side of the room, but only Admiral Orsaya spoke. "I doubt she considers it so."

MacClennan let the uncomfortable silence extend before he cleared his throat. "The automatic safeties on the suit clicked in, kept her alive."

"So she's unharmed while the rest of her crew is dead," Speaker Rhodes said. "Doesn't that strike you as suspicious?"

"She wasn't exactly unharmed." It was the first show of strong emotion Ean had seen from MacClennan. "She lost her legs."

Kari Wang was the sole survivor, saved because she had been in a space suit at the time. No one asked if she was a cripple. Prosthetic legs were better than human legs nowadays.

"Is she sane?" Admiral Katida asked.

MacClennan shrugged. "Time will tell."

The admirals liked MacClennan's answer even if the politicians didn't.

"No one could accuse Kari Wang of being pro-Lancian," Ahmed Gann said.

Ean saw the look both Katida and Orsaya shot Gann's way. He wished he had access to more lines than just the twos, threes, and fives in this room. He got the feeling Orsaya hadn't been expecting this any more than Katida or the Lancastrians had. Weren't Nova Tahiti and Yaolin working together?

"An experienced captain, you say," Speaker Rhodes said. "From Nova Tahiti." It was obvious the suggestion appealed to him.

"I have heard of her," Admiral Carrell said.

Admiral Orsaya thumped the desk in front of her. "There is no doubting her capability," she said. "But the woman has just lost her ship. Others have asked. Is she sane?"

It was the first time Ean had ever seen Yaolin and Nova Tahiti on opposite sides.

"We don't know," MacClennan said. "We do know she's a strong woman. If anyone can do it, she can. I believe we should let her try."

They debated it for another hour, but Ean could tell it was a foregone conclusion. The council voted one hundred to forty in favor of giving Captain Kari Wang a try.

"THAT came out of the void," Katida said, as she joined Michelle, Abram, and Ean, with Radko standing to attention as she normally did when she was on duty. Ean wished she would at least drink tea with them.

"That's because if we'd known about it, we'd have taken steps to halt it," Michelle said.

Even Orsaya, because Orsaya had been one of the forty voting against Captain Kari Wang.

"Maybe she'll be a good captain," Ean said. The council had asked lots of questions about her capability. Everyone agreed she was good. Even Abram had nodded once.

"We know she's a competent captain," Katida said. "Under normal circumstances, I'd vote for her myself. But she's just lost her ship, Ean. She cannot possibly be of sound mind right now."

AFTERWARD, Abram organized half a team of guards to escort them back into the city, to The Night Owl.

"This is starting to get silly," Ean said to Radko. "We can't move without guards around us."

Radko smiled faintly. "I'm a guard."

"Did you ever think, when you joined the *Lancastrian Princess*, you'd be following me around instead of doing what you were employed to do?"

If Vega had her way, the guards on the *Lancastrian Princess* would guard Michelle, and that was all they would do. They wouldn't spend half their time out on alien ships. They wouldn't have to trail around after linesmen. They would protect the heir to the throne of Lancia. Period.

It had been Radko's life before Ean had arrived. And Bhaksir's and her team. And Sale's team, too, although nowadays Sale's team spent more time on the alien ships than Ean did.

"I'm finding life interesting right now," Radko said. "And with Michelle on world so much, it would be boring otherwise."

It was boring with Michelle on world. Lonelier, too. Ean didn't want to think about it. He pulled out his comms and called Rigel. "I've finished what I needed to."

"Excellent," and Rigel's face creased into a smile that didn't reach his eyes. "Why don't I meet you at this Night Owl?"

Ean clicked off thoughtfully. He didn't like the feeling that Rigel was sitting around waiting for him.

ELEVEN

STELLAN VILHJALMSSON

THE MESSAGE ON Stellan's comms was coded and to the point. Meeting at the Night Owl 30 mins, along with coordinates and a link to what turned out to be a bar. So Linesman Lambert liked meeting in bars, did he? So did Stellan, for they were full of strangers. It was easy to murder someone in a bar. It should be easy to question someone there as well.

He changed into something as nondescript and unmemorable as his last outfit but this one suitable for clubbing, and left.

Stellan groaned when he saw the uniforms. A soldiers' bar. He hated working in soldiers' bars. It only took one alert patron to realize something was wrong and sound the alarm, and the rest of them would react the way they'd been trained to. Those who weren't too drunk, that was. He'd have to get Lambert away from here.

He groaned again when he saw the tall, white-haired woman at the back of the room. Dr. Randella Abbey. Markan should have told him if he was likely to run into someone he knew. Then, Markan probably hadn't known either. Abbey was Wallacian, and Wallacia was allied with Gate Union. She was, effectively, in enemy territory.

She looked like a Wallacian, too, with her tall, stick-thin body and the stark white hair. She wore a bejeweled white pantsuit, and her hair was tipped with silver. She stood out like a beacon.

Abbey raised a hand in greeting, then went back to talking to the blue-haired woman she was with. Blue was fashionable, for a number of people had hair that color, at least two of them with white tips over the blue. This woman's blue was solid.

Stellan nodded to Abbey, then headed for the nearest terminal to order himself a drink. As he waited for his order, he looked around.

He saw Morton Paretsky first. Paretsky was a big man although he'd lost a lot of weight since his last public vid images. He was talking to the second most exotically dressed person in the room, a man with white tips in his blue hair. Cartel Master Rigel. Rigel wasn't wearing a cartel uniform, nor was the woman with him. A linesman, Stellan guessed, for they both looked uncomfortable in their casual clothes.

They were at one of the tables at the back. You had to pay extra for the table, but it came with noise canceling and an in-table server. If you wanted to talk, it was the best place in the room to be.

Rigel was getting last-minute instructions—or a dressing-down—from Paretsky. Rigel nodded once or twice and looked up every time the door opened. The woman did, too, with a lot more eagerness.

Stellan edged his way carefully around to where they were talking, a listening device on the tip of his finger, ready to place as he "accidentally" bumped into Rigel. The bug was so small that if Rigel did see it, he would think it was a piece of lint and brush it off. Not that Stellan planned to place it where Rigel would see it.

Abbey cut across to Stellan. "I hope you're not working."

He could have said the same of her. He'd worked with her once. Roscracia and Wallacia, chasing a madman who'd liked to butcher soldiers in both fleets. By the end, he wasn't sure who was craziest. Their target or Abbey.

The blue-haired woman she'd been with scowled at them both.

"Friend of yours?" Stellan asked.

"My best work."

What sort of work would Abbey consider her best? Stellan forced himself not to look back over his shoulder or twitch. "Regen?" Abbey specialized in the area where nerve, muscle, and tissue systems worked together.

"You might say. I'm proud of it. You don't know her? She was military."

"There are hundreds of thousands of people in any one fleet. We don't all know each other." Abbey knew that as well as he did.

Abbey's lips curved into a smile. "You wouldn't recognize her for the same woman, anyway."

Not a regen, then. What else could Abbey do? Stellan glanced over his shoulder. The woman was still scowling. "You should have fixed the smile muscles at the same time. Stopped her from frowning."

"That would look unnatural," Abbey said.

Abbey was as crazy as some of her patients. "So what brings you to the capital of the New Alliance?"

"This is my home."

He didn't know why he was surprised. Just because she was Wallacian didn't mean she had to live on Wallacia. Stellan himself came from one of the Roscracian territories, not Roscracia itself. If you went back three generations, his own family was New Viking, and they were now part of the New Alliance.

"This used to be a nice world. Before the infidels took over. Now it's just a massive building site. Anything good is being knocked down, because suddenly it's the 'center' of the galaxy."

Once Gate Union won the war, it would return to being a backwater.

Lambert walked in the door then, and Stellan hadn't placed the bug yet. "Excuse me."

He was too late, for Rigel had seen Lambert, and was half-way to the door to meet him. Paretsky disappeared into the crowd.

TWELVE

EAN LAMBERT

THEY CAUGHT A cart up to the Night Owl. The carts were busy, but they got a compartment almost to themselves, except for a woman in Nova Tahitian uniform sitting in one corner. Initially, Ean thought Radko had arranged it that way, but at the next stop a group of noisy soldiers pushed their way in, glanced at the only other occupant, then pushed their way through to the next—packed—compartment. He looked more closely, and realized the woman wore commodore pips. In fact, he recognized her. After the council meeting, she'd gone up and spoken to Admiral MacClennan.

The woman saw him watching her and came over to them. "Clemence Favager." She held out her hand.

Ean shook.

"You'll like our captain, Linesman. She's a good soldier."

"Thank you." He hoped she hadn't made the trip just to tell him that.

It must have shown in his face, for she laughed. "Hardly. I would have collared you after the session. No, I come up here to look at the architecture." She stopped as more soldiers got on at the next stop. These were Nova Tahitians. They saluted her and kept moving as if they'd always meant to pass through.

"And sometimes to scare the rank and file," Favager said.

"Oh," and Ean picked up on the only word that felt safe for conversation. "Architecture?"

"Haladea was settled in the first wave after we got line ships. Back in those days, everyone based their buildings on Old Earth designs. That's why your own world has taken so much from the Chinese dynasties." He presumed she meant Lancia. "This one. Ancient Greece. We're losing it now, with all the new building that's going on, but there are pockets. Up here, for example, we have the finest Corinthian columns in the galaxy, and that includes on Earth itself."

The cart jerked to a halt. They got out. Favager's uniform gave them space and fast access to the exit.

Up so high, they could see the city spread out below them. Favager pointed to the central section. "Down there, that's all tidal land."

It looked like barracks to Ean.

"It used to flood when the three worlds came into conjunction. Until they built the tidal walls. Those walls are a hundred meters high."

"Behind us." Favager indicated the stone cliff, from which buildings had been hewn out. There was a wide stone pathway between the buildings, flanked by massive, carved-stone columns. "See those columns. That's based on the Temple of Zeus, from Earth. It's gone now, of course. Even the records are gone. Those Old Earth records can't be read by technology built on lines. Those that we can read—" She sighed.

"Have you been to Old Earth?" Ean asked. She made it sound so personal, whereas to him, Earth was just something that had happened so long ago, it wasn't real anymore.

"There's not much there," Favager said. "It's mostly desert. There'd be, what, 20 million people if you're lucky. They live on tourism, and there's not much of that. It's sad, really."

She kept up a monologue, describing each of the buildings as they passed them. "That's based on the Acropolis." It, too, had massive stone columns. "Not that it looks much like the original."

Favager, Ean decided, was an Old Earth nut.

She left them outside their destination with a final, "You *will* like our captain, Linesman." She continued on across the plaza, stopping occasionally to glance at one of the stone columns, or another piece of architecture.

"I know where I'll go when I want to learn anything about Old Earth," Ean said.

Radko laughed. "She's quite overpowering, isn't she?"

The Night Owl was set off to one side of the cliff face. There were dizzying staircases set into the rock at regular intervals leading down to the barracks. The staircases were full of soldiers making their way up or down. It made Ean's legs ache just watching them. He was glad they'd caught the cart up.

The bar was busier than Ashery at Festival time. Three-quarters of the patrons were in uniform. Most of them were simple spacers with pockets as bare as Ean's. He saw Ru Li and Gossamer, who ignored him. Or didn't notice him, he wasn't sure which.

Rigel was waiting for him, which was good, because he had no idea where to start looking. "I've hired us a table." He dragged Ean across to a reserved table where a woman was seated, and sighed with relief as the noise canceling came on. "You haven't changed your taste in bars, at any rate."

The bar Ean had frequented at Ashery had always been full of apprentices and lower-level linesmen. It was cheap, and it was close to the cartel house.

"I can't afford any better," Ean said.

He was on the same contract he'd signed with Rigel. It didn't pay much, and it had another ten years to run. As Michelle had told him once, "We'll make it up to you somehow, but we'd be stupid to change the contract. This way you're bonded water-tight to me."

Once Ean would have hated the thought of being bonded to a member of the royal family of Lancia. How times had changed.

He didn't recognize the woman until she stood up and hugged him. "Ean."

"Kaelea." He hugged her back. "What are you doing here?"

He turned to Radko. "This is Kaelea. She's a linesman from House of Rigel."

There was silence while the two women sized each other up.

"This is awkward," Rigel said, with forced jovialness. "If I'd realized—"

Ean realized what he thought. "Oh. Radko's not—"

Radko cut across him, "You're a level-seven linesman?"

Not that you could tell from the clothes Kaelea wore, but Radko wouldn't have cut across him if she didn't want him to shut up. Ean bit his bottom lip and didn't say anything more.

"Why don't we sit down?" Rigel said, with forced oiliness. He sat down himself, as if glad to.

Ean slid onto the seat opposite Rigel. Kaelea moved to sit

beside him. Somehow, Radko got there first and slid between them.

Kaelea looked put out as she sat beside Radko.

The joys of being a bodyguard, Ean supposed. People misinterpreted what you did and why you did it.

"Let's order drinks," Rigel said. He looked at Radko. "Maybe your girlfriend might like to—" He waved a hand at the crowd behind them.

"I'll sit." Radko sat back and closed her eyes. "It's noisy out there."

"She won't be in the way," Ean said. Normally, the cartel master would have been all over a beautiful woman, and Radko was attractive. She bore a distinct family resemblance to Michelle, except her hair was shorter and golden brown rather than black, and her eyes weren't the distinctive genetically engineered Lancastrian royal blue. Ean had never asked, but he suspected Radko wouldn't have to dig hard to find a direct ancestor to someone in the royal family. She had the same dimples.

It shouldn't have been awkward even if Kaelea was here.

Rigel looked around, almost as if he was looking for someone, then shrugged and perused the drinks menu. Ean ordered after him. "Tea," Radko mouthed, when he looked her way, even though she didn't appear to open her eyes to see him looking at her.

He punched the order through.

Rigel sat back. "I hear you've been busy."

What had he heard? Was he fishing for information about the ships?

"Same old, same old," Ean said. "Lots of lines to mend." Although Rossi did as much of that as he did, more, actually.

They were at war, and Rigel and Kaelea were on the opposite side. He needed to remember that.

It was a funny war when your enemies could visit you in what was, effectively, enemy territory. Why hadn't they locked down the Haladean worlds? Radko had said the other day that Lancia was closed to Gate Union ships now. Balian and Aratoga had closed their worlds as well.

"Given you're the only ten in the New Alliance, you're probably run ragged," Kaelea said. "I can see they've got you mending their warships. Co-opted you into the fleet, even," and she glanced at Radko, as if that explained how he came to be going around with a soldier.

There was also Rossi. "It isn't that much different to what I used to do with Rigel," Ean said. It wasn't a lie, not the line-repairing part. "When they ask me to fix lines, I fix them."

"And there's plenty of that," Rigel said. "The backlog from the confluence isn't going down much."

Their drinks arrived. Aged Grenache for Rigel and Kaelea, tea for Radko, Lancian wine for Ean.

"My," Rigel said. "Your taste has improved."

He hadn't even realized he'd ordered it. It was what they drank on the *Lancastrian Princess*. It had been automatic. Even now, it was a comforting reminder that Michelle and Abram were looking after him. He smiled as he raised the glass to his lips.

"I've developed a taste for it."

"On the contract you had with me, you couldn't afford wine like that. They must be paying you more." Rigel was fishing. Line contracts were Rigel's business. Changing a contract midcontract was as bad as walking out on one.

"I wish," Ean said. "My contract hasn't changed. I do a lot of work with Lancia. They offer Lancian wine on ship. And I'm busy. I don't have anything else to spend my money on."

Rigel nodded. "Busy times for all of us."

"It is," agreed Ean, savoring his chilled wine.

Radko sipped her tea with her eyes nearly closed, but he thought she gave a tiny smile of approval.

Morton Paretsky slid into the seat beside Rigel. Rigel looked relieved.

Ean had met Paretsky once, back when he'd been certified, and Paretsky had been grand master of the cartels. Ean's own certification had been unusual for a ten because he'd been certified through a public ceremony. Most tens went to the grand master for private certification. Rigel had made Ean do it in public, along with the dozens of other linesmen. It was only after he'd been certified as a ten by the tester hurriedly brought in to test his level that he'd been taken to the Grand Master to get his bars. Paretsky had been grim and angry.

"You should have brought him to me for personal certification," he'd said.

At the time, Ean had thought Rigel's choosing a public certification was because he was too mean to pay the money for a private ceremony. Now he was sure it was because Paretsky would have failed him. Ean's untrained approach to the lines hadn't gained him any followers in the higher levels of the cartel system.

Today, Paretsky was genial and smiling. "Guess who I met here." He looked up and out, into the crowd, and Ean thought he was staring at a white-haired woman with pale skin. Or maybe the blue-haired older woman beside her, who was glaring at their table. Until Paretsky added, "Fergus Burns," and Fergus slid in beside Paretsky.

"Hello, Rigel," Fergus said. "I haven't seen you in years." He held out his hand. "Last time I saw you was at Shaolin if I remember rightly. I must say, I like the hair."

Rigel smiled and almost preened. "Thank you. Done by DeGraves himself."

"And Kaelea," Fergus said. "Last time I saw you was at Confluence Station. You'd come to fix the lines."

Just like that they were relaxed and talking. Fergus could do that. He knew everyone; he knew what they liked to talk about.

"Lancian wine," Paretsky said. "I might have some of that myself."

Fergus chose a cheaper wine—at least, Ean presumed it was cheaper—which was surprising, because he knew Fergus enjoyed Lancian wine as much as he did.

The conversation roamed, from fashion, to travel—Rigel and Paretsky had no difficulty getting a jump—to linesmen Ean had only heard about. Janni Naidan, a ten from Laito. Geraint Jones, the ten from House of Rickenback. Which, of course, led to Jordan Rossi, who had been the other ten at House of Rickenback before Yaolin bought his contract.

"How is Jordan nowadays?" Paretsky asked.

"He's fine," Fergus said. He didn't tell them he wasn't Rossi's assistant anymore, even though they obviously assumed that. "You know Jordan. He hasn't changed."

"It must have been quite a blow, Rickenback's selling his contract like that."

Fergus shrugged. "You know Jordan," he said again.

Both cartel men laughed. Paretsky, in particular, laughed

until tears came to his eyes. "I feel for Leo," he said. "Rossi has a long memory for injustices done to him."

In his role as the new Grand Master of the line cartels, Leo Rickenback had recently visited both Ean and Rossi. Ean had found him a good match for Fergus, deprecating and unexpectedly kind.

Paretsky wiped his eyes. "I admit Leo's selling his contract was a surprise. Still, it was a perfectly legal exchange even if Leo shouldn't have done it." He turned to Ean. "Your contract, on the other hand. That was extortion, pure and simple."

Was he talking about the length of it? Most line contracts ran for three to five years. Ean had been desperate enough to sign a twenty-year contract, but he had known what he was doing when he signed it.

"I was happy to sign." Rigel had promised to train him in more than the lines, and he had.

Paretsky gave him an odd look. "The sheer effrontery of what Lady Lyan did. The arrogance of it."

He meant the signing over to Michelle. "It's perfectly legal," Ean said. Michelle's lawyers had gone over the agreement in agonizingly minute detail. They'd spent weeks on it.

"No, no," Paretsky said. "She marched into Rigel's home, held a gun to his head, and forced him to sign."

"It wasn't quite like that." She'd held the gun to Ean's head. Only it hadn't been a gun, it had been a disruptor. "She didn't have a weapon when Rigel signed over the contract."

Ean had destroyed the disruptor before that. Although, knowing Michelle, she'd probably had a second weapon.

"Lady Lyan tried to kill you," Kaelea said. "I was a witness to that, Ean."

"Then she demanded your contract," Paretsky said.

Ean looked at Rigel. Surely, Rigel would explain. But Rigel just smiled, and said, "We're here to fix a wrong that's been done to you, Ean."

Non-Lancastrians didn't understand the concept of revenge. "Rigel did contract a five out to Mi . . . to Lady Lyan when she asked for a six."

"I'm sure that was a mistake," Paretsky said.

"The five died."

"It was a misunderstanding," Paretsky said. "No doubt

Lady Lyan thought she was asking for a six when she actually asked for a five."

Ean took another sip of his wine while he considered what to say next. "Lady Lyan owns my contract now. She's my boss." They couldn't honestly believe Michelle would let him go back to House of Rigel even if he wanted to, and he didn't want to. He'd made a place for himself here. He wasn't leaving Michelle. He wasn't leaving the alien lines.

"Only because she forced Rigel to sign the contract over."

Rigel wasn't normally quiet, but today he let Paretsky do the talking. Ean studied his old cartel master's face, trying to guess the expressions. They should have done this on a ship or a station, then he might be able to pick up from the lines how happy Rigel was about all this.

"You'll never make it stick," Fergus said.

Did Fergus even know what had happened?

"We have witnesses," Paretsky said. "Rigel. Kaelea here. And Ean. It should be enough. After all, everyone knows the high-level linesmen should be in the cartels."

"I'm not saying she did anything wrong," Ean said. "And we're at war. The New Alliance won't hand my contract over to Gate Union." He hoped. Did Rigel have the right of it? Could he force him to go?

He might as well not have spoken.

"I'm prepared to say what Lady Lyan did," Kaelea said.

Radko gave her a sharp look.

"Even if they try to intimidate me."

"Against Lady Lyan." Fergus sounded dubious. "What does Leo say about it?" The Grand Master oversaw all contract disputes.

Paretsky made a dismissive motion with his hand.

"Rickenback won't be Grand Master much longer," Rigel assured him.

Paretsky intervened hastily. "You do know that Rickenback's position is temporary," he said to Fergus.

"I didn't realize it was a temporary role," Fergus said. "We don't get much cartel news out here. We're very isolated." Which was a lie. Fergus kept in touch. Ean himself knew more about current cartel doings than he'd ever learned at Rigel's. "Does the position automatically revert to you, Morton?"

Paretsky nodded.

"When does that happen?"

"These things take time," Paretsky said.

Fergus looked dubious.

Ean glanced around the room, wanting this over with. Ru Li and Gossamer were dancing, Ru Li with his typical showy abandon. When the music stopped, they were close to the blue-haired woman Ean thought Paretsky had been looking at earlier. Ru Li bowed to her and held out a hand. His message was clear. Dance?

She scowled at him, then scowled at Ean, as if she'd seen him watching them. Her gaze chilled him; he wasn't sure why. After which she turned to a tall, dark-haired man standing near them, and looked pointedly at Ean again.

The dark-haired man nodded and leaned back against the bar.

His jacket opened to show what appeared to be a long pendant that stretched from his chest to his navel. It was patterned with ochres and browns, around two centimeters wide at the top, tapering to half that at the bottom.

Surely not. A flick knife. When he'd been a boy, Marieke Cann had terrorized Ean with just such a knife. It still made him sweat, remembering it. The blade flicked out in a fraction of a second with enough force to impale a man—or a boy— without the holder having to do more than keep it steady.

He was glad he was with Radko, and that some of Bhaksir's team were in the bar. He turned his attention back to Rigel. It was his imagination, but he felt the blue-haired woman's eyes boring into him.

"I shouldn't have let the contract go in the first place," Rigel told Ean. "I did wrong by you. I'm trying to fix it."

The words coming out of Rigel's mouth sounded unlike him.

"I like my new job," Ean said. "I like my new boss. We both know the contract is legal. Lady Lyan did not force or coerce you in any way. I'll tell the Grand Master that."

"She tried to kill you." It was a feeble protest.

Ean stood up. "It was nice to see you again, Rigel," even though it hadn't been. He waited for Kaelea and Radko to let him out. For a moment he thought Kaelea wasn't going to move, but she did, after an obvious bump from Radko.

"It was good to talk to you again, Kaelea. Maybe one day when you're mending lines close by you could call me, and we'll meet."

With a war on, and her on one side and him on the other, that was unlikely.

Kaelea's gaze stopped at Radko, slid past. "I'd like that." She sat down again. Fergus moved from his place beside Paretsky to slide in beside Kaelea.

Ean hesitated, not sure whether to wait for Fergus or not. Radko pushed him on. "Let's go somewhere quiet," she said. Ean looked back as they walked away. Fergus was talking again to Paretsky and Rigel. He said something that made them laugh. Kaelea was watching Ean.

He half smiled at her.

"Your girlfriend?" Radko asked.

"No." Few linesmen had regular partners. "I slept with her occasionally." He didn't know if Radko had a partner. Would it be rude to ask?

Did he really want to know?

The dark-haired stranger followed them out.

"Do you see the man who was over near the blue-haired woman?" Ean asked.

"I do. Keep walking. Act as if you haven't seen him."

That was hard to do when he wanted to keep checking over his shoulder.

"He's got a knife."

"I'm betting he's got more than one," Radko said, grimly. "Sing my comms open to Bhaksir, Craik, and Sale."

"Sale's on the *Eleven*," but Ean sang line five.

Sale wasn't on ship. Ean could hear that her line was almost as close as Bhaksir's was.

"What do you want me to tell them?"

"Nothing," Radko said. "I want the channel open."

It was open. He could hear bar noises from Bhaksir's comms.

"A whole team left the bar after you did," Bhaksir said. "Following you. It might be coincidence." She didn't sound as if she thought it coincidence. "Turn left at the next corner. See if he follows."

Radko turned left.

This street was narrower and quieter, but there was still a sprinkling of pedestrians.

"They turned, too," Bhaksir said. She sounded as if she had started running. "Whatever you do, Radko, don't turn left again. The next four streets along are dead ends."

"Understood," Radko said.

"We're thirty seconds away."

There was a rush of footsteps behind them. Ean thought it was Bhaksir until the black-haired man grabbed his arm.

He tried to pull away.

Radko chopped down on the other man's wrist, hard enough to jar Ean's arm.

The attacker swung around to her instead.

Two more men came in to help the first. Ean bumped one out of the way. It was like hitting a wall.

Radko's knee connected with the black-haired man's crotch.

"Bitch." Although it was more of a wheeze than anything.

Thirty seconds till Bhaksir arrived. More attackers converged. How many were there? A whole team, Bhaksir had said.

Ean punched one of them. A feeble punch, but it felt as if he'd broken his hand. He bumped the attacker out of the way instead and tackled the second one.

Another man wrapped an arm around Ean's neck and jerked him backward. Radko kicked Ean's captor and punched another at the same time.

This was the longest thirty seconds outside of the void.

Passersby stopped to gawk. One passerby reached out and tripped up another attacker. The attacker turned on the rescuer.

"Thanks," Ean gasped, "but don't get involved."

Bhaksir thundered around the corner then, and made straight for Ean's rescuer.

Ean stepped in front of her. "No, no. He's on our side." He pushed the rescuer away. "I told you. Don't help."

Bhaksir kicked at the person who'd tried to strangle Ean. He went down, and stayed down. "Stay out of this, civilian."

The civilian backed away, to Ean's relief, but Ean didn't have time to be relieved for long for the black-haired man grabbed him again.

Ean tried Radko's trick, but Radko was there before him, punching the black-haired man away.

Two attackers converged on Radko, one high. She ducked away from him, and Ean used the bulk of his own body to bump the other one away.

"We're going to have to teach you to fight," Radko said.

Ean saw a flash of ochre and brown behind Radko.

The flick knife.

Desperation gave him strength and speed. He charged, knocked the flick knife away from Radko's back, and pushed down. Into the dark-haired man's thigh.

Ean pushed harder.

The dark-haired man howled.

Bright blood spurted.

Ean stepped back, shaking.

Nobody moved.

Ean became aware that Craik's team, and Sale, had arrived.

"Anyone else want to try with knives?" Sale asked. There was a member of Craik's team behind each attacker, pressing a weapon into his or her back.

"These are needle guns, incidentally. Feel the spikes."

Based on the careful way they moved, they recognized the weapons.

"Radko," Sale said, and gestured at the blood.

Radko knelt beside the black-haired man and took a mini medikit out of a pocket on her belt. "Keep still," she told him. "Or you'll bleed to death."

Ean stepped back to give them room. Stepped back farther as Bhaksir's team moved in with the plastic handcuff ties. He found himself next to the stranger who had tried to help. The man was wiping his hand, as if some of the blood from the man Ean had stabbed had spurted that far.

Ean forced away guilt. "Thank you for helping."

The stranger smiled. "It was educational. Two teams instantly at your disposal."

Was he being funny?

"How did you know it was *two* teams?" He was probably a military man, off duty, trained to respond like Sale and the others were. "Which fleet are you from?" Sale or Radko might put in a good word for his assistance.

He glanced back at Radko, and was surprised to realize he'd moved farther away than he'd meant to. He stepped toward safety.

Only to find something pressed against his stomach.

He looked down. Ochre and brown, spattered with the red-brown of drying blood.

THIRTEEN

EAN LAMBERT

"WE BOTH KNOW what this is," the stranger said quietly. "I know how to use it. And we both know the end result. Don't draw their attention. Don't do anything stupid. Move back slowly."

Ean moved back slowly. "Are you going to kill me?"

"If I wanted to do that, you'd be long dead by now."

Which was a relief although why did everyone want hostages nowadays. First Fergus, now him.

Ean's comms was still open. They heard Sale's call to Abram—although hopefully this man didn't realize she was calling Abram.

"Turn it off," the stranger said.

Ean hadn't turned a comms off by hand for so long he fumbled doing it.

"If you try to warn them, I *will* kill you."

They backed around the corner. A left corner.

The relief that flooded Ean made him shake. Bhaksir had said these were dead ends. This man couldn't take him anywhere except back the way they had come.

"Give me your comms."

Ean handed it over.

His captor tossed it away.

"What do you want with me?"

Their alley was little more than a court, with a building on both sides and one at the end. There were doors in each of the buildings. His captor chose the one on the left.

"Ean." Radko's voice. "Stay silent," his captor warned, and tried the door. The door was locked.

Shades of Fergus's race through the *Gruen*. It was a pity these doors weren't line controlled. Ean could have opened it to let the other man through, then sung it shut. Or the other way around.

"Ean." Voices, coming closer.

Ean tensed, ready. As soon as Radko and the others came round the corner, he would push this man—flick knife and all—and run.

His captor raised his knife, as if he'd realized what Ean was thinking.

Ean stepped back involuntarily.

The other man used the blade to push a wad of something between the door and the handle. He closed the blade, then released it again, quickly.

There was a quiet whumph. The door swung open.

"Ean." Radko and Bhaksir came around the corner.

Ean's captor shoved him inside the door and pushed it shut behind them. "Run."

Ean tried to trip him.

The civilian recovered midtrip and scissored his legs to trip Ean instead. "I want you alive, but you don't have to be whole. I'll break your legs and carry you if you get too clever."

He looked as if he meant it. Ean considered it momentarily. It would slow them down long enough for Radko and Bhaksir to reach them.

Maybe.

The civilian hauled Ean up.

They stopped at the lift. Ean's captor reached in, pressed three buttons, and stepped out again. "Move," he said to Ean, and they kept running, past the lift, onto the stairs.

They went down.

"What do you want with me?" Ean asked as he stumbled and regained his balance.

"Shut up and keep moving."

The civilian pushed Ean in front of him. "Move faster, or you may end up at the bottom in more than one piece."

It couldn't be far down. They had been at ground level. Ean ran, focused on where he put his feet. His captor pushed him to move faster. How were Radko and Bhaksir going to find him? They would have followed the lift.

"Stop." His captor pushed the knife toward him. Ean stopped, hands on his knees, breathing deep. He was fitter than he had been months ago, but if this man thought he wasn't, so much the better. As he waited, he listened for lines—any lines that might be around to help.

The building was old, preline. There was nothing he could use.

Or was there? One line. The other man's comms. He pulled in his breath to sing.

Another whump, and a lighter patch appeared where a door had been.

"Out." The civilian pushed Ean out.

He stepped onto a ledge and found the barracks spread far below him. Ean grabbed at the railing in front of him, which creaked, and moved.

The civilian grabbed him away. "I didn't bring you this far just to have you fall down a cliff."

"We're better back inside."

"With your friends. I don't think so." He pushed Ean to the left. "Save your breath. You'll need it."

Speaking of breath. Ean kept one hand against the wall as he made his way carefully along the path cut into the cliff. Just a tiny song, to the line that was close. *"Open a channel to Radko's comms,"* only he didn't have time to find Radko's line without the ship as an intermediary. He extended the song to include all ships on both fleets, in case his signal wasn't getting through. Surely someone would be listening and understand what he was trying to do.

"Are you *singing*?"

"I do it when I'm nervous." What information could he pass through that would help Radko? "Anyone would be nervous walking along the side of a cliff like this."

Now that he was getting used to it, he could see they were on a walkway between two sets of the steep stairs that soldiers climbed to get to the plateau that housed the Night Owl and other bars. In fact, they were coming close to one set of stairs now. It was blocked by a large iron gate.

That wouldn't stop this civilian for long.

"What happens when you run out of explosive to unlock gates?" Radko was used to interpreting for him. She might understand what he was trying to say.

"Do you ever shut up?"

He thought about saying, "Not often," but that would probably antagonize the other man. Instead, he waited while the other man pushed explosive into the lock and raised his voice around when the whump would come.

"Is anyone listening?"

"Listen," and Ean found the knife pressed against his stomach. "One more word—or note—out of you, and you'll find this through your side. It won't kill you straightaway, mind. You'll have plenty of time to do what I want first."

What did he want him to do? The distraction had come at the worst possible time, for Ean had missed any replies from line five, if there were any.

He didn't have time for any more singing, for the civilian forced him down the steps at a run, pushing other stair climbers out of the way.

"Sorry," Ean gasped, to one person he nearly knocked over.

They were two flights from the bottom when Ean saw guards in gray, running from the barracks. Three, four teams of them.

They'd heard him.

The civilian slowed.

There were shouts from above. The civilian glanced back. "Your friends found us quickly." It was almost conversational. Like it had been earlier, when he'd commented on Ean's having two teams come to rescue him. "So you have a trace."

A line was as good as a trace any day. If Ean had the breath, he'd have sung his thanks to the line five that had helped him.

The civilian took out his comms and punched in a code. "I need an out," he said. "Give me—" Ean only noticed the pause because he was used to it from Abram and Michelle and Helmo. This man was used to making quick decisions. "Attack on the New Alliance parliament building. And another one on the barracks."

Next moment, the whoop, whoop of the attack alarm sounded. From the loudspeakers on the ground; from the comms of every soldier around them.

"You're not seriously going to attack?" Ean asked.

Every soldier around them turned to run downstairs.

The civilian grinned. "What do you think?" He took hold

of Ean's arm lightly. "Keep up, or you'll get trampled. No one will stop for you."

They joined the flood of people running downstairs.

Running. He was glad for the other man's grip on his arm, because he was right, no one would stop if he fell.

Radko would probably make him run up and down stairs after this.

The gray uniforms below him made a wedge that the people coming downstairs flowed past. They stopped every Lancastrian they could, but they missed many.

The civilian pulled Ean off to one side, and they streamed past in a crowd that was mostly Aratogan camouflage brown and Balian blue, while the Lancastrians stopped three of their own from the center of the crowd.

Crowds could be used by both sides, and he'd have to move fast, or otherwise the civilian would separate him from this particular crowd.

Ean stopped so suddenly that the civilian almost lost his grip. It was enough. Ean wrenched free and darted into the crowd of soldiers heading toward the barracks.

Would Radko still be looking for him?

He wasted precious breath to sing to the fives around him, to open the channel to Radko as he had before. *"Here. Don't follow the other one anymore."*

He caught a glimpse of civilian clothing and put on a spurt.

The stranger would expect him to make for the safety of the Lancian soldiers. Or the safety of the biggest group.

Instead, he found a group of Balian soldiers and pushed into the middle of them, nearly tripping himself as he did so.

One of the Balians grabbed him. "You're heading the wrong way, soldier. Lancia's barracks are over there."

"Admiral Katida," Ean gasped. He didn't have enough breath left to explain.

The civilian had disappeared, and the Balian barracks was coming into sight.

The Balian looked at him and didn't loosen his hold. Fair enough, if it got him to talk to Katida.

If Ean had more breath, he'd have sung the comms around him open. He didn't.

They were three steps away from the gate when someone grabbed Ean's shoulder.

He squawked and tried to pull away, then realized that person was talking to him. "Ean."

"Radko. I have never been so glad to see anyone in my life."

"WE identified most of them," Abram Galenos said at the hastily convened meeting afterward. Abram, Katida, and Orsaya were there, along with Ean, Radko, Sale, and Bhaksir. Michelle wasn't. She was at one of her interminable functions. She wouldn't have come anyway. This was a military meeting.

"Their leader—the man Ean stabbed—is Mendez. He's ex–Roscracian military. He was kicked out, suspected of selling military secrets to anyone who would pay. The people with him were all ex–Roscracian military, too.

"We've footage from the Night Owl. We know that the woman who tipped Mendez off spent time talking to Randella Abbey. If we can't pick her up, we'll pick Abbey up."

Something in the grim way the other two admirals nodded made Ean shiver.

"They must know he'd be protected," Katida said.

"Linesmen don't normally need protection," Abram said. "Maybe they thought it would be an easy snatch. They know now, and have to be wondering why." He looked at Orsaya. "They may try to snatch Rossi next."

"It's covered."

"Make it visible," Abram said. "So they think we are simply protecting the higher-level linesmen."

"I hear you," Orsaya said.

"Maybe you should—" Ean stopped. If they didn't draw attention to the fact that Hernandez was a ten, too, she'd be safe.

They all looked up as Fergus came in. He'd changed out of his House of Rickenback uniform.

"We had to wait for the all clear," he said. "Did Gate Union really attack us?"

Sale shook her head. "Someone tried to snatch Ean and used that as a diversion."

"Gate Union?"

"Why would they bother?" Ean asked. "Rigel and Paretsky think I'll be back with Rigel soon. I'd be in Gate Union territory then."

Abram tapped the table eleven-time. "Gate Union supports House of Sandhurst, and Iwo Hurst wants to be Grand Master. I can't see them supporting Paretsky."

"If Markan heard that Rigel and Paretsky planned to meet Ean, he might take advantage of the fact that Ean would be in the open, ready to snatch," Orsaya said. She looked at the newscast replaying in silence on the wall. Panicked civilians packing the spaceport. Soldiers marching the streets. "Except I expected more from him."

How did you define more? Any way you looked at it, Ean's would-be captor had successfully stirred up everyone on Haladea III. They'd declared a state of emergency for tonight because of the panic. Those who hadn't tried to leave on the first shuttle they could get—shuttles were locked down now— had tried to raid the supermarkets. Others had barricaded themselves in their buildings. Even others had gone to the media and demanded the newly formed government do something about the attack.

What did they expect? There was a war on.

Abram's comms chimed. A text message. He thumbed it open and glanced at the message that came up. He forwarded it on to all of them in the room.

Mendez and companions escaped while being transferred to main jail. External assistance. Suspect military intervention.

There was a momentary silence.

"Was Rigel involved?" Abram asked eventually.

Ean shook his head. Radko shook hers.

"I don't think Rigel was part of whatever Mendez did," Ean said. Rigel had been . . . Rigel. "If anyone was making plans, it would be Paretsky."

"Paretsky left not long after you did," Fergus said. "I stayed to talk with Rigel. I can't work out if he sees a way to get back his ten, or if they've forced him into it."

Probably both. Rigel was like that. You could bully him, but he was always looking out for opportunities at the same time.

"But they can't make me go back," Ean said. Could they? Vega would be happy. Finally rid of him.

"No, Ean," Abram said.

Orsaya said, "Even if they try, we're at war. We'd just ignore them."

"I don't think this is aimed at you, Ean," Fergus said. "Paretsky sees this as an opportunity to get back his old position. He thinks he can't lose. He's already planning to call Leo Rickenback to sort it out. If Rigel gets you back, then Paretsky wins because 'he' negotiated it. If you stay here, then Leo looks incompetent because he's not doing his job. Paretsky and Rigel both know you'll stay here." Fergus ran his hands through his hair. Worried, Ean thought, for his old boss. "There's already a backlash against selling the higher-level contracts."

It was the Grand Master's job to sort out line disputes, but what if you weren't technically under the auspices of the cartel system anymore? Maybe Ean should make his own call to Rickenback.

AFTERWARD, Abram walked back to their transport with Ean. Bhaksir's team escorted them, four in front, four behind, and Radko in the middle with Abram and Ean.

"Everything's locked down, so we can't send you back to the *Lancastrian Princess* tonight. We've put you in the most secure barracks we have." Abram smiled. "Which coincidentally happens to be the same barracks we're placing the *Eleven*'s crew in as they arrive."

"All of them?"

He understood what Ean was asking. "Full linesmen and singles."

Ean's mouth was dry at the thought of it.

Abram said to Bhaksir, "We'll have to send mixed guards out to the barracks with you. A full contingent of Lancians will be out of place."

Bhaksir nodded. "How many of us?"

"Two from your team, in uniform. Two from Sale's." Who weren't in uniform. "They can be off duty. I'll ask Katida and Orsaya to send some along as well."

They walked in silence for a while. It was the first time he'd had to talk with Abram since he'd moved on world. Ean wanted to tell Abram that Michelle was missing him and ask if he would call her, but it didn't seem appropriate, not with a whole team listening in.

"Admiral MacClennan has been seconded to the Division for Alien Technology and Affairs," Abram said, as they turned into a larger corridor. At this time of the night, it was as empty as the last one. Or maybe Abram had made sure it was. "He'll be working with you and Captain Kari Wang to help her settle onto the ship."

"Do you trust him?"

"I don't know. He hasn't given us any reason not to, but Nova Tahiti blindsided us on this." Abram shrugged. "Maybe they simply saw an opportunity."

Or they could be trying to oust Lancia as the main power in the New Alliance. Ean had to remind himself that six months ago he would have been delighted to see that happen. He glanced back at Radko. Now he had a shipful of people who'd be devastated if Lancia was ousted. People he cared about.

Life had been simple once. Him, the cartel house, and the lines.

He looked around the gray corridors they were moving through. The only strong lines close were the twos, threes, and fives. He wanted to be back on ship with full sets of lines. He realized he'd stopped, and the others had all stopped, too, waiting for him.

"I think you should install a full set of lines here," he told Abram.

Abram smiled faintly. "That suggestion is never going to come from me, and I suggest it never comes from you either."

"Why not?"

"Because we both know what you can do with a full set of lines." Abram started moving again.

"What does that mean?" Ean asked Radko, as the two of them followed.

"It means he knows what you can do with a full set of lines."

What sort of answer was that?

FOURTEEN

STELLAN VILHJALMSSON

WHEN MARKAN CALLED, Stellan had to use iris, fingerprint and DNA identification to take the call. Markan was in real time, so he was somewhere in the Haladean sector.

"They're taking Lambert to the barracks at Nordia."

Nordia was a secondary barracks on the north edge of the city.

Stellan scraped his tongue against the bottom of his top teeth. He hated the bitter taste of the chemicals on the DNA swab. "So I'm not going anywhere near Nordia then." Why had Markan called in the middle of a job? He usually left Stellan alone to work.

"What? So you have me expend resources and risk my people just so you can say you're not going now."

"I didn't ask you to expend resources." Was he telling Stellan what to do now? Jobs didn't always work to plan; you allowed for that.

The look Markan gave him was strange. "Plus I object to expending resources on people who don't matter. Why in the lines didn't you use trained soldiers rather than a bunch of rejects we kicked out of the fleet?"

It was Stellan's turn to give Markan a strange look. "Why did you call, Markan?"

"Why? Because you demanded to know where they were going to put Lambert tonight. You made me risk half my covert-ops people getting your useless team out of prison. You should have used a real team."

What was going on?

"Talk to me, Markan. Don't get angry," for that was usually Markan's next emotion. "Tell me what happened."

Markan spluttered. "Tell you—"

"Markan."

"*You* tell *me* what happened."

That would be the simplest. Stellan sat back. "Lambert has a trace, incidentally." Maybe he could co-opt Randella Abbey to cut it out. Since she was here, and she knew who he was. "I don't have a team, useless or not. I'm working alone."

"What about—?"

"Wait. I haven't finished," Stellan said. "I followed Lambert out of the Night Owl. He and his girlfriend"—who wasn't a girlfriend, she was a bodyguard—"got about two blocks. Then they were attacked."

"Are you telling me someone in the New Alliance is trying to kill him?"

Stellan shook his head. "They didn't want to kill him. The ringleader was very handy with his knife. He could have stabbed Lambert anytime."

"Then who?"

"If we want to talk to him, Markan, there'll be others who want to as well. I'm sure you haven't told anyone outside Roscracia your plan. Worry more that they used Roscracians to do it if that's who you say they were. We could be being framed."

Markan looked at the comms in his hand, which he'd used earlier to push the details of Lambert's whereabouts through to Stellan.

"So you didn't ask for this?"

"I haven't gotten to the interesting part yet," Stellan said. "He had two teams on call. They were there in thirty seconds."

"Two teams?"

"And another four on call at the barracks." He thought about the chase. "I grabbed Lambert while the Lancastrians were mopping up. They were after him in half a minute."

"They probably tracked his comms."

"Teach your ancestor to hunt worms," Stellan said. "The first thing I did was throw away his comms. Yet they knew exactly where we were at all times. And they called in soldiers to come around the other way to block us off. They have instant access to a lot of soldiers."

If he hadn't let Lambert go, and used the crowd to cover his own escape, he'd have been the one sitting in jail right now.

"So if you say you were working alone, explain this evening's priority request to get your people out of jail."

"The only priority request I put through tonight was the attack alert."

"Someone used your code, and your name, and asked for an emergency op to get your people out before they were questioned."

Stellan realized he was rubbing his hand. He was glad Markan couldn't see him. Or register his heart rate, for the blood was pounding in his ears. Jobs could go to hell, but there had always been one absolute. Markan had his back, and he had Markan's. Now someone had breached that.

"There wasn't any request." Someone had to have hacked Stellan's account, used his codes to make the request look legitimate.

"Damn." Markan checked his comms. "They'll be long gone."

Stellan had to find out who the blue-haired woman was. "I'll get security vids from the Night Owl. I need you to identify a woman. Randella Abbey's best work, or so she says. She's military." Abbey had told him that much.

"That crazy—" Markan was smart enough not to finish it. "I'll get a list of people she's treated."

It would be a long list. "I'll see what I can do from here." Back to the real job at hand. "Markan, what aren't you telling me about Lambert?"

Markan looked as if he had no idea what Stellan was talking about.

"He's as closely guarded as Lady Lyan herself, yet I'd never heard of him before this job."

"And I'd never heard of him until Orsaya risked everything to bring him out to Confluence Station." He started to say something, stopped, rubbed his chin, then said it anyway. "Orsaya knew long before anyone else what was out there. She thought Lambert was the only one who could get the ship out."

That high up the Gate Union admiralty you didn't have to like the people you worked with, but you knew their strengths and weaknesses. Markan had never liked Jita Orsaya, but he had admired her work.

She had also been line obsessed.

"She owned linesman Rossi's contract by then, so she'd probably tried to get the ship with him and found he couldn't."

That certainly wasn't common knowledge. This was the most Markan had opened up about the whole fiasco that had led to the discovery of the *Confluence* fleet and the creation of the New Alliance. Stellan had heard parts of it, and ferreted out other parts, but Markan had never spoken about it.

"How long beforehand?"

Markan shrugged. "Who knows? She was in charge of the whole operation. She was *supposed* to be sharing information."

And Markan always shared information, too. Stellan bit down the obvious retort.

"I'm sure she knew not long after Linesman Grimes arrived back. If Grimes mentioned it to her cartel master, Hurst didn't mention it to me."

"Line business."

"Exactly. I'm sick of them and their damned line business."

Stellan hoped again that the line was secure even though he knew it was. This sounding off was better somewhere private. He changed the subject.

"I'll try to find another way to get close to Lambert." Which would be more difficult than he had first anticipated. Plus he had to hold him long enough to get some answers. "Let me know when you find out who cracked the codes."

"Speaking of which," Markan said. "I'm sending through a new code now. Don't give this one away."

Stellan made a rude gesture, then checked the code. It had the same accesses as the previous one. "Thank you."

FIFTEEN

EAN LAMBERT

THE TRIP TO the barracks site took half an hour. Radko and Ean wore Lancian uniforms. Hana, Ru Li, and Gossamer wore plain clothes. They were accompanied by two guards in Yaolin beige, two in Balian blue.

When they got there, they were greeted by Lancastrians on the desk. Why had Abram worried about a full Lancian crew? Everyone would think they worked here.

Then Ean walked into the rec room.

There were uniforms of every color from the New Alliance. The pale green of Eridanus, the mottled gold/green of Haladea, the gray of Lancia, the beige of Yaolin, the deeper beige of New Viking, the mottled purple-gray camouflage of Al Fawaris—which reminded Ean of the purple camouflage of Roscracia. Lots of colors. Lots of noise.

There were even people in casual clothes. Coming off leave or going on, Ean wasn't sure. His own group fitted well here.

Radko pushed her way through to a table that had spare seats on one end. The noise level dropped as people stopped to study them, then rose again. One old soldier in an Aratogan uniform—he looked ready to retire—nodded at them and slid along the bench to talk.

"Are you just in?"

The pocket below his name—*MAEL*—where the lines would be, if he had them, was blank. This was a single-level linesman.

"Arrived on planet today," Radko said. By now Ean was used to the misdirection. People heard what they expected to hear.

Hana and one of the Balians went to get drinks.

The girl who slipped into the seat beside Mael looked too

young to be a soldier. She wore a Haladean uniform. "One," pointing to Radko. "Two," to Ean. "Three. Four," to the Balians. "Five, six," to Ru Li and Hana. "Seven, eight," to the Yaolins. "Nine," to Gossamer. "Where's the other one?"

"Other one?"

"Matching pairs. Out here it's like being on a generation ship. Two by two."

Radko looked as mystified as Ean felt.

"Tinatin has a point," Mael said. "They do bring us in pairs." He looked around, then pointed to an Aratogan sitting with a Lancastrian and a Ruon. "That's my double over there."

His double was half his age, two-thirds his height, with group-leader markings on her shoulders. The Lancastrian and Ruon also had group-leader markings. Ean could see that they had bars below their names. At least four bars for each of them. They were linesmen and ranking soldiers.

"What?" Ru Li asked. "Like you're bonded or something?" Even though he knew they weren't. Ean never wanted to get into a lying contest with Ru Li. He would lose.

Mael's snort turned into a laugh that was nearly a choke. "That one. She couldn't bond to anything that isn't metal and solder. She's a machine."

"A robot?" Ean asked. Maybe Mael meant she'd had prosthetics, like Captain Kari Wang. Although they didn't say Kari Wang had prosthetics, they said they'd rebuilt her legs. Maybe she had metal bones.

"Sheesh," Mael said, and Ean got the feeling if there had been less people around, Radko would have said, "Figuratively, not literally."

Hana arrived back with foaming pots of something alcoholic. "You've got two choices here. Swill or no swill."

Ean took his glass. "So which one's this?"

"He's a raw one," Mael said, and everyone nodded. Ean supposed they were talking about him. He shrugged.

Hana held her glass up. "This, Ean, is swill. No swill is nonalcoholic."

"This isn't bad," Mael said. "You should taste what passes as alcohol out on the rim. Although there's some good stuff out there."

One of his companions rolled her eyes. "You and your black fire," she said.

Mael smacked lips. "One day I'll get some, and you can taste it. It's indescribable." He took an appreciative sip of his own half-finished drink. "They have real bars here on Haladea III as well. Off duty, I can take you around some."

"We're going to every bar in the city," Tinatin said.

Ru Li said, "At the rate they're building, you might find it hard to keep up. Looks like a new bar being added every day."

"Or more," Mael said. "We went to the Outlook center last week. They had three more bars since the week before that, which is when it opened."

Ean listened to them talk around him. It was harder than he'd expected to broach the subject of lines. Tinatin was a one. He could see the single bar below her name.

Except for Tinatin, he was in a group of single-level linesmen. The linesmen stayed together, by line or by seniority. He hoped that wasn't an omen.

Why wasn't Tinatin with the certified linesmen?

Because no one thought much of a level-one linesman. What could they do except fix line one, and the ones were found on ships. Who would take a level one when they could take a five or a six, someone who could fix more than just that one line?

He'd thought that once himself.

He looked away, ashamed. His gaze fell on the screen on the near wall. It was a news channel. They were still talking about the "attack" of earlier that day.

On screen, a well-dressed woman standing outside the new parliament house Ean had seen from the heights of the old, was protesting that, "They told Haladea, the New Alliance would be good for us. But what happens as soon as they arrive? We get attacked."

He shivered and looked away.

"Turn it off," an Al Fawarin at the next table said. "I'm sick of the sound of her voice."

"It was a false alarm anyway," another soldier at the same table said. "Probably testing the alert system."

"No it wasn't," Tinatin said. "It was a Lancian plot."

Ean turned to look at her.

"You have no idea, Tinatin," one of the other soldiers at the table said.

"No, no. It's true. I heard it while I was in the city earlier." She leaned close and said confidentially, "It was designed to show Nova Tahiti they shouldn't cross Lancia."

"But Nova Tahiti's on our side?" Ean protested.

Radko said, "Why would Lancia cause mass hysteria like that?"

Tinatin sighed. "You're Lancian. You don't understand. Lancia doesn't care about citizens. They just wanted to prove a point to Nova Tahiti."

"We are on the same side," Ean said again.

"That's the thing. Something happened today in the council. Everyone was there." She opened her arms as if to embrace the whole room, then leaned close again. "And in that council, Nova Tahiti did something that blindsided Lancia."

"Blindsided" wasn't a word Ean heard often, yet he'd heard it twice today. Or was it three times? How had Tinatin picked up on it? Not only that, she was remarkably well informed about what had been a closed council. "How do you get from the council to Lancia teaching Nova Tahiti a lesson by setting off a false alarm?"

"It's logical, isn't it? Lancia was unhappy about what happened today." She raised her finger to do quotes in the air. "They're 'sending a message.'"

Emperor Yu had "sent a message" before, back when his daughter was kidnapped in an effort to destabilize the old Alliance. That message had resulted in three worlds being kicked out of the Alliance, with twenty more worlds leaving. If it hadn't been for the *Eleven* back then, Gate Union would be the ascendant power now.

"What's the message?" although he could guess.

Tinatin leaned closer, so only Ean could hear. "Don't mess with Lancia. We're more powerful than you. Do it our way, or we'll let the enemy attack you."

"Oh." Ean realized he was rubbing his temples, like Abram did sometimes. "Do you think it's going to work? Their message, I mean."

Fergus slipped onto the bench beside Radko then, and

Tinatin turned to him. "Look, the missing link. I told you there had to be another one."

"Another what?" asked Fergus.

"We come in pairs, apparently," Ean said. "Two by two."

"What? Like a generation ship?"

"Exactly like a generation ship," Tinatin said. "I like you already. You *get* things."

"Thank you." Nothing fazed Fergus.

Ean's comms beeped. He glanced at it. Rigel again. He ignored it.

Fergus looked at the single bar on Tinatin's shirt with interest. "A single-level linesman."

He meant it respectfully—even Ean could hear that—but Tinatin hunched in on herself. "Just because you haven't met one before doesn't mean they don't exist."

"What use are they?" asked a spacer going past. He had six bars on his own shirt. "They can't do anything another linesman can't do."

Ean opened his mouth to say they could be useful, but Radko kicked him on his left ankle at the same time as Mael kicked his right ankle. Individually, both were hard enough to hurt. Together they brought tears to his eyes.

"I'm going to get another drink," Tinatin said, and left them. She walked straight past the bar and out the door.

Mael sighed. "That wasn't very bright," he said to Fergus.

"I wasn't trying to insult her," Fergus said.

"She got it from the cartel houses. She gets it from everyone here."

And she was still raw enough that she hadn't been certified long. She'd probably come straight out of the cartel and into fleet training, then out of fleet training to here. Her pocket was as bare as Ean's. He wondered if she'd even finished training.

"I don't know why she's so bitter," one of the other soldiers at the table said. "At least she *is* a linesman. What about those who went through all that training and failed."

He sounded bitter. And he didn't have any bars on his shirt.

Ean opened his mouth to say that it wouldn't matter soon, then closed it again.

The linesman came back with drinks. "Come over and join us, Linesman. There's a whole group of us over here."

"Group of what?"

"Linesmen, he means," Mael said. "See those bars on your shirt. It means you get to join the elite while the rest of us bow and scrape to you."

The linesman scowled at Mael.

The others at the table were looking at Ean as if they'd only just realized he had line bars on his shirt.

"They're only linesmen," Radko said. The linesman scowled at her, too.

Mael waggled a finger at her. "There's nothing *only* about linesmen.

"There's nothing *only* about a good soldier, either. You can't tell me you get a team half linesmen, half not, and the linesmen expect to be treated differently from the rest of you."

"I doubt we'll be in the same team," Mael said. "This group here. They're line heavy."

"Line is just an ability you have," Ean said. "Like some people are natural acrobats."

Ru Li did a complicated arabesque that turned into a bow. "Why, thank you."

If Bhaksir had been here, she'd have glared at him. "You shouldn't be separated just because you're good at something." Yet they separated linesmen out through the cartel houses, didn't they?

"You know," Fergus said. "A lot of linesmen in the military are in engineering. This ship will be top-heavy with engineers and low on fighters."

"Ship?" Mael asked, and Fergus shrugged.

"You've been listening to Tinatin," the six said. "So certain we're going on a ship. But we *are* all engineers here."

Was he talking just linesmen? Because none of the people at Mael's table had engineering badges. "Don't you even know why you're here?" Some of them must. The Lancastrians did, because Ean had been there when Abram told them.

The linesman looked at him as if Ean should know better than to tell the secret.

Ean would have gone over and talked to some of the linesmen, but it felt disloyal after what everyone had said. Instead, he stayed and talked to the people at his table, until he realized he was nodding off.

"I might go to bed." It had been a long day.

Radko yawned ostentatiously. "We're all tired, and who knows what tomorrow will bring. Why don't we all call it a night?"

They went out together in a loose group. They were still guarding him, Ean realized. "Why don't you all stay?"

"We want jobs tomorrow," Hana said, and Ru Li nodded emphatically from beside them. "You've never caught the edge of Bhaksir's tongue," he said feelingly. "Today has been fun, though."

Fun. Ean could think of better words to describe it.

THE changing music of the lines woke Ean.

He lay in the dark and tried to work out what was different.

Lines on world didn't have the sentience that lines on ship had. They seemed to require a full set of ten lines for that. Or the ability to jump through the void. Or maybe both.

He went through the lines he could hear.

There was a veritable chorus of fives. Everyone in the barracks had a comms.

The music of the fives sounded normal. No off notes, no stress. He could hear two soldiers—presumably in different bunk rooms—holding a whispered conversation about meeting in the laundry. Ean wished them luck with it. His experience with laundries was hard floors and nowhere to sit. Which was the point, he supposed, if they planned a midnight rendezvous.

That wasn't what had woken him.

He turned his attention to the other lines.

The barracks—like most planet-based buildings built in the last five hundred years—used line two for heating and cooling and line three for doors and other small mechanics.

Line three was straight. Not perfect, because there were minor repairs due, but it was as straight as it had been when they'd arrived. Ean would have thought that in a barracks half-full of certified linesmen, the lines would be perfect all the time, but that wasn't the case.

Line two was straight as well.

Maybe Ean was imagining it. His head was stuffy, his eyes ached, and there was a taste in his mouth that if he'd been on ship he would have blamed on the lines. It was probably reaction to the events of earlier that day finally catching up with him.

The taste in his mouth had the bitterness of triphene.

Ean swallowed. His mouth was dry.

And line two.

Line two had changed its song. That was what was different.

On a ship, line two controlled the lights and the flow of oxygen and other gases, and kept the ship at an equitable temperature for humans to live. Its song changed with a rise or fall in temperature, and changed if the composition of gases flowing through the ship changed. On a world, it controlled temperature and airflow.

The airflow had changed.

Someone had altered the gases coming into this room.

Ean sat up. Tried to, anyway, but found he was so lethargic it was easier to roll out of the bunk.

It was farther to the floor than he'd expected. He landed with a jar that jolted him more awake.

Ru Li and Hana, the guards on duty, looked at him and tried to rise. Ru Li fell forward in a slow-motion roll that mimicked Ean's own. Hana collapsed back.

They were both directly under the air-conditioning vent.

Oxygen was always close to high-level linesmen in the New Alliance. Ean dragged himself upright to get at the oxygen tank strapped to his bunk. He pulled on the mask, aware of Radko, so very still in the bunk above his.

She had drilled it into him, in her never-ending lessons on how to survive in space. "See to your own oxygen first. Always. Only then do you look after others."

She'd shown him how to share air, too—once he'd made sure his own supply was secure. Two breaths for one, two breaths for the other. Repeat as long as necessary.

Ean took two deep breaths of his own, then held the mask over Radko's face.

He could save Radko, but that wasn't going to save anyone else. Especially not Hana and Ru Li, who probably needed it the most.

He had to think of something else and fast.

Fresh air might help. But what if the whole barracks was being gassed?

He took two more breaths, then sang every door in the barracks open to the outdoors.

After that, he sang directly to line two. *"You're singing the wrong tune. This is what you need to be,"* and he sang the tune he remembered from earlier. He left the oxygen with Radko and kept singing as he staggered over to the next oxygen tank.

He had to stop singing and concentrate on moving. For a moment he wasn't sure he'd get there. He fell onto the tank and gulped in oxygen. That was one lapse Radko didn't have to know about.

More alert now, he resumed singing while he dispensed two breaths to Hana, two more to himself, and two to Ru Li.

He couldn't get oxygen to everyone.

Line two struggled to stay on the tune Ean had asked it to. He kept singing, helping to hold it there.

Radko had taught him other things in her emergency drills. Like the emergency override code you could use on the door to set off the alarm. He took himself and his oxygen over to the door, still singing line two into true.

The alarm didn't work.

Impossible.

He'd make his own alarm then. Ean snatched up the nearest comms, sang it open, and used it to sing every comms in the barracks open, sang them all up to full volume, and sang—because he couldn't have spoken right now—*"Emergency. Action stations"*—because he couldn't think of anything to say.

He set it to repeat, then ducked out to see what corridor he was in.

Tinatin and Mael came out of nearby rooms. Mael was grumbling. "Action stations. What sort of alert is that?"

Ean grabbed him. "What corridor is this?"

"Five E. Why?"

Ean said into his comms, "Gas leak, corridor Five E."

"Why didn't you say?" Mael ran back down the corridor, stopped at a cupboard halfway down. "Come on, Tinatin. You know what to do for a gas leak."

"But that's in space."

"Hurry," Ean said. "There are people dying in here."

"Not so fast," Mael said. "First rule of any gas leak. Protect yourself first; otherwise, you can't help anyone else."

Radko would like Mael.

Ean ran back into the room.

A man clad in a hazard suit similar to the ones Mael and Tinatin were pulling on, dropped from the ceiling.

Ean backed away.

Another man dropped. And a third.

"This's him," the first man said.

He'd heard the voice before, earlier that day. Mendez.

These people never gave up. Right now, Ean would have given the world to be back on ship, where they could fight on his terms.

"He's supposed to be unconscious," the man on Mendez's left said.

Two more suited figures dropped.

"I don't care what he is," Mendez said. "Just get him out before that alarm wakes everyone up."

Ean tried to remember which leg he'd stabbed. Mendez had been right-handed, and he'd aimed for Radko's back. Ean was left-handed; he'd pushed down. Left hand pushing right meant straight down.

He brought his oxygen tank down hard on Mendez's right thigh.

Mendez howled.

Ean ran. Slap into Tinatin and Mael, who were running into the room.

Mael had been talking into his comms. "Paramedics and—" The comms went flying. Tinatin and Ean went flying. Mael stayed on his feet.

"Out of our way," the man who'd complained Ean wasn't unconscious said. "We're getting this one to safety."

"Looked like he was running, to me," Mael said.

Mendez took out his blaster. "Move aside."

There was a crackle of blaster and the nauseating smell of cooked meat filled the room.

Tinatin's eyes widened. She yelled, louder than anything coming out of the comms, and jumped onto Mendez, belting him around the head, scratching, biting, kicking.

The man behind Mendez dropped.

Tinatin kicked Mendez's blaster out of his hand.

Ean dived for it; his fingers met Mael's.

Above them, they heard the crackle of the blaster again. Another person dropped.

"What the—?" Mael raised his head.

"Stay down. Give me a clear shot." Radko's voice.

The would-be kidnappers all turned, drawing their own weapons.

She couldn't hit them all.

Ean rolled, knocking as many off their feet as he could.

A crazy pattern of blaster fire crisscrossed the room.

"Sheesh," Mael said, covering his head.

At least two blankets caught fire. The occupants under them didn't move.

Ean ripped the burning blankets off the beds, dropped them onto the floor, and stamped out the flames.

"Mael," someone called from out in the corridor. "Where's this blasted gas leak?"

Mendez grabbed Tinatin, who yelled and tried to break away.

"Careful. He carries knives," Ean said.

"Tinatin," Mael said, "kick him where it's going to hurt."

Tinatin stopped struggling. "But you're dead."

"Just kick him. Now."

Mendez was already pushing her away.

Tinatin kicked up and back in a move Ru Li would have been pleased with.

Ean winced.

Mendez didn't waste any more time attacking. He and those left standing ran out the door. "Finally," said the person who'd called earlier from the passage. "What's going on?"

"Get these people outside," Mael said. "Get some oxygen into them. Although"—he looked at Ean—"not so sure they need it."

"They do." Radko's voice was husky. "Ean." She dragged him over to Fergus's bunk and handed Ean the oxygen bottle he had left with her earlier. She took out her comms and looked at it meaningfully.

He wished Radko was a line. Then he'd understand what she wanted him to do.

She made gentling motions with her hand. "But privately," she said.

She wanted him to turn off the alarm.

He went into the bathroom to do it because it felt like there were a hundred people in their room right now.

The silence was blissful.

"How did you know it was me?" he asked, when he got back.

"Is the sky on Lancia purple?"

"Yes, but—"

Radko took out her comms.

NOT long after that an armored troop carrier descended to take them back to headquarters. Ten soldiers exited and left at a run for the building where Mendez had last been seen. Four armed soldiers stayed behind and stood guard.

Two medics set up portable stations while two other soldiers set up lights for them. In minutes, the outdoor area was as bright as day.

"We already checked them," Tinatin said.

They examined Ean and Fergus first.

"I'm fine," Ean said. They always checked him first. He wished they wouldn't. "Look at the others."

"Told you he was important," Mael muttered to Tinatin.

"Of course he's important," Tinatin said. "He's got ten lines on his shirt. Haven't you noticed?"

"You didn't notice that before. Someone had to tell you."

The medic left Ean with a canister of oxygen and a mask over his face—"Don't take it off"—and moved on to one of the unconscious guards.

"I really get tired of oxygen masks," Ean said to Fergus, who was by now similarly masked. "Don't you?"

"Can't say it's been a problem for me to date," Fergus said.

Fergus was a single line, unaffected by the inhuman beat of line eleven. Ean couldn't think of anything to reply.

IN the barracks hospital, they were put into pressure chambers to normalize the oxygen in their blood. As he went in, Ean heard one intern whisper to another, "They're under guard. They're probably dangerous political prisoners."

It reminded him of Tinatin.

Afterward, he and Radko ate a late lunch with Bhaksir and Sale.

"Mendez had an aircar waiting," Sale said. "They were away before Radko called us. If I see him again, I'll kill him personally."

She'd have to get ahead of Radko, then, because Radko wanted to kill Mendez, too. She'd told Ean that, and there'd been a determination in her voice that had shocked him.

"We'll find him," Bhaksir said.

"We literally, or we figuratively?" Ean asked.

"We as in the New Alliance," Sale said. "It will take weeks. We're not doing it." She yawned. Ean yawned with her. "I want you back in space, Ean. Where it's safe. Unfortunately, Nova Tahiti is hosting a dinner tonight to welcome Captain Kari Wang. Ean's been invited."

"That was quick," Radko said. "They've been planning this awhile then?"

Sale shrugged.

"The consensus is that it's only been planned since the formal agreement to appoint a captain," Fergus said. "Somewhere between then and each world's choosing a captain to nominate, someone thought of Kari Wang. Most people think it was MacClennan, who's been watching her career."

Radko had once said Fergus could get gossip from a twenty-year-dry well.

Ean's comms sounded. He knew, without even looking at it, that it would be Rigel again. He didn't answer it.

SIXTEEN

SELMA KARI WANG

KARI WANG SOUGHT out Admiral MacClennan, determined to make him listen. She found him in his outer office.

"Captain." Sharp, with a bite to it.

She should have made an appointment. One didn't walk into an admiral's office and expect to be seen immediately. Especially not when said admiral was annoyed about something.

MacClennan turned to his aide, a swivel that ground his heel into the floor. "Get me the results of Dr. Fitch's Havortian tests. We'll send him instead. Provided nothing untoward comes out of *his* checks."

He turned back to Kari Wang, indicated his office with a jerk of his head, and waited until she entered in front of him. He closed the door with a bang.

"Our security check on Dr. Arnoud turned up a link to Redmond," he said, even though she hadn't asked. "He's been passing information to them for years. If we hadn't run these checks, we'd never have found out."

He looked as if he'd like another door to slam. "Enough of traitors. What can I do for you, Captain?"

"You want to put me into another ship."

He nodded, a single downward movement of his head.

"I do not want the job," she said. "It is inappropriate." Not to mention cruel.

He frowned at her. "Sit down," and went around to his own chair to sit down himself. Even that had a distinct thump to it. "Before you fall down," and waited until she sat before he spoke again. "I agree with everything you say." His frown lightened to a grim smile. "And everything you're not saying. But I will not change the decision."

"Then I resign." Once the fleet had been her whole life. Resigning from it would have been unthinkable. She'd have been better off dead. But then, she was better off dead, wasn't she?

"Amendment 184.2.1," MacClennan said.

Amendment 184 of the Nova Tahiti Charter had been brought in two hundred years earlier. Nova Tahiti had been under attack from a neighboring world. Back then they'd had difficulty getting soldiers to fight in the war. Section 2 dealt with conscription. Part 1 of section 2 was all about how the governing body of Nova Tahiti had a right to conscript any citizen in times of war.

"You can remain in your current position and retain the benefits of seniority," MacClennan said. "Or you can resign, and I will conscript you."

If she called his bluff, would he go through with it? Probably, because if he didn't need her, why would he want a broken soldier?

"Surely, Captain, you've been in positions yourself where you had to weigh up how to save the most people with the least loss of life."

"You're telling me this is a life-or-death situation."

MacClennan sighed. "No, Captain, this is politics, pure and simple." He pressed something on his comms, and, a moment later, an aide came in with two glasses of tea—which he couldn't possibly have had time to make in between the order and delivery. MacClennan waited until the aide had gone again. "I can't tell you much about this mission."

The tea was hot. Kari Wang left hers on the desk to cool. Like most spacers, she preferred her tea lukewarm, where if something untoward happened—like an unexpected gravity fluctuation—it wouldn't burn you if it slopped out of the glass. The admiral drank his hot. He'd been a long time out of space.

"What I can tell you." MacClennan paused. "This is a cooperative venture. You will have crew from all nations of the New Alliance. Two from each world, initially, then more once the first lot have integrated."

It sounded like a disaster in the making. "Who do they take orders from?" Each one of them would have their own chain of command.

"Their captain," MacClennan said, then added, "And whoever else they report to. On ship they will report to you."

Her tea wasn't cool enough yet, but she drank it anyway. It burned her tongue.

"Which ship?"

He didn't answer that.

The old Alliance didn't name their ships for their captains. She hoped the New Alliance didn't plan to either. She didn't want another ship to replace *her* ship. "Most fleets would have the decency to retire out a captain who'd lost their ship."

If the barb hit home, it didn't show on MacClennan's face. "This isn't about decency. It's about politics. The New Alliance needs an experienced captain. They don't come up often."

The relationship between ship and captain was undeniable. The commonly accepted theory was that because the lines were pure energy, and the Captain's Chair was built into the line chassis, the energy of the lines irradiated the person who sat in it. It was—whispered at the moment but gaining more credence each year—that the irradiation acted as an enhanced receptor in the basolateral amygdala of the brain, leading to a modified form of paranoia, which the recipient translated to something along the lines of "I can't live without my ship." Personally, Kari Wang believed the last was absolute rubbish, but it was a fact that once you chose to captain a line ship, that was as high as you went on the career ladder because you never left your ship until they forced you out at retirement. Or you died on the job.

Retirement was one thing she'd avoided thinking about.

"Worlds of the New Alliance are doing everything they can to cement their power." MacClennan scowled at his tea. "Nova Tahiti sees you as a piece on a massive gameboard right now. They're—" He corrected himself. "*We're* playing to win. Decency doesn't come into it. The fact that you should be on psychiatric leave doesn't come into it. You're a captain. An experienced captain who doesn't have a ship right now. You are our chance at controlling one of those ships." He looked up at her, his expression bleak. "You have no say."

"And Nova Tahiti's fleet motto?" *We look after our people.* If she killed herself—she should be dead anyway—they wouldn't have a captain.

The expression grew bleaker. "War makes monsters out of everyone, Captain." He finished his tea in one long draught although it must have been hot, then said, as if it were a normal reassignment, "You will report to Admiral Galenos of Lancia. And to me, of course."

"*Admiral* Galenos?" Last she'd heard Galenos had been a commodore, in charge of security for the Crown Princess of Lancia. Lady Lyan—the Crown Princess—had long been a thorn in Nova Tahiti's side.

MacClennan steepled his fingers. "And not before time, either. Unfortunately, his promotion means he manages this project by default, because Lancia did, after all, bring the ships out of the void."

Kari Wang picked up her own tea. She blew on it to cool it, thinking about what he'd said. And what he hadn't.

GOED Lutchen was hot and sunny. It reminded Kari Wang of the day Agda Ayemann had been elected to the council. The tarmac, as they walked out to the shuttle, heated the soles of her feet through her boots. Every step was hard work.

"You should preserve your strength," Jon suggested, inclining his head at the orderly who followed discreetly, wheeling an empty chair. "It's going to be a long day."

It already was a long day, but she was determined not to use the chair. She wished the shuttle they were making for wasn't on the outer perimeter of the landing field. "I'll be fine."

She had her own entourage. Jon Ofir, the psychiatrist, Benjamin Fitch, the doctor, and the aide with the chair.

It was the first time she had been outside since she'd arrived on planet. She'd last been off ship twelve months before that, when she'd spent a two-day furlough on Roscracia while a linesman serviced her ship.

"We're lucky we got a jump," Jon said. "They've been waiting for it for days."

Kari Wang concentrated on putting one foot in front of the other. That slight, annoying height difference was more pronounced on the unfamiliar surface.

Fitch moved closer to her. "I hear Admiral MacClennan commandeered the first jump to Haladea III." Out here in the sunshine, he looked nothing like Will; it was almost a shock.

The Haladean cluster was halfway out to the rim, so far

from other worlds they were in a separate line zone. They were politically affiliated with the Alliance—old Alliance, Kari Wang reminded herself—but they were poor cousins in that lumbering political party, tolerated more because they were founding members than for any power they had.

"Why Haladea?" Kari Wang asked.

They both looked at her, and she got the feeling she'd asked something extremely stupid. Even the aide was looking at her strangely.

"We forget, sometimes, that you don't know what's happened," Fitch said. "This must all be strange to you. Haladea III is the New Alliance headquarters. They've moved there from temporary headquarters on Confluence Station."

Everyone knew what was at Confluence Station. Alien spaceships. They'd all seen the vids. Her own crew had been talking about it before . . . She refused to think about that. Even she'd known it was the spaceships that gave the New Alliance the edge in the war between them and Gate Union.

Kari Wang had some catching up to do.

They finally reached the shuttle. When they stopped, Kari Wang's legs were shaking so much, she had to borrow the chair from the aide to support her.

Arnoud and Fitch had explained it to her. "The muscle in these legs have never been used. You have to tone them."

Why in the lines couldn't they have built her an old-fashioned pair of neo-alloy legs, where the strength was immediate, instead of grafting on real flesh and bone? She could take neo-alloy legs off when they ached, like her legs were aching now.

She could almost hear Will in her head. "Ah, but think of the stumps. They'd itch."

She looked at the steps in front of her. Thirteen steps. Right now, she'd give anything for a jetpack and an antigrav unit.

"We can help you up," Fitch offered.

She looked at him.

He stepped back in pretend fear. "It was a suggestion, Captain," and smiled tentatively.

She almost smiled back.

"You go up," she said. There was no sense all of them waiting out in the hot sun while she waited for her legs to start working again.

Nobody moved.

"At least two of you go up. Jon. Fitch." She glared at them. "Move." It would be unfair to order the aide to go, given that his job was to transfer her. "That's an order."

Jon scratched his head. "You can't order us, Captain." Even though she outranked them. "If it's your medical or psychiatric well-being that's at stake, we override your orders."

"Oh, for—" Surely they weren't going to draw demarcation lines here. "I intend to walk up those stairs. I need my legs to recover first."

"We'll make a deal," Fitch said. "You sit down while you wait, and we'll go up."

"Turn the chair around," she said to the aide, because now that she had stopped, she wasn't sure she could even walk around to the front of the chair.

He did so.

She sat.

Jon opened his mouth to argue. Fitch pushed him up the stairs in front of him.

"Thank you," Kari Wang said, and watched them go. Fitch would have made one hell of a psychiatrist if he hadn't chosen to be a doctor.

She wasn't foolish. She waited until she knew she could do it.

"Apologies for keeping you out in the sun," she said to the aide. She checked the name on his shirt, and his rank. "Spacer Grieve."

"It's not a problem, ma'am." He was so fresh-faced, he looked to be straight out of academy, but while his uniform looked crisp, his boots were worn in. Kari Wang suspected he'd still look fresh-faced when he was sixty. The sun didn't seem to bother him, anyway.

Kari Wang forced herself to move, and mounted the stairs one careful step at a time. At the top, she thought momentarily about using the chair again, then decided to enter on her own slow legs.

She was glad that she had, for when she entered the shuttle

cabin she found she hadn't merely been holding up her own
party. Admiral MacClennan was seated in the front row.

IT felt strange to be on a ship that wasn't hers.

Captain Abene Fierro greeted her briskly. "Welcome
aboard, Captain," with no betraying emotion in her voice, but
Kari Wang could see the pity in her eyes and was glad when
the captain turned to Admiral MacClennan without saying
anything else to her. "We've fifteen minutes before we jump."

MacClennan nodded and was polite enough not to say Kari
Wang had delayed them. Would they have sent someone out to
collect her if she had spent another fifteen minutes waiting for
her legs to stop shaking? She made for her cabin as soon as the
introductions were done. She didn't want to be on a ship that
wasn't her own. She shouldn't be alive.

She spent the rest of the ten-hour trip watching the news
feeds, concentrating on the political channels, interrupted at
hourly intervals by Fitch or Jon coming to check if she needed
anything. She told them the same thing. "I'm fine. Catching up
on news I missed while I was in the hospital."

She felt the ship change course just before Captain Fierro
called. They were an hour out of port. "We've been given permission to fly by the alien ships. The best view will be from
the bridge."

"Thank you," Kari Wang said. Her own crew would have
fallen over themselves to see this. She wasn't sure she wanted
to see it on her own. She stood up.

By now she knew it was the accusations and counteraccusations over the destruction of her own ship that had finally
catapulted Gate Union and the New Alliance into outright
war. It didn't bring anyone back, but there was a bitter pleasure
in knowing that the deaths of her crew had some effect.

There had been incursions, but no major battles to date.

She knew that Confluence Station—with its attendant alien
fleet—had moved, and was now orbiting Haladea III. Who in
their sane mind would move a station once it was set in place?
She knew that Lancia, Aratoga, and Balian controlled one fac-
tion of the New Alliance government, Nova Tahiti and Yaolin
another.

She also knew that most political commentators expected the New Alliance to fail spectacularly. Some gave it two years, some gave it ten, although one unfashionable observer predicted they'd last twenty. "After all," he told Galactic News reporter Coral Zabi, "there's no denying they have an edge right now," and he'd glanced significantly at the fleet of alien ships on the screen behind them.

Kari Wang opened the door, then paused to hear the rest of the broadcast.

"But, Professor Klerk," Coral Zabi said, "the New Alliance refuses to use the fleet at present."

Admiral MacClennan stopped for her in the corridor.

On-screen, Klerk made a dismissive motion. "It will take time to work out how to use alien technology. If Gate Union has any brains, they will attack before the New Alliance can work it out because once they know what they're doing with those alien ships, the New Alliance can take on Gate Union ship to ship and beat them."

Kari Wang stepped back to let the admiral go first, but MacClennan looked past her to the screen, where Klerk said, "There are two ways to win a war. Pound your enemy so they have nothing left to fight you with and are forced to surrender. Or stop supplies, so their economy fails and their own people will force them to surrender."

"And that's the truth," MacClennan said softly.

Zabi's eyes opened wide. "So you predict that the New Alliance will defeat Gate Union?"

"The New Alliance can never win," Klerk said. "Gate Union controls the void. The line cartels affiliate with Gate Union. They're squeezing the New Alliance now. Delaying jumps, refusing to fix their lines. If you can't jump through the void, and you can't fix your higher lines, you're stuck in local space. Over time, Gate Union will take more and more of the commerce. Worlds affiliated with the New Alliance will have to defect to survive. *That's* why Gate Union will eventually win."

Forcing an economic surrender was always preferable to killing off half a planet, but an initial quick show of force worked best. If you had the force, and with this ship surely the New Alliance had that but, as Professor Klerk had said, you couldn't simply take over a strange ship and have it magically work for you. You had to learn how to use it and how to supply it before it became useful.

"How badly are Gate Union squeezing us?" she asked, as she clicked off the vid and followed MacClennan.

"Badly," MacClennan said. "It's a massive problem getting jumps right now. Short term that hits us hard because worlds have based their economies around access to jumps."

They paused to let an excited group of off-duty crew make their way past them to the viewing center. Every ship had a room with a Plexiglas window, which looked out into space. It was usually tucked away in an unimportant area because space was huge and things in it were small, relatively speaking. You couldn't see much. The best place to view space was the bridge. It had a wall of screens and could zoom in on anything around it. Personally, Kari Wang would have made for the mess, which would have its own big screen. A good captain would patch the best feed through to that.

"Only short term?"

"One can hope," MacClennan said, but didn't expand.

Captain Fierro cracked a smile as they arrived on the bridge. "No one is allowed to approach this section of space normally. We are delighted you are aboard."

MacClennan grunted and looked at Kari Wang. She got the strangest feeling he'd been about to say, "It's not for me," and stopped himself in time.

"First ships coming up," the *Fierro*'s navigator said.

"Scouts," MacClennan said, as two small ships came into view. "Six crew."

Both captains looked at him, then at each other. Kari Wang gave a miniscule shrug.

"There are twenty of them," MacClennan said. "And twenty of these," as they moved past a larger ship. "Combat ships."

Kari Wang leaned forward. "It's damaged," she said. "It's been in battle."

"A lot of them are battle-damaged," MacClennan said.

They slipped past more ships.

As ship distances went, the alien ships were close. Kari Wang didn't want to be the captain who'd ordered that particular formation.

"Destroyer," as they passed a large, heavily armed ship bristling extensions. "We think those things jutting out there are weapons."

Kari Wang studied them. They might have been weapons. If so, they were like nothing she'd come across before. Will would have loved to see this.

"Patrol ship." Not as heavily armed as the destroyer, but some of the weapons were enormous.

They watched in silence as the ships seemed to slide past them.

"Mothership coming up," the navigator said, finally.

The ship on-screen was half the size of Nova Tahiti's smaller moon.

"That's the *Confluence*," MacClennan said. "On board are five hundred one- and two-man ships. It's like a city in there." He inclined his head toward a small, human-built habitation nearby. "And that's Confluence Station."

Kari Wang had been on Confluence Station. As stations went, it was large, but it was dwarfed by the ship beside it. Who in the lines had been crazy enough to put the station so close to a hundred ships? If it had been Kari Wang's navigator, she'd have busted him down a stripe.

MacClennan looked at the screen, and the star charts in front of him. He looked as if he was doing some calculations in his head. "Can you show us coordinates 234.1234.1343?"

Fierro nodded at the crewman on the comms board.

The ship that came up here was also alien. It looked like a series of linked hexagons. Kari Wang did some calculations of her own. Four times the size of her ship, which was big enough in itself, but nowhere near the size of the *Confluence*.

"That's the *Eleven*," MacClennan said.

SEVENTEEN

✦

SELMA KARI WANG

AFTER NOVA TAHITI, the autumnal chill of Haladea III went right through to Kari Wang's bones.

The spaceport was undergoing massive renovations. Enormous bulldozers pulled up the surface and pushed the debris into waiting carts to be carried away. The racket was immense. Because of the building works, the shuttle had landed at an external field, as far away from the spaceport as it had been on Nova Tahiti.

It was going to be a long walk.

A cavalcade of cars, with Nova Tahiti's emblem emblazoned on each one, dropped down beside the earthmoving machines, tiny beside them. A flock of what looked to be birds followed. The cars skimmed across the tarmac a meter above the ground, and pulled up outside the main barracks entry. The "birds"—which turned out to be media drones—swooped around the stationary cars.

The door to the first car slid open. Admiral MacClennan indicated that Kari Wang enter.

There was a protocol about these things. A captain did not enter a vehicle before her admiral, but a captain also didn't argue with her admiral. Not in front of the press.

"Captain," from a drone that was branded Galactic News. Kari Wang recognized the voice from the recent recordings she'd watched. Coral Zabi, self-styled leading reporter on all things alien. "How do you feel about—"

Kari Wang slipped into the car. MacClennan entered after her. The doors slid shut.

"Who in the lines told them what was going on?" MacClennan sounded irritated.

"The New Alliance is like a leaky sieve." The woman in

the front passenger seat wore a Nova Tahitian military uniform. So did the driver. "Someone was bound to say something." She tuned the vehicle screen to what was happening outside.

Kari Wang watched the screen. Spacer Grieve shepherded Fitch and Jon into the next car almost as fast as she and MacClennan had gotten into the first. Their own car started to move, the drones so close their cameras were like eyes, peering in the window.

"Such a pity we can't run them down," the commodore said. "Or even pick them off. I could use some handgun practice."

Kari Wang couldn't see her face, or the name on her shirt, but she didn't have to. This would be Clemence Favager, who worked closely with Admiral MacClennan and had a reputation for straight talking—even when it was inappropriate.

Favager turned back to look at Kari Wang. "Welcome to hell, Captain. I hope you have a tough hide because you're going to need it."

FAVAGER kept up a constant information dump as they moved level to the ground until they were past the spaceport, then rose past more cranes and earthmovers. They flew over at least four kilometers' worth, Kari Wang estimated.

"Most of the crew is in place by now although they're the most mismatched crew you ever saw. It's going to be a nightmare getting them to work together." This last was to Kari Wang.

Her new crew. For the ship she didn't want. Kari Wang looked out the window. They were moving over an industrial area now, mostly storehouses, based on the boxlike buildings.

"Balian has provided a full-blown seven."

"That's their second seven," MacClennan said. "Or did they give us that woman they're training?"

"Hernandez." Favager shook her head. "This is another one. I don't know where they're getting them from. I wouldn't be surprised if they had a cartel house right in the middle of the Balian military. Two sevens at least, and we all know the rumors about Admiral Katida now."

They did? Kari Wang didn't.

Favager looked back at her. "That's not common knowledge, by the way. Keep that to yourself."

"Yes, ma'am," but she was going to find out what that particular rumor was. And why everyone was interested in lines and line ability all of a sudden.

"Haladea III has given us a one. A spacer who's just finished basic training—and she may even have been pushed through early. She was a borderline fail until this business. I can't work out if they don't want to offer us any better or if they genuinely haven't got anything."

Below them the storehouses gave way to residential buildings.

"Maybe they don't have," MacClennan said.

"Aratoga's brought in some crazy old coot from the rim. He's two years off retiring, so old he looks like a good wind would blow him over."

Many fleets sent old soldiers they couldn't use out to the rim to work until retirement. Even Nova Tahiti did. They were usually sent for a reason.

"He used to be a subcommander. Whatever he did to get sent to the rim also got him booted all the way back to a spacer. Aratoga's trying to reinstate his rank."

Of course they would. After all, on a multiworld ship, it would be advantageous to have your soldier ranked highly.

"What level?"

"He failed certification."

MacClennan straightened up so fast he almost knocked his head against the ceiling as the car abruptly started to descend.

What was so significant about failing certification?

"Exactly," Favager said. She waited for the door to open. "Showtime. Let's give these drones absolutely nothing to report on, shall we?"

The Nova Tahitian embassy was built into the side of a cliff although it was rapidly being overshadowed by the new buildings going up all around it. Kari Wang could see the faint haze shimmering over the polished-rock exterior, along with the hum that signified a protective field. It might be an old building, but someone had gone to a lot of trouble to protect what was inside.

The drones moved in. Whoever was controlling the Galactic News drone should have been a fighter pilot. It had maneu-vered itself to the front again. "Captain. Do you believe you can pilot this ship?"

Kari Wang blocked her out.

The drones stopped at the door.

INSIDE there were people everywhere. "There's a big function in your honor tonight," Favager told Kari Wang. "Formal din-ner. Everyone will want to grill you."

An elaborately dressed secretary stopped in front of them. "First Councilor and Councilor Gann are ready to see you."

Favager took Kari Wang's kit. "I'll see this gets to your room," she said. She looked at Fitch and Jon. "I'll show you your rooms," and she and Grieve neatly divided Fitch and Jon away from the other two.

Kari Wang followed MacClennan and the secretary. She was physically and emotionally exhausted even though she'd spent ten hours sitting in her cabin. Maybe now she'd finally get some answers.

FIRST Councilor didn't look much different from that long-ago day when young spacer Kari Wang had stood beside her. She had more lines around the eyes, but she still stood slender and straight. Yet Kari Wang could sense a determination that hadn't been there before, almost a desperation.

"Captain," First Councilor said.

Kari Wang saluted.

"I am sorry for your loss."

Kari Wang couldn't speak. She nodded. It was the sort of thing Agda Ayemann would have said, all that time ago.

Ahmed Gann hurried in. "Captain. So delighted to see you here." He shook hands with her, then with MacClennan.

They sat, like civilized people, and First Councilor offered drinks all round.

"Thank you," Kari Wang said, "I'm on medication. Could I have water or tea, please?"

A secretary hurried to get both for her.

"I understand you are reluctant," First Councilor said. "I

don't want to embarrass you by saying how much we need this. It may not even succeed. We understand that."

Would somebody, for the lines' sake, please tell her what was going on?

"The power in the New Alliance is delicately poised at the moment. There are those from the old Alliance who mistrust those of us from Gate Union. There are others who are prepared to work with us." First Councilor took a sip of her drink. "And, of course, there are those who came over with us from Gate Union who thought things would change."

"What do you think?" Kari Wang asked bluntly. It was all very well to hear things in abstract. She wanted to know what she was working with.

"I think—" She could see First Councilor seriously consider her answer. It wasn't to consider what she thought, for no doubt she knew that already. No, she was considering what to tell Kari Wang.

"We can make Nova Tahiti a power in the New Alliance," Ahmed Gann said. "If we are smart and use to our advantage whatever luck comes our way."

First Councilor smiled. "I think," she said, "that most members of the old Alliance want change as much as we do. We are well positioned to take advantage of that. We have Ahmed Gann. But we are but twenty worlds out of seventy, and every world has two votes. I think we need to use some of that luck Ahmed talks about to help cement our position. You're our luck even though you may not agree with it at the moment."

She raised a glass to Kari Wang. "Admiral MacClennan told me you wanted to resign," she said. "Ahmed will tell you that there has been considerable discussion at this end on your mental suitability. Nevertheless, you are the only experienced captain currently without a ship in the whole of the New Alliance fleet. And there are 130 ships out there in need of captains."

MacClennan said, "But there are only two ships that matter right now."

They wanted to put her into one of the alien ships. With a mismatched crew who answered to their own world first, and to her second. "Which ship?"

First Councilor looked at MacClennan, who looked at Gann.

"It will be the *Eleven*. Almost certainly," and everyone except Kari Wang nodded, as if they agreed with his analysis.

THE function was held at the Aratogan embassy.

Fitch, uncomfortable in formal uniform, reminded Kari Wang of Will again. She forced back the wave of despair that threatened to engulf her.

"We might be able to slip away early," he said comfortingly. "We can use your legs as an excuse."

Kari Wang had news for him. It sounded as if they wouldn't be able to slip away anytime soon, and sure enough, the first of the diplomats approached even as they talked.

"President Rjinders of Haladea III on the left," Grieve murmured in her ear. "Governor Jade from Aratoga on the right."

Grieve had to be part of MacClennan's staff, whatever else he was. He was tremendously informed. Or maybe he had a minicomms secreted on his person, feeding the information to him even as they stood there.

"President, Governor," Kari Wang said.

Rjinders nodded. "I trust you are enjoying yourself," he said.

Governor Jade wasn't as polite. "So, do you think you can do it?"

"Of course," she said. It wasn't so much whether she could do it, it was more did she want to do it.

"You'll have to manage a multiworld crew, all answering to different bosses."

As if the thought hadn't already crossed her mind. "They'll answer to me on my ship."

"You might find that more difficult than you expect," Governor Jade said.

"Maybe," Kari Wang said. "But it's my ship. My rules. No matter where they come from."

"Well spoken," and Governor Jade turned away to speak to a man in an admiral's uniform. "She might do."

"Admiral Galenos," Grieve said quietly near Kari Wang's ear.

Kari Wang looked again. Sure enough, the man wore Lancian colors.

"Governor Jade," the admiral said. He smiled at Kari Wang. "Captain." Nodded to Fitch. "Doctor."

Aratogan and Lancastrian moved away, Governor Jade still voicing her opinion that Kari Wang might do.

An admiral in the mottled blue of Gallardia took Jade's place. "Captain, you lost your ship. You lost your crew. Are you up to this?"

"Admiral Ivov of Gallardia," Grieve said, under Fitch's protesting, "That's hardly appropriate right now."

She could see it wasn't going to be the last time anyone asked that question tonight. If she was going to crack up, she'd prefer it was in private. "Why don't you be the judge of that, Admiral? If you don't like it, why not take steps through the New Alliance parliament to have me ousted?"

"He already has," Grieve commented under his breath as the admiral walked off. "He was outvoted."

After that, a continuous stream of people came up to her. Most of them wanted to know if she was up to it. Grieve knew them all.

"You should sit down soon."

"I'll be fine."

"If you collapse now, you'll give them ammunition to get you kicked off ship, ma'am," Grieve said. "Nova Tahiti has worked hard to get you here. Best not to undo all that good work on the first night."

She heard the steel in his voice and wondered what he'd do if she refused. Was he the simple spacer his uniform made him out to be? He was very confident around all this brass. Whatever he was, he was right. Tonight wasn't the night to show weakness. Not at a function hosted by Nova Tahiti.

She had just sat down when a spacer approached her. He was one of the few uniformed people in the room who wore anything less than commodore's pips, and the others were all in her party. She watched him come. He was slender, and his movements were quick and light, but she would bet he had never undergone military training. His hair was long for most military.

He wore a Lancian uniform, unadorned except for the bars

below his name. She looked more closely. The bars went all the way across the pocket.

"Linesman Lambert," Grieve said softly beside her. "Don't be misled by the ten bars."

Kari Wang turned to look at him.

"Lambert is Lancia's chief linesman," Grieve said blandly.

Lambert was there now, smiling and offering his hand. "Ean Lambert," he said.

She took it automatically. "Kari Wang." What was a level-ten linesman doing wearing a Lancian military uniform? Why wasn't he in a cartel house?

"I know." Lambert pulled out the chair next to hers and sat down. "You're the captain of the *Eleven*." He grinned broadly. "And let me tell you, the *Eleven* is really looking forward to it."

"Looking forward to it?" Was he part of the crew?

"Maybe I am putting words into its mouth," Lambert admitted. "I'm looking forward to it. Ships need people, you see."

They were swamped by another round of dignitaries before she had time to ask him what he meant. This time the questions were aimed as much at Lambert as they were at her.

"Is the ship ready for a human crew?"

"Is it safe?"

"Is she emotionally stable?"

"I don't know," Lambert said, and she didn't know which one he was answering. He probably didn't either. "You've all seen the captain's record."

A diplomat in long green robes said quietly to another diplomat in a dark gray suit, "Her whole crew was destroyed. And her ship. That's her record."

Kari Wang didn't even realize she'd surged out of her seat—or tried to—until she felt the viselike hand on her shoulder that held her back. "Easy," and the woman who'd stopped her from proving to everyone just how emotionally unstable she was right now, said to the diplomat in green robes, "Doesn't it occur to you to wonder, Speaker Rhodes, what the *Kari Wang* was testing out there that led Gate Union to target them as the first ship they attacked after Nova Tahiti allied themselves with the New Alliance. Because *I* wonder."

"Admiral Katida. Balian," Grieve said quietly from behind her.

Kari Wang didn't need the introduction. Before she'd been promoted to admiral, Katida had been head of Balian's covert operations group. Every single world that had crossed from Gate Union to the New Alliance had come up against Katida's people at one time or another, Nova Tahiti included.

"Isn't that what the military is for, Admiral? To concern themselves with questions like that."

"Speaker Rhodes, if more politicians concerned themselves with questions like that, we might not now be at war."

Lambert winced, but he turned his face away so that only Kari Wang saw it.

The tall, dark-haired woman who was talking to Galenos not far away detached herself midsentence and came over to join them.

"Speakers." She nodded to Rhodes and the woman in the gray suit. To Katida. "Admiral."

"Lady Lyan, Crown Princess of Lancia." She didn't need any introduction either.

Lady Lyan turned to Kari Wang. "Captain. Lancia is delighted to have you aboard as captain of the *Eleven*."

"*Eleven*." Speaker Rhodes, who'd been edging away, stopped. "So the ship has been chosen?"

It hadn't exactly been a secret from where Kari Wang stood. Gann had known, and the Nova Tahiti power brokers had agreed with him.

Kari Wang looked thoughtfully at Lambert. Linesman Ean Lambert had known as well.

EIGHTEEN

SELMA KARI WANG

THE *ELEVEN* WAS a big ship. Far bigger than the *Kari Wang*.

"Suits on," Grieve said. "No helmets, though. We think we have the atmospheric mix right, but just in case."

Kari Wang picked up the suit, then froze. Last time she'd worn a suit, everyone around her had died. She pushed the suit away.

"It's rules, ma'am," Grieve said.

She shook her head.

Jon leaned over and said something quietly to Grieve. She couldn't hear it through the sudden roaring in her ears. Grieve tapped something into his comms.

"Stopping now," the shuttle pilot said, and the engines cut out. "Take hold."

A force grabbed the shuttle, and jerked.

"Shit," Jon said, and gripped his seat. Fitch hung on to his seat belt.

Another force grabbed the shuttle. Another jerk.

"Entry takes some getting used to," Grieve said. "We think when you work out how to fly the ship's own shuttles, it won't be so rough."

Jon sounded strangled. "You mean this is normal?"

"Yes." Something pinged on Grieve's comms. He looked at it, looked at Kari Wang, showed it to Jon and Fitch, then stood up as the all clear sounded. "Let's go see the ship."

They were met at the air lock by a voice raised in song.

That was almost as worrying as Grieve, Fitch, and Jon conversing quietly behind Kari Wang's back. Grieve wheeled the chair he'd carried the day before.

Linesman Lambert was the singer. He was surrounded by

a team of Lancastrian guards. They all wore suits, helmets down their back.

The team leader in front of Lambert frowned at Kari Wang's lack of suit. She opened her mouth to speak—presumably about the suit—but both Jon and Grieve shook their heads.

Kari Wang ignored them.

Worst of all was that she knew how she would react to someone on her own ship behaving like that. She wouldn't make them put on the suit, of course, but she wouldn't let them step out of the air lock, either. They'd be heading back with the shuttle, placed under the care of a psychiatrist until they could work out their issues.

The rules weren't there for fun. If they wanted her suited up, there was a genuine danger the air on the *Eleven* could go at any time.

Lambert stopped singing and smiled at her. "Welcome aboard the *Eleven*," he said.

She inclined her head. She couldn't speak yet.

"Let's give you a tour," Lambert said, reassuringly, and she knew, by the way he patted her hand as he turned away, that he had registered her discomfort and chosen to ignore it.

One of the spacers handed her some goggles. "UV filter," she said. "You'll find them easier to see with, at least initially."

It was a big ship. Kari Wang watched each section as they passed through. "This ship must take a thousand people when it's fully staffed."

"There were 1024 aliens on board," Lambert said.

She supposed she should think about the previous occupants, but right now the current occupants disturbed her more.

"Don't worry—" Lambert caught his breath, and stumbled. One of the soldiers with him grabbed an oxygen mask off a nearby wall and pushed it over his face.

Lambert pushed it away. "I'm fine." He sang, breathlessly, and seemed to listen.

There were oxygen stations everywhere, Kari Wang realized. The only real signs of human habitation.

One of the Lancastrian guards held out an oxygen mask to Kari Wang. She pushed it away. "What's going on?"

"Line eleven," said the guard who'd loaned Kari Wang her

goggles. The name on her pocket was *Radko*. "Affects linesmen."

Suddenly, MacClennan's insistence on line testing made more sense. "I'm not a linesman."

Radko's gaze swept over the other Nova Tahitians.

"None of us are linesmen."

Radko nodded, then turned back to Lambert. "Are you finished yet, Ean?"

"Fine," Lambert wheezed, and made off down the corridor.

Radko reached out and grabbed him. "Wait for us."

He waited.

"These oxygen stations?" Kari Wang asked.

"Are necessary. You get strong linesmen in here, and you're going to need them."

"All of your people will get special training in dealing with line-related issues," the team leader—Bhaksir—said. "It's a real pain."

They continued through the seemingly endless corridors. Lambert kept up a song for most of the way. No one seemed to find it unusual.

"I tell you something," Fitch muttered, as Kari Wang ducked under another bulkhead. "If we'd known about this ship, we'd have built your legs forty millimeters shorter. I wish they'd told us."

She managed the first smile of the day.

"Average height of the aliens is eighty percent of human norm," Bhaksir said. She seemed to be everywhere, listening in. "Bridge is coming up." She looked at Grieve. "You might need that chair ready. It can be a shock first time you see it."

Lambert's song rose, and amplified around the great space they entered that was the bridge of the alien ship. The humans on the bridge looked around. Some smiled a welcome. One, with group-leader pips, detached herself from the group in front of a board and came over to greet them.

"Captain Kari Wang. Group Leader Sale."

Kari Wang nodded, only half listening.

The panels were flickering bars of light. She could vaguely make out what looked to be a star chart on the main screen, but she had no idea what the rest of the screens showed. There were colored bars of light everywhere on the star chart.

How in the lines was she going to work out what was happening on ship?

Sale must have caught her expression. "Exactly," she said. "You'll require a lot of faith in the people you work with, for this is a line ship, pure and simple." She tapped a secondary set of boards, placed around the Captain's Chair. Familiar equipment. With an obviously alien-designed screen right in the center. "We've put some human boards in, and some sensors, but we don't know what we're covering, so this is all you have."

It was little better than a scout ship. "And how is anyone supposed to run it?"

"That's what your crew is for." Sale tapped one of the weaker-colored bars on the huge star chart that took up one wall. "Ships," she said. "That one is"—she checked her comms—"Scout 5." She tapped one of the three strongest sets of lights on the chart. "The *Confluence.*" Another strong set. "The *Lancastrian Princess.*" The third strong set. "The *Wendell.*"

"The *Wendell*?"

"It's part of the *Eleven*'s fleet."

According to the news vids Kari Wang had watched on the *Fierro,* Wendell and his crew had been with Yaolin when the New Alliance had been formed. Their own world, Wallacia, had declared them outlaws. She felt sorry for Piers Wendell. She liked him, and he was in almost as bad a position as she was.

"As you can see," Sale said. "The lights have nothing to do with the size of the ship. It's all about the strength of the lines." She tapped the screen again. "Ean, give her the tour."

Sale's pocket was covered in badges, as was everyone else's on the bridge—except Lambert's. Every badge, without exception, displayed the glyph that marked the wearer as among the top 10 percent for that particular qualification. Every wearer—without exception—also wore braid on their shoulders that proclaimed them members of Lady Lyan's personal guard.

How did Lady Lyan's personal guard get to work on this ship?

Lambert guided her over to the stool underneath a hooded canopy, where Kari Wang could see the whole room. "The

Captain's Chair. The line chassis is here," and touched the canopy, almost affectionately. "Sit down, and I'll introduce you."

She sat, glad to have a reason to. Her legs ached.

The stool was hard, and short, but if they made it much higher, she'd be blinded by the canopy.

Sale made a sympathetic noise. "Pity you're not shorter," she said.

"She'll be fine," Lambert said. Bhaksir and Sale made faces at each other, as if they didn't quite trust his optimism.

"You'll probably walk around a lot," Sale said.

It was a pity she didn't have the legs for it right now.

Lambert sang, the same waterfall of sound he'd been singing before.

Introduce her, he'd said. "Who are you introducing me to?" she asked, when it was over.

"The ship."

She was aware Sale and Bhaksir were watching her intently. They'd probably been told to watch her. This whole unpreparedness might even be a setup to see how she reacted.

Let them watch.

"Line one," Lambert said. "The crew line. Or crew and ship, really. On the screen in front of you."

He meant the alien screen in among all the smaller ones she was familiar with.

He sang, light clear notes this time, and she imagined, as part of that song, that the ship welcomed her.

Kari Wang refused to listen. It wasn't her ship. It wasn't her responsibility. Instead, she looked at the screen—if that was what it was, for it was dull, and seemed to vibrate. She put her hand close. Sure enough, she could feel vibrations.

Lambert stopped singing. "You can see that line one is weak."

She couldn't see a thing except a few vibrating colors.

"Line two."

This time the song was a soft chatter that made Kari Wang think of light and air and warmth. The image on screen was stronger.

"Line two is still getting used to human conditions," Lambert said. "Sometimes, things go wrong, which is why you have to wear a suit all the time." He looked at her, at her suit-lessness, then hurried on.

"Line three."

More chatter, and intermittent lights across the screen. "We haven't worked out all that's wrong yet."

Line three controlled small mechanics, and things like doors, and other ship machinery. From the looks of the screen, half the doors on the ship weren't working. If she was reading the screens properly, which was doubtful.

"Line four." Gravity. This time Lambert's song was a staccato on/off.

Kari Wang looked around at the working soldiers. They were all watching her with half their attention, but they had their own tasks, too, and they were doing them. They were used to this.

"Line five." The ever-vital comms.

She was glad there were only ten lines. Or were there eleven? Her crew would have wanted to know.

"Comms looks strong," Kari Wang said, for the colors were stronger here.

Sale snorted. "That's because Ean's been singing his heart out to them every day. All the lines. You should have seen how weak they were when we started."

"Singing?" Fitch asked.

Sale shrugged.

"Line six," Lambert said, cutting across their talk. This song was heavy and strong. The lights were strong, too.

When he sang, he had the seriousness and absorption of Will, when Will talked about his own favorite subject—weapons.

"Line seven." A comfortable baritone.

"Line eight." Rich, and warm and pleasing to the ear. Also strong.

Line nine was a deep, resonant dirge. Ten, high, clear notes. Both were strong.

"Line eleven," Lambert said, and started a beat that sent him to his knees. "Not so strong," he begged, still in song.

Radko moved over to the nearest oxygen unit.

Lambert pushed her away and struggled to his feet. "I'm fine."

Kari Wang watched them. The ship seemed less alien than the humans on it. Her own crew would be fascinated. She could imagine Kelan—long a student of human behavior—watching avidly. The others. They'd be watching the ship, asking questions she herself would normally ask. Where were the engines? How did they plan on running the ship? What about the weapons bays?

Lambert hadn't even shown her the weapons bays. Instead, he'd sung to the lines. And seeing all this alien technology, when her crew wasn't here to see it with her, made her numb inside.

She forced herself to sound interested in something although she didn't care about the answer. "How many lines are there?"

"Twelve," Radko said, and looked toward Lambert, who flushed, but didn't argue the count.

AFTER lunch Kari Wang wanted to rest. Instead, she met with Admirals Galenos, MacClennan, Katida, and Orsaya.

"You shouldn't be doing so much so soon," Fitch said. "They should give you time between to relax."

"Fitch, is there anything wrong with my legs except lack of muscle tone?"

"No, but—"

"I'll be fine." There had been a time, hundreds of years ago, when losing one's legs would have been debilitating. Nowadays, they replaced them with neo-alloy legs, which provided instant strength, even if the wearer had to get used to the impulses sent through the nerve endings by the artificial legs. Why had they given her real legs?

Because they could, she supposed. So here she was, five months after such an accident with legs where the only thing wrong was lack of muscle tissue.

And a slight height difference, as she tripped over her own toes and nearly fell.

Or maybe it was a problem with nerve endings. Who said they had retained all the nerve endings she'd had before? Or even put them in the right place?

Grieve looked meaningfully at the chair he wheeled around like some sort of prop. She pretended not to see.

She also pretended not to notice as Grieve deftly separated her from Jon and Fitch at the meeting-room door. "Doctors, why don't I show you the fleet hospital while the captain is speaking with the admirals."

She rapped on the door and went in.

AS well as the four admirals, there were two captains.

One of them was immaculately dressed in Lancian gray and black. Captain Helmo from the *Lancastrian Princess*, Lady Lyan's personal ship.

The other was tall and skinny, with white skin and dyed maroon hair. His uniform barely made regulation. Captain Wendell, from the *Wendell*. Kari Wang's mouth curved into a smile. "Piers."

Wendell looked thinner than ever, and there were black rings under his eyes that she hadn't seen before. He smiled for her, though. "Selma."

She looked at his uniform. He wore the green of Wallacia, which wasn't one of the seventy worlds that made up the New Alliance. She didn't ask. She'd ask later.

Admiral Orsaya said, "Don't be fooled by the uniform, Captain. Wendell and his crew are dual citizens of Yaolin and Lancia, and part of the New Alliance fleet. They will wear the same uniform as your crew. *If* the uniform committee ever gets around to agreeing on a design."

"Let's hope they don't choose that dreadful orange thing they were so set on," Katida said.

Everyone shuddered.

"I've asked Ean to join us," Galenos said. "He had some line business to attend to, but he'll try to come by."

Galenos brought up a list of names on the tabletop screen. "Your crew," he said. "Two from each world, as agreed by the council. They're still undergoing security tests."

He split the names into two groups. "We asked for one linesman, one failed linesman from each." He tapped the left list. "The linesmen. Mostly sixes, with two exceptions. Balian sent us a seven."

Everyone looked at Katida.

"That's your second seven?" Orsaya said, and it was a

pointed question. "Didn't you also provide a seven for line training?"

Katida skirted the question by explaining to Kari Wang. "There are two groups of linesmen. Ean is already training the first group. They will go back to their own worlds when they're done. The second group is your crew."

"We noticed you avoided answering that question," Orsaya said.

"So I did." Katida tapped the table. "The other exception?"

Galenos might have hidden a smile. "Haladea III sent us a one."

"An insult?"

"Do you think they have anything better?" Helmo asked.

"No, I don't."

They all looked at the list for a moment. Galenos broke the silence. "The single linesmen." He tapped it. It was shorter than the other one. Kari Wang did a quick count. Around fifty names.

"We have the military of every New Alliance world scouring their databases for failed linesmen. Unfortunately, most of them don't consider military careers."

"Nyan has five of them," Orsaya said. "There's little else to do on Nyan except join the military. There's no other job for a failed linesman if he or she goes home."

"Most of them don't go home. That's the problem."

"Who would?" asked Wendell. "They've seen what life can be for linesmen. *I* wouldn't want to go back to my old life. Especially not as a failure. I'd go as far away as possible."

Early in her career, Kari Wang had worked with someone who had undergone line training, then failed certification. The girl had been unprepared for the military and totally unsuited. She'd left two months after graduating. "Why do we want failed linesmen?" It was the craziest thing she'd heard so far, and after watching Lambert sing to the lines earlier, she hadn't thought anything could be crazier than that.

"Because they're linesmen," Galenos said. "They'll work as well on your ship as certified linesmen." He steepled his fingers. "Current line testing is flawed. There's an assumption that linesmanship starts at one and goes up. The tests start at line one. If you recognize line one, you go on to be tested for line two. If you recognize line two, you go on to be tested for line three, and so on. Maybe you stop at six, because you don't recognize line seven. You're certified. You become a linesman level six."

Few linesmen made level ten, the highest level. Highest certified level, Kari Wang corrected herself, for hadn't Radko claimed Lambert was a twelve. Could they even test for that? Or was he simply an exceptional ten and the New Alliance didn't have the experience to know any better?

If Kari Wang had been certified a linesman, she'd want to be a six. The cartels didn't want you. The sevens and above stayed in the cartel houses and were contracted out on repair jobs. The sixes could choose any job they wanted because everyone needed lower-level linesmen and line six controlled the Bose engines that powered spaceships. The military or the big manufacturing companies snapped you up so fast, you didn't even have time to say good-bye to your fellow linesmen after the certification ceremony.

There had been two sixes on the *Kari Wang*, plus a three. All of them engineers.

She considered what Galenos hadn't said. "You're saying that even those who failed certification are still linesmen."

"Some of them are, at least. The ones we know about have a single line. One thing we do know is that all of those we have tested can hear and see the lines on the alien ships."

"Hear?" It sounded ominous given that Linesman Lambert had introduced her to the ship in song.

"Line testing is flawed," Galenos said again.

Kari Wang didn't know much about line training, but the higher-level linesmen were famous. "And a level-ten linesman I've never heard of is telling you this. Are you sure he knows what he's saying?"

If there'd been any physicality to the way her words changed the atmosphere around the table, her hair would have been standing straight out with the static.

Wendell broke the mood by laughing. "Be careful whom you insult," he said. "Lambert is the most protected civilian in the galaxy right now." He indicated the admirals with a wave of his hand. "Not to mention their pet project." Then he added,

"For what it's worth, I don't doubt Lambert myself. He's the best linesman I know."

"And I," Helmo added.

Interesting. "Understood," Kari Wang said, before the silence got too awkward. She wasn't sure she did understand. But she would.

"He does clean lines," Wendell said.

How much of Wendell's approval was tied up in how well Lambert fixed the lines? But then, she'd always liked a good line repair herself.

"We've learned a lot about the lines recently," Galenos said. "We're at the start of a giant leap forward in line knowledge."

Katida and Orsaya nodded. MacClennan didn't. Nor did Helmo or Wendell, but she could see the two captains agreed with Galenos. MacClennan must have known something, though, for he had implied by omission that the New Alliance had no problems getting ships fixed. Because if you could find single-level nines and tens, you no longer had to rely on Gate Union to fix your ships for you.

"There's another advantage with the single-level linesmen," Galenos said. "Line eleven can be . . . strong."

"Debilitating," Katida muttered.

Orsaya's eyes gleamed. "Are you saying, Katida—"

"The stronger the linesman," Katida said, over the top of her. "The worse line eleven affects them. You've heard about the confluence?"

The *Kari Wang*'s annual service had been pushed back three months because the nines and tens were out at the confluence. It had still been waiting for that service, in fact, when it had been destroyed.

"That effectively took all the nines and tens out of service for six months. Most of them aren't fully back yet."

Kari Wang nodded.

"Single linesmen don't have that problem," Katida said. "Because they're blind to eleven."

"Don't you mean deaf, Katida?" Captain Helmo asked.

"Deaf, blind, drugged out of their brain." Katida waved a dismissive hand. "Nonfunctioning."

Kari Wang looked at the shorter list of names on the

tabletop screen. "You think all these people are single-level linesmen?"

"Yes, we do," Galenos said. "The *Eleven* is a ship you can't run without linesmen."

She wasn't a linesman.

Galenos touched the longer list. "Your other crew will be overcome by the *Eleven* when it's strong."

So she was to crew a ship she couldn't read the panels on, with half a crew that needed oxygen on a regular basis, and the other half with who knew what skills.

Wonderful.

NINETEEN

EAN LAMBERT

"WHAT DO YOU think?" Ean asked, after he, Radko, and Craik had seen their visitors off.

"I think that not wearing a suit on a ship like this is asking for trouble," Radko said.

Craik shivered. "Grieve said it was close to a full-blown panic attack."

"More fodder for Speaker Rhodes." Ean turned away. He hoped she'd work out. He walked back to the bridge, singing to the lines as he did so. Their mood was hopeful. They wanted this to work out as much as he did.

ONCE Ean had thought that the lines on the *Lancastrian Princess* reflected Michelle's feelings because the ship picked up Michelle's thoughts. And it did, but it was more complex than that. He was coming to realize that the ship reflected Michelle because to everyone else, from Captain Helmo down, Michelle was the most important thing on ship.

He would have liked to discuss it with Abram, but Abram was on Haladea III now. He missed Abram.

So did Michelle, and Ean was never, ever going to tell her how clearly that came through the lines. Sometimes, especially late at night, the lines keened with loneliness. One night it was so bad it woke Ean. By the time he realized what it was, Helmo was tapping on Michelle's door with an apologetic, "Sorry to wake you so late, ma'am, especially when you don't get much time to sleep, but—" The pause was imperceptible in real time but was a big green snap through the lines, and Ean still didn't know if his own lines listening in had guided

Helmo's next words. "I would like some guidance on what to do with Lambert."

Michelle swung out of bed as if she were glad to leave it. She didn't seem to find it strange that Helmo would come and wake her in the middle of the night to talk about Ean, of all people. If Helmo was discomforted to see his boss dressed in only a short silken shift, he didn't show it. Ean, sitting on his own bed, arms around his knees, was more so.

Michelle indicated a corner nook with two chairs and a small table. "Please, sit down. A drink?"

"Thank you." Helmo sat. "Not just Lambert. Burns as well." He studied the drink Michelle had poured. The smell that came through the lines was smooth and mellow. Ean couldn't always differentiate what was in his own immediate vicinity and what was on other parts of the ship. Helmo sipped with obvious pleasure, then sat back. "Lambert."

There wasn't any more of the green snap with the words. He'd made that one decision earlier to use Ean as the excuse to come in and talk; now he was following through on it. "I suspect Vega will try to move him off ship, claiming he's a security risk. Burns, too."

Ean knew, as clearly as if Helmo had said it aloud, that the real reason Helmo was there was because the ship had registered Michelle's discomfort. Had the captain recognized it specifically as loneliness, or just as something not right with the lines? It wasn't something he could ever ask.

He couldn't tell what Michelle thought. He could see her, though. Her and Helmo, both with a full spectrum of visible colors and beyond. He could smell the clean fizz that he associated with Michelle, and the sharp, metallic overtones of Helmo.

"I want Ean on ship." It was quick and instinctive.

Helmo nodded. "She'll want to move him off this floor."

"Because he's a threat." Michelle sounded bitter. "She has no idea what's a threat and what's not."

"She has a big reputation to live up to."

"Maybe if she stopped trying so hard she'd—" Michelle took a deep breath. "Sorry."

"We've all got some adjusting to do." Helmo stared at his glass. "Sometimes I wish we hadn't been so successful." He looked at Michelle. "Maybe we were getting too comfortable. I don't know."

"Comfortable. Is that what you call it?"

Ean would have called it happy, and he really shouldn't be snooping through the lines like this, but it wasn't something you could turn off.

Helmo dragged the conversation back. "So. Does Lambert stay on this floor, or do I move him off when Vega asks?"

He said when, not if, Ean noticed.

"He stays," Michelle said.

"And Burns?"

"Can't he stay in the VIP quarters? He's Ean's assistant."

"He'll be the only person there."

They spent the next fifteen minutes discussing where to house Fergus, something both of them would normally have decided with a five-second snap decision.

He couldn't stay in crew quarters. Vega didn't like civilians in with the crew. There wasn't any room in the space set aside for Michelle's personal staff, and Helmo wanted to close down most of the modules that had housed the VIPs to save on air and heating.

Ean, sitting up in bed, could feel the tension in the lines easing.

"Leave one of the VIP modules open," Michelle said finally. "I think it will be the best solution."

"That will work." Helmo stood up. "I'd best let you get back to sleep, ma'am. Thank you for your time."

Absolutely nothing had changed with regard to living quarters for the linesmen.

After Helmo left, Michelle went back to bed, where she fell asleep almost instantly. Helmo walked the corridors of the ship first, then went to bed himself and to sleep almost as quickly.

Ean had lain awake for the rest of the night.

HE didn't see Michelle before she left the next day for the sitting of parliament, but as they came back into range after line training, he could tell from the lines that she was back on board. The first thing he was going to do was find her and talk to her.

His comms chimed as he stepped out onto the shuttle deck proper. It was Vega. "Meet me in my office." The anger she was hiding was sour and blue.

Ean checked on Michelle. She was in the workroom, immersed in whatever was on her screen. The lines were quiet. She was okay for the moment. "I'll be down," he told Vega.

Vega met him with, "This is not a public meeting place, linesman. And we're not all here for your convenience."

"Maybe if you explain what the problem is," Ean said. He was tired of Vega's superrighteousness. Or maybe he was simply tired. He had been awake most of the night. "I'm not a mind reader."

She was only doing her job, and he should remember that. All he could think of was Michelle's loneliness of the previous night. Why couldn't Abram have stayed?

He wasn't sure if he was angry at Vega or Abram.

Vega looked at him, and for a moment, he wondered if *she* was a mind reader. He watched the muscles in her throat tighten and saw the effort it took to relax them. Her voice was civil when she eventually said, "Grand Master Rickenback requests permission to come aboard the *Lancastrian Princess* to visit with Linesman Ean Lambert," but there was a tic at the left of her mouth that she couldn't quite stop.

The Grand Master had every right to request to see a linesman, especially if said linesman had asked for an audience. That was part of the Grand Master's job. To assist linesmen in disputes with cartel houses.

If Paretsky had been Grand Master, would he have come so readily?

"I'll meet him off ship," Ean said. Maybe he could use the Night Owl again.

"*You'll* choose. *You'll* decide."

The sour blue behind the words was so strong, Ean stepped backward. The top of Vega's head came to his chin, but Ean had no doubt that if she attacked him—and he wondered for a moment if she was going to—then she would beat him to a pulp. "Vega, I am trying to help."

"As Grand Master Rickenback pointed out, he has a legal right to see you at your place of work."

What, technically, was his place of work? "You want him

to come to the *Eleven*?" He wasn't going to ask for clearance for that. Even Vega knew he wouldn't get it.

The tic grew stronger. "Rickenback will be here at 16:00 hours. I have made meeting room two available." She paused. "I have also explained to him that he is on a secure ship. He will be searched."

"I am sure he understands."

Vega made a dismissive motion with her hand. As Ean turned to go, "Lambert."

He looked back over his shoulder.

"This is not a social visit."

"Understood," Ean said. Did that mean he couldn't even offer Rickenback a drink? He'd have to ask Radko.

BY rights, he should have gone to his own quarters, but until Vega officially stopped him, he would spend time where he always had. Michelle and Abram's workroom.

Michelle looked up and smiled as Ean entered. "Hello."

The shadows under her eyes were cleverly hidden with makeup, but Ean was looking.

"What?"

Ean was aware he'd stared too long. He shrugged.

"What?" Michelle asked again.

"Your makeup is very well done."

Michelle laughed aloud. "That's a backhanded compliment." She poured him a glass of tea.

Ean took the tea. "Have you seen Abram lately?" And if she hadn't, he was going to make sure that she did. Even if he had to drag Abram here on a manufactured excuse about line ships.

"Hmm. I can hear some determination in the lines there."

She hadn't answered his question. Ean didn't push it.

"So Leo Rickenback's visiting," Michelle said.

Ean was surprised she knew.

"He called Lin, who told him to call Vega. I told Vega to invite him here, that you weren't going off ship to see him."

Vega hadn't told Ean that. "I can meet him elsewhere."

"Ean, people try to kill you when you're elsewhere." It was followed by a red-mint-cinnamon spurt of amusement.

"People try to kill you all the time," Ean said. Radko had told him that once when he'd asked why they needed a whole ship to protect Michelle. Six or seven times a year, she'd said. Half the ship was devoted to intelligence gathering, trying to work out who and why and when.

Even Ean wasn't naïve enough to think the intelligence gathering stopped with Michelle's safety. Katida had hinted as much once when they'd been talking about covert operations, and she'd said, "If Lancia wanted a decent covert operations team, they'd have put Galenos in charge of it."

It had been the same morning they had spoken about fathers and mothers, and Katida had implied—although she'd said the opposite—that Abram was more Michelle's family than anyone else.

"Do you see the rest of your family much?" Ean asked Michelle now, thinking of that morning.

Emperor Yu had taken part in the signing of the deed for the formation of the New Alliance, which had been held in a modified cargo hold on Confluence Station. It had taken four weeks to set up.

And six weeks to take down.

Michelle's brothers and sisters had been there. They hadn't looked comfortable with their older sibling. None of them had visited the *Lancastrian Princess*.

Michelle shrugged.

"I don't see my family, either," Ean said. He hadn't seen his father in ten years. He might even be dead by now. Juice itself didn't normally kill you, but you forgot to eat, and it made you violent. Pick on the wrong person, like another juice addict, while you were high—or worse, coming down from the high—and they'd kill you. A lot of people stole to feed their habit. That was dangerous enough on its own.

"Do you want to?"

Ean shook his head. Abram and Michelle would have researched Herman Lambert when they'd looked up Ean's records, back when they'd realized he was Lancastrian. They probably knew more about Ean's father than he did. A concerned hum from the lines made him realize he'd hunched over instinctively. He straightened, self-conscious.

"My family wasn't that bad," Michelle said.

"Strangers?"

She shrugged and rubbed her eyes. "The *Lancastrian Princess* is my home now."

Except it wasn't a home any longer. It was empty and lonely.

EAN asked Radko if it was acceptable to offer the Grand Master a glass of tea on a nonsocial visit.

"I'll organize some," Radko said. "Leave it to me."

Ean was glad to, for Rigel's lessons had been emphatic on treatment of the Grand Master. You always offered him a drink. And refreshments. He wasn't sure how he could have provided tea anyway. When it was for Michelle or Abram, he could call up the galley and someone would bring it up for them. When it was for himself he went down to the mess and got a glass from there.

Fergus joined Ean as he went down to meet Rickenback's shuttle.

"I hope it's okay, but I'd like to say hello to Leo."

"Why don't you join us?" Ean said. There was nothing he had to say that Fergus couldn't hear.

"Surely you would rather talk privately?"

"I'd be grateful if you came."

Fergus looked doubtful.

"I mean that," for Fergus was a good barrier between the old cartels who'd thought nothing of Ean, and the New Alliance. Although he probably shouldn't rely on him like that.

Fergus grinned. *"Since you put it that way."* Every line seven came in as a chorus as part of the answer. He winced. "I'll get the hang of it one day. I will."

They waited while Vega subjected Rickenback to the most exhaustive security check he'd probably ever known.

"I bet you don't get that at Gate Union," Fergus said, when Vega finally announced the Grand Master clean and fit to pass onto the ship. He came over to shake Rickenback's hand, but it was half a hug, really.

"It's almost as bad," Rickenback said, smiling as broadly as Fergus. "You can't move nowadays without being checked for weapons." He turned to Ean and shook hands. "Linesman Lambert."

"Grand Master."

"Leo, please."

Morton Paretsky had never told Ean to call him Morton. At least, not that first time they'd met. Or even the second.

"And I'm Ean." He glanced at Vega, who was glaring at them as if they were cluttering up the shuttle bay. She looked meaningfully in the direction of the lifts. "Let's find somewhere quiet to talk."

A quartet of guards followed. Bhaksir's people.

"I bet you don't get that either," Fergus said. He glanced around. "Where's Radko?"

Getting some tea, Ean hoped. "She's around." Radko didn't spend all her time on ship babysitting Ean.

They made small talk as they waited for the lift. After months of talking to admirals and politicians, Ean was getting better at it. Fergus, of course, was a master.

Rickenback looked around with interest. "Not many linesmen get onto the *Lancastrian Princess*. House of Sandhurst services their higher lines." He glanced at Ean, and amended, "Serviced."

Fergus laughed. "I'll bet Iwo Hurst is annoyed they don't do it still. It would have been a job to boast about."

Given the sanctions, and the fact that the cartels weren't servicing any New Alliance ships at present, House of Sandhurst couldn't have serviced the ship even if it had been asked to. Although Gate Union might have asked them to, even with the sanctions, for who better than a linesman to pass on information about an enemy ship.

Radko followed them into the meeting room with glasses, a pot of tea, and some pastries, then moved to stand against the wall, one boot flat against the wall in her characteristic working stance.

"Thank you," Ean said. He hesitated and looked at the empty seat at the table. Radko shook her head. A tiny shake but a definite no.

"So. Rigel," Rickenback said, while Ean poured tea. "What exactly is the problem?"

It was good that he was direct. It was better than skirting around the issue.

Ean knew too much about the alien fleet and line eleven for

the New Alliance to ever let him go back to Gate Union. Even if he wanted to, which he didn't. But he couldn't tell Rickenback that, for the Grand Master's job was to protect linesman. Supposedly, anyway.

He had asked Rickenback to come because he wanted the matter sorted; he wanted Rigel and Paretsky off his back. The cartel houses were constrained by the cartels, so if the Grand Master told them to back off, they'd have to. However, he needed Rickenback to trust him before Rickenback would tell them to back off, and if the Grand Master learned Ean had kept something back, that trust would evaporate. Therefore, he couldn't lie to him because Rigel would tell what had happened the night Michelle had visited the cartel house.

He thought about that now as he picked through what he was going to say. No surprises. Which meant the truth.

"Rigel and Paretsky claim my contract is illegal and that I will have to go back to House of Rigel. I don't want to do that."

"Why are they claiming your contract is illegal?"

Start at the beginning. Ean took a deep breath. "I need to talk about Vicki Singh first. I don't know if you knew her?"

Rickenback shook his head.

"She was a five. A strong five. She was at House of Rigel."

Rickenback nodded.

"Michelle bought a contract for a linesman level six. Rigel gave her Vicki."

"He does oversell occasionally," Rickenback said, and Ean was surprised that anyone outside Rigel's house knew he did.

"They got her to fix the Bose engine." Because Tai had been busy on something else, and because she was there. She wasn't a soldier. She'd only been on ship because they were using the time they transferred her to Lancia to explain the job in detail.

"The engine spiked. She had a heart attack." He still hadn't worked out how a line she supposedly couldn't hear had induced such a response in her. "A real heart attack I mean, not a—" Line-induced one, he'd been going to say, which wasn't a heart attack at all, it was the body trying to force itself into a different rhythm.

Rickenback blinked, but he didn't ask what a nonreal heart attack was. Fergus nodded.

A regular myocardial infarction. The medic had been insistent. Pain in the chest, nausea, vomiting, sweating, shortness of breath. Engineer Tai had been slowly fixing Vicki's damage to line six. It had still been slightly off true when Ean had joined the *Lancastrian Princess.*

Ean paused. "How much do you know about Lancastrians?"

"Only what I've seen on the vids, and that's probably half-wrong."

"They have a strong revenge culture. An eye for an eye, a tooth for a tooth. You kill one of my people, I kill one of yours."

Rickenback nodded although a faint frown appeared. "What's this to do—?"

"Because Vicki was part of Michelle's staff, Michelle had to avenge her." Ean rolled the glass around in his hands. This was difficult to explain. "A linesman for a linesman, and she knew what would hurt Rigel most."

He had their undivided attention. The combined gaze was more unnerving than being interrogated by a full parliament.

"So rather than try to kill someone, she took Rigel's ten," Rickenback said.

Ean winced. Paretsky would tell it, even if Rigel didn't, because you could get anything out of Rigel if you bullied or flattered enough, and Paretsky would have done either, or both. Or paid him.

"A linesman for a linesman. She tried to kill me."

Rickenback moved back.

Even Fergus looked horrified and faintly nauseated. "It was only for show. I mean, she didn't kill you."

Ean wanted to let them believe that lie, but it would come out. "She used a disruptor."

"I can't believe you're still alive."

"I *am* a ten." A ten was the only human who could turn back a disruptor because a disruptor was made with a full set of lines.

Fergus twitched at that. Radko put her foot down. Fergus put up his hands, Rossi-style. "Sorry," he said to Radko.

Radko changed legs and put the flat of her boot of the leg she had been standing on back against the wall.

"That's Radko, by the way," Fergus said to Rickenback, who looked as if he had no idea what was going on.

"Hello, Radko," and Ean knew that like Fergus, Leo Rickenback would never forget her name from now on.

Radko nodded but didn't speak. Rickenback took his cues from her and turned back to Ean. "So she tried to kill you."

A disruptor cost as much as a small shuttle because it was made with lines. Ten of them. Ean supposed, when he'd destroyed the disruptor, he'd effectively murdered the lines. How did lines feel about being part of a disruptor? Were they like the stations, lonely and crying out to be heard?

"But you were strong enough to turn the lines," Rickenback said.

Ean nodded. "So Michelle said she'd take my contract instead."

"She tried to kill you and *still* took your contract."

"Otherwise, she wouldn't have gotten her revenge, would she?"

"I don't understand how that was revenge," Rickenback said. Then, "No, actually. I do. Take away Rigel's only level-ten linesman, and you've taken away half his income. And you were the only ten working at that time." He looked momentarily haunted. "So she threatened Rigel and made him hand over your contract."

"She didn't threaten Rigel," Ean said. Rickenback had to understand this. "She said she'd buy my contract. And he signed the papers."

"I call firing on someone with a disruptor a major threat," Rickenback said.

"There was no threat to anyone except me. I had already destroyed the disruptor. She didn't have another weapon." Not that he and Rigel had seen.

"It was a mighty big assumption that you would destroy it. A dangerous one."

Ean didn't correct the misapprehension. He'd told the truth. If Rickenback chose to believe that Michelle expected Ean to survive, he wasn't going to say otherwise.

Rickenback sat back in his chair. He ran a hand through his hair, glanced at Radko, then at Fergus, and ran his hand through his hair again. He opened his mouth to speak, closed it with a snap.

"Michelle took me in. She looked after me. She gave me a job I love." She'd given him the lines, but while Ean was prepared to tell Rickenback about Michelle and Rigel, he wasn't going to tell him about the lines. He looked directly into Rickenback's eyes. "I'm right where I want to be, Grand Master. I'm staying here."

Rickenback stared back, as if trying to see into Ean's soul. It was a pity he didn't have lines. The lines would have told him Ean was telling the truth.

"For what it's worth," Fergus said quietly, "Ean does love working with the lines here."

"Thank you," Ean said.

"What about Lady Lyan?" Rickenback asked. "She tried to kill you once. What if she tries again?"

If she tried again, she would succeed. And she would kill him if he became a threat to Lancia.

Michelle had kicked off her shoes and was sitting with her feet curled up on the couch. She didn't relax often. Her head was against the back of the couch. She was smiling. The feeling coming through line one was affection.

"She'd do it to my face. And she'd have a good reason." Ean looked around the room for the camera. There had to be at least one. He couldn't see any, and he knew if he asked Radko where it was, Rickenback—and Fergus, too—would shy away like they had before. Instead, he sang under his breath softly to line five. There. And there. And there. He looked toward the nearest camera and smiled.

He got a spurt of cinnamon–red-mint amusement in return.

Rickenback glanced at him, then at Fergus. "Let's assume you want to stay contracted to Lady Lyan. Rigel seems to have a fair case."

"She didn't threaten Rigel."

"Maybe, but if it goes to court, it could be argued that she did."

"I've never heard of line business like this actually getting to courts," Fergus said.

"No." Rickenback agreed. "That's what the Grand Master is for."

You would want the Grand Master to be on the side of the linesman, then. Would Morton Paretsky have been on Ean's side? No. So a single linesman was powerless really. It was stupid to feel so disillusioned since he knew that Paretsky would have failed his certification if he'd been given the opportunity.

"We're at war," Ean said. "The New Alliance courts won't recognize Gate Union courts and vice versa. Neither Michelle nor I plan on attending a Gate Union court." It would be like walking into a trap. "No one, not even you, could guarantee our safety."

"Linesmen are supposed to be neutral."

"Look me in the eye and tell me you believe that."

Rickenback's mouth twisted down momentarily. "Point taken." He rubbed the bridge of his nose. "Rigel might agree to a payoff."

Rigel was going to ask a lot of money. "I'll talk to Michelle." It wasn't Rigel they had to worry about. It was Morton Paretsky. "You know that Paretsky is using this to get back in as grand master."

"I understand that." Rickenback almost smiled. "It might be a relief, actually." He said it as much to Fergus as he did to Ean. "But while I am in this position, I will do what I was elected to do. If you want to stay here, then I will facilitate that."

"Thank you."

Rickenback stood up. "I'll talk to Rigel, see what I can arrange."

TWENTY

EAN LAMBERT

MICHELLE JOINED THEM on the shuttle deck.

"Grand Master Rickenback," she said, and sounded almost surprised to run into him. She glanced at Ean. "Is it line business that brings you on board?"

Ean was sure he'd never have been able to say it with such a straight face.

"Lady Lyan." Rickenback shook hands. He, too, glanced at Ean. "Yes, it is. It's about one of your contracted linesmen actually. Are you aware Cartel Master Rigel claims the contract with Linesman Lambert is illegal?"

Ean expected her to smile, but the lines were serious, and so was she. "Lin, my assistant, mentioned that." She glanced at Ean again. "Understand that we're very happy with Lambert's work."

Ean bit his lip to stop his smile.

"I'll talk to Rigel," Rickenback said. "I may be able to arrange a financial settlement."

"I would be happy to pay it, of course," Michelle said.

Rickenback nodded, shook hands with Ean again. "I'll let you know what happens." He nodded at Fergus and exited into the shuttle.

They watched as the bay door closed and waited the full minute until the light went green, signaling that the shuttle had left.

"That was quite a tale you told," Vega said, from behind them. "Is there *anything* you omitted to tell?"

Ean turned. Vega was so angry his line-addled brain imagined sparks coming off her. "Did you want me to lie? Imagine how Rickenback would have felt about that."

"I'm imagining how he felt about what you did say."

Ean glanced at Fergus.

"If he's anything like me, shocked, but coming around," Fergus said.

Vega pounced. "Coming around?"

Fergus shrugged. "You had to admit, Rigel had it coming to him. He was known for ripping off people who didn't know better."

That was so unfair. "Why does everyone think Michelle wouldn't know better?" She was the smartest woman Ean knew.

"Lancastrians don't know anything about lines?"

Ean had to listen hard to hear if he was serious. Fergus certainly looked serious.

"I'm Lancastrian." Not that he would have admitted to that six months ago.

"The line cartels think anyone not directly connected with the lines has no idea what they're doing. Lancia doesn't turn out many linesmen."

"There were other linesmen on Lancia." Tai and the other line engineers on the *Lancastrian Princess*. The Cann siblings, when Ean had been a boy, and a handful of others whose names Ean couldn't remember. But he'd heard the music in them.

"They never made it into the top cartels. And your reputation—" It was the first time Fergus had ever mentioned the reputation Ean had among the other linesmen. Fergus looked sorry he'd mentioned it.

"Why does every conversation on this ship come back to Lambert eventually?" Vega demanded.

"It's an interesting topic," Michelle said.

Vega's look toward Michelle was almost as withering as the one she'd given Ean earlier. She indicated that Ean should walk with her. He did.

"Whether Rigel's reputation is known or not, it doesn't excuse your telling Rickenback the story of what happened to you."

Michelle said something quiet to Fergus. He nodded, and turned to go. Michelle followed Ean and Vega.

"He'll hear it from Paretsky. How would he feel if I told him it was a simple transaction, then he hears Michelle threatened Rigel?" Ean thought about what he'd said. "Threatened me, I mean. With a disruptor."

"So you admit Her Royal Highness threatened Rigel." Vega paused at the door to her office and ushered Ean in.

"No. She threatened me." He thought about that. "She didn't threaten me. She just tried to kill me."

"And you don't call that threatening?"

"It was a threat." Michelle followed them into the room. "Rigel knew that. I knew that."

"Why?"

"Because someone died." If Vega didn't understand that by now, she never would. "What else could she do?"

"Maybe not get caught doing it."

It seemed to Ean that Vega was so exasperated, she actually forgot, for the first time, that Michelle was her boss. He liked her better for it. "She didn't do anything wrong."

Vega bit down hard on whatever comment she'd been going to make. Ean could see from the way the muscles in her neck bunched just how tightly she was biting. When she could speak, her question was aimed at Michelle. "What in the lines were you doing on Ashery attempting to kill a Lancastrian citizen?"

"I can't ask my staff to do something like that."

Vega opened her mouth to say something, closed her mouth, tried again. "You were alone. What was Galenos doing letting you go alone? The only witness we have is a linesman from the House of Rigel."

"I can't ask my staff to witness something like that, either."

"What are you smiling at?" Vega demanded.

Ean hadn't even realized he was smiling.

"This is not a laughing matter. It should never have gotten this far."

"Rigel will take the money if he can," Ean said. All this other business about the lines and the cartels was foreign to Rigel. "Except Paretsky is pushing him." He hoped Fergus's trust in Rickenback wasn't misplaced. Jordan Rossi had said Rickenback would be devoured by line politics. "He'll ask a lot, though."

"The money's not a problem, Ean," Michelle said. "You're worth every credit we haven't paid yet."

"We could hand him over," Vega said.

Vega wanted him gone. This would be a simple way to get rid of him, and she was in charge of security. If Abram had said he was to go, Michelle wouldn't have questioned it.

Ean hoped Rickenback would sort it out fast and send Rigel and Paretsky home.

"No," Michelle said. "We are not letting Ean anywhere near Rigel again. After two failed murder attempts and one snatch, Gate Union has to be wondering why we're protecting him so carefully."

"*I'm* wondering why you're protecting him so carefully." Vega held up a hand as Michelle started to speak. "I know what you told me. Line twelve, plus a different way of communicating with the lines. So far, all line twelve has done is link ships—and we could have done without that."

Michelle opened her mouth to speak again.

Another hand to keep her silent. "We know about the singing. We have Linesman Rossi half-trained. We have linesmen from other worlds in the New Alliance half-trained. If Lambert died tomorrow we wouldn't be any worse off."

"It's not—"

"Are we protecting him simply because you like him?"

"Michelle would never put me before her duty."

There was a spot of color high on each of Michelle's cheeks. "Isn't it enough that he is the only twelve the galaxy has? Isn't it enough that only he can control the alien ships?"

"We trained people in alien line technology five hundred years ago when we discovered the *Havortian*. We can do it again." Vega thumped her desk. Ean couldn't stop his flinch. "My job is to protect you. So far, what I see is half my staff diverted to protect a man who would normally affiliate himself with Gate Union. He accused you outright just now of threatening someone. He is not important enough to risk your reputation. I say hand him back to Rigel and close this whole thing down before it becomes public."

Michelle had never lost a fight that Ean had known. He forced away a sudden worry this would be the first.

"I won't send him back to the cartels," Michelle said. "There's more to this than you know."

"Send him to Admiral Galenos on Haladea III then."

"He needs to be on a ship."

"So, send him to Confluence Station."

"You're prepared to send half this ship to protect him?"

"Of course not. Galenos can provide protection."

"No. He's my staff. *I* protect him. He stays here."

Vega stared at Ean. Her eyes were like lasers. "Give me a reason to expend so many resources to protect a linesman. A better reason than being a line twelve."

"There's nothing she—"

"No, Ean," Michelle said, then to Vega, "A better reason?"

Vega nodded. They seemed to have come to another understanding Ean wasn't part of.

"There is no better reason than his being a twelve," Michelle said. "But I will show you what he can do that no other linesman can, and why I am dispensable while he is not."

"You are what's keeping the New Alliance together right now," Ean said.

"I am one of many, Ean, and all of us know that if we can't beat Gate Union at their line games, we have no hope. You are our only hope."

He'd never heard Michelle speak so bleakly about their prospects.

"I haven't seen any signs of his saving the world so far," Vega said.

Ean was grateful for her cynicism. Did Michelle truly believe they had no hope?

"He is the only linesman who can get the ships to do things."

"We have other tens coming through. Jordan Rossi. Ami Hernandez."

Ean hadn't told Vega about Hernandez. How much snooping did she do?

"Rossi can't—and never will—talk to line eleven. Nor will Hernandez. You won't even be able to take them away from the fleet ships. You've seen what happened to the linesmen at the confluence."

"A minor problem in the scheme of things. We have two eleven ships. We can make more."

Ean lost track of the conversation momentarily. How did

you make lines if they weren't cloned? Lines must have a way of reproducing somehow. Something else to put on his long list of things to find out about lines. Maybe that was line seven's role.

"Linking, keeping together." It was a whisper in his mind. Not reproducing lines.

He came back to the conversation in front of him at Michelle's raised voice. "You don't understand what line twelve does, and you want to throw that away. Because he doesn't fit your idea of a tidy life. Because the only thing *you* understand is weapons."

"Michelle."

Michelle ignored him. "If weapons are all you understand, then let me spell it out for you in terms you *do* understand. Here is the greatest weapon the New Alliance has at their disposal, and you want to give it away."

"I wasn't planning on giving it away. Just moving it."

"People try to kill him when he's away from here. Or kidnap him."

Vega glared at Ean as if he were something that had crawled onto the ship uninvited. "I don't see evidence of a world-destroying weapon."

Michelle paused. "You don't?" She smiled, and Ean smelled ozone through the lines. It came out in the frozenness of her expression, too. "Let's remedy that." She was calm suddenly. "Show us something line-based Ean. Something only you can do. Show her what a weapon you can be."

Ean wasn't a weapon. He was a person, and Vega was right. He wasn't going to save the world. "It's Vega's job to protect you, Michelle."

"There are more important things now. Our future, as an Alliance and as a world. Go on. Something only you can do."

What could he do? Open line five so they could hear other parts of the ship through the comms? Vega would say they had equipment to do that. Unlock doors? They had equipment to do that, too.

He could always override an air lock. But what would that prove? Jordan Rossi could do that if he tried.

Maybe he could use line eight to throw her across the room like he had that day to Gospetto. Gospetto had spent a week in the hospital and was still a little scared of him. Unfortunately, Ean didn't know what he'd done back then, except panic. Line eight had done the rest.

On the bridge, Captain Helmo was sniffing the air, almost as if he could smell the argument. Or maybe he could hear it.

"Helmo will kill me," Ean said. He would. Literally.

Michelle flicked the screen on her comms. Helmo answered the instant the call came through. "Captain," Michelle said. "We're going to do a line experiment."

If she was in any way nervous, she didn't show it. Ean was. Nervous and showing it. He shook his head.

"What, exactly?" Helmo's voice dropped twenty degrees. The ozone smell was back. Ean shivered.

Michelle looked at Ean.

"Um," which wasn't the brightest answer.

"Something that's going to scare the lines out of Commodore Vega," Michelle said. "Help her realize how dangerous Ean is."

The ozone should have gotten stronger. Instead, it faded as Helmo stared down at his comms. "Do you think that's wise?" he asked eventually. "You don't really want to scare her."

Ean thought there might have been a slight emphasis on the "really." Helmo hadn't asked the obvious question, either, which was what sort of scaring did they want to do?

"I don't scare easily, Captain." Vega's voice was frosty.

"I do. You may regret this, Commodore." Helmo paused. Ean could see him at the captain's station. Thinking. The sound of the lines had a worried blue edge to it. "I do not recommend this, ma'am." But there was also approval, and a bit of relief.

"We need to do it," Michelle said. "We can't keep tiptoeing around reality. Vega is right. She needs to know."

More worried blue thinking. Helmo said eventually, "Maybe we could arrange something." He hesitated, then added. "Of course, there's no point if Vega can't see who is controlling things. Your Royal Highness, Commodore, Linesman. Why don't you join me on the bridge."

"Our pleasure." Michelle made for the door.

Vega followed, her back straight.

"Ean," Helmo said, as Ean followed them. He'd clicked off his comms, and was just talking out loud, the way he had the day Vega had arrived. "Don't do anything until I say you can start, but when I do, I want you to take the lines down. In the following order, if you can. Line two first, then line four. Then line five. Then line three, and lastly line six. Do you hear me? Do you understand me?"

"Yes," Ean said aloud, but, of course, Helmo didn't hear him. "Do you?"

Ean sang the feed of the camera just near them in the corridor onto Helmo's comms. "Yes."

Vega looked around at him.

Helmo clicked off his comms again—or tried to. Ean had to sing it off. "Good. Now remember, I want my crew prepared. I'll say when you can do it."

Ean nodded even though Helmo couldn't see him anymore.

Vanje Solberg, Helmo's second, was on the bridge, too. He'd heard the instructions.

"I think this is unwise."

So did Ean.

"It's a considered risk, Vanje," Helmo said. The lines were full of Michelle and Vega when he said it. "It might clear some tension."

It wasn't clearing any tension at the moment. As they got closer to the bridge, the lines seemed to stretch tight. Was Helmo regretting his decision?

His face was expressionless as he greeted them at the entry to the bridge, but the lines grew tighter still.

"Commodore Vega, requesting permission for Her Royal Highness, the Crown Princess Michelle, to enter the bridge," Vega said.

She didn't ask for Ean or herself.

"Permission granted," Helmo said, and all three of them stepped onto the bridge.

"With your permission," Helmo said. "I need to warn people of what is to happen." He tapped the board at the captain's chair. An alarm sounded through the ship. "Attention all crew. This is a line-twelve drill. Full suits."

Full suits meant space suits. The alarm that accompanied it was for full suits as well. Michelle and Vega made for the nearest suit station.

All over the ship, crew were reporting to team leaders once they were suited, and team leaders were reporting to group leaders.

Three crew members checked Michelle's, Ean's, and Vega's suits. Vega pulled away, looking affronted, then let the crew member check the suit anyway.

The crew member gave a thumbs-up. "Secured, sir," she said to Helmo.

Helmo was suited as well now.

"Group leaders report," Helmo said.

As the group leaders reported to Helmo, lines went green on the screen in front of him. "Commencing drill," Helmo said, when all the lines were green. "It's all yours, Ean. And don't damage my ship."

His voice was steady, but Ean could see that his hands gripped the arms of his seat.

Ean checked the ship from end to end. Everyone was accounted for. Everyone was suited.

Take down the lines, Helmo had told him. What would that show Vega? That he could take life support off-line, he supposed.

He cleared his throat nervously. He sang to the lines, all of them, to explain what he was doing. An exercise, to show what could be done. The lines were as nervous as Helmo, but somewhere in the middle of Ean's song Helmo said, "Permission granted for this exercise," and the lines calmed.

It was Helmo's worry they were projecting.

"Close down life support," he sang to line two. *"Quiet, quiet. You stay strong, just hold life support back."* He wasn't sure how else to explain it to them.

The other lines resisted. He included them all in his song. *"This is to show Vega—"* What? That he could dampen the lines?

It took lines one, two, and eight working together to do it.

They plunged into darkness, the only lighting the emergency panels on the floor. The flow of air—which Ean hadn't even noticed until it stopped—ceased. Line two stopped, mid-chatter, and Ean's head was filled with the hum of it.

Even with a suit on, it was quiet without life support.

"Problem?" line eleven asked.

"No, no problem. Ship is doing an exercise."

He hoped he didn't muck up on the line order Helmo had given him. He glanced at Vega and Michelle. His own voice was unsteady as he sang line four down. He had to sing line eight and one into the chorus as well before he could make it happen.

Helmo clipped on a belt. Michelle grabbed a handhold. Vega's boots clicked—as did the crew at the boards—as they fastened themselves to the floor. Some form of magnetism in the boots, he supposed.

Ean rose slightly. He'd have to ask Radko how to use the boots.

"Line five," he said to Vega, and he and lines one and eight sang line five down. The big screen Helmo used to communicate with other ships—the only thing that was still lit at present—went black.

Vega glanced his way sharply, then glanced down at her comms, which was also black.

Wendell called them up. *"Lancastrian Princess, we have lost communication. Please answer."*

Naturally, the *Lancastrian Princess* didn't hear the message. Maybe Ean or Helmo should have explained it to every ship in the *Eleven*'s fleet

"No problem," Ean sang, but Wendell persisted.

"Lancastrian Princess, please answer."

Ean sang the line up. "I don't think he's going to stop," he said to Helmo. Wendell was unpredictable, and when he did things, he was fast. If Wendell thought something was wrong, the crew of the *Wendell* would be setting out to board the *Lancastrian Princess*. In fact, right now Wendell was choosing a team.

"Let me talk to him," Helmo said.

Ean sang a line open.

"Everything's fine here, Piers," Helmo said. "We're doing a line-twelve exercise. Seeing how far we can go."

Wendell looked past Helmo. What could he see? Everything dimmed by emergency lights. He chewed his bottom lip. "You don't know where line twelve will stop." The *Wendell* lines flooded with anxiety. "How long will this exercise last?"

"Another two, three minutes."

It felt like an hour already.

Wendell clicked off.

Ean sang line five down again. "Line three." It was getting harder. He sang the full ten lines in to pull it down.

He didn't see much change—everything was in emergency mode already—but Vega did, for she clicked her boots off and pushed herself over to the door. She studied the door, then looked back at Ean.

Ean took a deep breath. "Line six," he said, and started to sing line six down. The whole ten lines again, concentrating on using them to lower line six.

As the line quietened, line one grew agitated. It came in waves. From Helmo, from everyone on the bridge. Even Vega. Rolling off them, even though they all stood quietly, watching him.

He stopped. "I'm not going to do this."

A wave of giddy relief—from everyone—deafened him. Followed by determination from the ship lines—from *Ship*.

"You have to, Ean," Helmo said. "Otherwise, this whole exercise is pointless. You have to show you have total control."

"He's made his point, Captain," Vega said. "And if it's all right with you, I'd rather not leave us helpless in space while we waste ten hours and a payload of fuel turning the Bose engines back on. Just so he proves he can turn them off."

Ean didn't wait for Helmo's approval. *"Back on,"* he sang to the lines. *"Back at full strength. All of you."*

Returning power was deafening; returning light was blinding. Returning gravity crashed him to the floor. He wasn't expecting it. Naturally, he fell. He picked himself up, wincing at the pain in his knees. *"Thank you,"* he sang to the lines as he stood. *"Thank you."*

At the boards, crew did status checks. It was the same all over the ship.

Helmo finally gave the all clear.

Ean climbed out of his suit. He was drenched with sweat, shaking like he'd run a marathon. Only then did he look across at Vega. Her face was bloodless.

"And any high-level linesman can do this once they're taught?"

"No," Captain Helmo said. "Other linesmen can work with

single lines at a time. Rossi, for example, would be able to break line six. But to take the whole ship off-line like that, the lines have to work together. It seems to be a function of line twelve."

"You see, Commodore," Michelle said. "It's not about the alien ships because we can't separate them, and as soon as Gate Union realizes that, they'll attack us."

Vega moistened her lips and tried to speak. Couldn't. Ean wished she would sit down. She looked as if she would faint.

"It's about what we can learn from Ean to protect us. Or to attack, if required. We can't hand that to Gate Union."

Vega finally sat down. "I concede he's a powerful weapon, but he's a menace to any ship you put him on. He's a monster. We need him off here right now."

Ship line one surged, and the other lines with it. Ean hurriedly put a hand on Michelle's arm. Her muscles were bunched. It took all his strength to hold her. "It's all right," and he sang to calm line one as much as he did to calm Michelle.

"What's he doing now?"

There was a frozen standoff, then Helmo laughed. "So that didn't prove what we wanted it to."

"No," said Ean, for neither Vega nor Michelle looked ready to answer.

Helmo rubbed his chin and looked at the two women, then at the time display comfortingly back at the bottom of the screen. Three minutes. That's all it had been. "Dinner is in half an hour," he said. "Join me at my table." He looked at Ean. "All of you."

AFTERWARD, Ean went to the fresher, but he couldn't clean Vega's "monster" accusation from his memory.

He eavesdropped unashamedly on the lines.

Vega called Helmo and said she couldn't make dinner. Helmo fixed her with a stare Abram would have been proud of, and said, "Captain's orders."

"I outrank you."

"On my ship, I outrank everyone unless it's to do with the welfare of Crown Princess Michelle. I will see you at dinner, Commodore."

Afterward, he listened in on Helmo, in Michelle and Abram's workroom—where Ean would normally have gone but he didn't feel it was appropriate right now. Helmo sat on Ean's couch. No one sat on Abram's couch.

Michelle was fresh from a shower, too. Ean could see it in the way the hair curled damply around her face.

"Vega is right when she says you are personally involved. She thinks that is coloring your judgment."

Ean had never heard Helmo speak so bluntly to Michelle.

"Do you think it is?" Michelle asked.

"Not in how important Lambert is. Just in the way you deal with it. He scares people. He scares me sometimes, and after today's demonstration, he scares me more than he used to."

Helmo had suggested Ean use life support. Had he simply not realized the effect it would have.

"He doesn't scare me," Michelle said.

"He should."

"But—"

Helmo spoke over the top of her. "Recognize that other people feel differently. You have succeeded today in showing Vega why she should protect Lambert. Or destroy him. Now that you have shown her he's a ticking bomb, tonight you have to convince her that he's *your* bomb, and you control what sets him off." Helmo stood up. "If you'll excuse me, I've a dinner party to prepare for."

Ean waited until Helmo had gone before he entered the workroom.

Michelle looked up and smiled wryly. Her dimple showed. "*My* bomb," she said.

"I didn't mean to eavesdrop."

"Lines are lines, Ean. That's what they do."

Some lines should learn human manners. It wasn't polite to eavesdrop.

"Besides, I'd only have to explain it to you if you hadn't." Michelle crossed her arms across her chest, almost defensively. "Eventually all level-five linesmen will be able to listen in, I suppose."

Listening in to the ship was more an overall thing, much like what he'd had to do earlier to take down the lines. "Line five can only listen on comms." He thought about what he could do with a comms. "I think a level-five linesman can move comms from one channel to another. Divert it, multiply it, or even make their own connections. But they still need something to get the messages, something for it to come out on."

"That's a relief," Michelle said. "One of you is enough for the moment." She grimaced. "I'm sorry I put you through that. Especially since it didn't have the desired result."

"It's fine. I've a thick skin." After learning what the other high-level linesmen thought about him, Ean should be inured to people thinking he was a freak. Vega wasn't much different. He leaned over and gave Michelle an awkward hug. "A bomb is better than a monster, though."

Michelle's dimple showed, full and deep. "Thank you." She sighed and stood up. "And I'd better get dressed for dinner."

BOTH Captain Helmo and Commodore Vega wore formal uniform, while Michelle dressed in a long midnight blue sheath dress that showed off a lot of leg. She wore a choker of Girraween opals and a bracelet of the same that went halfway up her arm. Ean was glad she wasn't around the Lancian slums. She wouldn't last two minutes wearing jewelry like that.

Or maybe she would, if she had a team of *Lancastrian Princess* guards with her.

Dinner was in a small room off Helmo's office. He had two spacers waiting on the table.

Helmo served black liqueur in thumb-sized glasses. "This is from one of the rim worlds. Onanganang. They call it black fire."

Ean thought of Mael, one of the single-level linesmen being recruited for the *Eleven*, smacking his lips over black fire.

"It's potent, so beware." Helmo downed his drink in one swallow. He smiled, and his tongue and the edges of his teeth were black. "Don't worry. It's not a permanent stain. It's actually good for your teeth."

Vega and Michelle threw their drinks back the same way.

Ean looked at his own drink doubtfully. How long did a nonpermanent stain stay around? He hoped Helmo didn't plan this as part of some bizarre bonding ritual, where the four of them spent the next month going around with black teeth to show that they were all friends.

Still, if the others had done it, so could he. He downed it the same way they had.

Fire was a good way to describe it. It burned all the way down and settled in his stomach in a ball of hot flame that spread out and warmed him through, and kept burning for a minute afterward.

"That's quite a drink," Vega said eventually.

Helmo grinned, and Ean could have sworn his teeth were blacker than they had been. "It's traditional to serve a dish called keep-the-fire-burning afterward, only we don't have the ingredients on ship, so we're serving the poor man's version—battebrot."

Battebrot turned out to be a thick bread with green, purple, and red chunks through it. The purple chunks were tart, maybe a berry. The red junks were rubbery and chewy and tasted like dried flam fruit. The green chunks melted in your mouth. The trick, Ean found, was to chew them all together and the taste changed again as the ingredients reacted with the saliva in his mouth. In his stomach, the heat from the black fire flared up momentarily after he swallowed.

"I thought I knew more weird food than the rest of you combined," Michelle said. "But this is the weirdest I've come across in a while."

"Battebrot is quite tame," Helmo said. "Compared to some of the food from Wossworld, for example."

"Wossen spores," Vega said, with the heartfelt hatred of someone who knew them well.

Ean wanted to ask when she'd come across them but figured it was better if Vega forgot he was at the table.

"They get into the air-conditioning and reproduce, and before you know it, the spores have coated everyone's lungs, and they can't take oxygen in. Worse, take some into your lungs, then next time you climb into a suit, you've contaminated the suit."

"So how do you get rid of them?" Then Ean remembered he was trying to be seen and not heard.

Vega looked at him. The drink might have relaxed her, or

otherwise she was trying as hard as Michelle was to be civil. "Water. Plain and simple. Flush the air-conditioning system out with water. Better yet, replace it altogether—after you've flushed it. Destroy the suits. And hope to the lines you got to the personnel in time to flush out their lungs, because otherwise you have to replace them. If you realize what the problem is before they suffocate to death."

Vega had definitely seen Wossen spores firsthand. Ean shuddered.

"Exactly." Vega bit off a piece of battebrot and chewed it. "If I had to kill a whole ship," she said reflectively, "that's a good way to do it. Particularly if the ship can't get a jump."

Everyone shuddered this time, Vega included.

"Although," and Vega took a breath, as if debating whether to say the next, "if I had access to a line twelve, I might rethink it."

Ean hoped she didn't plan on using him like that. He wouldn't do it. He was glad Helmo laughed.

"Despite what we were trying to prove earlier, Ean doesn't destroy ships as a rule. He's far more likely to use the *Eleven* to link your enemy ship to the *Eleven*'s fleet instead. *That's* what you have to watch. He's a true line in that respect," and he patted the wall beside him. The emotion that came out through line one was tangy affection. "They don't necessarily take sides."

It wasn't that bad. A ship knew its ship people's enemies. But only through its humans' emotions, Ean supposed.

"Speaking of killing people," Michelle said. "That's an impressive collection of ancient weapons you have on your wall. I'm told that's only a quarter of it."

"More like a tenth," and Vega launched into a description of the weapons room at her home on Lancia.

Judging from the impressed hum of line one, it was an impressive collection. One whole wall was for weapons with artificial intelligence. "I've even got an early Brimstone missile from Earth," Vega said. "It's primitive, but fascinating to see how far we have come." She looked sideways at Ean, and said, "I don't have any functioning, reasoning weapons, though."

Jordan Rossi would have said, "Functioning, yes. Some of

the time anyway. Reasoning. That's questionable." Ean was glad Rossi wasn't there.

"It would be interesting to test his limits."

The trouble with functioning, reasoning people was they didn't like to be used, not when they had plans of their own that didn't include being a living weapon.

"This one's for my wall," Michelle said.

Ean wiped his palms down his sides and knew that some of his relief seeped through line one. Helmo would have registered the reaction even if Michelle didn't.

Vega nodded, and changed the subject to talk about the exercise regime on the *Lancastrian Princess*.

They finished up at 02:00, on a lot friendlier terms than they had started, and Vega even said good night to Ean as well as to Michelle and Helmo.

He walked with Michelle back to their rooms on the fifth floor.

"That ended better than I expected," Michelle said. "I made a mistake earlier, thinking that showing her how you could be a weapon would get her on our side."

"It could have been worse. She could have found out by accident."

Only time would tell if it had made things worse for Ean, but for the moment they seemed to have a temporary truce. And Vega couldn't—now—say she didn't know Ean was dangerous. Even better, something had changed between Vega and Michelle. The beginnings of acceptance? Which was probably what Helmo had been aiming for.

"Captain Helmo's quite sneaky, I think."

Michelle laughed as she moved off toward her own rooms. "You only think."

TWENTY-ONE

SELMA KARI WANG

THERE WAS NO sign of her usual clinging escort when Kari Wang left the admiral's office. She reveled in the chance to be alone and relaxed for the first time since they'd installed her legs. Or had they grown them? She wasn't sure.

There was no sign of any transport, either.

Kari Wang looked out across the building site that made up most of the current headquarters. There were temporary paths among the mayhem, and people on them. Fleet tarmac that would become parade grounds once the offices were built.

She thought about calling a car, looked at the people walking, and decided to walk herself.

After fifteen minutes, she regretted her decision. She—who could have navigated her way out of an unknown sector of space with a star chart and some starting coordinates—was hopelessly lost. Worse, the temporary paths were gravel, making every step she took an effort. Her legs ached, and she was losing her sense of balance.

She paused, holding on to one of the temporary fences that separated the works area from the path she was on, and considered asking a passerby for help.

Maybe there was a public cart close by. She pulled out her comms, and pulled up carts, public.

Someone shouted. She looked up as two figures crashed into her and pushed her down. Her comms went flying. The fence she was leaning against fell flat. An aircar swooshed over the fallen fence, so low it pushed the fallen fence aside, nearly tipping itself over as it went. The heavy concrete support of the temporary fence base slammed into her side.

"Sheesh, lady," said one of the people who'd knocked her down. "Don't you pay attention?"

The aircar righted itself and hopped across the construction grounds, eventually plowing into an earthmover in its way. It settled with a crash and screech of folding metal.

"Stay there." Her rescuers sprinted across to the crash site.

Kari Wang pulled herself up. She picked up her comms, which was crushed. She wouldn't be able to call for help on that. Her legs were shaky.

Her two rescuers came back, the older one—the man who'd chastised her for not paying attention—shaking his head. "Nobody in it. It's on auto. I got the registration, but I doubt it will help."

He called it in.

"Are you okay?" his companion asked Kari Wang. She was a young girl, hardly old enough to wear the generic coverall favored by off-duty soldiers. Hardly large enough either. She would fit easily under the bulkheads on the *Eleven*.

"I'm fine," Kari Wang said, although the adrenaline of the near miss had left her shaking.

"She's not okay," the older man said. "Shock," he told the girl. "They're full of bravado, and say they're all right, then all of a sudden, splat. You're picking them up off the ground."

"I'm Mael," he told Kari Wang. "Mael St. Mael. And this here's Darejani Tinatin."

"Thank you for saving my life." For they had saved her life. How would Admiral MacClennan and Ahmed Gann have explained that away? "That captain we acquired for you. She died in an accident."

She had to choke down a bubble of insane laughter.

"Told you," Mael said to Tinatin. "They *say* they're okay, but they're not." He patted Kari Wang's arm. "Don't worry, Captain. Your breakdown is safe with us."

Maybe. He looked the sort who'd confide anything to anyone.

"Thank you," Kari Wang said. She took a deep breath. "I wouldn't mind some help. I need to get back to barracks, and I'm lost."

"You can't even say it's a maze, can you? It's just a mess. Come this way."

As they walked off together, Mael muttered softly to Tinatin, "See the way she's shaking. Her legs can hardly hold her up. That's a bad sign."

"'She' is not deaf," Kari Wang said.

Mael grinned unrepentantly. "Teaching the youngster some basic first aid. They don't teach anything at academy nowadays."

They both reached out to steady her as she wavered off track.

"Although I must admit," Mael said. "Three days spent learning how to administer oxygen to heart-attack victims is overkill. We did get basic training."

Kari Wang stopped. After what she'd learned earlier, who would receive training like that except the crew of the *Eleven*? She'd been rescued by two of her own crew.

"They even took us out into space and made us learn what to do if you had a heart attack in a space suit," Tinatin said. "Like it was the most important thing we'd ever have to learn."

"You never know when you're going to use something like that," Kari Wang said, studying them. What was it Commodore Favager had said? Some crazy old coot from the rim, so old he looks like a good wind would blow him over. As for Tinatin, she didn't look old enough to have left home. "Let me guess," she said to Mael. "You're Aratogan. You're just in from the rim."

"That's hardly news," Mael said. "I've already heard about two heads and how things have changed around here. Like hey, alien ships. We do get the vids out there, you know. Even if they take time to get there." He looked at her reprovingly. "And if you don't mind my saying so, a captain should be above that sort of thing."

Kari Wang started to laugh. She didn't mean to. "I need a seat."

Mael looked at her. "I know your legs aren't too good at the moment, but if you don't move, we'll be late back on duty. Which is not good because they send out search parties."

"We can't even be five minutes late without a 'please explain,'" Tinatin said. "It's like being in prison."

If her comms wasn't broken, she could get Grieve to fix that for them. Assuming that Grieve had jurisdiction over other worlds' crew.

"Can I borrow a comms?" She held out her hand for one as they half carried, half dragged her along.

"We'll be late," Tinatin said.

"Slow down, and that's an order." She put some force into it. "And someone loan me a comms.

They slowed reluctantly.

"Meeting a strange captain's no excuse for being late," Mael muttered.

"I'm not so strange," she said, plucking the comms he pulled out of his pocket out of his fingers. "You'll be sick of me soon enough."

She had no idea who to call. She gave it back to him. "Call your commanding officer."

He took it almost sulkily. "Yes, ma'am," and made a face at Tinatin that no doubt she was meant to see. No doubt he also expected to be disciplined for it, based on the way he paused before he connected.

"Just do it, please," Kari Wang said. She was exhausted and all she wanted to do was sit down.

She took the comms back. He'd called a team leader. "Team leader. This is Captain Kari Wang here."

Behind her she heard an awed whisper from Tinatin. "Kari Wang."

"I have broken my comms, so I have borrowed Mael's." Which should stop the initial questions about what a captain was doing using a spacer's comms. She hoped. "I have also borrowed two of your team. Mael and Tinatin. They will be late back on duty."

The team leader opened her mouth to speak. Kari Wang spoke over the top of her. "Patch me through to Admiral Mac-Clennan's office, please. I need to report why I am delayed."

No one stood in the way of another soldier's apologizing to an admiral's office for tardiness. The team leader pushed her through.

Favager answered the call. "Captain, we've half the base out looking for you. You're not answering your comms."

"My comms is broken."

Favager raised an eyebrow.

"It got in the way of an out-of-control aircar."

The eyebrow raised higher.

"Is Grieve there?" One didn't bother commodores with tasks like smoothing over irate team leaders.

"He's out looking for you."

Kari Wang nodded. "Get him to call me on this comms, please."

"Shall do. Are you all right?"

"I'm fine."

Favager clicked off.

Not long after that, an aircar came speeding straight toward them. Grieve, no doubt, although he was supposed to call. At least, she hoped it was Grieve, because otherwise another out-of-control aircar was headed for them.

"You're captain of the *Eleven*." Tinatin's voice still held some awe. "What's it like?"

Kari Wang thought of the endless corridors, and the lights on the unreadable boards. "Interesting," she said, as she handed Mael back his comms. "Thank you," and smiled at Tinatin. "It will suit you. You're tiny. You and me"—for Mael was as tall as she was—"we'll learn to duck quite fast. I hope they're teaching you how to deal with concussion as well as heart attacks."

She saw Mael's eyes narrow, and his expression became thoughtful.

Maybe they should give everyone a hard band to wear across their foreheads. There would be a lot of bumped heads initially.

They stepped aside as Grieve pulled up. "We've been calling you." Jon and Fitch were with him.

"My comms is broken." She smiled placatingly at them all. "These two helped out. Any chance of a lift back to base for us. I've delayed these two spacers, and if we can deliver them, it might save them some trouble."

Grieve looked at her companions and did a double take. "I know," Kari Wang said, before he could say anything.

Mael watched them.

"Sure," Grieve said.

They squeezed into the car, and the airspace around them miraculously cleared.

"She wasn't shaking because she was scared," Tinatin said in a whisper to Mael. "She's got no legs."

"How can they shake then?"

"What's this about shaking legs?" Fitch asked.

"Overexertion," Kari Wang said. "I couldn't walk straight. You'd understand that, Fitch."

"There's such a thing as overdoing it."

Today, she honestly felt as if she had.

Grieve dropped Tinatin and Mael off right outside their barracks door.

"We might not even be late," Tinatin said optimistically, as they scrambled out.

Grieve lifted off again almost before the car door had closed behind them.

"You will make sure they don't get into trouble?" Kari Wang said to Grieve.

He nodded.

"And in the training. I want everyone to recognize concussion, and to know what to do when someone is concussed." She watched the two spacers run for the door. "Is the girl Aratogan, too?" It was an unlikely pairing, old man and young woman.

"She's native Haladean," Grieve said. "She's their one."

On reflection, Kari Wang couldn't say she was at all surprised.

KARI Wang woke the next morning stiff. She'd never have admitted it to Fitch or Jon or Grieve, but yesterday's tumble had left her sore.

She winced as she stood up, didn't notice Fitch was in the room until he said, "So, maybe you'll take it easier today."

It would be nice to be unobserved for a change. Kari Wang sighed. "What's on the agenda for today? I hope it includes breakfast."

Fitch smiled. "Hunger is a good sign."

"Sometimes it would be nice to have a little less cheer."

"So you want me to be dour?"

"Glower at me over breakfast, why don't you." Provided she got breakfast. "So that I wonder what I've done wrong."

"You'll wonder, all right. Today you're getting a physical. And a psych test. Then the admirals want to talk about your reactions to the ship. This time Lambert *will* be there."

Lambert hadn't arrived yesterday at all. He'd been caught

up in other things. It was interesting that they'd waited until Lambert arrived to get her opinion rather than asking for first opinions while they were fresh. To be honest, she didn't have opinions yet. Yesterday had been exhausting.

She thought about the ship while she ate breakfast. No way did she intend to rely on her staff to monitor her ship for her. She'd have to do it herself. Otherwise, they'd be smarter to get a linesman to captain it.

Except it would need a ten, and based on the ribbing of Katida yesterday, that was a bad option. What was Katida, exactly, to get that ribbing in the first place?

"You're quiet," Fitch said.

"I'm always quiet." She'd never been a noisy captain.

"Quieter than normal, I mean."

She tapped her head. "Hear that whirr. It's my brain. I'm thinking."

He smiled again. "So while you think, let's do. I want to run full tests."

She found that somehow she'd eaten her way through a full serving of Haladea's nut-paste with winter fruits, along with two glasses of tea. She followed him to the medical center. After yesterday, even that was too far.

What would Fitch do if she asked for the chair?

EAN Lambert joined them and settled down on a nearby vault. "Will I be out of your way here?"

She nodded.

One of the spacers who'd been on the ship yesterday accompanied him. Radko. She took up a position against the wall, one foot raised and pressed back to rest against the wall.

"Sometimes I'd like to see the old Haladea," Lambert said. "To see what it was like when it was nothing but an agricultural world."

Kari Wang concentrated on Fitch's tests. "Is that what it was?" She'd have expected something more, given that Redmond had been so keen to annex it less than twelve months ago.

"Their big export was starfruit."

She might have known. "Those things that smell like something died?"

"They have a reputation," Lambert said. "Aphrodisiac," then laughed, and made a face. "They do stink, but Abram says there is some truth in the rumor. They contain alkyl nitrates."

Which she took to mean that alkyl nitrates were some form of aphrodisiac.

"Anyway," Lambert said. "They've gone from being an unknown agricultural world to one of the most important worlds in the galaxy. They're building to match their new reputation."

Kari Wang concentrated on the warm-up exercises. "Why choose here?" Of all the places in the galaxy, the Haladean cluster was the last place she'd have chosen for headquarters.

"Everyone asks that."

Fitch put up a hand. "You're favoring your right side," he said. "I want to see."

She sighed and obediently moved over to the examining table.

"I'll come back later," Lambert said.

She was used to being examined in public. "Stay and talk." She certainly wasn't going to get one-on-one conversation later, and nor was he. "You were saying why Haladea III was chosen as the New Alliance headquarters."

"If you're sure."

"I'm sure."

"Right." Lambert blew out his breath in a manner reminiscent of Galenos. "No one could complain about Haladea's giving advantage to one or more of the New Alliance worlds because they wouldn't. They're nowhere near anywhere else."

That was an understatement.

"What the hell is this?" Fitch demanded.

Kari Wang and Lambert both craned to see.

"It's a bruise," Lambert said.

It covered the whole of the right side of her back, right down to her thigh. No wonder she was sore. Over it and around it were scrapings from gravel rash.

"I can see it's a bruise," Fitch said. "But how did she get it?"

"I fell," Kari Wang said. "Yesterday. Remember, I broke my comms."

"Don't you think you could have told me you were hurt?"

"Fitch. I moved aside to avoid an aircar. I fell. Mael and Tinatin picked me up and looked after me. It wasn't important."

"It must have been some fall."

It had been, with two solid bodies on top of hers and the fence slamming into her. "I haven't got any control of my legs, remember." She might as well get him to look at it properly. "It might have gravel in it," she said meekly.

Fitch pulled out a scanner. "It's no shame to fall, Selma, but you have to tell us when you do."

Kari Wang nodded. "What other reasons did they choose Haladea III for?" she asked Lambert.

He pulled himself away from his fascinated study of her back. "That's some bruise," he said. "It has to hurt."

Radko coughed.

"Sorry. Okay. So the Haladeans found the ship near here. Well, near in space terms but a long way away, really. Abram's worried about aliens."

"Admiral Galenos," Radko said, from her position against the wall.

"Thank you," Kari Wang said.

"Sorry, Admiral Galenos. And all of them—Abram, Katida, Orsaya—are worried about why Redmond attacked Haladea in the first place. Because there isn't any reason." Lambert moved back to his vault. "Plus, the Haladean worlds are agricultural. With Gate Union restricting the jumps, they can still feed everyone."

Logistics. So vital to any war.

"But enough about politics," Lambert said. "I want to know what you thought of the *Eleven*."

Did he want her real answer? How was she going to captain a ship she couldn't even read the screens on? With a crew who had been enemies with each other four months ago.

"I'm wondering how I'll go with the screens," she said.

He nodded sympathetically. "It's like being blind, isn't it?"

Which didn't make her feel any better.

"Or deaf, rather, because you can't hear what it's doing."

Which wasn't any more encouraging.

"Don't worry. Because the *Eleven* wants this crew. It will do everything it can to help."

Here may be the reason for Lambert's almost-unaccompanied visit.

"From what we can tell, both the certified and the single-level linesmen can read the whole panel, so it's not as if your crew is blind or deaf." Only her. "Though they can only communicate with their own lines."

"How do my crew communicate?"

She knew what the answer would be before he said it. Lambert had sung to the lines.

"They sing."

This was going to be the noisiest bridge she'd ever worked on. A change from her own bridge, where her crew had bordered on the quiet side.

"Do they know how to sing?"

"Not yet." His cheeks colored again, for no reason she could see. "They'll need to come to line training." He said it almost apologetically.

Radko waited until Fitch moved out of earshot. "This method of communicating with the lines is one of the biggest secrets in the New Alliance at present. Another is single-level lines."

A *spacer* was telling her this, rather than one of the admirals. Kari Wang gave her a sharp look.

"Need to know, ma'am," Radko said. "It's something you need to know now." She moved, to change the leg she currently had propped against the wall. "Your crew hasn't been cleared yet. It's a long process because every world is doing its own clearances on the other worlds' crew. They won't get to line training until that happens."

"Every world?" How inefficient was that?

Fitch came back.

"Every world," Radko agreed. Her comms chimed. She glanced at it and pushed herself away from the wall. "You're wanted, Ean."

Lambert made a face. "We do have three tens."

"THREE tens," Fitch said, after they'd gone. "I heard they'd executed Rebekah Grimes for war crimes. Apparently they didn't." He packed up the scanner. "Just do the warm-up exercises today. We'll let the bruises settle."

Kari Wang went back to the warm-ups. "Couldn't you give me something to prevent the bruising?" He'd already sprayed them with painkiller. She felt a lot better.

"Maybe if you'd told me about it yesterday, I could have prevented half the bruising."

"Sorry."

"There are rumors they're looking for failed linesmen," Fitch said, and Kari Wang had to remind herself that he hadn't been at her meeting with the admirals yesterday. "They want to use them as experiments on the ships. It would be interesting to know how."

No matter what Radko had said, you couldn't keep something like that a secret for long, and Fitch would come across single-level linesmen soon enough. "You saw the bridge yesterday," Kari Wang said. "I'm sure they're trying everything they can think of to see who can read the boards."

She walked carefully along the horizontal line marked on the floor. Given that Radko had chosen what she said, and when she'd said it, Kari Wang would have to balance her own words as delicately as she did her body.

"Mmmh." Fitch looked at her critically. "I think we should start you on stairs soon. Stretch out some of those muscles. Your balance is improving. Half of what's left is psychological. You *think* they're not your legs, so you haven't accepted them."

Why would she even think that? She could feel them. They ached every night; they gave out on her all the time. "Fitch, maybe someone should give you a new pair of legs and see how you'd cope. Things are not quite in the same place."

"They are, you know. We created them exactly."

Kari Wang didn't believe him.

TWENTY-TWO

STELLAN VILHJALMSSON

SO FAR, LINESMAN Lambert hadn't gone anywhere a civilian could get to him. Yesterday morning, someone had leaked the story of Lady Lyan's forced takeover of the contract. Stellan had heard five versions since. It had been cleverly done, for sympathy was with Rigel.

Markan denied anything to do with the leak. "You think I want to draw more attention to him than I have to? If the New Alliance thinks he'll go back to House of Rigel, they'll double their guard."

"If they double the guard, he'll have more than the Emperor of Lancia himself," Stellan said. Markan still didn't believe how many guards Lambert had around him.

If Markan hadn't leaked it, Stellan's money was on Paretsky. Good publicity for a man trying to get back into a position he had lost.

Meantime, Stellan had to find a new way to get Lambert.

He'd slept with Kaelea twice. She was like other high-level linesmen Stellan knew; aware of her importance as a linesman, looking down on nonlinesmen like himself.

Kaelea had told him that Lambert hated Lancia.

"He'll be so grateful Rigel has come to rescue him." Why she thought Rigel could or would rescue Lambert was something Stellan didn't pursue. Typical linesman, she seemed to forget there was a war on. The cartels didn't have the power anymore, no matter what they thought. If Lambert knew as much about alien technology as Markan thought he did, Lancia wouldn't let him go, whether he wanted to or not.

By the second night, it was obvious Kaelea was having as much trouble contacting Lambert as Stellan was.

Still, there had been some history between Kaelea and

Lambert, and an ex-lover might be able to slip through where others couldn't.

He twisted a strand of her hair around his finger and considered how to use it. "I've heard rumors," he said, and made himself sound cautious, as if he wasn't sure he should be repeating it. "Lancia won't let Lambert go. He's been on the alien ships, you see, and they're worried he'll take the secrets over to Gate Union with him."

"They can't stop him. He's a level-ten linesman. He can do what he wants."

"I heard," and he stopped twirling her hair to give his next words emphasis, and chose every word carefully. "Rebekah Grimes tried to go back, too, and they made up some story about war crimes."

Rumor was Lancia had killed Rebekah Grimes, and those sorts of rumors often had a basis in fact.

Kaelea stiffened. "They wouldn't," but it was uncertain.

Stellan shrugged. "You know Lancia," he said, and left her to think on it.

WHILE he waited to see what became of that, Stellan looked around for other opportunities.

He tried Cartel Master Rigel, of course.

Rigel spent a lot of time at the Night Owl. Since it wasn't the sort of bar Rigel looked to normally frequent, Stellan assumed he was hanging around hoping his former employee might return. Kaelea, he was pleased to see, didn't come here.

Stellan was fast becoming a Night Owl regular himself, although no one who'd seen him that first night would recognize him now.

Stellan had introduced himself the second night Rigel had been there. "You look about how I feel," he told Rigel. "Let me buy you a drink."

Rigel had looked him over. What he would have seen was a man of medium height, human-standard stock, with brownish blond hair—spiked into the latest fashion, much like Rigel's own but without the color—dressed in regular business clothes. Stellan looked like a midlevel executive. Rigel would have dismissed him immediately as no one high enough in a company hierarchy to sell line business to; just another person in a bar wanting to talk.

"Thank you," Rigel said.

Stellan ordered Glenn spirits, which was around what a midlevel executive would buy.

"You're here on business?" Rigel had asked.

"Business." Stellan made his voice bitter. "I finished my business days ago. I booked out on the *Sagittarian Queen.*" The *Queen* ferried corporate trade. "We've been waiting for a jump for two days now." He downed his drink in one gulp. The mods in his stomach turned alcohol into harmless sugars almost instantly. He had to watch his weight, unfortunately, but it was worth it because people would say things when you were both drunk that they wouldn't say otherwise. "Our company has a contract with the Sagittarian Line in this sector, so my boss won't even let me switch to another ship. I've watched five ships leave while I wait here. Five." He held up five fingers, as if he was already half-drunk and had to emphasize it.

"That's too bad," Rigel had said sympathetically. "I wish that was my problem." He downed his drink. "Another?"

"Thanks."

They were nodding acquaintances now, occasional drinking partners when they were both alone.

Tonight, however, Stellan had other prey.

The line trainees. He'd researched all twenty of them. Some were housed on ships from their home worlds. Five more were housed on Confluence Station. But twelve were based here on Haladea, and three of those had become friends who visited the Night Owl regularly when off duty.

He sighed when Rigel saw him and came over.

"Can I buy you a drink?" Rigel asked.

Stellan forced himself to smile because he couldn't afford to alienate the cartel master. Rigel might still deliver. "I'd love the company." He made it enthusiastic.

Rigel hesitated, as if he could feel he wasn't welcome.

"Sit down, man. I've had a depressing day. It will be good to have someone to talk to. I thought I had passage off this hellhole, but it was a false alarm. I almost checked out of my hotel."

"That would have been bad," Rigel agreed. "You'd never

get another room." He settled onto the stool beside Stellan. "I've been stuck in worse places. Not many more expensive, though."

Stellan raised his glass when their drinks came. "To company expense accounts."

"I wish," Rigel said.

Stellan's quarry entered then. Three young soldiers laughing together. One in Aratogan caramel, one in Barossa two-toned brown, and one in Eridanus green. He watched them hunt for spare seats. They'd be lucky tonight. They even looked toward the private booths at the back until the Aratogan shook her head. He could see her mouth, "Too expensive."

They were expensive, and they charged by the hour, but one of those booths had already been booked by Stellan in the hope the line trainees would be here tonight. Now all he had to do was get rid of Rigel, plant a bug on one of the three, and settle in to listen.

Rigel followed his gaze to the soldiers. "You've high hopes," he said. "I think everyone in this bar has hit on her at one time or another," for the Barossan—Aurelia Solvej—was an attractive woman.

"One can hope." Sex and romance were age-old assistants to spies and assassins everywhere. Get an attractive person in the group you wanted to follow, and you always had an excuse to approach them. Even if you were rebuffed, you got close enough to plant a trace.

He drained his glass and ordered another drink for them both. "I'm just ducking into the bathroom," and left Rigel shaking his head.

On the way back he detoured via the bench the three had found, and offered to buy Solvej a drink.

"Thank you, but no."

Stellan leaned forward to show her his comms, and his contact details. "If you ever want a decent dinner," he said.

"Thank you again, but no." She was polite about it, but turned immediately back to her friends. Stellan looked disappointed and turned away, brushing lightly against her, slipping the microbug close to her collar, where it couldn't be seen, as he pulled his comms back.

At the bar, Morton Paretsky was talking to Rigel. The

former Grand Master was in casual clothes although he still wore the ten bars of the highest-level linesman on his pocket. What else could he wear? He wasn't Grand Master anymore. He wasn't affiliated with his old house, Aquarius, either. Stellan thought Paretsky might be feeling unsettled right now.

Personally, Stellan would have managed getting his old job back differently. Paretsky had spent most of his time at the confluence in the hospital with heart problems. He'd missed the brunt of whatever it was that had happened. With so few powerful tens working at capacity right now Stellan would have demanded his old line job back, and worked his way back into favor from there.

Stellan picked up his drink. "I'll leave you to talk."

For a moment Rigel looked panicked, and Stellan was tempted to stay for the goodwill it would generate. But he wouldn't need the goodwill if he could get a better way to Lambert through the line trainees.

Rigel's expression changed to relief so suddenly that Stellan wondered if he'd lost five seconds of time and had offered to stay anyway.

"Leo," Rigel said.

Stellan looked back. The man behind them wore midnight blue. He had a leaping rickenback stitched in gold on the pocket of his cartel uniform. He displayed no bars of a linesman. Leo Rickenback, Grand Master of the line cartels, cartel master for House of Rickenback.

It was interesting he dared to dress so openly in cartel uniform.

"Rigel," Rickenback said. "Morton." He nodded to Stellan.

It was a strategic time to retreat. Stellan took out his comms and made a show of looking toward the booths, then "booking" the one he'd prebooked.

He slid into the seat and turned the silencer on. Peace descended. Stellan ordered another drink and some of the fried root that was a specialty on Haladea III, put a receiver into one ear, and listened.

He was on his last fried root before the trainees started talking about what he wanted to hear.

"Do you really think Lambert knows what he's doing?" It

was Solvej of the lovely looks. "I mean, he was nobody before—"

"Shh," the other two cautioned.

Solvej scowled into her drink. "Sometimes I need to talk about it. Tasker's a six, and he says—" She stopped. "I know what we're doing is experimental, but you should hear what he says about Lambert. I need to talk to people who understand."

Klim, the Eridanian, said, "We'll be surrounded by people who understand soon. After the fuss about Hernandez, I hear they're going to move us together."

"If you sell the contract, Morton, you have to expect the linesman to move out of the cartel house. Or do you expect the New Alliance to start their own house, and that's what has you worried?"

Stellan stopped himself—just in time—from looking around as Rigel, Rickenback, and Paretsky arrived at the table behind him. Someone had bugged Rigel. Or Rickenback or Paretsky, and his listening device was picking it up.

Which meant that whoever was bugging Rigel was picking up the linesmen as well.

"One might say the same of you, Leo," Paretsky said.

"What, that I'm worried about the New Alliance starting their own cartel house? Or that I didn't expect my linesman to move out once I sold his contract? Part of that contract is board and salary. Of course he'd move out. And it's inevitable they'll end up creating their own gates—and therefore houses—if Gate Union continues to block access," Rickenback said.

Paretsky said, "That's—"

"Unthinkable, Morton? No, what's unthinkable is us not thinking that will happen. Eventually, the galaxy will split into two, and the only people who will move between will be free traders affiliated with neither and prepared to wait and jump to the rim."

Underneath, the third linesman, Chantsmith, said something that sounded like, "Never did get that business with Hernandez."

"Didn't you hear?"

"But that's not what I'm here for," Rickenback said, over

the top of Klim. "I've just come from seeing Ean Lambert and Lady Lyan."

Rickenback's voice was as strong as any linesman's.

"Back when they moved the fleet to Haladea III," Klim said. "You know, when Lambert had to go off and do whatever he had to do. And we got two days off."

"Is Paretsky blackmailing you, Rigel? Or threatening you?"

"The only person who's threatened him is Lady Lyan," Paretsky said.

"Keep out of this, Morton. Besides, according to Lambert, Lady Lyan didn't threaten Rigel at all. She threatened Lambert."

"Threatening a linesman is as bad as threatening a cartel master. Especially a level-ten linesman."

"Anyway, Hernandez was really obnoxious about missing line training. You know how she gets."

"Don't we ever. It's like she's on a drug."

Stellan perused the menu in the center of the table without really seeing it, trying to look as if he weren't listening to either conversation. He jabbed an item at random, as if he'd finally decided on more food, and sat back. He should have recorded this. Except, all he'd been hoping for was something to help him get to Lambert.

"Why, Morton." He could hear the anger in Rickenback's voice. "As a former grand master yourself, you know that every linesman is equal in your eyes. That's what the grand master is for, to look after *all* the linesmen, not 'especially' the tens."

"Such naivete, Leo. You won't last long with that attitude."

"She was so bad," Klim said, "that her team leader sent her out on a job that day. It was that or put her in jail."

Stellan had studied the twenty linesmen trainees so carefully he knew more about each of them than their fellow trainees did. Hernandez was a scout pilot.

"Isn't that what this is about, Morton? Usurping me as grand master because I'm not doing my job?"

"Leo, the job should never have been yours anyway. We had an incumbent Grand Master."

"Who'd been in the hospital for six months. If you can't do your job, someone has to do it. Let's not forgot, you're not the only one who wants the position. Iwo Hurst is looking for it, too, and he has more support right now than you do."

So far, Rickenback was making an excellent grand master. It was a pity Markan didn't support him.

Stellan's order arrived then. The same fried roots he'd had before. He bit into one. It was hot enough to burn his tongue.

Behind him, Paretsky laughed. "The cartels don't want Sandhurst in charge."

"Iwo has close to the numbers. It will only take a few to cross, and he'll have them. He also has Gate Union support. It's a different world out there now. The cartels made some bad mistakes. The worst of which was sending our nines and tens out to the confluence. We lost a lot of power. We don't have it back. The military is ascendant now."

"Of course it is," Paretsky said. "There's a war on."

Klim lowered his voice. Stellan forced himself not to lean forward. It wasn't going to make him hear any clearer. "They got attacked. One of her team died."

Rickenback said, "If Gate Union wants House of Sandhurst in charge of the cartels, they'll make it happen. And speaking of Gate Union and Sandhurst, let's address Lambert's other worry. That Rigel will hand him straight over to Gate Union as soon as he gets him back."

So Lambert had some brains at least.

"Of course I wouldn't," Rigel said. "I'd make him work. Do you know how many people have offered to pay triple and more to get Ean to work on their ships?"

Paretsky laughed. "Only Lambert would think he's that important."

Along with the whole Lancian fleet, who were prepared to expend a lot of manpower to keep him safe. Proven, as Markan had rather snarkily confirmed, by that unsuccessful attempt to kidnap or kill Lambert that first night. Stellan had to bite his tongue hard when he'd heard. It wasn't his job to tell Markan his business, and he knew as well as Stellan did that Markan had a big security problem somewhere close to him.

The fried roots had lost their allure. Stellan ordered a bowl of what the menu mysteriously called gher-wha, with no further explanation. He took out his comms, and settled back in the corner of the seat, facing outward, and pretended to watch his comms while he listened. It gave him a view to some of the room.

"There was this big fuss," Klim said. "Why had she been allowed to go? And she's supposed to be traumatized. I mean, Hernandez."

Stellan could imagine the eye roll that went with it.

"Probably traumatized because she missed line training," Solvej said

Rickenback was pitching doom and gloom for the line cartels. "You think you want to be Grand Master again, Morton. Have you looked at what you're getting into? The cartels are a mess. Half of them are going broke, the military is trying to buy up the high-level lines."

"That's why," Klim said softly, and Stellan had to stop the instinctive leaning forward to listen again. "That's why they're talking about putting us together. On a ship. So it doesn't happen again."

"If it's a mess, then whose fault is that?"

"Partly yours, Morton, since you were supposed to be in charge for much of that time." Then Rickenback shook himself impatiently. "It's *our* fault, of course. We were too complacent, too used to the way it was. Our whole economy runs on lines, and we were all too stupid to realize someone—something—had effectively disarmed us all. Six months' failure to supply is bound to go close to destroying any business, no matter how important we think we are."

"You have no idea—"

"The *Eleven*?" Solvej asked eagerly.

"We built our ship, we have to pilot it. No one trusts us anymore to deliver. Half the nines and tens still have problems working." Rickenback shook himself again. "Gah. I don't know why I'm talking to you. Take time out from trying to get your old job back and find out what's happening. And I want to talk to Rigel without you around."

"I'm here to ensure he gets treated fairly."

"And I'm here in my role as Grand Master to talk to Rigel about a linesman for whom he is causing trouble. Read the rules, Morton. The linesman has a right to a private hearing. Go away, or I'll throw the regs at you. I'm simply doing my job."

"Of course it won't be the *Eleven*."

"But they're crewing—"

"We're not part of the crew," Chantsmith said. "They would have told you that when you signed up for this mission, Solvej. We're going back to our home fleets."

Paretsky didn't move, so Rickenback took out his comms. "Record," and held it up to the table, to take in the three of them. "Witness. This is the Grand Master of the Line Cartels, Leo Rickenback, in the case of Lambert versus Rigel, request number L258394. Linesman Lambert has requested assistance from the Grand Master. Date." He pressed the on-screen button to record the date. "At Lambert's request, I am attempting to discuss the issue with the former owner of Lambert's contract, Cartel Master Rigel from House of Rigel. Linesman Paretsky, I wish to speak to Rigel alone. Please leave us."

"You can't be serious."

"So where are we going then?"

"You're on record," Rickenback said. "This is going back to the cartel houses. Please leave."

"It's obvious," Chantsmith said. "There's only one place that's got any room. Lonely ship."

Paretsky turned on his heel and walked away. Stellan was glad for the silence that followed, the chance to listen to a single conversation for a moment.

"Lonely ship." Solvej and Klim groaned in unison.

"We'll be miserable all the time," Klim said.

"It's not so bad," Chantsmith said. "It likes people around, that's all. And we do a lot of training there now. Anyway, we should be getting back. My dorm has a curfew even if yours doesn't."

More than the three of them were leaving. A lot of people had curfews it seemed. In the noise of their all leaving, Stellan almost missed Solvej's grumbled, "A hundred thirty ships to choose from, and they put us on the *Gruen*."

If the trainees were stationed on the *Gruen*, and if, as Chantsmith had said, they sometimes trained on that ship anyway, all Stellan had to do was get onto the *Gruen* on a day when they were training there. Linesman Lambert was the trainer.

The gher-wha arrived. Cold noodles in an unappetizing clear broth.

"Would you like a drink?" Rickenback asked, making Stellan jump.

He hoped no one had seen him do so.

"Just don't make it Lancian wine. I'd choke on it."

Stellan couldn't see what Rickenback ordered, but he heard the weight of the glass hit the tabletop. A liquor, not a wine.

"This one's almost as bad," Rigel muttered, then sighed with pleasure. "Tastes good, though."

"Last time Morton came to visit me, he called me a traitor for serving it," Rickenback said. He mimicked Paretsky's slower, heavier tones. "They're our enemy now." He laughed. "But he drank two glasses and hinted for more."

"Enemies." Rigel was bitter. "Linesmen aren't supposed to be affiliated. I've been here days. I could have had my whole house working. Good work. Do you know how many jobs I've turned down?"

"You don't have to turn them down."

"Don't be stupid."

"Mmmh," Rickenback said. "Abram Galenos offered to set my house up here on Haladea III. So did Jita Orsaya. I think they're desperate for linesmen."

Stellan decided to eat cold soup. This he could take back to Markan.

"But that's not why we're here."

"Lady Lyan threatened me, she threatened my linesman. I was scared. I gave in to her demands."

"Then waited months before you tried to do anything about it."

Rigel didn't answer.

"You can't afford this, Rigel, any more than I could."

Rickenback dialed them both more drinks. "Rigel, has Ean talked to you about what he thinks will happen if he goes back to your house?"

"Ean hasn't talked to me at all since I saw him that first night. He refuses to answer my comms. He refuses to see me."

Rickenback was silent awhile, then, "Kaelea thinks Lancia will kill him if he leaves."

"Kaelea." Rigel waved a dismissive hand. "She's got some crazy idea, but Ean's a linesman. Why would anyone kill a linesman?"

"Why did Lancia kill Rebekah Grimes?"

"*If* they killed her." Rigel didn't sound as confident anymore. "You don't think . . . I mean, Ean."

The soup tasted as bad as it looked. Stellan forced it down.

"You're the Grand Master, Leo. Why don't you ask Ean?"

"I would if I could trust his answer," Rickenback said. "But he's surrounded by guards. He'll say what they want him to say."

"Oh dear."

"Exactly." Rickenback's tone turned grim. "So instead I asked Fergus Burns if Lancia would kill Ean if we got him back."

There was a pause. Stellan badly wanted to turn to see the expression on Rickenback's face.

"I like Fergus," Rigel said. "He's a good man. What did he say?"

Another long pause.

"He hesitated, then said it didn't matter anyway because Ean didn't want to go back."

"But—"

"So I dropped by to see Jordan Rossi. Asked the same question."

"What did he say?"

"He said, 'What do you expect? He's been on the alien ships. He knows too much.'"

"So what are you going to do?"

"Do." Rickenback dialed more drinks. "I don't want to be responsible for anyone's death. I am going to pretend I believe Ean when he says he's happy here, and I'm going to negotiate a settlement for you. I'm going to take Lady Lyan for every credit I can get. She won't know what hit her. And I'll make sure Ean gets a cut. If he is being forced to stay, then they had damn well better pay for it."

The conversation in the booth behind was deteriorating, both in comprehension—they had both put back a lot of those heavy little glasses of liquor in a short time—and in interest. It had reverted to general line discussion. Who had moved to which house, what the cartels were doing, who had the most promising apprentices.

"One of my new apprentices is strong," Rigel said. "The best I've had since I took on Ean."

"A ten?"

Rigel laughed. "Are you kidding?"

"When did you know Ean was a ten?"

"I didn't. Not for a couple of years. The trainers said he'd never amount to anything. Yet he was so determined he was a linesman. I haven't seen anyone with that sort of determination since . . . I thought he'd be a three or a four. I thought—" Rigel broke off. "His keep and his training weren't going to break me."

"Do tell. Rigel feeling sorry for someone." Rickenback must have been drunk, for the man Stellan had listened to berate Paretsky earlier wouldn't have said that.

"It wasn't sympathy," Rigel said. "Have you ever had a dream, Leo? Have you ever wanted that dream so much you—"

Stellan couldn't see the gesture that went with the words.

"Oh, I calculated everything carefully. I wasn't going to be out of pocket for his expenses. I never expected . . . a house like mine should never have had a ten. At first even *I* didn't realize what I had."

Stellan swiped his comms to off and stood up. He had better things to do than sit around listening to two drunk cartel masters talk about their star ex-employees. He had to find how to get onto the *Gruen*.

TWENTY-THREE

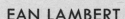

EAN LAMBERT

AFTER HELMO'S DINNER party, Ean and Vega avoided each other. Ean had the advantage, for he knew where she was on ship, so they only came across each other when Ean was engrossed in what he was doing and hadn't noticed she was around, or when Vega sought him out.

Today, she'd sought him out. She'd come down to Engineering, where Ean was working with the *Lancastrian Princess*'s linesmen, and waited until he finished. He'd been aware of her, but the lines enjoyed their time with the crew, so he hadn't stopped.

"Is it true they're going to move all the trainees to the *Gruen*?" Tai asked, once they were done.

"Yes." They should have done it from the start.

"Me, too?"

Tai had been working with the lines; his own lines were clear. While he understood it would be good for the trainees to be together, he didn't want to leave his ship. His lines were here. Ean understood that.

He glanced at Vega. "I'll see what I can do." Lancia would be accused of favoritism again, but they did have to shuttle Ean across every day. It wasn't as if they weren't going there anyway.

"Thank you."

"No promises, mind," Ean said. "You may have to go." He turned to Vega. "Commodore."

"Linesman Lambert," and she walked with him back to her office.

Radko marched behind. Ean glanced around once. Vega acted as if she weren't there but dismissed her at the door of the office.

Vega indicated a chair. "Someone bugged your trainee linesmen the other night."

"Bugged them?" For a moment, he didn't understand what she meant and had to check the lines to translate it. "Listened in to their conversation?" Was she accusing him? "I didn't do it."

"No. They planted a bug on Solvej's uniform. Some of us still need to do it the old-fashioned way."

Vega had learned a lot about Ean since Helmo's dinner party. Probably a lot of it incorrect.

"The lines don't work like that," Ean said. "I'd need line one and line five to hear through the lines, and probably other lines as well." Maybe that was what line seven did. "And if they were on a ship I knew," because he wasn't convinced he could read a strange ship yet.

"Admiral Orsaya thinks you could communicate mind to mind if you wished to. You snoop into Linesman Rossi's mind on occasion."

"Only by accident." It was true he sometimes accidentally dipped into Rossi's lines—especially after training, when the lines were wide open—but Jordan Rossi wouldn't have admitted that to anyone. Line business was for linesmen. Orsaya wouldn't have admitted it either. She was fanatical about lines, but in her own way, she protected Ean. Vega had done some snooping of her own.

Maybe he should try sending thoughts the other way. He shuddered, imagining what Rossi would say to that.

"But you could do it if you wanted to," Vega said.

"The lines would have to be receptive."

She nodded, as if he'd confirmed something she'd suspected. "So, who would bug your trainee linesman, and why?"

Wouldn't that be obvious? "They want to know what training we're doing."

She pushed a transcript of the three trainees' conversation over to Ean. "Read it, it will be faster than listening to it all night."

Ean wasn't a fast reader. "Why don't you tell me?"

"Read it."

So Ean did, carefully and thoroughly, while Vega paced the room.

Her sighs were distracting. He had to reread some parts. He was glad to finish. "They didn't say anything wrong."

"Didn't . . ." Vega visibly pulled herself together.

"Unless you count the bit about my being strange."

"They gave away their new location. They discussed the weakness of one of the linesmen."

Ean stood up. "Everyone needs to talk sometimes. What they talked about were things other people might know already." Like how obsessed Hernandez was with the lines. "Or things they will know soon." Like the fact that the linesmen were moving to the *Gruen*.

"Why was someone listening that particular day?"

"Nothing unusual happened if that's what you're asking." She nodded. She was.

"How do you know it was only that day?" Maybe they bugged them every day. "You must know. Otherwise, they could have been bugged every night."

"We've been listening to Cartel Master Rigel," Vega said. "He goes to the Night Owl most nights. We think he's going there for you."

"Rigel? Did he—" Ean stopped, not sure how to ask.

"Grand Master Rickenback said he will negotiate a deal."

Yet no one had spoken to Ean about it.

Vega looked at his face. "Sometimes you overthink things, Lambert."

Sometimes she overprotected things.

"Rickenback will do his job. Meantime, I'm trying to do mine. If you hear anything, I want to know immediately."

TWENTY-FOUR

✦

SELMA KARI WANG

THE DAYS TOOK on a routine. Exercise and physical checkup first, followed by a trip out to the *Eleven*, where Kari Wang wandered around the ship and tried to familiarize herself with it. She spent half the time on the bridge, trying to work out the boards. Nothing made sense. The afternoons were spent with the admirals, going over the crew, the ship plans, and line information.

Afterward, she came back to her quarters and spent two hours doing more physical exercises.

Fitch wanted her to spend more time on her legs—and she did half an hour of that—but she spent most of the time on the bars and balance. There was nothing wrong with her upper-body strength, and any spacer should be able to move through the whole ship using handholds.

Fitch and Jon spent the afternoons out with her crew, running comprehensive medical and psychiatric tests one person at a time.

"It's amazing what level of fitness the different militaries accept," Fitch told her.

Kari Wang thought it was more likely they'd waive extreme fitness to get the type of recruits they wanted.

She wasn't sure who had arranged it so Fitch and Jon didn't arrive back until after she had finished exercising, but she was grateful for it.

Launching herself off the bars, twisting, using her own body strength to move from one bar to the next to get her around the room was the closest Kari Wang came to being at peace. She didn't think about her ship then, or her crew, but the familiarity of the exercises somehow brought them closer.

Only when the muscles in her upper body shook with fatigue did she go back to the exercises Fitch had set. The stairs, which she loathed.

They'd found an old fire escape that wasn't used because it bordered on one of the construction sites. When Grieve had first offered its use, Fitch had taken one look and gone so white Kari Wang had grabbed onto his shirt for fear he'd faint and fall. It was clear there had once been a building beside this one, and thus no need for a railing on the stairs.

Even Grieve had paled. "We'll put a barrier up, of course," and his voice shook. "It's a good spot because it's private. Even the media drones can't get around here."

Spacer that she was, Kari Wang had no problems with the stairs, eight flights open to the gaping hole of the building site next door. It reminded her of the vastness of space.

"Do we have to put a barrier up?"

"Yes," they'd both said.

Put up a barrier they had. A massive thing of steel and plastic that made Kari Wang feel as if she were in a cage. Sometimes all she did was hold on to the bars and look out over the building site. This was her life now. Caged. Out of her control.

EVERY third afternoon she had a psych session with Jon.

He talked to her about her crew. "It's the weirdest mix you have ever come across," he said. "Linesmen, I understand, because you're working on a line ship. But the others. Some of them barely make regulation. Like Mael, that old man who rescued you the day you dropped your comms, for example. They sent him out to the rim for a reason. He's half-crazy. As for following orders, I don't think he knows what an order is. No wonder he was demoted. I'm going to recommend he be removed from the project."

"I doubt anyone will listen to you." The admirals had high hopes of Mael, for some reason. Besides, she liked someone who would rescue a stranger.

"Because Aratoga's so powerful." Jon made a face. "I have never seen so much politics in my life. They're always arguing over who's got seniority, and why."

* * *

ONE afternoon the admirals sent Kari Wang, Helmo, and Wendell out to the barracks where her crew were quartered.

"Not that they know they're your crew yet," Galenos said, "and we'd appreciate it if you didn't mention it until the security clearances come through, but we're sure you'd like to meet them."

No one could replace the crew she'd had on the *Kari Wang.*

The admirals didn't say, but it seemed to be part of some bizarre bonding program. They'd told her the ships were linked, and that everywhere the *Eleven* went, Wendell and Helmo would follow, and vice versa. Along with the *Gruen* and the two media ships. Edie Song, captain of the *Gruen,* had been invited to join them, but she'd had other plans.

Barracks 24, where the *Eleven* crew were stationed, was at the edge of the city, surrounded by golden paddocks. There were no other buildings close. Off to one side—but still four hundred meters from the barracks itself—was a stand of vegetation. Not quite trees, for the branches grew up from a central stalk. Each branch was studded with large, oval globules. As they exited the car, the stench of something rotting, but sweet, almost overwhelmed them.

"Starfruit," Helmo said. "I bet that's a popular night trek."

Kari Wang bet it was.

They found the crew exercising halfheartedly on the obstacle course outside the building.

"Get your lazy asses into gear and do some work," a trainer screamed at them as they jogged past. "If you want to play triball after this, you'd better work for it."

"I don't think they're even raising a sweat," Wendell said. He frowned at one man in a New Viking uniform who was jostling a smaller man in Ruon uniform.

The exercisers were running so slowly, Kari Wang could hear snatches of conversation as they passed. The odd couple of Tinatin and Mael jogged by. Tinatin was saying, "Lambert's the worst ten ever, according to the woman who accompanied his cartel master here."

"So why have the cartels come to collect him then?" Mael asked.

Kari Wang caught something about, "Line business," but the rest of Tinatin's answer was lost.

"You've got some work ahead of you," Helmo said.

He was so right.

Second time around the circuit, Kari Wang stepped in and snagged the New Viking out of the crush. A captain controlled her own crew, but she could see Helmo and Wendell both ready to step in. That was fine. She would have done the same.

She looked at his shirt. "Spacer Mikaelsson," she said. He had six bars below his name and team-leader pips on his shoulders. "We don't tolerate bullies here. Consider this your first warning."

"It's team leader," he said.

"That's worse."

She became aware other spacers had stopped.

"Will you look at that?" Mael said to Tinatin. "Captain Legless."

The trainer ran up. "Get your scummy selves back on the course." She was the only one in the whole group who moved with any speed. "What in the lines is up with you all?"

"Visitors, Group leader," Tinatin said.

"That doesn't give you a reason to stop," the trainer said. "Keep moving."

They kept moving, Tinatin looking behind her as they went. The result was inevitable. She ran into someone else, who knocked her over, but picked her up, too, and as they ran, Tinatin explained, with backward gestures, about their visitors. Or maybe about the legless captain.

Kari Wang sighed. Normally, she liked a challenge, but she didn't want to build another crew into a cohesive unit.

She let go of Mikaelsson. Her arms and hands were strong, even if her legs weren't. He'd have a bruise on his shoulder tomorrow where she had gripped him. "Remember this," she said. "Go." The man he'd been tormenting was halfway across the course now.

"Visitors report to security," the trainer said.

"We did that," Kari Wang said.

The trainer checked her comms, saw they had, and scowled. "So what do you want?" She turned and bellowed at the trainees. "Come on, you useless lot. You're on show here.

Not to mention you have exactly"—she checked her comms—"forty-five seconds to get back to the line, or you're out of this afternoon's match."

Everyone picked up the pace.

"What's the match?" Kari Wang asked.

"Triball," the trainer said. "It's the one thing I can bribe them with. There's no motivation here."

Kari Wang's own crew had just started a triball tournament when they'd been killed. She breathed deep and tried not to remember that.

Helmo and Wendell noticed. Of course they would. They were both good captains.

"Can we pick the teams today?" Wendell asked. She wasn't sure if it was to give her time to recover or his way of helping her get over the bad memories by forcing her to relive them.

The trainer looked at them doubtfully, looked at her comms again, looked at Kari Wang. "Why not?"

Triball was a strategy game played by three teams. Each team had a token, and the aim was to place the token in the team goal. Three center players—one from each team—started with their team token and passed it on to other members of their team. It was a combination of speed, defense, and fooling the other sides as to who had the token.

Team numbers varied, but it was usually played with between ten and thirty people per team. You could play it on planet or in space. Captains loved the game because it allowed them to gauge how fit their crew was, and how they cooperated with each other. The team that didn't cooperate lost. Always. Even if they had the fastest movers on their team.

Not only could you learn about how your team cooperated, you could learn a lot about the coaches by the way they played their team. If her ship was tied to the *Lancastrian Princess* and the *Wendell*, this would be a good way to see what the captains were like.

"Send them around once more," Kari Wang said, without giving the trainer time to argue. "Then we'll pick teams."

There was a chorus of protest when the trainer sent them around again. "You said we could play triball when we were done," Mikaelsson said.

"So I did, and these captains are going to pick teams. So work for a change."

They watched them go around, critically this time, looking for the strengths required for triball.

This time when Tinatin ran past, she was explaining to the spacer who'd helped her up earlier. "Ransomed back the first time. Then the Alliance caught them again, so Wallacia said, 'Enough, we're not going to send good money after bad', and refused to have them back. So the New Alliance is stuck with them."

Kari Wang wondered if the girl ever shut up.

"So they're enemies inside the New Alliance," the spacer she was running with said.

"Exactly," as they jogged out of hearing again.

Further, Kari Wang wondered if Tinatin always got her facts a little skewed.

JON joined them as they were choosing teams.

She'd forgotten Jon came out here every afternoon to work with the crew. Fitch would be around somewhere, too.

It seemed the captains looked for similar things in players, for most of the time Helmo and Wendell chose the same people Kari Wang would have. Except Wendell chose Tinatin for his third pick, which was unexpected. Kari Wang wondered if he did it out of sympathy.

"Right," she said to her team. "Any strategies?"

Unfortunately, they had plenty. All of them contradictory. She held up a hand. "You, you, you, you." The four who'd come in front on the final lap. "You're our initial runners."

"If I'd known that, I would've run faster," grumbled one who'd come in a long way back.

Maybe it would teach him to try harder in the future.

"One minute," the trainer said.

Kari Wang gave final instructions and stepped back to see how well they carried them out.

"You haven't seen these people work together," Jon said, as the game started. "Some of them out-and-out hate each other. You'll be putting quite a few of them into the brig when the interworld rivalry comes to a head."

Kari Wang looked at him. "There'll be no interworld rivalry on the *Eleven*," she said. She turned to look back at the field. It was obvious who had Helmo's token. A tall, willowy woman whose skin had the green tinge of Nyan. It seemed half the field was after her.

Tinatin was still talking. Tagging after one of Kari Wang's own team, mouth and hands moving as she talked volumes. Eventually, Kari Wang's team member turned and yelled at her to go away.

Tinatin scampered.

"No," Kari Wang said, for she realized how close the two were to the Wendell goal. Everyone else was following Helmo's latest runner. "Tell me he didn't do that. The bastard."

Sure enough, the buzzer rang as soon as Tinatin reached the goal square.

A trick like that should have only worked once, but Tinatin did it again just before the final bell.

The game finished 6-3-3 in Wendell's favor.

The three captains shook on it. "We must try that again with our own crews," Helmo said to Wendell, and Kari Wang agreed. When they did, her crew would be working together like a real team. And maybe as sneaky as Wendell's.

"That was fun," Kari Wang overheard Tinatin say to Mael as they made their way back toward the barracks.

"That's because you scored two goals."

"I've never scored in triball before."

She was unlikely to score again for a while. This whole crew knew that particular trick by now. She'd end up the most marked woman on the field.

They returned to the main barracks to meet a flurry of media drones.

"Captain Kari Wang, is it true your crew consists solely of linesmen and failed linesmen?"

"Captain Kari Wang, were you aware of this?"

"Captains," for some of the drones that couldn't get to Kari Wang homed in on Wendell and Helmo. "Why do you think they chose failed linesmen to crew the *Eleven*?"

Kari Wang ignored the drones, as did Helmo. Wendell, though, looked straight at the camera and said, "Why don't you tell us? After all, doesn't the media always know before we do?"

Which silenced the drones long enough for all three captains to enter the building.

KARI Wang had half an hour left before dinner. She used it to exercise on the stairs. In truth, she'd have preferred to be on the bars.

The building next door was up to six stories. They were using prefabricated Supacrete walls. Just slot and bolt, according to the ads Kari Wang forwarded past when she watched the news. All the infrastructure built in.

One day to lay the floor, three days to set the walls. They hadn't mentioned the day in between to move the cranes, and that you had to build it in two halves so the cranes had something to work with. Still, it was faster than anything Kari Wang had seen built on Nova Tahiti.

When she had arrived on Haladea III, they'd been working on the third floor. Now they had completed the first half of the sixth floor, and had moved the cranes to the seventh floor—directly beneath her—ready to finish assembling the second half of the sixth.

Kari Wang herself was on the ninth floor. She leaned against the bars of her prison to watch. It wouldn't be long before her view was gone.

She sighed and started down. Step after step after endless step. Except on the fifth step she tripped, and went tumbling down the stairwell.

She grabbed at the railings, only to have them fall away as her weight crashed against them.

There was no way she was going anywhere except over the edge. Kari Wang couldn't stop herself in time, no matter what she tried, so she didn't try. Instead, she used what little strength she had in her legs to springboard herself away from the stairwell to give her momentum a boost.

She dived toward the cranes she had been watching earlier.

Two floors onto Supacrete might not kill her, but it would be close, and even if it didn't, she'd be left so crippled she'd take years to rehabilitate. Unless Fitch and Arnoud could come up with another miracle cure.

If she could slow herself enough to catch onto the builder's scaffolding at the bottom, it might not be so bad.

She calculated velocities and fall rates as she fell, and twisted her body halfway down to turn. In space, a miss was as good as forever. She was going to catch the links on that crane, or she didn't deserve to be in space.

The crane approached fast. Distances on world were tiny compared to those in space, and gravity was a major factor you had to calculate for. She grabbed at the chain, so small from the stairwell, each chain link as thick as her arm up close. If her upper-body strength had been standard, she wouldn't have held on.

The chain spun crazily. Down below, the workers scattered. She slid partway down the chain, let go before the slide burned her, and grabbed again farther down.

She used her momentum to push herself away, aiming for the railings that surrounded the drop between the sixth and seventh floors and swung in a dizzying loop of acrobatics to slow down even more.

The scaffolding gave way, but she'd slowed enough by then to jump away and land on her feet.

Where her treacherous legs immediately gave way under her.

Footsteps pounded up the temporary metal stairway between the sixth and seventh floors. Someone in workman's boots stopped in front of her.

"You crazy bitch. You could have gotten yourself killed."

Kari Wang stretched her legs to see if they were broken. "The aim was to not get killed." She couldn't feel anything, which might or might not have been a result of the adrenaline still pounding through her body.

She stood up carefully. "Apologies for this." The shaking was definitely due to adrenaline. At least, she hoped it was. She looked up at the blank space in the stair guard opposite them. "The railing broke. I fell."

He looked up, too, made an "oh" at the hole. "Lady, you lead a charmed life."

She thought so, too, and her legs wouldn't hold her up much longer. Stupid, inconvenient things they were. Why hadn't they gone with an old-fashioned pair of neo-alloy legs? They'd have been crushed right now, but they could withstand the pressure of a two-story fall.

"Sit down," the man said, and she was glad to. "You need something for shock."

His name was Sten, and he was the building foreman. He gave her hot tea and called the site doctor. "We need to see if anything is broken. And I'll have to fill out an incident form."

Kari Wang blew on her tea to cool it. All planet-bound people drank their tea too hot. Worse, this particular batch was like tar. Sweet tar.

Her biggest hope was that their elevator was working. The thought of walking down seven flights of stairs was daunting.

She looked around for her comms. She should call Fitch. He'd want to make sure she hadn't broken his precious legs. Better yet, call Grieve. He could sort things out.

Her comms was gone.

Sten brought it up to her before the doctor arrived. "One of the men found this down on the sixth. Is it yours?"

It had shattered. Her second since she'd arrived on Haladea III.

"Thank you."

The site doctor pronounced her lucky and with no permanent damage. "You'll be sore tomorrow. And very stiff."

She rather expected that herself.

"And if you're going to do any form of gambling tonight, don't. You've used up all your luck for the next ten years."

There was luck and there was preparedness. Although, it took two coincidences—her to trip, and the railing to fail—for the bad luck she'd had today. She had tripped before, often. This time it felt as if she'd fallen over something on the stair.

"You should call someone," the site doctor said. "I'd prefer if you didn't go home alone."

Home was next door, but she dutifully borrowed Sten's comms and called Grieve to come and get her.

"From where?" Grieve asked.

"The building site next door."

"And why aren't you calling on your own comms?"

"I dropped it."

"Again?"

She didn't want to explain it over the comms. "Why don't you come collect me, and I'll explain."

Grieve brought the chair because, naturally, what else would he think except that her legs had given out? Kari Wang was glad Sten and the doctor escorted her down to the ground floor rather than have him come up to the seventh.

Sten was apologetic about that. "Regulations," he said. "No one allowed on the site without clearance."

"It's fine." She signed a waiver to say she didn't hold the building company responsible, and signed the incident report as well.

"Thank you again."

Sten nodded, and said to Grieve, "Now you're a smart man." He helped Kari Wang into the chair. "She's one very lucky lady."

Kari Wang settled into it without protest.

"You should make sure she sees her own doctor," the site doctor said. "And no matter what she says, she'll be in shock."

Everyone on the building site came to wave her off.

"I'm not even going to ask," Grieve said. "Not until we get inside."

"Thank you." Kari Wang sat back and let him push the chair. "Didn't they give you a motorized chair?"

"Motors take room, they're heavy, and you're stubborn." He pushed over a rough piece of path. She felt it all the way to her nerve ends. "I'm not carrying around extra weight I don't need if you refuse to use the chair. What happened?"

"You weren't going to ask until we got inside."

"Look at your hands. They're scraped raw."

Her hands were scraped, but they didn't hurt. The site doctor had sprayed something on them. They were about the only thing that didn't hurt.

They reached the entryway. She was glad of the smoother floors indoors. "I fell," she said. "I can walk now," although she wasn't sure she could.

"Humor me. Pushing you lets me take my anger out on something."

She humored him. "Why so angry?"

"Because you're stubborn, and you refuse help when it's

offered. You fell again." It wasn't a question, it was a statement of fact.

"I fell again," she agreed. She almost wasn't going to tell him where she'd fallen, but someone would have to fix the railing on the stairs. "I was doing stair exercises. The railing gave way."

The lift arrived then. Grieve pushed her in. If Kari Wang hadn't pressed the button for her floor, they'd still have been sitting in the lift on the ground floor.

They were joined on the next floor by a commodore and two captains from Nova Tahiti. Kari Wang moved her chair out of the way so they could get in.

"I thought we'd agreed on the stairs you could exercise in," Grieve said, as the bell pinged for their floor, making the commodore and captains look at him strangely.

"That's right." Grieve didn't move, so Kari Wang stood up and exited the elevator, leaving him to bring the chair.

Her legs ached, and maybe Grieve could wheel off some of that aggression he had. She settled back in the chair.

"You're telling me the railing on the stairs out there gave way." He waved a hand roughly in the direction of the stairwell. "Those railings were triple-bonded, alarmed, and *padded* so we'd know the second you fell."

She hadn't known they were alarmed. "So you already know about this?"

"No," he said. "I didn't."

GRIEVE brought in a team of experts who went through the railings with enough equipment to run a small ship.

Their findings. Shoddy workmanship.

"The alarm system never worked," the team leader said. "It wasn't hooked up. Except at the top, which was probably where you tested. As for the railings themselves. Yes, they're triple-bonded, but the bolts were low-grade. They were always going to fail as soon as something hit them with force."

"So you're telling me we paid a fortune for top-of-the-line protection, and we got this," Grieve said.

"It's common nowadays," the team leader said. "The good contractors are booked out for months. If you want a fast job you'll only get fly-by-nighters."

* * *

AT Kari Wang's next meeting with the admirals, MacClennan told them Grieve had offered to resign.

They all looked at her.

She knew, if she asked for it, he'd go. Maybe they'd kick him out of the fleet, maybe move him on to another, less prestigious job.

"We all have mistakes on our record," she said. "This isn't as bad as some."

"Thank you," MacClennan said.

"It's an unusual error for Grieve," Admiral Katida said. "He's so efficient I was starting to think you'd replaced his brain with a computer. After all, you can replace everything else."

Which was high praise for the man indeed.

Kari Wang made her way back to quarters in a thoughtful mood.

Grieve was waiting for her. Alone.

"I want you to know it won't happen again," he said.

Kari Wang looked at him. "I'm sure it won't," she said.

"I don't know how it happened. I checked the contractors thoroughly."

He wanted her to say something. To yell at him, or sack him, or even dock his pay. She could feel his need, desperate, under the surface. Anything to acknowledge he'd failed, instead of this blanket, "Don't let it happen again," he was getting.

Kari Wang got them both tea. Weak and lukewarm, like a spacer took it.

"If you want to do penance, Grieve, let's do something useful. I want you to work out exactly how you were taken in. There has to be something that would have tipped you off. You work out why, so you don't make that mistake again, and we'll call it quits. Okay."

He looked at his glass, not at her, "Thank you," then gulped his tea as if it was water for a thirsty spacer. He grimaced at the taste, or maybe at the temperature. "Thank you," he said again.

TWENTY-FIVE

EAN LAMBERT

THE *GRUEN* MADE a good training ship, for its lines went out of true easily. No matter how clean the lines were when the trainees left it, by the next day, they needed fixing again.

It missed its old crew. It was unwanted, unloved. Even the trainees were reluctant to be there because the lines cried out with loneliness. The teams who manned it had picked up their captain's attitude. This was a dead-end job. The sooner they were out of it, the better.

The ship knew it wasn't wanted.

Maybe that was why it clung to the little kindnesses when it got them. Esfir Chantsmith—who always had time for the ship—got special attention. But Chantsmith alone wasn't enough, and he was due to go back to his own ship when line training was finished. What the ship needed was a captain who cared for it, and a full crew to keep it.

There was no science yet to prove it, but Ean was sure line ships were more sentient when they had other sentients around them. Ships needed people. People who wanted to be there.

It was time Captain Song took responsibility for her ship.

Ean's schedule was planned to the minute. Mornings were spent with the trainees, afternoons on the *Eleven* or the *Confluence*—unless he needed to attend one of the interminable council sessions—and evenings training the *Lancastrian Princess* linesmen or working with Fergus on line seven. Occasionally, he was required to attend functions. In between all this he answered line questions. From Abram's Department of Alien Affairs, from politicians, from the military. Luckily not from the media, though. Abram and Michelle answered those.

He wasn't going to get time out if he didn't ask for it. The question was, whom did he ask? Abram and Michelle were constantly busy. In the end, he went to Vega.

"Don't I have enough people assigned to you already."

"I wasn't looking for a minder. I'm telling you I'm going down to Haladea III."

"Yet I have to organize not only your regular crew, but another team to accompany you. And ensure there are crews on call on planet if required."

"I just want to visit someone."

"Every time you go anywhere, Lambert, you get into trouble. I have to rearrange everyone's schedule to accommodate you. These schedules have been planned weeks in advance."

Vega, Ean decided, liked to be organized. "What if something unexpected happens?" Like the arrival of a captain for an alien ship. Ean had broken his carefully planned schedule for that before.

"On my watch, everything's planned for."

"So you must have planned for me wanting unexpected trips down to the planet, as well."

Vega's face puckered in what might have been a scowl. Or a smile. She inclined her head. "Bhaksir's team will accompany you, with Craik and her team on the ground as immediate backup—and note, I have to take them off their work on the alien ships to do this."

"Thank you." Ean escaped before she could say anything else.

AS Ean stepped onto the shuttle to go down to Haladea III to see Song, Abram called. "The final security clearance for the *Eleven* crew came through five minutes ago. You can start line training tomorrow. They'll arrive on the *Gruen* after your session with the other trainees."

They had discussed whether to train the *Eleven*'s crew on the *Eleven*, but Ean wanted them used to singing to the lines first, and the *Gruen* was their de facto training ship. He also wanted the two groups of trainees together for that first session. Those who had been training for a while might be able to help with the newcomers. After all, 130 people were a lot to train.

Maybe Edie Song would be there tomorrow if he could convince her to come out to the ship. Then they'd see what the lines could do.

Song's quarters were on barracks, close to the rooms they had set aside for the Nova Tahitian party. On their way, they passed a room with an open door where Fitch was arguing with Kari Wang.

"You've just had regen."

"So I've new skin now. You don't need to treat me like an invalid."

Kari Wang's arms and legs—and the side of her face— showed the mottled pink of new skin grafted alongside the old. In parts, there was bruising as well, so she was tricolored, and she moved carefully.

"Your muscles will be sore."

"But not my walking muscles."

"Walk down the room and tell me it doesn't hurt."

Kari Wang stood up. Her face was turned to the door— away from Fitch. She winced, then saw Ean watching her and frowned instead.

Ean stepped inside. Radko followed him in.

"If you're here to tell me how grateful the ship is that I'm safe, I don't want to hear it," Kari Wang said.

"She's a little grumpy today," Fitch said. "She's sore, and she won't admit it."

"I think I'd be grumpy, too," Ean said, watching the careful way she put each foot down.

"So what do you want?" Kari Wang demanded.

Fitch was right. She *was* grumpy. "I'm going to see Captain Song. Talk to her about spending more time on her ship."

Kari Wang reached the end of the room. She turned. "You can't force a captain to be with a ship they don't want to be with." Ean was sure she wasn't talking about Edie Song. "If someone doesn't want to be there, you should get rid of them, give the ship a chance to get a captain who will care for it."

"Sometimes you have to take what you can get," Ean said.

She stopped when she got close and glared at him. "And sometimes that's the stupidest thing you can do. To the captain, or the ship."

"I don't want unwilling captains for my lines any more than you want them." The lines didn't need them. "If I could do something about it, I would."

Unfortunately for both of them, she didn't have any choice. Ean didn't either. He had to live with it. And so would she.

Radko moved between them. "We're on a schedule," she reminded Ean.

Fitch had moved across to Kari Wang and had a hand ready to hold her back. "Easy," he said.

Ean and Kari Wang stared at each other. Ean realized he was breathing hard. He looked at Radko and managed to make his voice normal. "You're right. We are on a schedule."

He nodded to Kari Wang and Fitch, and turned and left the room.

Behind him, he heard Fitch say soothingly to Kari Wang, "Your heart is racing as fast as a rookathook. I'll get something to calm you down."

"Rookathook," Ean said, because half of Bhaksir's team was out in the hall with them, and he didn't want to show them he was upset. "What's that?"

"It's an animal," Radko said. "They move and look something like a crab, but without the hard exoskeleton. They're closer to a rodent."

Ean couldn't imagine it.

"Their heart beats 250 times a minute."

Kari Wang would be dead then if her heart were beating that fast. Ean knew a lot more about hearts than he had six months ago.

Behind them, Kari Wang's irritated reply faded away.

"Interestingly," Radko said. "In their natural habitat, rookathooks are pied in color. Much like Captain Kari Wang's skin back there. But it's an optical illusion. When you photograph them, their images show smooth brown fur." She frowned. "Most people don't see them in their natural habitat. They're native to Redmond."

"But you have."

"Yes. Back when I was a child and my parents thought I might make a diplomat. I spent six months there perfecting my accent."

"Your Redmond accent? It's a wonder Abram never used you as a spy."

Radko didn't answer that.

Abram probably had used her as a Redmond spy.

CAPTAIN Song wasn't in her rooms. They finally tracked her down in the gym, running on a treadmill. She looked as if she'd been at it for hours.

"Captain Song," Ean said.

"Linesman." She kept running.

Back when he'd been a linesman in the cartel system, hardly anyone had known him. Now, it seemed, everyone knew him by sight, even though he wore a simple soldier's uniform.

Ean looked around the gym. There were four other users, one of whom was scowling at him. He wasn't sure why, until the officer said, pointedly, "This is an officer's gym, soldier."

It was good to be reminded there was a world out there, full of people to whom the lines were unimportant.

Another of the exercisers leaned over, and said quietly to the officer, "That's Linesman Lambert."

"Oh," said the officer.

So then, of course, everyone watched them, waiting to hear what Ean had to say.

Ean looked around again. "Captain Song. Could we talk outside?"

She looked at the other exercisers, pressed *Stop*, then picked up her towel and led the way out without a word.

"What?" she demanded, out in the corridor, as she wiped her face with her towel. The towel was as wet as she was. Ean hoped her red face was from exercising and not from annoyance.

He looked around to be sure they were alone. How did he say this without accusing her of deserting her ship? Or maybe he should do that. After all, that's what she was doing.

"The *Gruen* needs its captain on board."

"What?" Whatever Song had expected, it wasn't that.

"It's a line ship," Ean said. "You're dragging it down by staying away. You need to be on ship more."

If her face hadn't already been red, it would have reddened now. "Are you telling me what to do on *my* ship?"

"That's the problem. You're not *on* your ship. It needs you. Training for the new linesmen starts tomorrow. Can't you at least be there for that?"

She looked at his uniform, at the braid on his shoulders. Or lack of rank, Ean supposed.

"A Lancian. A simple *soldier.* Telling *me* what to do on my ship."

"I'm not a soldier," Ean said. "I'm a linesman. I'm responsible for the welfare of the lines on those ships out there. And one of those ships is yours."

She turned on her heel.

"Captain Song. You are negligent in your duty toward your ship." He didn't want to raise his voice, but he wanted her to hear him. He used a technique he had learned from Gospetto, filling his lungs with air and letting the sound carry.

She swung around so fast Ean stepped back. Radko stepped forward at the same time—faster—so for a moment she and Song were standing face-to-face.

Song looked past Radko to Ean. "Don't you ever tell me what to do in relation to my ship. Especially not while you're the one who's keeping it where it is. It's a dead-end ship, it's a dead-end job. They should have turned it into scrap."

"It's a fleet ship," Ean said. "We can't do that." He didn't want to think about what happened to old ship lines. Did they die with their ship? Probably. "And while it's a fleet ship, while its lines are under my care, I say you are not doing your job."

"What job? What is there to do on a ship stuck orbiting a planet? You know what they gave me? Two teams. Eighteen people. To run a warship. A warship that can't move without *your* say-so."

"It's not my—"

"What can the *Gruen* do? Last I heard you were using one of the cargo compartments for line training. As if it's better than sitting there, empty. It would be smarter to close the whole ship down."

"We can't do that." Didn't she understand?

"Don't you come to me about the 'welfare' of my ship. It's a useless heap of junk, and the worst day of my life was when they gave me that commission."

She turned on her heel again and strode back into the gym.

Ean watched her go. "That was a mistake, I think," he said to Radko.

"Maybe not," Radko said. "You had to do it, Ean. Think of it more as the first round of hostilities."

Hostilities. Even Radko thought it would be a fight. Ean took a deep breath. This was one fight he had to win.

EAN arrived on the *Gruen* early, and gave the original twenty trainees their lesson first. They were doing well.

"We've got new trainees today," he told them, as the last song died away.

They'd just been singing to the lines. Their emotions were as clear as if they'd voiced them aloud. The predominant one was jealousy. This was their secret.

Jordan Rossi chuckled. "Weren't expecting that, were you?"

"You're reading my lines, Rossi."

"Isn't that what you're teaching us to do?"

Vega was right. Linesmen could communicate mind to mind. Except, why did it have to be with Rossi, of all people?

Ean took a deep breath and tried to concentrate. "The new trainees are the crew of the *Eleven*," he said. "They'll be doing the same training you are. I want you to look after them." He frowned at them all. *"Be nice to your fellow lines.* If you treat them well, they may even invite you onto their ship one day."

He'd always planned to take the trainees to the *Eleven* to experience lines there, but a little bribery didn't hurt.

The overall emotion became more speculative, even calculating.

Sale took over. "They'll be arriving in three shuttles." One hundred and twenty people made for a lot of visitors.

She separated the trainees into two groups of seven, one of six. "Make them welcome, help them if they have problems. You know the drill, they don't."

Ean's hands were shaking. He tucked them under his armpits as he watched the group divide. "How long should we train this lot for before we send them back to their ships?" he asked Fergus and Radko. Every trainee was talking to the lines now. If they knew enough to help train the *Eleven*'s crew, did that mean they were ready to return to their own fleets?

"Depends what you want them for," Fergus said.

"And what damage sending them back half-trained will do," Rossi said.

"Even you, Rossi, fix lines straighter than you used to."

"And you think that's enough?"

"What do you think?"

Whatever Rossi thought was lost in his crossed arms and raised eyebrows and the arrival of the first shuttleload of *Eleven* crew onto the *Gruen*.

DAREJANI Tinatin was first off the ship, followed closely by Mael St. Mael.

"What is this place?" Tinatin asked. "It's sad. Just sad."

"Sick maybe," Mael said, looking around, his gaze stopping at the paramedics, and then at the oxygen stations along the wall. He shivered a little and checked his suit readings. Then leaned over and checked Tinatin's.

Ean heard a low hum of approval from Radko.

"We don't have to wear them," Tinatin said. "Just put them on."

Wasn't that wearing them? "How do you mean sad?" Ean asked.

"It's just—" Tinatin waved her arms around, almost braining Ean as she did so. "Sad. Someone should fix this ship."

"So what's wrong with it?" How strong was she if she could pick up the underlying emotion of the ship so quickly?

"She has no idea." The accent was Balian, short and sharp. Jem Abascal, the Balian seven. "She's guessing. She has no *real* line ability. She's a one."

Ean didn't need the nodded greeting to Ami Hernandez to know the two Balians had worked together in the past. Their lines were comfortable together.

"Yes. What would she know?" That was the six from the other night.

"I didn't say it was the lines," Tinatin protested. "I said it was a sad ship."

One of the linesmen already on the *Gruen*, Esfir Chantsmith, said, "It's not the ship's fault its lines are bad."

Chantsmith always defended the ship. Even when he wasn't

on it, like the time at the Night Owl, when Ean had read the transcript of his conversation with Solvej and Klim.

Ean smiled at them all. "It is about the lines, you know. And you're right. It is a sad ship. That was a good call. Line one is the crew line, and this ship doesn't have a strong line one."

"Crew line?" Mael asked.

"A ship with a well-knit crew who got on well together."

He'd bet the *Kari Wang*'s line one had been strong, but he'd never say that to the *Eleven*'s new captain, even though it was a compliment.

"Kari Wang was supposed to be on this shuttle," Sale said. She made for the shuttle door, but Mael stood in her way. "The captain will be out in a moment," he said. "She's just getting her legs together."

They looked at each other. Sale moved first. "Get this lot into the big cargo hold," she ordered the trainees assigned to mind them."

Mael made sure she moved away from the door before he moved.

Sale came over to Ean. "Tell me what's going on." She made it quiet.

Ean sang gently to line five. He couldn't see what was happening on the shuttle the way he could on a ship, but he could pull one of the camera feeds out through the line. And the audio.

It looked like a standoff, with Grieve holding a suit, saying, "We don't know what damage these untrained linesmen will do." Kari Wang didn't have a suit on yet. It looked as if everyone was holding their breath while they waited for her to decide.

"Not this again." Sale watched the comms over Ean's shoulder. "That woman has a real problem. You tell her," as Grieve opened his mouth to speak. "She can't keep doing this."

Kari Wang held up a hand. "Don't say anything. Jon, Fitch, leave please."

Jon would have argued, but Fitch pushed him out into the shuttle bay. Bhaksir went down to head them off.

Ean could see drops of moisture on Kari Wang's face. She was sweating badly. "Sorry," she said to Grieve. "Some days it's harder than others."

"I don't understand," Grieve said. "It saved your life. I would think you'd love to put it on."

"Exactly. It saved *my* life. When everyone else died."

Ean bit his bottom lip. Even Sale was quiet.

Kari Wang took a deep breath and struggled into the suit as clumsily as Ean had the first time he'd worn one. She sealed it with a little more finesse, leaving the helmet hanging down her back, then walked stiff-legged to the air lock.

SEVENTY certified linesmen, fifty presumed single-level linesmen—plus Kari Wang and her entourage, Sale and Bhaksir's teams, Ean, Fergus and Rossi, and who knew how many paramedics—filled the largest cargo space on the ship.

Ean made his way over to a temporary dais that had been erected on one end.

Tinatin, who had joined Mael, gestured toward the guards, then to Ean. He whispered a quick song to line one, to hear what she was saying.

"They're to make sure he doesn't escape. His cartel master has come back to collect him, but the New Alliance won't let him go."

Sale joined him on the dais. He stepped back to let her speak first.

"Note where the nearest oxygen cylinders are. Note where the paramedics are. Note where your assigned buddies are." Some of the assigned buddies were grinning, thinking they knew what was to come. They'd be disappointed, for fifty of the newcomers were single lines, and so far, single lines had not been troubled by line eleven.

It was the same talk she'd given to the original trainees.

"If you're in trouble, signal a paramedic. If the person next to you is in trouble, you've all been trained in how to deal with heart problems. You know what to do."

"I'll say," one of them close to Ean muttered. "They're anal about it. How many times in your life do you treat victims with heart problems?"

Fergus, who was standing nearby, murmured, "About twice a day, on average."

Ean hid his smile.

"All yours, Ean."

Ean sang the now-familiar explanation to the *Gruen* lines. *"Introducing more linesmen."*

"Mine?"

"Not this lot," and the hum of disappointment it returned made Tinatin frown. And, he noticed, Chantsmith wince.

Ean had to do something about Song. A ship shouldn't have to tolerate an absent captain.

When he was done, Ean put his comms on the podium in front of him and sang to open the lines to the speakers in the hold. "We're going to sing. Let's start with some warm-up exercises. Sing along with me."

One hundred and twenty musically gifted people made an impressive choir. No one complained. Had they already heard about line training?

Fergus moved through the crowd. He tapped the shoulder of a woman who was singing halfheartedly, and moved his hand up to show she should increase her performance. Even Rossi scowled at one less-than-enthusiastic performer.

The original trainees watched.

"Right," Ean said, after ten minutes of exercises. "Now we'll sing to the lines." There were a few uneasy mutters at that. Mostly from those with bars on their pockets. Ean ignored them. "We're greeting the lines, saying hello to them one at a time." He smiled. "And if you genuinely believe you are talking to them, don't be surprised if some of them answer back."

There were more uneasy looks, and lots of feet shuffling, but he didn't give them time to think about it. "Line one. You sing what I sing." He launched into song. *"Hello, hello, hello."*

There was a lot more halfheartedness about this particular exercise.

At least he could rely on people like Tinatin, who sang with gusto.

Ean stopped singing. "Line one is replying now," he said. "Some of you may hear it," and line one replied.

Tinatin's eyes widened, then rolled to show the whites. Kari Wang and Fergus both hurried forward, but Fergus was there first, putting a hand on her shoulder to support her. He must have been watching her.

Tinatin blinked at him.

Fergus smiled and gave her a thumbs-up, then rounded his thumb and forefinger in the universal "spot-on" sign.

He left her then, to move through the crowd and give the thumbs-up to other white-eyed individuals.

Tinatin didn't sing again.

AFTER line training Ean sought Tinatin out.

"What did you hear?" Tinatin was asking Mael.

"Me. I heard lots of people singing."

"When it talked back, I mean."

"It didn't talk to me," Mael said.

Ean joined them. "What did you hear?" he asked Tinatin.

She looked at her feet and shrugged.

"Come on," he coaxed. "What did you hear?" He wanted it in her own words.

She shook her head.

That was a pity, but the more he pushed, the less likely she was to answer. Ean considered what he should do next. "I heard it," he said. "It said hello back."

Her eyes widened.

"Come for a walk with me," Ean said.

She looked doubtfully at Mael.

"Team leaders won't be happy with us if we wander," Mael said.

"This is line work," Ean said. "This is important."

"Important for you, maybe, but you haven't got bosses like ours."

That was easily fixed. Ean called Kari Wang, who was at the shuttle. "Captain," he said, "I want to talk to two of your crew." He would have preferred Tinatin on her own, but Mael was obviously going to come along. "They may be delayed."

"Let me guess." She sounded resigned. "Tinatin and Mael."

"Yes." Why did it have to be them?

"Her crew?" Tinatin said to Mael behind him.

"I'll get Grieve to square it. If they miss the transport, you'll take responsibility for getting them back to barracks."

Radko moved up closer to the comms. "Yes, ma'am."

"Thank you." Kari Wang clicked off.

"How did she know it was Tinatin and Mael?" Ean asked Radko.

"I don't know, Ean. Maybe it has something to do with the way Tinatin heard the lines."

"Could even be because we're not on the shuttle," Mael said.

"Could be that, too," Radko agreed.

Fergus joined him and Radko as they started down the corridor. For a moment, Ean didn't think the spacers were going to follow.

"We got permission from the captain," Mael said to Tinatin. Ean heard it through the lines. Mael's voice didn't carry. "Don't you want to know more?"

Tinatin hurried after them, Mael more leisurely, but he had longer legs. "If she's our captain, does that mean we're crewing the alien ship?" she asked Mael.

"Probably."

"If it's not general knowledge, maybe you should keep it to yourself," Radko said.

"Captain Legless has been around enough that some of us were wondering already," Mael said.

Mael seemed the type who would pick up information like that. Michelle had told Ean the Aratogans had a lot of faith in Mael. They'd brought him back from the rim especially for this job even though they had a dozen failed linesmen to choose from, and other worlds didn't agree with their choice.

Mael's psychiatric assessments had pointed out some real problems. There had been one made by the Aratogan medic, the other made by the psychiatrist who'd arrived with Kari Wang.

The Aratogan report had been brief. *After so much time out on the rim may find it difficult to adjust to a more controlled environment.*

The Nova Tahitian psychiatrist had been blunt. *Sanity questionable. Has been demoted once. Does not follow orders well. Recommend he not continue with the program.*

If Mael worked out, Ean wanted whoever had chosen him to be on the team that chose future linesmen. Still, today, Ean wasn't here to talk to Mael although he would like to know what line he was. He was here to talk to Tinatin, who'd heard line one.

"What do you think lines are?" Ean asked Tinatin.

"Lines of energy. Havortian fields."

"Not what they tell you in the cartels. What do you really think lines are?"

She looked at him as if doubting his sanity.

"What does line one do then?"

"Nothing." Her reply held the bitterness of personal experience. "Nothing useful, anyway."

"It's the crew line," Ean said. "It tells you how the crew and the other lines on the ship are."

"You realize that's not how they put it in line training," Fergus said.

"It's not?" Ean had always known what line one did. He'd never considered he had it wrong. "What is it, then?"

"Let me remember. It was a long time ago."

Mael looked at him sharply.

"Something about the strength of the other lines."

It was that, sort of, but it was much more.

Fergus took out his comms and called up Rossi, who they'd left talking to Hernandez. "Jordan, what's the official definition of what line one does?"

"The bastard version or the cartel version?"

Behind him, Tinatin sucked in an awed breath. "That's Jordan Rossi," she whispered to Mael. "He's a level-ten linesman."

"So's that guy," Mael said quietly back, nodding at Ean.

"But Rossi's famous."

"Cartel version," Fergus said.

"It shows the strength of the other lines," Rossi said. "The health, if you want to put it in Lambert terms."

"Thanks." Fergus clicked off.

"You have Jordan Rossi on one-click on your comms." Tinatin was almost too awed for words. "And you don't even have to say who you are when you call him."

She obviously hadn't seen Rossi back in the training room. "He does have some friends," Ean said, then added hurriedly, in case Fergus thought Ean was talking about him. "Rossi, I mean." Fergus had hundreds of friends.

Fergus laughed. "Foot in mouth, Ean." He sobered. "They don't talk much about line one in training. Not from what I remember. I think it's mostly used by lower linesmen as a gauge to tell when they need a higher-level linesman for repairs."

"That's pretty much what they taught me, too," Mael said. He looked at Fergus. "You did line training?"

"Failed certification," Fergus said.

"Me, too."

Fergus nodded. "This is the best place to be right now for people like you and me."

"You are amazing," Tinatin told Fergus. "You get things. You know important people."

"Thank you." Fergus smiled at her. "Right now, one of those important people wants to talk to you about line one."

He didn't have to put it quite that way. Mael gave Ean a sharp look. Ean hoped he wasn't as pink as he felt.

"Line one. As Rossi said, the people and line health."

"I was *that* far away from someone talking to Jordan Rossi."

Ean wasn't sure to whom she was confiding. Maybe she wasn't sure herself.

Mael pushed her gently toward Ean.

Ean knew how to get a linesman's attention. He sang to the lines, especially to line one, and explained to it how the other line one wasn't listening at all.

"I *am* listening," Tinatin said.

He had to stop his triumphant "hah," for he hadn't actually spoken the words. "Why don't you sing with me then?"

She went shy on that.

Ean didn't push her. He could see she was the sort who might practice on her own, given enough encouragement. "I think we should go to another ship," he told Radko. "One that's not so sad."

"Confluence Station," Radko said.

He would have liked the *Lancastrian Princess*—Ean was as proud of her lines as Helmo was—but Radko wouldn't have agreed.

"Confluence Station," he agreed, and they made their way down to the shuttle, where Bhaksir and the rest of the team joined them.

They left the *Gruen* contented for the moment. After all, it had just been boosted by linesmen, but Ean knew he'd have to do something about the ship eventually. He also knew what Abram, Katida, and Orsaya would say. "Not important enough to worry about right now." He'd have to come up with a reason to make it important.

Tinatin spent half the journey to Confluence Station being awed by the fact that she was sharing a shuttle with Jordan Rossi, then regained some of her natural effervescence. "Did you know Confluence Station used to be at the confluence?"

"It was all over the vids," Fergus said, straight-faced.

She gave him a look that said her opinion of him was slipping. "I went there once. While it was the confluence. I didn't get any of the awe and wonder. Everyone else went 'ooh, aah, isn't it magnificent,' but it wasn't. It was ordinary." She cupped her chin in her hands. "Line ones don't even get that."

If they trusted her, now was the time to tell her the reason she hadn't gotten any of the awe was because she was a single level, not because she was a line one. Even Ean was smart enough to keep his mouth closed. He didn't need Radko's warning pressure on his arm to keep quiet.

"I thought it was ordinary, too," Fergus said.

Ean's comms beeped. It was Kaelea.

"Don't cut me off, Ean. For old times' sake."

"I'm listening," Ean said, for what else could he say? He moved away so Tinatin and Mael didn't hear as clearly, but they could, of course. Everyone could.

"You should talk to Rigel again. I know you think he did badly by you, but he's trying to help now."

"I don't think he did badly." He wished he wasn't holding this conversation on a ship with strangers. And Jordan Rossi. "I like it here. I like my job."

"You're a ten. You should be in a cartel house."

"Not going to happen, sweetheart," Rossi murmured, almost to himself.

Was he talking about Ean or thinking about himself?

"Ean. Are you—?"

He waited. There was a long pause.

"I need to talk to you."

"I'm not going back, Kaelea." The shuttle chimed for landing. "I have to go." Ean clicked off.

He could feel Rossi's amusement through the lines. That was normal. Ean could ignore that.

"The girlfriend?" Rossi's question was almost malicious.

"No."

But Rossi wasn't looking at him, he was looking at Radko. Radko looked daggers back.

Tinatin pursed her lips, but she didn't say anything as the shuttle had pulled into Confluence Station.

They exited onto the station as line eleven surged. How much did that surge have to do with Tinatin's disapproval? Or Radko's?

"Sometimes you need to get the whole story before you make snap judgments," Radko said to Tinatin. She lifted an oxygen tank off the wall.

"Don't need any." Although Ean did stagger a little as he made his way down the passage. "Listen to line one, Tinatin. What do you hear?"

He heard disappointment. Loud and clear. Coming from Tinatin. Maybe a bit from him, too, because he expected people to be continually impressed with the lines. He moved away to sing a greeting—for after all, he was on Confluence Station, so it was only polite to greet the station lines.

The lines greeted him back.

Tinatin didn't sing, but she heard.

"What did it say?" Mael asked.

"It said hello, like the other one." Tinatin glanced sideways at Ean. "And don't upset the other line. He's *our* line."

TWENTY-SIX

SELMA KARI WANG

HER DIVE OFF the stairs had unsettled Kari Wang.

If she hadn't tried so hard to save her life, she could have simply fallen to her death. Which was as it should have been, given her whole crew—and her ship—had already died. If she'd had time to think about it, would she have let herself fall?

After line training, Sale and her team took Kari Wang over to the *Eleven*, as if they expected that the more time she spent there, the more she would bond with the ship. She wouldn't.

She wandered the *Eleven*, melancholy and alone.

What could she have done to save her ship? Her crew?

Anything?

Nothing?

Something?

The *Eleven* was huge, but she was determined to walk the whole of it, no matter how long it took her, no matter how much her legs complained. It was her own penance, in a way, for surviving when everyone else had died.

The ship was made up of interlocking hexagonal blocks— six sides around, with a top and a bottom—linked together in a honeycomb. Some of the more modern Gate Union ships— the GU *MacIntyre*, the GU *Burnley*—used a similar honeycomb. The center hexagon housed the bridge with its line chassis. Each hexagon was surrounded by its own hexagonal corridor, with openings into other hexagons.

Kari Wang stopped to examine one of the openings.

It was thick enough to act as an air lock, and could close on demand. As yet, only Ean Lambert had managed to close them with any regularity.

"Line three," he'd told Kari Wang as he'd sung them closed. "You'll have lots of people who can open or close them."

Kari Wang had held her breath until he'd opened them again, and decided that meant her crew would have to go around in pairs, for single-level linesmen would never be able to close the doors.

They'd traced the airflow, heating, and cooling. They *thought* each hexagon could be self-sufficient. If they could work out how they were fueled.

As for the fuel source. That was built into the exterior surface of each hexagon, and so far as they could determine worked together to produce power similar to the way a Bose engine did. Kari Wang was glad so many of the crew were sixes. The way they explained it to her, every wall was part of the engine. The propulsion units were hundreds of tiny jets built into the same surface. It was, as Spacer Craik said, a bitch to drive. Although, once they worked out how to pilot it, it was going to be the most accurate ship anyone had flown.

Where had the hexagonal design come from?

Young Benita Chay, from her own ship, would have known. Chay had been passionate about ships, spending all her off-duty time with the engineers. So much so that Kari Wang had investigated what training had been available to turn a spacer into an engineer.

The reply from Fleet was still unread in her comms.

She pulled her comms out now, and had to work out how to scroll through old messages.

"State of the art," Grieve had said, when he'd given it to her.

"I'll try not to break this one."

The joke had gone flat. Grieve wasn't responding well to lighthearted right now.

She found the message.

Yes, a spacer could become an engineer. Even better, Fleet offered traineeships, which meant Chay could earn while she learned and spend most of her time on her home ship if her captain was agreeable. Chay would have loved it.

Kari Wang deleted the message with a savage swipe. Except, of course, she wasn't familiar with the new-style comms and the message wouldn't go. It took three tries, and by the end of it she was blinking so furiously, she couldn't see the screen.

* * *

KARI Wang reached the outer edge and followed the ramp up to the top level of hexagons. She ended up in a storeroom. Most of the storerooms were still half-full. A ship partway through a long voyage, Kari Wang decided.

Much like her own had been.

The day before the end, she'd walked with Will through chambers like this.

Sure, the computers could tell her what was there, but she liked to get a feel herself. A half-full store told a better story than figures on a screen. Plus, it was a good place to think, or to talk privately.

Will had wanted to talk about the tests they were carrying out.

"I'm worried about them," he'd admitted.

"I thought they were going well."

"Too well," he'd said. "They're giving us exactly the results we're expecting. It's like we're testing weapons that have been in service for years. So much so I wonder what we *are* testing, if it's not the weapons themselves."

"So you think they haven't given us the real thing?"

"I don't know what they've given us," Will said. "Maybe we're decoys while they test it elsewhere. Or maybe we're not testing the weapons at all. Maybe we're testing something else."

Gate Union had spent 10 million credits modifying Kari Wang's ship for this mission, and a billion credits on the weapons they were to test, so they were testing something. But Will had good instincts. "What else could it be?"

"I don't know. Maybe the equipment we're using to test it with. Why else give us something we can predict the results on?"

"They look like new weapons."

Will gave a disparaging snort. "A pretty package doesn't make any difference. I'm telling you, those weapons are not new." He'd worked with weapons all his career. He'd know. "You know what I'm worried about. That someone promised Gate Union weapons they couldn't build, and now they're trying to cover it up. And we're part of that cover-up."

"I'll check it out," Kari Wang had promised.

It was another thing she hadn't finished.

Kari Wang sighed and looked at the boxes stacked in the storeroom. This particular storeroom was full of empty packaging.

Aliens and humans had a lot in common. They both recycled their rubbish. Which was common sense. In space, waste was your enemy.

They both used nets to secure their cargo although the alien nets were made of a light metal-carbon mesh and took two people to secure—four-handed aliens meant Kari Wang's crew would perpetually work in pairs—while human nets were lock and click.

And, of course, there was the hexagonal shape of the modules the ships were built with.

She didn't want to return to the bridge, so she made her way to one of the weapons bays on the outer perimeter of the ship. The place where her own crew would have congregated. Not everyone was convinced they were weapons bays, but Kari Wang *knew* they were.

Ean Lambert joined her there, the ever-present Radko beside him.

"Tinatin and Mael are on their way back to Haladea III." He looked as if he was about to say something else. Didn't. Instead, he sang softly to the ship. A song of comfort. She got the impression the song was directed as much at her as it was at the ship.

Kari Wang wished he'd go away. "Why don't you take that elsewhere?"

Lambert stopped singing. Listened. Then sang again. "She's miserable. She's sore. Her other lines died. Give her time."

A rush of adrenaline carried her across to him. Spacer Radko stepped between them. "He's a line, ma'am. It's how he communicates. Lines share information, whether you like it or not."

Lambert didn't even notice. "Sore? Like . . . broken lines." He glanced her way, stepped back, as if startled at seeing her so close. "No. Not fix. Human lines. They're fragile."

"All your crew will communicate aurally," Radko said. "Lines share. Nothing is private. You'll need to get used to it."

Kari Wang turned away.

She looked around the weapons bay, trying to shut them out. Spacer Radko loomed tall and menacing nearby. She was harder to shut out than Lambert himself, and Kari Wang had no doubt she'd protect her charge by any means necessary.

Lambert had gone back to his original song of comfort. Coaxing the lines, calming them. At least, that was what it sounded like.

If only he would shut up.

She ran her hands over the outside casing of the bay. It didn't fit right. Will would have decreed it damaged.

Lambert stopped singing again. She heard voices in the corridor. Grieve and Fitch, coming their way. Her blessed isolation was rapidly filling with unwanted people. She blocked them out and turned back to the casing. "This mechanism is damaged. It must be fixed before anyone uses it."

Lambert's silence was different this time. She turned and glared at him. He hurriedly started singing again, an obvious explanation of what she had just said. He broke off halfway through. "Yes. That's exactly the problem." His face split into a wide smile. "The ship is happy you understand."

"We need to go back," Grieve said.

Kari Wang gave a last backward look as she went. It was like leaving something familiar.

Like leaving the *Kari Wang*.

Surely not.

"Are you okay?" Lambert asked.

"I'm fine," she said. "I need to visit—" a ship like her own, whose weapons bays would be similar to the *Kari Wang*'s. "The *Wendell*."

"Right now?" Grieve asked, and she detected a hint of martyrdom in his voice. "Because we've a schedule."

"After I've finished for the day," she amended, and added, "I'll let you wheel me back to the shuttle." It would be a slow trip back if she had to walk it, for the long walk around the ship was starting to catch up with her.

He opened the chair for her.

Lambert and his song followed them all the way back.

* * *

AS soon as the shuttle was under way, she pulled out her comms and called up the *Wendell*.

"Piers," she said, when Captain Wendell's face came up on her comms. "I want to come out to your ship. I want to look at your weapons bays."

"That's not going to do you a lot of good," Wendell said. "Unless you want to see empty space. The New Alliance pulled out the weapons when they captured the *Wendell*. They haven't put most of it back yet. We've six working cannons, and that's only after we promised, on our life, not to fire at anyone."

She didn't have to listen hard to find the sarcasm. "Damn."

"What was it you wanted to see?"

"I'm not sure. Something familiar, I think."

Wendell must have stepped back for a better look at her face, for his own face receded, then came back into view. He ran his fingers through his hair, which needed a redye. She could see the white-blond coming through underneath the maroon. His real hair was as white as his skin.

"What about the *Gruen*? I don't think they pulled it apart."

Why would they pull the innards out of one ship and not the other?

She'd been on the *Gruen* earlier, when the *Eleven* crew had done their line training. She'd never looked at their weapons bays. Maybe she should simply wait until they went over again. No, she needed to see it while the thought was still fresh. "Sure."

He arranged to send someone to collect her after her meeting with the admirals. "You'll have to organize it. I'm not cleared for the *Gruen*."

"Why, because it's got weapons on it?" They were on the same side, for lines' sake. Even if the rest of Wallacia wasn't.

"Something like that," Wendell admitted.

GETTING clearance for Wendell took some talking but she got it—with the proviso that Captain Song be present while he was there, and met Wendell for a quick trip over to the *Gruen* later that day.

"It's probably the first time Edie Song has been on her ship in weeks," Wendell said. "It's almost a demotion for her, given she's stuck in a fleet she can't get out of, with only a skeleton crew. She resents it."

Lambert had sought out Song the previous day. What had he said to her? Kari Wang was torn between a sneaking sympathy for the captain who would have had dreams of glory, only to find she was in charge of a ship that would never be used in war, and disgust that a captain could neglect her own ship so.

"She doesn't spend much time on her ship," Wendell said. "Definitely not enough to bond with it. I'm not sure how you'll go with your ship, actually. Not if you can't jump in it."

Why would Wendell assume you needed to jump to bond with your ship?

"We're here." The trip had been so smooth, Kari Wang hadn't felt the deceleration. Or the docking.

Captain Song and Team Leader Perry met them there. Song was younger than Kari Wang had expected, and her Standard was upper-class. Grieve had said Song's promotion was political. Kari Wang had seen promotions like that on Nova Tahiti. They didn't always make good battleship captains. The *Gruen* was a good ship for her, given it was unlikely to ever go into battle.

Kari Wang handed over her comms, with the approval thumbed by all four admirals. "We want to see your weapons bays."

Song didn't even look at it. She nodded at Perry, who led the way around to the first bay.

"As you can see, they've left me with nothing."

"At least you have a full complement of weapons," Wendell said.

"What use are weapons if you never get to use them?"

"You never know when you might need them," Wendell said.

Her glance was contemptuous. "As if *you'll* ever use weapons again. Face it, Captain Wendell, you're a prisoner in enemy territory. You're lucky they let you keep your ship."

Kari Wang felt a surge of anger on his behalf.

"No one takes my ship away from me," Wendell said. His voice was relaxed, but Kari read determination in Wendell's demeanor. He smiled. "Or from my crew." He glanced around the weapons bay. "But if you're looking to off-load any of these useless weapons, you know where to send them."

Kari Wang couldn't tell if he was serious.

The weapons bay could have been found on any Gate Union ship. And no doubt on most of the New Alliance ships. There was nothing about it that reminded her of the *Eleven*. Nothing in any of the bays reminded her of the *Eleven*.

Afterward, the three of them went back to a bar on Haladea III. The more Song drank, the more bitter she became about her "promotion."

"My former captain said he'd rather jump into the void and stay there than travel on a ship I commanded. I showed him. Then they gave me this piece of shit."

Kari Wang was glad they were off ship. You didn't insult your ship while you were on it. Most captains didn't insult their ship off it, either.

"Another drink?" Song asked.

"Not for me," Kari Wang said. "I'm still on medication."

"And I'm on duty when I get back on board," Wendell said. "Can't set a bad example."

"Who cares what example you set? You're a prison captain on a prison ship. No one cares."

What did the woman want? To twist the knife?

"I care. My crew cares."

"Your crew—"

Song could insult Wendell as much as she wanted to, but you never insulted Wendell's crew or his ship.

"Enough on the negatives," Kari Wang said sharply. "We're all in the same situation. Let's dwell on the good for a change."

"There isn't any good," Song said. "Another drink?"

When Song passed out, they helped her to her quarters. Afterward, Kari Wang walked back to the spaceport with Wendell.

"What are we going to do about Song?" Wendell asked, as they paused at the gate.

She'd been wondering that herself. "Lambert paid her a visit yesterday. He might convince her to spend more time on her ship." After which it would be their job to merge her in as a functioning member of the team.

Not that Kari Wang wanted to be a member of that team, either, but she didn't say that to Piers Wendell.

THE next day Jon, Fitch, and Grieve all asked if she'd enjoyed her night out, and teased her about her nonexistent headache.

"I've some salts if you need them," Fitch offered.

"I'll suffer," she said.

The mystery of the familiarity of the *Eleven*'s weapons bays continued to haunt her. That afternoon, as she listened to Admiral MacClennan outline Speaker Rhodes's latest grievance, it finally struck her what it was.

She sat up, cutting across MacClennan's words. "The new weapons we were testing on the *Kari Wang*. They were based on alien technology."

The admirals looked at her as if she were alien herself.

"That's not logical," MacClennan said.

"It has to be." She looked around the table. "The weapons setup we were testing. The weapons bays were *exactly* like those on the *Eleven*." Or close enough to it that she could recognize them.

"Gate Union doesn't have alien technology," MacClennan said.

"They do." What's more, they'd had it for a while. "Weapons aren't the only things they've built based on that technology. The *MacIntyre*, the *Burnley*. They're building ships based on it."

Galenos blew out his breath. "What makes you think that?" He looked exhausted.

"Other than the weapons bays they built on the *Kari Wang*?" He nodded. "Ships, you say."

"The honeycomb design they're using for the newer ships."

Orsaya said, "I can honestly say I never heard any mention of alien ships or alien technology while I was at Gate Union."

"Me either," MacClennan said.

Neither had Kari Wang. "They've got an alien ship somewhere," she said. "They've had it awhile. Will was right. We weren't testing new weapons at all. We were testing the weapons bays."

* * *

AFTER the admiral's meeting, as Grieve took Kari Wang home, he said, "I've done some research on those contractors. The ones who did the stairwell. They're dead. All of them. Their bodies were found three days ago."

"What? They fell through one of their own jobs?" but Grieve still wasn't responding well to jokes.

"They'd been dead seven days."

The stairs had been done six days ago.

"Are you sure?"

"The coroner's sure. They got dumped in the Darling trench, which is twenty kilometers out to sea."

Murdered, he was saying. The day before they'd worked on the stairs.

Grieve's smile was grim but triumphant. "Opinion is the bodies weren't dumped by a local because the locals know you never dump anything there, even weighted. There's a microscopic sea creature that feasts on dead flesh. It fastens on and starts to dissolve flesh, bone, and muscle. Eventually, body parts drop off." Grieve gave a half shrug. "They float up. The coroner can tell from the growth patterns and thickness of the growth on the limbs how long the sea creature has been reproducing."

"How long before that did you hire them?"

"Two days. They checked out. They still check out." The last was almost defiant. A subconscious attempt to tell her *he* hadn't slipped up. Even if he didn't realize it.

"How many jobs have these imposters done since ours?"

"None," Grieves said. "Everyone is crying out for tradesmen. They could have kept going until the police arrived to pick them up. But they didn't. After they did your stairs, they disappeared." She didn't need him to spell it out, but he did. "Someone weakened that frame deliberately. They wanted you to fall."

The aircar pulled up at the barracks. Kari Wang stood up.

Grieve blocked her way. "Somebody tried to murder you," he said. "Is it wise to go out of the safety of your own rooms before we determine who it is?"

"Someone tried to murder me on my own ship, too." Her voice was brittle.

"That was different. Back then, you weren't the captain of an alien spaceship."

For a moment she saw black rage. "You say my crew is less important than this? My crew's being murdered is nothing, compared to now, when I was almost murdered because of what I can do for you. When I—" She pushed past him, so hard, she knocked him against the door of the aircar. She misstepped, and tumbled out onto the landing floor.

It hurt, and she wasn't sure she hadn't done more damage.

"Don't say anything," she said to Grieve, who'd jumped out behind her. "And don't, whatever you do, call Fitch," for he'd taken out his comms. "Or Jon."

"But you might be—"

"Give me a minute." Captain's voice. Commanding. "Let me sit until I recover."

He put his comms away and hovered.

She sat on the ground until the nausea subsided. "Thank you," she said when she could stand up. "Can you help me up please?" He would anyway, and she'd prefer she controlled the stand-up.

He helped her stand.

"I apologize for my behavior before."

"*I* apologize," Grieve said. "I shouldn't have made it sound so trivial."

She cut him off before he could dig himself in deeper, or before she misconstrued whatever he said next. "The workers on the frame. Did they look like the original crew, or didn't they bother to disguise themselves?" She didn't want to know, but she didn't want to talk about her crew.

Thankfully, it turned the conversation.

"Right down to the eye color," Grieve said. "One of the murdered men was a native Gallardian, with that distinctive purple ring you get around the iris."

Kari Wang nodded.

"They brought in a native Gallardian to replace him."

It was the sort of puzzle that would have fascinated Will. He'd be looking at all the nuances around it, too. Like how, when everyone was complaining about getting jumps, could they possibly have gotten a native Gallardian in time to replace someone who'd only been booked two days earlier.

And how much rank had Grieve pulled to get the job done so quickly, given the long waiting list for work.

Grieve might have been reading her thoughts. "We pulled in a lot of favors. It's one of the reasons we didn't pick it up earlier. Everyone thought the workmen were still doing our job—because they hadn't done anything since."

Forcing someone off the side of a building was usually a sure way to kill them. Kari Wang shivered. She'd been lucky to get away with skin scraped raw and some bruises.

She remembered the last time she'd been badly bruised. The out-of-control aircar, and Mael and Tinatin pushing her to the ground. What if that had been deliberate?

"You're certain someone is trying to kill me?"

"Yes."

"Remember the first time I broke my comms, when Mael and Tinatin picked me up."

"How could I forget? We had half the barracks out looking for you."

"Maybe you should investigate that. I think someone might have tried to kill me then as well."

TWENTY-SEVEN

EAN LAMBERT

VEGA WAS WAITING for Ean at the shuttle bay when he arrived back on the *Lancastrian Princess* after training.

"Linesman," and she walked with him.

He hesitated. He'd planned on going back to his cabin, wasn't sure what he should do now. She hadn't asked him to come to her office.

"This won't take long."

He kept walking.

Vega glanced at Radko, who followed them. "If you're going to listen in, you might as well come closer, so I don't have to raise my voice."

"Yes, ma'am," and Radko moved up so she was only two lengths behind them. Ean glanced back at her. He couldn't tell what she was thinking. He couldn't tell what Vega was thinking, either.

"The investigation into the incident at Barracks 24 is complete."

The "incident" where Radko and the others had nearly died. Where Radko had saved his life. Again. He couldn't tell what Vega thought. There was the usual hint of impatience through the lines he always associated with Vega but no strong emotions like irritation.

"They got in through the ceiling."

Ean could have told her that.

"The gas they used knocks you out after ten minutes, kills you after thirty. They carried oxygen. We surmise they planned on waiting till everyone was unconscious, giving you oxygen, and sneaking you away, leaving the others to die."

They wouldn't know Bhaksir's team carried oxygen with them everywhere.

"We have confirmed that the two people who died were part of the team that attacked you earlier that night, which means both attacks were from the same source."

Ean knew that as well. The other man, though, the one who'd "helped" in the first incident, hadn't been at the barracks. He was sure of that.

"Luis Mendez," Vega said. She gave a sour smile. "Luckily—or maybe unluckily for you—you aren't the only one people are trying to kill. Captain Kari Wang took an unexpected dive off a building recently. Most people wouldn't have survived it. Sometime before that, she was almost hit by an out-of-control aircar. You admired her bruise, I believe."

Kari Wang hadn't said someone had tried to kill her back when she'd had that first bruise.

"That makes at least three times," Radko said. "If you count the destruction of her ship."

"Yes," Vega said. "It's almost as if having missed killing her the first time, they'll keep trying until they do."

Ean shivered.

"That's Nova Tahiti's problem," Vega said.

"She's captain of the *Eleven*," Ean said. "We have to keep her alive."

"She's doing fine by herself so far. And you can be sure Nova Tahiti will do its best. It is to their advantage, after all. She's not my concern."

Ean waited. There must be more.

There was.

"Remember Professor Gerrard, whose ship was destroyed the same way Kari Wang's was?"

How could he forget? "You think whoever destroyed Gerrard's ship, and the *Kari Wang*, have come back to kill Kari Wang?"

"I'm sure of it," Vega said. "What's more, we now know who sponsored Professor Gerrard's research. Research that conveniently took him away from studying line ships. A company called SevenHills Consolidated."

She paused, as if expecting Ean to recognize the name.

Radko rescued him. "Redmond?"

"Redmond," Vega confirmed. "And it may be coincidence, but SevenHills Consolidated is a major shareholder in the company that designed the weapons the *Kari Wang* was testing."

"You think Redmond is trying to kill Kari Wang?"

"Probably," Vega said. "There's more. Our friend Luis Mendez was kicked out of the Roscracian fleet on suspicion of selling military secrets. They couldn't pin it on him— otherwise, he'd be in prison now, not free here on Haladea III. He sold those secrets to SevenHills Consolidated.

EAN wasn't surprised when Abram called him up the next day and arranged to meet him on the *Eleven* before line training.

Abram brought Kari Wang, Piers Wendell, Jita Orsaya, and Marsh MacClennan with him. They stopped at the air lock of the shuttle bay and let Kari Wang enter first.

"Requesting permission to come aboard," Abram said, formally.

It made Ean shiver.

Kari Wang was equally formal. "Permission granted."

Ean hadn't seen an admiral on the ship since the early days. Come to think of it, this had to be Wendell's first trip.

He let Kari Wang lead the way and fell in beside Wendell. "It's impressive, isn't it?"

Wendell nodded as he looked around.

"So what's this about?" Ean asked. No one looked likely to tell him if he didn't ask.

"We're trying to work out if Redmond has an alien ship hidden away somewhere," Abram said. "Or maybe saw these ships before Haladea did."

After Vega's pronouncement, it wasn't unexpected. "Maybe someone sold them pictures of the *Eleven*."

Abram shook his head. "If they have one, they've had it for years."

Redmond had tried to take over Haladea before the war had escalated. The then-Alliance had sent in ships in exchange for access to the *Eleven*. Maybe Redmond knew the ships were nearby. Maybe the *Eleven* hadn't been alone.

"Let's look at the weapons bays," Orsaya said.

Ean let Kari Wang lead.

"On the way, we'll check how the sections interlock," Abram said to Wendell.

They stopped at each of the sections, so Wendell could see.

"Maybe," Wendell said after the third. "The *MacIntyre* does link together in a honeycomb like this."

Captain MacIntyre had shown Ean over the whole GU *MacIntyre*. He'd been proud of his ship. "The sections are made of titanium-bialer alloy," Ean said, digging the knowledge out of his memory. "They can withstand the direct hit of a million-terajoule bomb."

All three admirals turned to look at him.

Ean colored. "Captain MacIntyre—" had been the first captain who'd treated him like a level-ten linesman. "He was proud of his ship."

"He *was* proud of it," Wendell said. "Justifiably so."

Ean dug out more memories. "If one section gets damaged, you can unlink it from the rest."

"Much like you can with the *Eleven*, I imagine," Abram said. He tapped eleven-beat on a nearby console. "Let's see a weapons bay."

Wendell took one look at those and shook his head. "Never seen anything like these."

"Not even on the *MacIntyre*?"

"The *MacIntyre* had the same weapons we had."

"So they had ship knowledge before they had weapons knowledge. They've had it for years, and none of you had heard about it."

Orsaya and MacClennan shook their heads. Kari Wang, too. Wendell, frowning, didn't.

"The weapon system we were testing was designed by a private company," MacClennan said. "We all knew about it, but it was horrendously expensive. Too much for a single world. It was a Redmond company, but Redmond didn't have the ships or the money to test it. They proposed a joint trial. There was no mention of alien technology."

Orsaya nodded.

"Gate Union put up half the money on condition a Gate Union ship tested it. Roscracia tried hard to have one of their ships test it, but they were overruled because Will

Merricks"—he nodded respectfully to Kari Wang—"the *Kari Wang*'s third-in-command, was a weapons expert."

"There was no mention of special ships when they installed the weapons system," Kari Wang said. "My crew would have picked up on that."

Ean dropped behind to walk with Wendell on the way back. "You knew about the weapons?"

Wendell shrugged. "Gossip only. Ric MacIntyre had it from one of the engineers who worked on his ship. They mentioned a weapons system and implied it was line-based."

Alien ships. Linesmen. That made sense. "If it's based on alien technology," Ean said, "there has to be a ship out there. How could anyone keep that a secret?"

"We don't know how long the *Eleven* was here before Haladea found it," Abram reminded him. "They still haven't said how long they knew about it before they called us in."

"Even the confluence was discovered by accident," Orsaya said.

Wendell said, "The *MacIntyre* was a prototype, the first of four. A company called TwoPaths Engineering built them."

Another Redmond company? How significant was that?

Orsaya wrinkled her nose as if she smelled something bad. "All these alien ships appearing in human space suddenly. I'll take the coincidence of the *Eleven* and the *Confluence* fleet. I somehow feel they're related. But I can't believe a third ship just 'appeared,' given the last and only ship we have found before this was five hundred years ago."

"If two ships can appear, why not three?" Abram asked. "Provided we assume they all arrived at the same time."

When MacIntyre had given Ean the grand tour, he'd told him they'd spent years designing and building the ship. How could ships like the *Eleven* and the *Confluence* have been around so long without anyone's finding them?

TWENTY-EIGHT

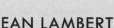

EAN LAMBERT

THEY'D REACHED AN impasse on line seven. Community, linking, completeness, and a very strong sense of the void. Ean was starting to wonder if Fergus was right, and line seven did something in the void that humans weren't equipped to work with. For most humans—except him—the time in the void was a microsecond. Maybe they didn't stay long enough to discover what line seven did.

Next time he was in the void, he was going to ask the lines there, but no one would let him jump just to ask line seven a question.

Meantime, they kept trying.

Maybe they were asking the wrong ship. Most of their testing was done on the *Lancastrian Princess*.

Maybe it was time to bring in others.

He took Fergus, Rossi, and Hernandez out to the *Eleven* with him. And Radko, of course. Captain Kari Wang hadn't arrived yet. It was the day after the revelation that Redmond was building their ships to an alien design. Ship mood was somber.

Rossi looked at Ean. "Someone's depressed."

It was Ean's mood the ship was reflecting.

"So this is the famous *Eleven*," Hernandez said, saving Ean from having to reply to Rossi. "It looks like . . . a ship."

"Mine?" the *Eleven* asked, a line chorus of hope, all the way up to eleven. It sent Rossi and Hernandez to the floor and Ean to his knees.

It took Ean a moment to understand what it was asking. *"Not this one. You know who yours are."* The crew might not have come on ship yet, but they sang to the *Eleven* every day.

Instead of becoming disappointed, the ship brightened. It took Ean another moment to realize that the shuttle bearing

Kari Wang had arrived. *"This one's mine."* It wasn't a question, it was a statement.

"Yes. This one's yours."

They waited to greet the captain. It was only polite on her ship.

Kari Wang was accompanied by her usual retinue. Doctors Fitch and Ofir and Spacer Grieve. Did she ever get time alone?

She greeted them with frosty civility. "As you were," she said.

That felt strange, too, someone's telling Ean to relax on a ship that hitherto he'd had free rein on. Worse, the other linesmen felt his discomfort, for they all looked at him strangely.

He concentrated on what they were there for. "Let's sing to the ship, ask line seven what it does."

He tried to relax as the song soared in the large space. The *Eleven* had superb acoustics, no matter where you were on ship.

Rossi and Hernandez sang directly to the seven on the *Eleven.* Fergus, as usual, sang to all the sevens. He really couldn't sing to just a single line. He was aware of the ship seven, and singing directly to it, but he was singing to the other sevens at the same time.

All the sevens answered him back, too.

As Ean listened, he thought about Abram's visit of the previous day and the discovery that Redmond had access to an alien ship.

The Alliance had only discovered the *Eleven* after Redmond had tried to annex the Haladean cluster. Maybe Redmond's reason for attempting to take over Haladea in the first place was because there were alien spaceships nearby. In which case, the ships would be in this sector.

The linesmen finished their session with no more idea on what line seven did than they had before they started.

"Any other bright ideas?" Rossi asked.

Not about line seven, no, but, "I want to contact other ships," Ean said. "You can tell the difference between human and alien ships, can't you?"

"Of course." Each alien ship was unique, but the human-built line ships all had undertones of the *Havortian.*

"So you'll recognize another alien ship if you hear it." If this worked, it would be so simple. "I want us to sing to every line five we can hear. There's another alien ship out there. I want to find it."

"Another one?" Fergus said.

Rossi didn't look surprised. Orsaya must have already mentioned it to him.

"Some real work at last," Hernandez said.

"If you think I'm singing to every ship and shuttle in the Haladean sector, you can think again," Rossi said. "You're talking thousands of lines."

He had a point.

"Why don't you ask your precious lines to find it for you? They'd do it faster."

"If there is another ship, *I'd* like to find it," Hernandez said.

"Sweetheart, there are a thousand ships around Haladea III right now, and the lines know how many shuttles as well. We're not all like the one-man choir here. *We* have to contact them one at a time. We'd be at it the rest of our lives."

Ean was glad Fergus asked, "Can you only talk to one line at a time?" because otherwise he would have. "I thought you could hear them all."

"Hear, yes. Talk to and get an answer. That's one-on-one."

"So the lines and I talk, and you listen." Ean tried not to be daunted by the numbers Rossi had given. He could use line one and line five, so he was just talking to ships, not to ships and shuttles. It was still a lot of ships. At least Haladea wasn't one of the busy commercial hubs—or not yet, anyway.

"We're talking to all the ships we can contact," he told line five. *"I want you to contact the ones on each ship. Say hello, and how is your ship."*

He sang with line five.

The noise of the replies drowned him. He couldn't stop it. He couldn't block it. The sound crashed down on him.

He came around to an oxygen mask over his face, and Radko wadding her jacket under his head. "Let's not try that again," she said.

"Lines a little strong for you, Linesman?" Rossi asked.

Rossi and Hernandez were both fine.

*   *   *

EAN couldn't tell if any of the ships that had replied were of alien origin. There had been too much noise. And Rossi was right, it would take a long time to talk to each ship individually. Not only that, ships jumped in and out of the sector all the time.

There had to be a better way to discover alien ships. But how?

The first thing Radko did when they got back on the *Lancastrian Princess* was take him down to see the medic.

"I'm fine," Ean said. He avoided the medic when he could.

"Whether you are or not," Radko said, "you're going to see him."

One didn't argue with Radko when she'd made up her mind.

"What's he done now?" the medic asked.

"He was singing to the lines," Radko said. "He collapsed."

Which was really going to endear him to the medic, who was convinced Ean would someday turn them into a crazy ship, like the *Balao*.

"Let me look at him." The medic prepared him for the first test. This involved putting a sensor net over Ean's head and taking readings. He had twenty such tests, none of which had existed before Ean had come on board. They were the medic's own invention. Ean wasn't sure if they worked or not, but he was sure of one thing. The medic liked building gadgets. "What exactly did you do?"

"I was singing to ships. Other ships. Lines one and five."

"They've never knocked you out before." The medic compared the readings against a chart of old readings.

"The first time he was on the *Eleven*, he collapsed," Radko said.

"He *said* he was over the alien ships' knocking him out."

Sensory overload, and Radko was right, as usual. "These weren't alien ships," Ean said. "These were human ships. I just contacted a lot of them at once."

"Strikes me you shouldn't have been contacting a lot of other ships anyway," the medic said. "Outside of the alien fleet, I mean. Sing to line one."

Everyone had ideas on what Ean should and shouldn't be doing. He obediently sang to line one. *"Testing my line. How is the ship?"*

The line answer was a mix of sound—*"Lines are good. Ship is good"*—colors, scents, and images. Ean saw a quick succession of Captain Helmo talking with his second-in-command, soldiers going about their business, other soldiers climbing on the big nets in the cargo space Helmo had emptied for them, and, lastly, a berry-scented image of one of the engineers asleep in a bed in the medicenter.

"What's wrong with Jaffir?"

"Fell down the stairs coming back from the Night Owl," Radko said, when the medic just grunted. "Lucky he only fell one flight."

If they were the stairs Ean had run down after his own visit to the Night Owl, Jaffir was lucky indeed. "Is he hurt?" He was careful to say "hurt" and not "damaged." Sometimes he forgot and used line terminology for everything. Radko understood, but the medic took it as a sign of a crazy line.

"Watching for concussion," the medic said. "He hit his head. Now, I need some blood."

Not that Ean knew what blood had to do with line ability, but this was part of the ritual.

He followed the medic's instructions automatically and thought about what to do next. Redmond had a line ship, according to Abram, but if he couldn't start from that ship, where else could he start?

Through the lines, Vega's voice rose in exasperation. "Luckily—or maybe unluckily for you—" Someone else was getting a tongue-lashing from her.

It seemed to be a favorite phrase of hers. She'd said the same thing to him the other day. "Luckily—or maybe unluckily for you, you aren't the only person people are trying to kill," she'd told him. She'd been talking about Captain Kari Wang.

After which they'd gotten on to Redmond, then Professor Gerrard, who'd presumably sold a secret about the *Havortian* to Redmond in exchange for funding for Gerrard's project.

Maybe whatever Gerrard had told them had allowed them to find this other alien ship.

If he couldn't find the ship itself, maybe he could start by finding out what Gerrard had discovered.

HE called Orsaya once the medic had finished with him.

"Admiral Orsaya. You must have checked Professor Gerrard's work on the *Havortian*. Before he stopped it, I mean." How did you ask in a nice way if she'd stolen his research?

She looked as if she could see right through him. She probably could.

"You think you can get something when I've had a team working on this for five years. Longer."

When she put it that way, it was unlikely. "I've had more experience with alien ships," Ean said. "Maybe I'll find something you missed."

"Maybe I should have put Linesman Rossi onto it," but seconds later the information started scrolling through to Ean's comms. Exabytes and exabytes of it.

"Thank you," Ean said. All that data. It was almost as bad as talking to all the ships in the sector at once.

There had to be a better way.

He clicked off and scrolled through the data. Orsaya was right. She'd already been through this. There'd be nothing here to find.

If *he'd* been Professor Gerrard, he wouldn't have given Redmond the only copy of his work. He'd have a backup somewhere. Orsaya should have found it already.

Unless Gerrard carried it with him. It would be too precious to leave behind. He'd have taken it with him to the edge of the galaxy. Orsaya would have been too busy with New Alliance politics to follow up on Gerrard.

This time Ean called Abram. "Gerrard's ship," he said, without even waiting to say hello. "Did they collect the bodies?"

"Every single piece they could," Abram confirmed, and Ean remembered that some of the bodies would have been in pieces. How big a job had it been, collecting them all?

He grimaced. "I need to see everything Gerrard had on him."

TWENTY-NINE

―✦―

STELLAN VILHJALMSSON

STELLAN HEARD ABOUT Lambert's visit to Song but hadn't been able to get anywhere close. He knew the linesman's movements well by now. The mornings were spent training other linesmen. They did that on New Alliance warships—if there were any booked up for repair—or on the *Gruen*.

Of all the things the New Alliance had done in this war, keeping the *Gruen* irked Stellan the most. There were two possible outcomes for a ship captured in battle. You took it to the scrap heap and turned it into parts, or you stripped it of anything remotely belonging to the defeated party, renamed it, and brought it back into service as a new ship.

Instead, the *Gruen* sat there—untouched, unmanned—like a trophy they flaunted in the face of those who had lost the battle.

In the afternoon, Lambert usually went out to the alien ships. Getting to them was about as likely as flying to the largest moon of Haladea III without a suit. There was a four-thousand-kilometer exclusion zone. Get any closer without permission, and you got fried.

Stellan didn't plan to go near the alien ships. Nor anywhere near the warships. They were too well guarded. The *Gruen*, now. Captain Edie Song spent a lot of time on planet. But she did, on occasion, go out to her ship.

Stellan already knew Captain Edie Song better than her crew did.

Not that she had much of a crew. Song must have pissed someone off badly to end up with a barely manned ship. Two teams of soldiers—eighteen people—who shared time on the *Gruen* between them. Three days on, three days off.

Song and her crew were Aratogan.

With Markan's help, he acquired Aratogan uniforms and had a team ready for when he called.

"I hope you're not planning on walking around as Aratogan," Markan had said, when he'd called Stellan up to say they'd been dispatched. "You're no actor. You can't carry it for long."

"I'm a quick in and out, Markan. I know my limitations. But I need a team ready on demand."

Markan grunted.

Stellan's plan was simple. Find out which days Lambert would be on the *Gruen*. Formulate an incident that would require Song to be on ship. Accompany her out to the *Gruen*. Markan had organized clearances for him and his "team." Thus getting out to the *Gruen* would be easy. Getting onto the ship once they were there was the hard part. They needed clearances for that, and Stellan didn't have them. Markan couldn't get them for him, either.

"I think our original plan was better," Markan said. "Rigel looks ready to make a deal with Lady Lyan. Lambert will come down for that."

"Markan, Lambert is as well protected as Lady Lyan herself. And they're using Lyan's bodyguards to do it. I could assassinate him for you." From a distance, and he'd want a quick escape route.

"I need you to question him, not kill him. At least not until we have answers. Do you still have the dromalan truth serum?

"Of course."

THEY had a name for the blue-haired woman—Neela Cotterill—but nothing else. Randella Abbey denied ever having said the woman was ex-military. She was lying, but Markan refused to pull her in for it.

"It's not important," he said. "She's useful to us in other ways."

Despite Markan's misgivings, Stellan wore the Aratogan uniform. It allowed him to blend in and get close to people he wanted to.

He didn't use bugs anymore. Whoever had bugged Rigel would be listening for that. Instead, he made himself known to the soldiers from the *Gruen* when they were on leave.

Luckily for him, this crew frequented a different bar, for he didn't know what he'd have done if they'd gone to the Night Owl, where Rigel still spent time.

The Aratogans weren't as close-mouthed as the linesmen doing training. From them, Stellan learned that the linesmen had, indeed, been stationed on the *Gruen*.

"They go around singing all the time," one of the soldiers complained. "It drives you crazy."

Lambert was known as a linesman who sang. Known to be crazy for doing it, too.

"I don't mind them," another soldier said. "They help with the small line repairs. And you have to admit, the ship does run smoother after they've done their training."

"So what sort of training is it?" Stellan asked.

"Not in our need to know," the crew member said. "They go into the cargo bay, and that's it. That Sale—or even Bhaksir— she'd shoot us if we tried to go in."

If Lambert was on the *Gruen*, one or both of Bhaksir and Sale's teams would be, too. If Stellan turned up unannounced, they'd shoot him.

He had to find a way to get onto the ship, and he had to find it soon. Moreover, once he got his information from Lambert, he had to get off the ship without anyone killing him.

THE drinks were more expensive at the Bar on East, where the crew of the *Gruen* used to drink. Stellan was the first there— as he'd planned.

What he hadn't planned was for Rigel and Rickenback to walk in five minutes after him. Or sit at the bench behind him.

Stellan sank low and hunched in on himself. He'd changed his hair, and had new contacts coloring his eyes, but he hadn't made much other effort to disguise himself. He hoped it was enough.

A woman with dark hair—getting on to a blue-black—but with the same white tips as Rigel's, stopped by Rigel's table and looked them over. Down one side of her face she had a striking tattoo—blue-black like her hair, fading into lighter blues and whites. The tattoo extended down her shoulder, onto her arm. She was dressed in a wired corset and short shorts, both of which showed she was too old to be flaunting her body.

"Lady Lyan made an offer," Rickenback said to Rigel.

"You know Lancia," Rigel said. "I bet it's as paltry as her first one."

"Gentlemen." The woman's voice was low and throaty. "Are you after a good time?"

"We're not interested," Rickenback said. "Find someone else."

They waited until she moved on. She stopped at Stellan's table.

"Go away," Stellan said.

There was something familiar about her. He looked more closely. "Have we met?"

She gave a rasping laugh. "If I had a credit for everyone who's asked me that while I've been on this forsaken place, I'd be a rich woman." She slid into the seat beside him. "I'm Neela."

"Not interested." Stellan said it automatically, but he eased his comms out of his pocket. Neela was an unusual name.

"It's a generous offer," Rickenback told Rigel.

"It is generous actually," Neela said, softly into Stellan's ear.

"I said I wasn't interested." He kept his comms in the hand that was away from her, ready to thumb in the overriding access code.

"Twenty million credits," she breathed, just before Rickenback, behind them, said, "Twenty million credits."

Rigel choked on his drink.

Stellan wanted to choke on his. The last time a level-ten linesman had switched contracts, Lino Abeu had gone over to House of Sandhurst. Iwo Hurst had paid 10 million credits. Given Lambert's reputation, Lyan should have offered somewhere between 2 and 5 million—enough to get Rigel interested. Lady Lyan wasn't known for her largesse. She was looking for a quick solution.

Stellan glanced over his shoulder, in time to see Rigel lick his lips and shake his head. "Paretsky will—"

Neela said something Stellan didn't catch.

Rickenback said, "Does it matter what Paretsky thinks, Rigel? Can he offer you that sort of money?"

"No one can offer that sort of money."

"You need to come with me," Neela said.

Stellan shook his head.

"I'm still concerned about this deal," Rickenback said. "That amount of money could almost be construed as a bribe. Regardless, Lambert is going to get something from this. Your portion is eighty percent, Lambert's twenty percent. It's up to you to agree."

Something sharp pricked Stellan's side. He looked over at Neela.

"Capraxis," she said, still close to his ear. "On most people, it has no effect except to make them instantly drunk. If your stomach has been modified to convert alcohols to sugars, however, capraxis reacts with the contents of your stomach to make a nerve serum. You should start feeling the effects in about"—she looked at her comms—"four, three, seconds."

Stellan thumbed the emergency code into his comms. "You crazy—" He could already feel a numbing in his fingers. Or maybe that was psychosomatic. His finger muffed the last number. "What have you done?" except it came out unintelligibly, for he couldn't move his mouth to form the words. He couldn't feel his feet either.

Two paramedics raced in with a stretcher. "Make way, make way."

It was too early for anyone to have called them.

Neela caught Stellan as he fell, caught his comms with her free hand, and supported him until the paramedics reached them.

"Why?" Stellan couldn't articulate the word, but she seemed to understand. Or maybe she was guessing.

"Perhaps you should have talked to me instead of listening in on lost causes. You might have found out."

The man who bundled Stellan onto the stretcher looked familiar. Stellan had last seen him the night someone had tried to snatch Lambert.

Neela had to be the blue-haired woman who had been with them that night. Neela Cotterill.

Rigel was still deep in conversation with Rickenback. He didn't even notice them wheel the stretcher out.

THIRTY

EAN LAMBERT

ABRAM SENT THROUGH a list of items that had been found on Professor Gerrard's person. His comms had survived intact, and Ean breathed a sigh of relief at that. If the notes were anywhere, they'd be on his comms. Which was just as well, because Gerrard had kept a lot on his person. A chain he'd probably worn around his neck. It had a flat square plastic medallion hanging off it. At least three bracelets, four pieces of metal, two ceramic items, and a pair of pliers. Plus a tab of choco-limone, a pack of menthos, four cream biscuits, and a strip of jerky.

Professor Gerrard had been fond of his snacks.

"Can I see the comms?" Ean asked Abram. Or was the comms too obvious? "Could I see all of it?"

"A dead man's belongings," Abram said. "Part of an investigation? You'd need a good reason, Ean."

He didn't have a good reason. "I was trying to trace the ship Redmond found. I thought they might have found it through whatever Gerrard discovered. Gerrard might have kept a copy of whatever he gave Redmond. If he did, he probably kept it close; otherwise, Orsaya would have found it."

Abram blew out his breath. "Maybe. It's worth a try. I'll send someone up with the items."

He didn't mention the obvious. Like, if they really wanted to know what Gerrard had found, they should just hand them over to Orsaya. If she thought there was something, she'd find it.

Ean was grateful for that.

VEGA insisted on being present when Gerrard's personal effects arrived.

She pulled the knife out of her belt to pick through the contents. "The man liked his sweets sweet," she said, pursing her mouth at the chocolimone. "And in quantity . . . hello, what have we got here?"

She lifted the chain out of the box.

"A neck chain," Ean said. Would Vega mind if he took the comms now? Or should he wait until she gave the all clear.

Vega put down her knife to hold the chain by the square that dangled from it. The black was faded in places, which meant the plastic was old. It was an ugly thing to wear around your neck, but who was Ean to talk? He didn't wear jewelry.

"I wonder." Vega did something with both hands. The little square seemed to snap—or that's what it looked like to Ean—then he realized it hadn't snapped, she'd opened it.

Vega's voice held wonder. "I haven't seen one of these outside a museum. Or my own collection." She stood up and moved over to her collection of weapons. To one particular weapon that Sale had told him was pre-expansion. Beside the weapon, in a clear case fixed to the wall, were two items—a metal key and a small piece of plastic that looked a lot like the one Vega carried in her hand.

"Gerrard carried part of an old weapon with him?" It didn't make sense to Ean.

"No." Vega compared the two. "They're storage devices. This particular one"—she tapped the plastic on the wall—"carried the instructions and codes for this." She tapped the weapon. "This one." She looked down at the square in her hand. "Who knows what this one might hold."

Ean knew, with a sudden, line-dizzying certainty. "Vega. You are a genius."

THEY couldn't read the records.

Even though he knew it was preline, Ean tried to coax the lines into giving up the information to him. They didn't understand what he wanted. To the lines, there were no records.

When he left for line training the next day, the tiny storage device was still unread.

He was halfway through line training when he realized who could help.

"Favager," he said to Radko, making the trainees look at him strangely. He was used to that, although he wasn't getting as many strange looks as he had at the start. "You remember Clemence Favager. We met her on the way up to the Night Owl. She loves Old Earth. If anyone will know how we can read it, she will."

He called Favager as soon as he got back to the *Lancastrian Princess*.

Favager looked at him with interest. "Linesman. What can I do for you?"

"Do you have anything that can read preline databases?"

"Depends. From where?"

Did it matter?

Favager might have been reading his mind. "Earth technology moved on, but new worlds didn't. They were too busy trying to survive."

Gerrard had been from Ruon. Was it safe to assume the reading device was from there? "Ruon." Then he added, "Maybe."

"Ruon. I might not have anything that old. Let me see what I've got."

DESPITE her misgivings, Favager did have something. She delivered the reader personally. Vega accompanied her to the small meeting room and stayed while Favager set up the reader for Ean.

"You need to be careful," Favager said. "Use the wrong reader, and you can do untold damage. Even wipe the records."

"I appreciate your coming out this way to help," Ean said.

"Not a problem," Favager said cheerfully. "Anyone who wants to read old records, I'm interested."

Most people would have used it as an excuse to talk to Michelle. Ean thought Favager genuinely meant what she said.

"Provided I get to control the equipment, mind. They don't make readers like this anymore." She finished setting up. "Let's look at your data."

Ean looked at Vega. He didn't have the plastic knowledge store. She did. Vega silently handed it over.

Favager made some adjustments. "First Wave." She sounded

impressed. She adjusted more. "It's old, even by Earth standards."

Information scrolled onto the screen. Favager looked as pleased as if she'd performed a miracle by herself. "And here we have it."

Ean and Vega moved in to read over her shoulder.

"Ship records," Vega said. "No, wait. Metal. Scrap metal."

"It's the records of a shipyard," Favager said. "This is amazing. And they kept such meticulous detail. Every ship or piece of metal that passed through."

"He or she had a tidy mind," Vega said.

Ean would have called it obsessive, for the next record was for four screws, but both commodores nodded approvingly.

How could they find if one of those ships was an alien ship? "Can we search?"

Favager did something on the screen.

"Let's look for Havortian."

"Havortian," Favager said. "This is getting interesting suddenly."

That search revealed nothing.

Ean looked at the records in front of him. Metal, scrap. What did they know about alien ships?

"Hexagonal shapes." The composition. They tried them all. Nothing.

What did he know about the *Havortian* from his line-training days? Havortian had bought his piece of alien ship from Red Javed, who had owned a scrap-metal business on one of the smaller planets in the Chamberley system. His clientele had been prospectors looking for minerals, and small cargo ships that traded between worlds. He was known for one thing. He'd sold the most famous piece of scrap metal in history to a man named Havortian.

"Try Red Javed."

Favager added the search code. "No Red Javed," she said, "but on landing date 82.189, some scrap metal was sold to a man named Kai Javed."

Vega tapped something into her comms and nodded at what was returned. "Kai Javed was Red Javed's father."

"I'll be—" Favager said. "Look at the manifest here."

And there it was. A piece of metal ten meters by six by six, sold to one Kai Javed. Part of a ship that had been broken down for scrap.

"Let's track this beastie down." Favager's fingers flew over the controls. "Here's what he paid for it."

Ean read over her shoulder. "Received in return from Javed. One damaged cargo container, forty-five by ten by twenty. Steel-ceramic. Hull breached, obvious impact from multiple meteor storms. Internal chamber contained three percent oxygen, two percent nitrogen. Cargo of fifty Earth sheep, dead." Even the composition of air had been documented. "I wonder." He called up the specs of the *Eleven* on his own comms. "Search on this combination. Oxygen, nitrogen, xenon, and radon."

Those were the gases common to the alien ships before they changed them to suit human bodies.

It took five minutes. When it came up they stared at it for twice that time. Every piece of scrap that came into the salvage yard had been documented in detail.

Here, in front of them, were plans and vids and notes of the *Havortian*.

"I don't understand how they didn't realize the ship was alien," Ean said.

"I do," Favager said. "Now line ships are made by two factories, and they all look the same. But back in those days, everyone designed their own ships. They were unique. Furthermore, I've heard that if you're not a linesman, you can't hear the boards. You can't even tell that half of them *are* boards."

"Admiral Galenos needs to see this," Vega said. "Can you copy it?"

"Sure." Favager pulled a small device out of her bag and connected the reader to Vega's comms. "Wouldn't mind being there when you tell him."

She handed over the copy. It hadn't taken long.

Vega hesitated, then, "Why not do it now?" She looked at Radko, standing at ease close to the wall, and nodded at Radko's comms. Radko handed it over. Vega handed it to Favager. "Spacer Radko can go back with you."

Favager copied the files again.

"I'll let Galenos know you're coming," Vega said.

Ean went down with them to the shuttle.

"Thank you," he said to Favager.

"My pleasure. Anytime you want old records deciphered, talk to me."

He would, too.

It felt strange to see Radko go off in a shuttle without him. He watched the lights recycle back to green before he turned away.

"Linesman Lambert," Vega said, as he started toward his quarters. "Next time you invite all and sundry from other fleets to assist in your research, I want to know about it first. Understand?"

"Understood," Ean said.

THIRTY-ONE

EAN LAMBERT

BY NOW, EAN knew what line each of the single-level linesmen was. Mael was the only nine. There were three eights, two sevens, ten sixes, nine fives, twelve fours, five threes and eight twos. Technically, Tinatin was a single-level line as well, the solitary one.

It was time to introduce them to their ship.

He traveled with them in the first shuttle, and used Fergus's unclenched hands as a barometer to know when they should all be hearing the lines.

"We should sing," he said. "A greeting to the ship we're going to. You know the *Eleven*.

"All of you sing," he said. "Sing to all the lines you know. Greet the ship. You don't have to start at one."

Tinatin didn't bother singing anything but one. Mael sang them all, but only became animated when he got to the sonorous song of nine. Ean sang them all, too, but gave lines ten and eleven a little more. After all, who else did they have to sing to?

"We're coming. I'm bringing your crew."

The lines made a happy chorus of pleasure back.

"Next time maybe you should wait till we're on the ship before you do that," Radko said, after he was done. "Oxygen's harder to get to on the shuttle. It's in the suits."

There were oxygen canisters fastened to the wall, but there wouldn't have been enough to go around.

"Sorry." Line eleven had been calm. It was trying not to break these fragile little lines but no one seemed to understand that except Ean. He sang a song of apologetic consolation. Eleven and the other lines swirled around in the song, reassuring him, telling him it was fine, and they would manage.

He stopped singing when the safety chimed for landing, to find the whole shuttle silent, staring at him.

"What did I do?" he asked Radko. He hadn't had that kind of freak reaction for weeks. Except for Vega, and hers was monster, not freak.

Radko shook her head. "I'm no linesman, but it sounded impressive. Harmonious."

"You're a one-man choir," Fergus said, unbuckling and standing up as the all clear came on. "To me it sounds as if you're amplifying the lines, but a human larynx can't do that. Not all those different sounds at once. I think you're pushing the lines straight into here." He tapped his head. "It's a bit like telepathy."

"Telepathy isn't like that," Tinatin said as she followed them out. "Telepathy is useful. You can talk to each other. This is just singing."

"Ah, Tinatin. Maybe you should try listening to the words of the song."

"The Hello Song," one of the sixes said as they followed them out. "I feel like I'm back at junior school. You know, where they make you learn the letters of the alphabet and numbers."

Ean hid his smile. That was exactly what it was.

Sale and her crew waited for them on board.

On ship, the strength of line eleven stopped most of the multilevel lines. Ean gave them time to recover.

"Do you want to say anything?" he asked Kari Wang.

She shook her head. "I want to observe their reactions."

Ean looked at Sale. She always had something to say.

"Oxygen," Sale said, and raised her voice to the new crew. "You all know the drill by now. Look around for the nearest oxygen cylinders. You'll find there are plenty on board in the main compartments between here and the bridge, not so many in the lesser-used rooms. For the moment, stick together and don't get lost. It's a big ship. It could take us days to find you."

As a joke it fell flat, for Ean knew he could ask the lines where the crew were. He rubbed his nose and didn't say anything.

"Right," said Sale. "They're all yours, Ean."

They stopped in the main rec room, so the crew could look at the huge image on the wall.

"There's one on every ship," Ean said. "Usually in a large room like this but not on the bridge."

He moved over to Tinatin while they looked at it. "How does this ship feel to you?"

She looked at him as if wondering if he meant what he'd asked.

"I mean it. I want to know how it feels to you."

Another soldier said, "Tinatin is all—"

"T'Fika," Kari Wang said sharply. "No negative comments."

T'Fika subsided, scowling.

Ean saw the hint of an approving smile on Mael's face. "What does the ship feel like?" he asked Tinatin.

"You always ask me." She crossed her arms and glared at them both. "What does it feel like to you, Mael?"

He considered the question. "Itchy," he said finally. "Like a band that likes to be stretched but isn't."

At least half a dozen of his crewmates turned to look at him.

"No it doesn't," Mikaelsson said. "It's rusty, like a piece of metal on a planet that's been exposed to oxygen, and it's starting to rust."

"It's resting." Misty Dubicki was one of the single eights. "Waiting to be useful."

Ean wouldn't have used any of those descriptions although he supposed they were all apt.

"It's excited," Tinatin said. "Happy we're here. Happy it has a crew."

Mikaelsson shook his head. "You can't get anything right, Tinatin."

"It is looking forward to having a crew again," Ean said. "It is happy." Mikaelsson was a full six. He should have been getting some of that anticipation.

"You say that like it's a sentient thing."

"Maybe you should start thinking of it like that. You have six lines, Mikaelsson. You and Tinatin both have line one, but Tinatin's doing a better job of picking line one than you are. You can't ignore it because you think it beneath you." He raised his voice so everyone could hear. "Those of you with multiple lines need to remember you have more than one line.

Don't concentrate on your highest line to the detriment of the others."

Tinatin turned away. "So there."

"Tinatin," Kari Wang said.

Tinatin looked sideways at her.

Dhalmans was another multiple line. She challenged Ean a lot in training. She reminded him of Sale sometimes. She said now, "You're asking us to disbelieve our training. Everything we have been taught tells us we go to the top line."

"That's right. You will find a lot of what you have learned in the past is—" Not wrong, exactly, but definitely not right either. "It doesn't apply to the alien lines. These are lines as the lines are supposed to work. Not lines forced into the pattern humans force them into."

"Twisted," Tinatin murmured, and Ean had to stop himself saying, "Exactly."

"Line one on this ship is not inferior to line six." Maybe they should have had this conversation off ship. "Line one is the line that monitors the strength of the crew and of the lines. Probably of the whole ship, we don't know yet. Line six is the line that works the engines."

He left it at that. "Let's go and see the bridge. It's rather impressive," and led the way.

THIRTY-TWO

✦

SELMA KARI WANG

BIG AS IT was, the bridge couldn't hold 120 people. They viewed it in groups, while Sale and her team took smaller groups off to see the cargo holds and other parts of the ship. Bhaksir's team watched Ean.

None of them were interested in the weapons bays.

That was the first place Kari Wang's own crew would have asked to see. They would have wanted to know each weapon's capabilities, capacity, and how it was fired.

But her own crew was a fully trained battleship crew, ready to fight. These—half of them were engineers, the other half not much better. There were only two really good fighters among the whole lot.

Kari Wang made her way over to the Captain's Chair. This short-legged chair didn't help. How could you even work as a captain when you couldn't get comfortable?

She shouldn't be here. This wasn't her ship. It wasn't her crew.

She should have been dead with her crew. She should have bought herself an old tramp ship ready for scrap and jumped into the void with it. Maybe she should still do that.

Yes. That's what she would do. Find some way to escape Grieve—and Fitch and Jon—and jump into the void.

THIRTY-THREE

EAN LAMBERT

THE DIRGE THAT swept through the lines knocked Ean off his feet. As he picked himself up, he was aware of Tinatin, on the bridge, saying to Mael. "The ship's sad now. It should have died."

Radko and others in Bhaksir's team surrounded him in a protective circle. "What's—?"

He could hear the lines preparing to jump. "No," and frantically sang a negation.

But the ship had already entered the void.

In the eternity of the void, he realized line ten hadn't come in at all. The ship wasn't going to jump. Didn't plan on jumping.

"We're staying here," line nine told him.

The thump-kerthump of line eleven was a steadying influence. Which he needed when he realized there were seven other nines in the void with him. The six nines of the *Eleven*'s fleet plus one other. Abram wouldn't be happy if he brought another ship into the fleet.

He tried to sing to the new line, but it wasn't listening. He turned his attention back to the nines who were.

"Why are we here?"

"That's what we have to do."

"No you don't."

Underneath, he could hear the funereal song of depression and loss from line one. The other ones were catching the tune now. They should have been dead. Like their ship. Like their crew.

It could only have come from one person, and she was sitting in the Captain's Chair, amplifying the sense of loss.

Ean sang a desperate countermelody.

He didn't sing happiness. Kari Wang would never buy that, and right now the ships wouldn't, either.

He sang a song of hope and of new beginnings. He sang of the ships and of how they had been alone for so long. Captainless. Crewless. Lonely lines. Nothing in space. It was a desperate bid to drag her out of her own depression and into someone else's. Saying, "Cheer up, be happy," wasn't going to work. She needed to stop thinking about herself. She needed to stop thinking about taking a jump into the void.

He sang of simple things, like the pleasure of a well-tuned ship. Of how he had felt when he'd arrived on the *Lancastrian Princess* and sung line six back into perfection. Of the way line one reflected the crew a ship had. Of how bad the lines on the two media ships had been when he'd first come across them.

Nothing worked.

Line nine still wanted to stay in the void.

What could get her out of her funk?

The reminder of the media ships gave him an idea. She was a good captain.

"Forgive me," he whispered to line two, and sang it out of true.

It worked.

The captain's attention switched off the track it had been on. Ean's next plea to line nine got them out of the void.

"Ean." Radko's voice was urgent in his ear. He found he was on the floor. "Are you all right? Ean." She reached out to touch his shoulder.

He launched himself at the Captain's Chair.

Kari Wang wasn't expecting it, but Ean had no strength. She landed off the chair. Ean landed on top of her.

Ean crawled to his knees and sang line two straight. Then he knelt on his hands and knees and dry-retched.

Kari Wang was already on her feet.

Radko came over to pick Ean up.

"Don't let her back in that chair."

She changed direction and moved over to guard Kari Wang. "I'm sorry, ma'am. Best you stay here for the moment."

Ean hoped her blaster was on stun, for she had it out.

Bhaksir came over to Ean.

"Keep away from me." He'd just been in the void.

Two comms channels beeped for attention. Helmo and Wendell.

Ean sang them both open.

"What is going on?" Wendell got in a second before Helmo.

Ean was too exhausted to pull himself up. "It was an accident. It won't happen again."

He'd opened visuals as well as voice. Both captains looked around the bridge, assessing what was happening.

"We're not sure what's happened yet," Bhaksir said. "But it seems to be over."

Through the lines, Ean could feel the snap decision both captains came to. Do nothing, wait for the report. After so long in the void, his lines were wide open. Helmo had been working out. Ean could smell the sweat. Wendell had been drinking tea. Ean could taste the tea.

"I expect a full report." Wendell clicked off.

Helmo didn't ask for a report, but then, he knew he'd get one soon.

Bhaksir moved over to Kari Wang, her weapon out. She nodded to Radko, who moved over to Ean.

"Let me help you up," Radko said. "I'm used to my hair sticking out." She holstered her weapon and hauled Ean to his feet. She helped him to a seat, for he couldn't do it on his own.

It wasn't the Captain's Chair. Ean was glad of that. As he sank into it, he became aware that everyone on the bridge was staring at him.

"Will you look at that?" Mael sounded as hoarse as Ean. "Her hair really does stick out." Then he crumpled into a heap on the floor.

"Oxygen," Bhaksir said, gesturing to Mael, and two by-now-well-trained guards moved in with an oxygen cylinder.

Ean felt as if he'd been in the void forever.

"Get her off this ship," he said to Radko, and there was no question who he was talking about. "Get her off now."

"Get her out of here." Bhaksir nodded at Ru Li and Gossamer. They stepped forward, weapons in hand.

"If you'll come with us, Captain."

"Now hold a minute." Mael pushed the guards away and sat up. He looked as green as Ean felt. "What's with the weapons? What's she done?"

"Mael's right," Ean said. "She hasn't done anything wrong. Just please, get her off the ship."

Kari Wang held her arms up in surrender. Ean couldn't tell what she was thinking.

"Take her weapon," Bhaksir said.

"But she hasn't—"

"Shut up, Mael, or I'll arrest you, too."

Kari Wang didn't hand them her weapon; she put her hands on her head and let Ru Li come and take it.

"Apologies for this, Captain," Bhaksir said. "But you must understand we protect the linesman first."

"The linesman who said it was an accident," Mael pointed out.

"You're under arrest, Mael." Bhaksir gestured with her blaster. "Take his weapon, Ru Li. Uh-uh," as Mael put his hand to his holster. "Like your captain did. Hands on your head."

Mael put his hands to his head although he was shaking so much, he almost couldn't do it.

"Why are you arresting him?" Tinatin demanded. "He hasn't done anything either."

"Because I said if he didn't shut up, I would arrest him. And he didn't shut up." Bhaksir moved her blaster to take in the rest of them. "Does anyone else want to be arrested? Tinatin?"

"I haven't—"

"Tinatin," Kari Wang said. "Let's find out what the problem is first."

Tinatin bit her bottom lip hard. Ean thought it might have been to force herself to say nothing more.

At a gesture from Bhaksir, Ru Li and Gossamer took Kari Wang out. A discreet wave of her hand told them to leave Mael with her.

Ean crooned a song to the lines as he watched Kari Wang go. Another apology to line two, a check to see how line nine was going, an overall song to all the lines.

Mael was still green. How often had he had to work under less-than-ideal conditions when he was feeling wretched, like he was now?

Bhaksir called Sale. "We're done for today. Send everyone home."

Sale didn't ask why. "Okay. We'll take them back to the shuttle."

"What about the ones who haven't seen the bridge?" Ean asked.

"They can see it next time," Bhaksir said. "We're getting you to a medic." She looked at Mael. "Him, too."

Ean didn't need a medic, but Bhaksir wasn't listening to reason right now. He climbed wearily to his feet. He felt like he had the first day Radko had made him do the standard soldier daily exercises. Sore all over.

"I can walk," as Radko came over to help him. His voice was husky. Voice coach to the stars—Messire Gospetto—whom Ean went to every morning for exercises to prevent voice strain, was not going to be impressed.

Bhaksir indicated to Hana to walk with Mael.

"How long were we in the void for?" he asked Radko, as they staggered after the silent crew. They would have a lot to talk about on the way home, at least.

Radko guided him away from the wall. "I don't know if it was the void. There was this awful, I don't know, and you were on the floor." Radko was normally clear. If she couldn't describe it, it must have been bad. "Between one blink and the next. Literally. I didn't see you fall. Then you knocked Kari Wang off her chair."

"All that time," Mael said. "And you couldn't tell something was wrong."

Radko guided Ean off the other wall. "It was awful, but it wasn't long. Of course, when both captains called up, we knew something had happened."

"We went into the void." Ean couldn't stop the shudder. "For a long time. The ship didn't want to come out. It took all the ships with it." Because it was the *Eleven*. "We'd have been there forever, and no one would know."

Except him, and that mysterious other line that had been in there with them. Which had to have been Mael, because logically the nine would have been the only one who'd known they were in the void and thus known time was passing.

Bhaksir was talking into the comms, getting clearance for Mael to come onto the *Lancastrian Princess*. Vega didn't want him to come.

"He needs medical attention, ma'am. Attention only our medic has experience to deal with."

"No," said Vega.

"I'm bringing him anyway," Bhaksir said, and clicked off.

One day, Vega was going to put them all in jail.

Bhaksir looked at Ean, clicked back on, and continued the conversation as if she hadn't clicked off at all. "Ma'am. Linesman Lambert also needs attention. If I don't bring Mael to the *Lancastrian Princess*, I will need to take Lambert—and the medic—to Confluence Station."

This time it was Vega who clicked off.

"She was sweating," Bhaksir said, to no one in particular. "Literally, I mean."

ON the shuttle back to the *Lancastrian Princess*, Sale sat down next to Mael. "How do you feel, Linesman?"

He was getting some color back. "Like I've lived a hundred years."

"Ean can be a little heavy-handed sometimes."

"*I* didn't do a thing," Ean said.

"This has all the hallmarks of one of your escapades, Ean."

"Escapades?"

"It looked line-related to me."

"There were a hundred linesmen on that ship." One hundred and twenty-two in fact. "And it wasn't a linesman who did it anyway."

Sale raised an eyebrow.

"I sent Kari Wang back under guard," Bhaksir said.

"And I'm under arrest," Mael said.

"That was for talking back to a superior officer after you had been warned."

"In another fleet?"

Sale and Bhaksir exchanged eye-rolling glances. "I get that one," Sale said. "What did Kari Wang do?"

Even now, Ean shuddered thinking about it.

"I have no idea," Bhaksir said. "See what you can make of it."

She brought up a recording from the bridge. One of the cameras that showed the Captain's Chair and its surrounds. Over to one side, the new crew crowded around a screen, talking to each other. Ean and Fergus conversed quietly, while Kari Wang sank into the Captain's Chair.

Then everything stopped for five seconds. Stopped talking, stopped moving, some of them midstep. It was almost as if someone had paused the recording, except that Ean fell to the floor, and Mael swayed on his feet. Then Ean lunged for Kari Wang and knocked her out of her chair.

Seconds later, both captains called up.

Bhaksir clicked off after Ean's, "Get her off this ship."

"Let's see what happened on other parts of the ship," Sale said.

They checked six other cameras. The crew all looked as if they had been momentarily paused. Radko timed them all. "Exactly 4.97 seconds, every single one."

"Shit. And only Ean and Mael reacted. What do you two have in common?"

"Line nine." Ean's stomach knotted just thinking about it. "We went into the void. Line nine takes you into the void."

"It's almost like olden times," Sale said. "Sometimes I feel nostalgic for all this line business."

"I had no idea what was going on," Bhaksir said. "But something happened."

"Kari Wang wanted to stay in the void," Ean said. He cast his mind back to what had happened. So long ago now. "She thought she should have been dead. Like her ship. Like her crew."

"A suicide jump?" Like the captain of the *Davida*, whose ship had been damaged beyond repair. He'd saved his crew, dumped them at the nearest fleet outpost, and taken himself and his ship into the void.

Ean shuddered. "The ship listened to her."

"Well, it answers two questions we had," Sale said. "Will the *Eleven* accept her? And how will she control it if she's not a linesman herself?"

"She's not getting back on that ship."

"Ean, you said yourself it was an accident." Sale moved over to check Mael, who'd gone green again. She handed him a sick bag. "You'll be fine," Sale said, and her voice was almost gentle. "The lines haven't killed anyone yet. Not like this, anyway."

"He'd probably like some sandwiches," Ean said, remembering back to his own earlier jumps. Food had helped.

Mael groaned and clutched the bag closer.

"Yes," Ean said. "He needs sandwiches."

Sale flicked on her comms. "Note to self. Sandwiches in the linesman's survival kit." She flicked off.

Ean looked at her, wondering if she was joking.

Fergus hid a snort of laughter. "Let's hope they don't carry the same set of sandwiches around for weeks."

"You would be surprised at how long food can last in space, Fergus," Sale said.

"I don't think I would," Fergus said.

ON the *Lancastrian Princess*, Vega waited with the medic.

"What's he done now?" the medic asked, running the scanner over Ean's body.

Ean was becoming tired of being blamed for every line-related problem. "Why don't you thank me for saving your ship?"

Vega's lips tightened along with the medic's.

"Maybe because from where I'm standing, I didn't see you save the ship." The medic checked Ean's pupils with a light, then shined the light down his throat. Ean didn't know why he bothered, for the image was up on-screen. "Except you've strained your voice again. Those lines of yours won't keep fixing it forever, you know."

He turned to Mael. "Let's look at you." He ran the scanner over Mael and checked Mael's pupils and throat. "You haven't been doing as much singing, at any rate. Your voice is good. What about other symptoms? Chest pains? Thirst? Dry mouth?" He ran his hands over Mael's. "I suspect you're mostly over the initial shock. How bad was it?"

Mael shrugged.

"Yes, well." The medic looked at everyone crowded around him. "Perhaps we could have some privacy here."

"What happened?" Vega asked, out in the corridor.

Ean wanted to talk to Michelle and Abram.

"Captain Kari Wang triggered something," Radko said.

"The ships entered the void. Ean got them out again." She looked queryingly at Ean.

He nodded.

"It doesn't seem much," Vega said.

Not much. "We could have stayed in there forever." Ean's voice shook although he tried to stop it. His hands shook, too.

Bhaksir looked at Radko, who gave a slight nod.

"I may have acted inappropriately, ma'am," Bhaksir said, and proceeded to walk down to Vega's office with her. "I disarmed Captain Kari Wang and we escorted her from the ship. A slight overreaction."

Radko pulled Ean back when he would have followed. "Let's go to the mess. Get some of those sandwiches you were talking about."

He wasn't hungry.

"We can order some for Mael, too. I doubt anyone has done that yet."

FORTIFIED with sandwiches—which made him feel a lot better—Ean was prepared for the conference call with the admirals.

To observers outside the linked fleet, the ships had disappeared for 4.97 seconds. They'd watched recordings from the *Lancastrian Princess*, the *Wendell*, the *Gruen*, and Confluence Station. On board each it looked as if everything had paused for the same amount of time. Both media ships had lost 4.97 seconds of broadcasting as well.

"She took the whole fleet into the void," Ean said.

"A cold jump?" Abram asked, for who would think of taking a ship into the void and stopping there.

"No. Just into the void." Ean shuddered. "I wasn't sure we'd ever get out."

"How? She must have some control over the ship then."

"Did she know what she was doing?"

"Was it deliberate?"

The questions came together. Ean held up his hand to stop any more. "She didn't know what she was doing." He was sure Kari Wang would never endanger the lives of the people on five ships and a station like that. "But that makes it worse because we can't control it. What if it happens again? What if I'm not there to fix it next time?" It had been hard enough to fix this time. "What if I can't fix it?"

"How long do you think you were in the void for?" Orsaya asked.

Ean shuddered. "It felt like forever." He didn't want to remember the helplessness, the time toward the end when he had started to wonder if he could get them out. "I'm only a linesman. I can't fix everything." He realized how plaintive that sounded. "I'm sorry."

"There are things that scare us all," Abram said.

"Four point nine seven seconds," Orsaya said. She shivered as if she were cold. "What if the real time that passed outside was years? How do you think the people in the void would react? Would no time have passed for them? Or would something change over such a long period?"

"Like how long?" Katida asked.

Sometimes Katida and Orsaya picked up on each other's conversations as if they were reading the other's thoughts. Ean could tell by the way they looked at each other that this was one of those times.

"Ten years," Orsaya said.

Ten years. She was talking about the crazy ship, the *Balao*, and Ean could well believe the people on board the *Balao* had gone crazy if they'd been in the void that long. He tried to do a quick calculation. Four point nine seven seconds times how many to make ten years? The thought of it made him want to retch.

"I don't see how," Katida said. "The others on board had no sense of time passing."

"So do you think this is what happened to the *Balao*?" Orsaya asked.

Who knew? But Ean had seen the terror on the faces of the people on the *Balao*, and he could well understand that terror based on today's experience. They were all watching him, waiting for his answer.

He shrugged. "Maybe. Possibly."

They absorbed that in silence. "We need psychiatric assessment," Katida said finally. "To see if Kari Wang is a bomb primed to go off." She looked at MacClennan, who hadn't spoken yet. "I don't know what we'll do if she's too dangerous to have on ship. We can't go back on a council decision. Not without explaining what the problem is, and most of them won't believe us anyway."

"She's dangerous," Ean said. He wouldn't always be on ship when Kari Wang went into depression.

"Which begs the question," Orsaya said. "How did she convince the ship to go into the void? She's not a linesman. She can't read the instruments. Yet the ship obeyed her."

"She's the captain," Ean said. He'd introduced her to the *Eleven*, told it she was its captain. He was responsible for her being on ship, and for the ship's accepting her. You could say he'd sung Kari Wang into the fleet. You couldn't sing a line out of the fleet. That would be cruel. Or would it? He was starting to wonder if he'd have to do that anyway, to separate the ships. The aliens must have had ways to separate them, and it was more urgent than ever now because Kari Wang could destroy them all.

"She's not coming back on ship." He'd sort it out with the *Eleven*.

Abram blew out his breath. "Ean." His voice was gentle. If he'd been on ship, Ean knew that the lines would be pouring out reassurance, and he didn't need lines to know what Abram was going to say next.

"She's too dangerous."

They were all looking at him sympathetically now, but each had the same implacable expression.

"We don't have any choice," Abram said. "The council has voted. They won't let us take her off the ship."

"Even though she'll kill us all." His voice cracked at the end.

"Even then."

The lines sang comfortingly in his head. They knew something was wrong. They were trying to fix him. Ean forced himself to concentrate on the meeting. Otherwise, he'd have to face the other fear he'd been avoiding since he'd pushed Kari Wang off her stool.

He was scared to go back into the void.

"Captain Kari Wang will undergo psychiatric assessment

tomorrow to ascertain her state of mind," Abram said. "We'll reconsider after that."

They were empty words, for Ean knew as well as everyone else what a prize the *Eleven* was, and how most of the council would view taking Kari Wang off the ship as a power push from Lancia.

"I'm sorry, Ean. But we'll be relying on you to stop her if she does it again."

Suppose he couldn't. All his friends would die.

MICHELLE arrived on ship around 04:00. She wasn't supposed to be here. Ean had seen her schedule. She wasn't due back on the *Lancastrian Princess* until the following evening.

Ean hadn't been able to sleep. Instead, he stood in Michelle's workroom, practicing breathing, singing to the lines. All of them.

"You shouldn't strain your voice," Michelle said. "Or can you ask the lines to fix it?"

He'd lost his voice once before, and the lines had fixed it for him.

"I don't want to ask."

Michelle looked exhausted.

"You should get more sleep," Ean said. The makeup wouldn't cover how tired she was forever. How long could she go on, alone?

He made them tea.

Michelle took a long mouthful. "Seriously, you shouldn't be singing."

"I'm worried that if I don't, I won't be able to." He could admit it to Michelle. The fact that he'd been powerless in the face of line nine's determination to stay in the void.

Michelle held her glass out for more tea. How long had it been since she'd relaxed. As Ean made the tea, he sang through the comms, asking for sandwiches. Would whoever answered it at the other end get the message?

"I remember when I was fifteen," Michelle said. "I used to love weapons. The blaster; the knife; you name it, I used it. I was so proud of myself. Then one day, Mu Kwan tried to assassinate my father. He had a ceremonial trishula, what they call a three-spear, a long stick with three metal prongs on the end. I didn't think. I saw what he planned and stepped in the way. It was instinctive." She shuddered. "Abram." She shuddered again. "He's slowed down a bit, but back in those days, he was fast, and, of course, an excellent shot. Mu Kwan splattered all over me. There was all this blood, and the smell of burned flesh. It was horrible." She rolled the glass in her hands. "I didn't want to touch a blaster again because now I'd seen what they could do, and they scared me."

But she'd continued to use the weapons. Enough to use a disruptor on Ean when she needed to. It was her duty.

It was Ean's duty to maintain the lines, to keep the ships safe. Even if Kari Wang got depressed again.

"Blasters still scare me," Michelle admitted.

The void would probably scare Ean for a while, too, but he couldn't let that show. Not to the lines. Not to Kari Wang.

The sandwiches arrived, delivered by an orderly who looked alert and awake, which was more than Ean or Michelle did.

Michelle leaned back and sighed. "So, if the rumors are correct, you arrested half the crew of the *Eleven*, attacked the captain on her own ship, and unjustly imprisoned another of the crew—who, incidentally, still hasn't returned."

Ean stared at her. "Where are you getting these rumors from?"

Michelle's dimple showed. "I don't know her name. Small. Young. Haladean. She stopped me on the way back from parliament. She's worried about her friend—the one we've locked up. She thinks we should let him go."

"Tinatin." Of course it would be Tinatin. Who else could force her way in to see Michelle? Who else would think to approach Michelle, of all people?

"What did you tell her?"

"I said I would find out what was happening."

"The medic kept him overnight for observation. In case of shock."

Michelle studied him carefully. "What about you? Are you in shock?"

Michelle's schedule had been planned for weeks. Yet she took time out—time that she couldn't afford—to come back to check that he was okay. Ean blinked. His throat was tight. "I'm fine." Or he would be. He hoped. "It was unexpected, that's all. And not pleasant."

"I imagine it wouldn't be."

Michelle patted the couch beside her. "Talk to me. I want to be sure you're okay."

"I should let you get some sleep." She got little enough as it was. Instead, he moved over to her couch—sacrilegious— and she leaned against him. The fizzy smell of her tickled his nose.

They didn't talk, just relaxed together. Ean listened to the song of the lines and found peace for the first time since they'd come out of the void earlier that day.

"Thank you," he started to say, then realized Michelle's breathing had evened and deepened.

She was asleep.

THIRTY-FOUR

SELMA KARI WANG

"MUST HAVE BEEN quite something on the ship yesterday," Grieve said, as he and Kari Wang made their way out to the isolated barracks that Kari Wang's crew currently called home.

He was fishing.

"You were there."

"I missed all the excitement. I was doing the grand tour of the cargo holds."

Yet no one had wanted to see the weapons bays.

"And of the cabins. Each crew member has their own cabin."

Kari Wang had tried to give her crew their own cabins where she could. She and Medic Halliday agreed that people needed a place where they could get away. So much so that she'd preferred to run her ship slightly understaffed to give her crew more personal space.

"You know as much as I do about what happened."

She could almost read Grieve's thoughts. If she didn't want to talk about it, he wasn't going to push her.

"You've got a psych test after this," he said finally. "Jon needs to present to the admirals before they see you this afternoon. Whatever you did got them in a tizzy."

She'd bet the admirals hadn't known about it—whatever it was—until Lambert's dramatic, "I want her off this ship." *She* still didn't know about it.

Her comms pinged. It was a copy of a message from Lin Anders, Lady Lyan's personal assistant, to Tinatin, of all people. What had Tinatin been doing talking to Anders?

She switched the message to text and scrolled through it. Linesman Mael was in the hospital, for observation.

Kari Wang knew that. She'd had a similar message from

the medic on the *Lancastrian Princess* last night. But what was Tinatin doing receiving the same? From Lady Lyan's personal staff.

THE crew were running laps. She was pleased to see Dhalmans talking to Dubicki as they ran. Two weeks ago, that wouldn't have happened.

Tinatin angled off as soon as she saw Kari Wang. "They've still got Mael," she said accusingly.

"Didn't you get a message this morning? He's being kept for observation."

"He didn't need to go to the hospital yesterday. He was fine before they took him away."

"I seem to recall him on the floor for a while." Yesterday, everyone had been busy tending the linesmen. Today, she wanted answers. She planned to get them at this afternoon's meeting.

"They don't even know who he is." Tinatin pulled out her comms. "Look. They called him linesman. They're talking about Lambert. Mael's probably still in jail."

It was a good pickup, but Kari Wang knew that Mael was a single-level linesman. Which meant that Lady Lyan's staff did, too. How secret was this supposed secret?

"What were you doing approaching Lady Lyan's personal staff, Tinatin?"

"I didn't approach her staff. But Lambert wears a Lancian uniform, and I knew Lady Lyan was in parliament."

"So you approached Lady Lyan herself." It was a wonder she hadn't been shot.

"She is head of the Lancian fleet. She should know what her soldiers are doing."

"Technically, her father is head of the fleet." If Jon found anything at her psych test later, it would be because Kari Wang was worried about what Tinatin would do next. Still, she'd done well all the same. Kari Wang scrolled through her comms, found the one the Lancastrian medic had sent the prior evening. "I got this from the ship medic last night."

She didn't say which ship. Tinatin was likely to raise a rescue party. "Why don't I call Mael, Tinatin?"

"I tried that. I can't get through."

Surely a captain would have better access than a simple spacer. "Let's see," Kari Wang said. She called Mael's comms and got Commodore Vega.

"This isn't a line hotel," Vega said.

"No, ma'am." There was no point introducing herself. Vega knew who she was. "I'm checking on one of my crew. Your medic has him in your hospital."

"Linesman Mael." She didn't say anything more, just switched her through.

"See?" Tinatin said. "They have no idea who you mean."

The crew on the *Lancastrian Princess* obviously knew about single-level linesmen. Everyone would soon if they kept using the title in front of Tinatin.

Mael looked as if he hadn't slept at all.

"How are you feeling?" Kari Wang asked.

"Good enough to come home, I guess. Although the medic here wants to run some more tests."

Tinatin leaned into the comms to see him. "You look terrible. What sort of tests?"

Mael shrugged. "Who knows? He's got his own gadgets here. He made them himself, he said."

"So he's *practicing* on you."

"Tinatin," Mael said. "I'm having a rest from all that training they're making us do. You should be envious. I bet you're running around in circles still."

Tinatin scowled, but she didn't say any more.

"Call me if you need me," Kari Wang said. "You've got my code." She pushed it through in case he didn't.

"I'll check again this afternoon," she told Tinatin after she clicked off. "I'll find out what the problem is. Now, as Mael pointed out, you are missing training."

JON'S psych test was as thorough as that for a new recruit, and Fitch did a medical afterward. As he reasoned, "If they think something happened, it's likely to manifest itself physically. How do you feel?"

Exhausted, with the beginnings of a headache, and depressed. She wanted her ship back. She wanted her crew back. She didn't want to be here.

She didn't tell Jon or Fitch that.

Jon gave his findings to the admiral without her present, but she was allowed to watch it on video. She wondered if the pretence of confidentiality was for her or Jon.

"This is a woman who has suffered a major loss, who has not yet allowed herself to grieve."

"Is she depressed?" asked Orsaya.

"She hasn't allowed herself to be depressed yet."

"So you think the worst is to come."

"Maybe," then, "Yes. Probably."

"And what is this worst?"

"Well, depression. Possible suicidal thoughts."

"Suicidal thoughts?" Orsaya asked, sharp-voiced as ever.

"Wish-I-was-dead type thing." Jon shrugged. "It's normal in situations like this."

"I should go and jump in the void and stay forever," Katida suggested.

"Possibly. But she won't do it. She's a strong-willed woman. She would have done it by now if she'd been going to."

From the way the admirals looked at each other, they thought that was what she had done.

What had she done exactly? Thought about her ship and her crew. That wasn't a crime.

"Thank you," Galenos said eventually, and they waited until he was gone before they called Kari Wang in.

"I don't know if you are aware," Galenos said, "but yesterday you took the *Eleven* and its whole fleet into the void."

Fleet was a joke. One alien ship no one knew how to work. One royal yacht. One understaffed captured fleet ship. Another undergunned captured fleet ship. Two media ships and a space station.

"One doesn't enter the void by mistake. It takes preparation—and a trigger—to do so," Kari Wang said. The safeguards were there for a reason. No one, alien or human, would allow such a dangerous maneuver without safeties in place. And on the *Eleven*, how could a nonlinesman like her enter the void anyway?

"The danger seems to be in coming out the other end," Admiral Katida said. "It's probably quite safe going into the void."

Admiral Galenos said, "These are alien ships. We don't

know why they do what they do or how they do it. What were you thinking about before . . . before the incident?"

He couldn't very well say before his soldier pushed her off her chair, could he? Not that Lambert was a soldier.

She tried to be honest. "I was thinking about my crew." She looked at them all. They looked back. She couldn't read any of the expressions. "I was disappointed. None of the crew here are real soldiers. For most of them, the lines are their life, or were until they failed certification. Naturally, I'd be disappointed." She said it defiantly. "I had a good crew. They were *soldiers*."

Orsaya and Katida nodded. Kari Wang thought Mac-Clennan might have, too, but he was better at hiding it.

"Disappointed. Is that all?"

She knew what Galenos wanted to hear. "I was thinking I might get an old ship and jump into the void and stay there forever."

"Forever is a very long time," Katida said.

If that had been the void, what was the point? It hadn't felt a long time at all. "It won't happen again."

"How can you be sure of that?" MacClennan asked.

She thought carefully before she answered. She didn't want this ship. They knew that. But she also needed them to know that she wasn't going to sabotage it either. Or their puny fleet. It was a matter of honor.

"There is a perception that diving into the void is final. That it solves everything because effectively you die. Lambert says we went into the void," and she still wasn't sure they had, but something had scared Lambert. And there was Mael's reaction. "But I didn't notice a thing. Since nothing happened for me, there's no point to doing it, is there?"

She let them think about that.

"Also, I would not deliberately take a whole ship crew with me." And definitely never multiple ships. "If I go, I go alone. Now that I understand the problem, I will endeavor to ensure it doesn't happen again."

She hoped.

The ship had to learn that people indulged in occasional melancholy. That didn't mean it had to take everything literally.

Galenos tapped the table in front of him, a slow tap, tap-tap. "Depression is hard to recognize sometimes. It can strike without warning and with ferocity. It is not something you can control."

"Isn't the danger that I might take the ship into the void? What can I do?"

Orsaya and Katida looked at each other. "What else can she do?" Orsaya asked.

"Decide that the New Alliance is the cause of all her problems and choose to bomb them out of existence."

"Start feeling defensive and accidentally turn on the defense system."

"Crack, and take it out on anyone and everyone in the vicinity."

"When you ladies have finished scaring the rest of us," Galenos said. "What can we do to prevent it?"

Orsaya waved a hand as if that was foregone. "Keep her out of the Captain's Chair."

It wasn't that comfortable a chair anyway.

"Other than that?"

"Make her aware it might happen and have her watch it." Orsaya leaned forward. "Can we stop talking about the dangers now and talk about the good things. The ship accepted her."

She hadn't accepted the ship. She didn't plan to, either.

"It followed her orders, even though it had a level-twelve linesman on board."

The conversation shifted to how much Kari Wang's prior captaincy had contributed. To the changes in brain activity observed since she had taken on the role. To whether or not they could use current captains to take on other alien ships.

"You can't take a captain away from her ship." What did they think they could do? Switch captains and ships around as if they were disposable items. The blood that surged up made Kari Wang's arms and legs ache. She made a conscious effort to smooth her hands, but she couldn't stop the bite in her voice. "Surely you understand how cruel that would be." She thought of Edie Song on the *Gruen*. "Not to mention, for most of us, it is, effectively, a demotion."

Katida pounced on the words. "Demotion? How?"

"These ships can't go anywhere. They're stuck."

"They can move."

"But only as a group, which means to all intents and purposes they're so much junk. Static storehouses, if you like." Even the *Eleven* was although she felt disloyal thinking in those terms. "People will soon realize that. If you work your way up to captaincy, you don't want to be left minding the store." Even if it was an alien store.

Katida sat back. "That's an interesting way to put it."

It was the truth.

"Let's not tell Lambert she said that," Orsaya muttered.

Everyone laughed, except Galenos, although Kari Wang couldn't see any reason to.

"When you were thinking about your crew, just before you went into the void," Galenos said. "Did the ship feel different?"

"No." She wouldn't have noticed even if it had. She'd been too busy missing her crew. She still missed them.

THIRTY-FIVE

EAN LAMBERT

ENTERING THE VOID again scared Ean. He was terrified he would be stuck there forever. He had to get over it, and the best way to do that was to go back into the void.

"I know it's stupid," he told Radko, as they waited for a voice lesson with Gospetto. "I *trust* the lines." At least, he wanted to. "But what if it happens again? What if I can't get us out this time?"

Radko, who'd listened silently through his outpouring, said, "It's a perfectly understandable reaction. I'd be worried, too."

"I have to go back in." He didn't want to.

"The sooner the better," agreed Radko. "What's our plan?" He wished she'd tried to talk him out of it.

"We need to keep you as safe as we can." Radko swapped from her left leg to her right leg. "We probably shouldn't tell the admirals. You're too valuable to waste." She put the last word in air quotes.

"I'll be wasted if I don't get over this."

"I know," she said. "That's why we need to do it fast. So you don't have time to think about it. You'll need someone to pull you out, if they can, which means you'll need Rossi."

Ean wasn't sure which was worse. The worry that he might drag Rossi into the void with him, or the fact that he'd have to admit a weakness to Rossi in the first place.

"You'll need Kari Wang because she controls the ship."

"She's not going back onto the *Eleven*."

"Ean, you have no choice about that. She's got the whole of the New Alliance behind her. And if she's helping you, she won't be going into black depressions, will she?"

Suppose she couldn't help herself.

"She's not going—" He couldn't keep repeating the same thing over and over. Particularly since no one was listening to him. As Orsaya had said, the ship had accepted her. She was dangerous. He'd find a way to stop her damaging the ships and the people on it.

"We'll need the other two captains in on it."

There were only two other captains as far as most people were concerned. Ean wondered sometimes what the captains of the two media ships thought, or Captain Song. Or even the manager on Confluence Station.

"Hmmm," Radko said. "Too many people to keep it a secret. We need a cover. Maybe say you're doing an experiment—" She hesitated, and they heard the ticker tacker of Gospetto's shoes as he hurried down the corridor toward them—plastic toes were in on shoes. "Why don't we say that you heard something while you were in there? Maybe bring a couple of other linesmen in. Do an experiment for real. Use people we know. Like Fergus and Tai."

That was going to make Abram, Katida, and Orsaya think they had something. It was almost like lying. Ean blew out his breath. They'd be disappointed when they found nothing.

"We should ask Mael if he wants to take part in it, too," Radko said. "I'm sure he doesn't like the void any more than you do."

Radko thought of everything. "I don't know where I'd be without you."

"You'd survive, Ean. You're resilient."

Bendable, like pseudorubber.

"I meant that as a compliment."

"You want to be careful, or I'll make your hair stick out again."

"No, no, no," Gospetto said as he reached them and heard the last part of the conversation. "What have you done to your voice now? Do my lessons mean nothing?"

"I'm sorry," Ean said meekly.

RADKO must have worked while Ean had his lesson with Gospetto, for when they were done, Radko said, "Tai's on duty, but everyone else is available. Sale will collect Captain Kari

Wang after her meeting with the admirals. Mael, too. Rossi."
She shrugged. "I've left him to Fergus. You'll need to let Wendell and Helmo know."

"So soon?"

"You don't need time to think about it." Radko fixed him
with a glare. "Go and explain to Helmo that you're taking the
ships back into the void."

He'd prefer to wait until they were about to do it, but one
didn't argue with Radko.

"Right." He took a deep breath.

"Go."

So he went. All the way to the bridge, where he realized he
should have requested permission before he came, but by then
it was too late, he was there.

"Linesman Lambert requesting permission to come onto
the bridge." One day Kari Wang would make him do that on
the *Eleven*. If she remained captain of the *Eleven*, and that
was one thing both Abram and Michelle were adamant about.
They couldn't order a change of captain.

"Permission granted." Ean heard it through the lines,
straight from the Captain's Chair.

"We're planning an experiment with the lines later." Did he
sound as nervous as he felt? "We're going to take the ships
back into the void."

Helmo looked as if he could see right through him.

"For how long?"

Ean couldn't help his shudder. "Not for as long as last time."

"I see," and it seemed to Ean that Helmo did see. "Have
you invited Linesman Mael to join you?"

Ean nodded.

"Let me know before you start, please."

Ean nodded again. "Thank you."

He left and waited until he was two corridors away before
he took out his comms to call Wendell. His hands were
shaking.

Ean was halfway to the shuttle bay when Helmo caught up
with him. "Ean." He held out a small bottle. "Give this to Mael.
It might help."

Helmo did know what they were doing, and why. Ean took
the bottle awkwardly. "Thank you."

*   *   *

SALE arrived with Tinatin in tow as well as Kari Wang and Mael. She shrugged at Ean's raised brow. "She's convinced we're doing dastardly deeds. Brainwashing him or something. I nearly told her that we didn't need him close to brainwash him, but she'd believe that. She thinks Lancia does horrible things."

Ean was Lancastrian, and he thought Lancia did horrible things.

He looked down at the gray uniform he was wearing. Once, it had been something to fear. Now the uniform signified his home. The only family he had.

Line one from the *Eleven* chimed chidingly in his head. The *lines* were his family.

They were, too. Ean bowed in the direction of the ship lines. *"Thank you."*

Tinatin watched them all mistrustfully.

Fergus arrived then. He had gone with Ru Li and Gossamer via Confluence Station to collect Jordan Rossi.

Tinatin's eyes widened.

Ean hoped he wouldn't spoil it by saying something cutting, like, "What's your problem, sweetheart?" Rossi had no tact.

Instead, Rossi looked around the ship. "This is cozy. Just us."

"And two teams of guards," Sale said.

Ean looked at Mael. "Will you be okay with this?"

Mael shrugged. "Can't say I'm looking forward to it. But it needs to be done." His hands were shaking.

"If you don't want to do it, Mael," Kari Wang said.

"I need to do it, ma'am. I'll be scared of this ship forever if I don't."

Most of the soldiers nodded approvingly. Except Tinatin, who looked around suspiciously. "What are you going to do?"

"I'm sorry I put you through this, Mael," Kari Wang said. "I wouldn't have if I had realized what I was doing."

Mael shrugged. "You didn't mean to, ma'am."

"Let's get this over with," Sale said. "You," to Kari Wang. "In the Captain's Chair." She said in an aside to Bhaksir as Kari Wang settled herself, "We should have brought the medic."

Tinatin's voice rose. "What are you going to do?"

"What are *we* going to do, sweetheart? *We're* going to sing to the lines—you included—while the bastard here drops the ships into the void. And maybe brings them out again." Then Rossi added maliciously, "If he can. That's what we're here for, to give him a lifeline out."

"Don't mind Jordan," Fergus said.

"But look what happened last time. Mael went to the hospital."

At least it was an improvement on "Mael being arrested."

"What if he can't?"

"Tinatin," Kari Wang said. She held up a hand for silence. "This is my ship. I control when it goes in and out of the void."

That was the trouble. She couldn't control it.

"It's not up to Lambert. It's up to me. It's nice of you to be concerned, but if you want to be part of this, shut up and do what you're told." She looked at Ean. "For what it's worth, now that I understand what I did, and that it's no solution, I won't be wishing for it again."

He nodded. It wasn't any consolation, no matter how sincere she sounded, for if she hadn't known what she was doing the first time, how could she prevent it another time?

He'd planned what to do on the way over. "I need you to sing to your lines on this ship—and the other ships in the fleet if you can hear them—and to me."

"Like we've been doing in line training?" Fergus asked.

"Exactly like that." Ean took a deep breath. "Let's practice first. Rossi, I want you around the edges, helping if we need it."

"Line twelve, asking a mere ten for help. Unbelievable."

"Hah," Fergus said. "You just admitted it. In front of witnesses. I'm not going to let you forget that, Jordan."

"Let's practice," Ean said hurriedly, before Rossi could think of a cutting retort. "Start singing. Greet your lines. All of you. You, too," to Rossi, who might scoff, but he hated to miss line training, and Ean had heard him through the lines on Confluence Station, practicing. He wasn't going to mention that fact. Ever.

"Talk to the ship," he told Tinatin. "Sing line one." He sang the music for her. An explanation of what they planned to do. "Like this. Sing with me."

"I don't know the words."

"Make up your own. Ask it how it is?" He was struck with an idea. "Tell it what happened to Mael."

He turned to Mael. "Sing line nine," and as Mael hesitated, "It's safe here. We're not in the void yet."

Fergus didn't need to be told. He was singing to line seven, explaining what was happening.

Ean opened his own voice, weak as it was, and sang to the lines. Rossi's voice joined his. The lines surged in strong around him. Rossi's lines weakened, and he was vaguely aware of, "Shit," from Sale.

Line eleven wasn't even strong today.

"If he goes on about the glory again," Sale said, "I'll kill him myself." She looked at Craik, who was getting oxygen. "Bring two, just in case."

Ean finished his explanation. Tinatin had stopped singing and was listening, nodding occasionally at what made sense. Mael was doing the same.

The song died away.

Ean glanced over to Kari Wang, sitting in the Captain's Chair. He hoped she wasn't too depressed.

"Let's do it for real now," Sale said.

"I need to call Helmo and Wendell first." Ean sang two comms open. "Ready to enter the void, Captains," he said.

Even Kari Wang nodded.

He closed the lines the same way. "Let's do it."

Mael had started to shake again. What if he couldn't help Mael? Then Ean remembered Helmo's gift. He pulled the small bottle out of his pocket and handed it across. "Captain Helmo asked me to give this to you." At least it would give Mael something to think about.

Mael unstoppered the lid and sniffed at it. He sniffed again, more deeply. "Black fire," he said wonderingly. "Do you know how much this stuff costs?" He downed it in one mouthful. Then he smiled. His tongue and his teeth were black.

"What have you done to him?"

"Tinatin," Kari Wang said.

"Let's go into the void," Ean said. "Start singing. I'll take us in when we're all communicating through the lines."

Mael was still smiling, singing his heart out, as Ean took them into the void.

IN the void it was just Ean and Mael and Rossi.

And line seven. Ean could hear Fergus, linking all the sevens—Ean included—with his song. Could see the interlinked chain of the sevens like twisting ropes of light. It was so amazing he stared at them for a moment. He could feel it—see it—going all the way to the thump-kerthump that was line eleven.

They hadn't been there last time.

Then he remembered. They were only to be in the void for a moment.

"Take us out," he sang to line nine, and line nine, as reliable and friendly as it had ever been, took them out.

THIRTY-SIX

EAN LAMBERT

OUTSIDE OF THE void Ean sang a thank you to the lines—especially to line nine, which had not failed him.

Rossi was on the floor, dry-retching. Ean became aware he was on the floor, too. Flat on his back. The Lancastrians were just starting to react.

Radko got to Ean first, with oxygen. He shook his head.

Rossi pushed Sale away. "If you have done anything to my lines, bastard."

Mael stood above them, grinning euphorically. "That was amazing," he said. "It was so clear and close and—"

His teeth weren't black anymore.

"Sing to line nine," Ean suggested, but Mael shook his head. "Amazing," he said again.

Ean rolled over onto his knees. It was like when he'd first gone onto the *Eleven* and kept blacking out. He was weak, and his muscles weren't working properly. Radko helped him up.

"Your hair really has some static in it," Mael said.

"I'm used to it." Radko's voice had picked up some of the lines. She still always sounded like Helmo's ship.

Ean went over to Fergus. "How do you feel?"

"Me?" Fergus looked at him as if he'd asked something strange. "I'm fine."

Kari Wang moved over to ask the same question of Tinatin, with much the same result. Tinatin looked at her oddly. "I'm not the one laughing crazily like they fed me poison. Or lying on the floor being sick. Or just lying on the floor."

"I'm not lying on the floor now," Ean protested.

"I think," Tinatin announced to the room at large, "that he's crazy."

Rossi managed to stand up under his own steam. "You only think that. The rest of us know it, sweetheart."

Her hero worship of Jordan Rossi was fast dissipating if the look she gave him was anything to go by. "I'm not sure which one of you I'm talking about yet." She moved over to Mael.

"I'm fine," Mael said. "It was amazing, Tinatin. There was this music. Deep and . . . deep and—"

Tinatin was fine, and Mael would be, too.

"What happened in the void?" Ean asked Fergus.

"In the void? Nothing."

Ean blew out his breath, then realized it was getting to be a habit. One he hadn't had before he'd met Abram. "You were in the void. All the sevens together."

Fergus shook his head.

Rossi staggered a little as he joined Ean and Fergus. "We were in the void forever," he said, and Ean had to look at him to see if he really meant it. "It's normally over in a blink."

"That wasn't long," Mael said. "That was friendly."

Friendly was one way of putting it. How would Rossi have coped with the earlier time in the void, which truly had been long? Would he have come out of it as well as Mael had, or would he have come out of it worse? Crazy even?

Ean was glad Rossi had been off fleet, mending a Yaolin destroyer, when Kari Wang had inadvertently taken them into the void the first time. That was something to think about for the future.

"Did you see the lines?" he asked Mael. "The sevens? All interconnected like someone had tied them together."

Mael shook his head.

"I heard them," Rossi said. "All green and pink and smelling like Centauran basket palms and icy like dripping water."

"You should hear yourself," Tinatin said. "You sound like you've been drinking."

Yes, the awe was definitely gone from that relationship.

"Tinatin." Fergus's voice was gentle. "That's the lines talking. You yourself will start to mix up smells and sounds and sights soon."

"And taste and touch," Radko said. "What does this ship taste like, Tinatin?"

"Tinatin," Kari Wang said, when it looked as if she was

going to remain silent. "Answer the question." She was testing the air herself. Ean would bet the ship had a taste for her, too.

Tinatin opened her mouth to deny it. Kari Wang glared at her, so she said sulkily, "It smells like the sound the waves make on a beach."

"Don't you mean smells like the salt in the waves?" Mael asked.

Tinatin shook her head.

They were saved any further semantics by Wendell's opening a comms. "How long before you start this thing?" He sounded a little irritated. Through the lines, Ean could feel blue edges. Wendell didn't like waiting around on other people. He liked to be in control. There was a lot of blue in the *Wendell* lines nowadays.

Ean should have told them the experiment was over. "We've finished, sorry."

"So you're not going into the void?"

Ean stared at the comms. Even through the lines, it sounded like a genuine question. "We've already done that," he said.

"I know when my ship goes into the void," Wendell said. "We didn't go anywhere."

If anyone knew, Wendell would. He and Helmo had both recognized they'd entered the void last time.

"Hold on a minute." Ean sang a line open to Helmo.

Behind him, he heard Mael whisper to Tinatin. "Watch him. He never touches anything when he does that."

If they wanted to keep that particular talent a secret, Ean had better start opening the comms the way everyone else did—even if it was faster and you could do more with it when you opened the lines directly.

"Is there a problem?" Helmo asked.

Why would he assume there was a problem unless he thought they hadn't gone into the void either? "Did you feel us go into the void just now?" Ean kept the line three-way, so Wendell heard the answer, too.

"You haven't gone in yet." Helmo was as definite as Wendell was.

"But we did."

"You didn't."

"You didn't notice anything at all?"

"No." The only thing more decisive than a captain's saying no was two captains saying it at the same time.

Ean looked around the bridge of the *Kari Wang*. "Did we go into the void before?"

Fergus shrugged. Mael nodded. Rossi groaned. Kari Wang nodded, too.

"We did." Ean was sure of it. So what had changed between this time and the last?

The line sevens?

"Can we try something? Can one of you take the ship into the void?"

He could hear them shudder through the lines.

"We need another side to come out," Helmo said.

Wendell's was a flat, "No."

Okay, so he was the only one who could take them into and out of the void without problem. They'd put a lot of trust in him earlier then, when they'd let him do it.

"I'm going to take us back into the void momentarily." He swallowed, and tried to make his voice normal. "I want to know if you feel this. I'll make it fast."

He sang to line nine on the ship. "Take us into the void."

He was in the void again. The normal eternity that he felt, with just him and the lines. This was friendly, too, and he knew now he could fix any line here in the whole fleet.

The line sevens, the knots, they were there. Faintly, but there. They'd always been there; he'd just never known what they were till now.

"Out again, please."

They were back in real space. Mael and Rossi were just starting to react. Rossi was saying, "No."

"That was the void," Wendell said.

Helmo nodded.

Kari Wang nodded.

"What about this?" Ean looked at Fergus. "Sing to the sevens. Like you always do. Tell them we're practicing."

"Sure." Fergus started to sing although he looked at Ean strangely.

"No," Rossi said—almost begging—and Ean wondered if he should stop, but the sevens were already confirming back.

Ean sang to line nine again. "Take us into the void."

Inside the void was a strong chain of sevens, linked to each other, linked to the *Eleven*.

"Take us out again, please."

Outside, he sang his thanks to line nine, patient enough to humor him.

"You do what lines have to do," line nine told him.

"How was that?" Ean asked Helmo and Wendell.

"Nothing."

"This ship went into the void," Kari Wang said. "Although I don't have any instruments to tell me that."

Ean suspected neither Helmo nor Wendell did, either. Or maybe human ships did have a warning. But they usually warned before they entered the void, not when they did it. It was probably some infinitesimal ship change the captains were attuned to that no one else could pick up on.

"And it was Burns's singing that triggered this?" Wendell said.

Ean thought it out as he talked. "The links were always there." If he'd been smart enough to notice. "But Fergus." Fergus couldn't sing to a single line. He sang to all the sevens. "What exactly did you tell the lines, Fergus?"

"I said we were taking the *Eleven* into the void."

"Just the *Eleven*?" Wendell asked.

Fergus thought about it. "Yes. Just the *Eleven*. I explained the problem." He looked apologetically at Ean. "As far as I knew it, anyway."

There was no privacy with lines. What one line knew, the others knew. Ean nodded. "I don't think we've ever spoken specifically to the sevens like that before, not going into the void." Lines and humans had been working together for months now as well. They understood each other better.

The sevens had always said the void, and communications. And linking. Next time a line said it worked in the void, Ean was going to take it into the void and ask it there.

Both captains started to speak, stopped together. Ean had never seen either of them so animated—physically, or through the lines.

"You first," Wendell said.

"How can you be certain you entered the void?" Helmo asked. He stopped, a blue snap of instant decision. "Let's not discuss this over the lines."

The lines were as safe as Ean could make them.

"Let's meet in my office." He glanced at a screen. "At 23:00 hours. Burns, are you available?"

Fergus looked as excited as Wendell and Helmo, and who wouldn't. This might be where they finally unraveled the mystery of line seven. "I'm available."

"Good." Helmo said to Wendell, "I'll get clearance for you. Selma?"

"I'd appreciate that," Kari Wang said.

"Linesman Rossi?"

"I'll be there." Rossi sounded as if he'd rather be elsewhere, but Jordan Rossi was never the sort to miss out on major happenings. That meant Orsaya would know before Abram and Michelle did. Although Rossi wasn't one to share line information.

"I will see you all at 23:00 hours." Helmo clicked off.

Sale broke the silence that followed. "I'll get you two back to base," she said, looking at Mael and Tinatin.

Tinatin looked as if she was going to say something, but didn't.

Ean bowed to them both. "Linesmen," he said. "Thank you for coming."

Mael nodded. "It helped." He took Tinatin's arm. "Let's go home."

Through the lines, as the two of them walked to the shuttle with Sale's people in front and Sale's people behind, Ean heard Tinatin say, "Even he calls you linesman. You'd think, because he was a ten, he should know who you are."

"So far as I can tell, he's not a ten," Mael said. "Not from what everyone's saying."

"He's got ten bars on his shirt."

"Linesman Rossi called him a twelve."

"Linesman Rossi should know better."

Oh yes, the luster had well and truly gone.

"And it's cruel, calling you a linesman all the time. They should know better."

"Maybe they do know better." Mael sounded thoughtful. "Maybe we're the ones not listening, Tinatin."

Ean was definitely going to find the Aratogan who'd rec-
ommended Mael and see if he had more single-level linesmen
to recommend.

"And they didn't even invite us to their meeting," Tinatin
said. "Even though you're the one they poisoned, and they
made you go into the void like that."

"Tinatin." Sale was one of the soldiers behind them. "You
wouldn't want to chat with Captain Helmo even if you could.
He's one scary bastard."

EAN was glad Helmo had arranged the security. He could
imagine what Vega would have said if he'd asked if Wendell,
Rossi, and Kari Wang could come aboard.

The meeting room was crowded. Helmo and Wendell
between them exuded so much energy, the room seemed too
small for anyone but them. Kari Wang was quiet, taking
everything in. Rossi looked to have a headache, and he took
the glass of wine Helmo offered him with more alacrity than
politeness.

Fergus couldn't stop smiling. "I don't know what I did,"
he'd told Ean as they walked up to the meeting together. "I
have no idea what to tell them."

"Tell them the truth," Ean said. "They can't do anything
but listen, can they?"

Wendell and Helmo pounced as soon as they arrived.

"Linesman Burns, can you do it again?"

"Do you think you can do it on this ship?"

"Give him some room," Ean said. "If you scare him into a
heart attack, he won't be any use to you."

"He's a single-level linesman," Wendell said. "He doesn't
have heart attacks."

"You know, there are more than just line-related heart
attacks," Ean said. "There's the old-fashioned kind. The one
where you scare someone to death."

Helmo and Wendell looked at each other. "Apologies,"
Wendell said to Fergus, while Helmo said, "Let's start at the
start, shall we, and work out exactly what happened?"

"I wanted to go back into the void," Ean said. He hesitated.
This was the awkward bit.

"You don't have to explain," Helmo said. "We understand the reasoning. You were on the *Eleven*, you called to tell us you were going into the void. What happened next?"

That was easier than he'd expected. "We sang. We started singing before we went into the void. There was Fergus, Mael, Rossi, Tinatin, and myself. Mael's a single nine," he told Wendell. "Tinatin's a one."

Wendell nodded.

"Inside the void it was . . . different."

"Lit up like pleasure planet," Rossi said. He shuddered. "And the music. That deep tone of line nine. The baritone of line seven. And behind it all, the beat of eleven."

It was the first time Ean had ever heard Jordan Rossi admit to hearing music.

"And knots everywhere."

"Knots?" Ean hadn't seen any knots.

"Tying everything together. This ship to that ship to that ship."

"They were lines to other ships," Ean said.

Wendell thrust his comms at him. "Draw it. You, too," to Rossi. "Who else saw it?"

"I didn't," Fergus said hastily, and no wonder for it looked as if Wendell would snatch his comms out of Ean's hands to get Fergus to draw it instead.

"What about Mael? You say he's a nine. He was in the void."

"He didn't see anything." He'd said it was awesome, but he hadn't seen or heard the sevens. "He heard line nine."

"But you two, having both lines, did."

Ean nodded, and began sketching the approximation of what he'd seen. Lines, coming out of each ship, going into other ships. Line seven to line seven. And a thicker, heavier line from each ship, going to line eleven.

He finished around the same time Rossi did. Helmo put them both on screen.

Rossi's diagram was similar to Ean's, except he knotted the ends of his lines, and he didn't have the thick lines going to line eleven.

"What's this?" Wendell pointed to the thicker line.

"Line eleven." Eleven to seven, or seven to eleven, he wasn't sure which.

"Which proves one thing," Helmo said, and added, when everyone looked at him, "Lambert sees more lines than other linesmen."

"He claims he *hears* them," Rossi said.

Ean had never claimed he heard more lines than anyone else. Sure, he might hear them differently, but that didn't mean he heard more of them. It was time they brought the conversation back to the topic of interest.

"We came out of the void. Rossi—" He stopped.

Kari Wang took over smoothly. "Rossi appeared to feel a lot of time had passed. Mael and Lambert didn't seem to notice the time."

"Except Mael's teeth weren't black anymore," Ean said.

"How long since he'd drunk the black fire?"

"Just before he went into the void."

"It takes a couple of hours for the black to wear off," Helmo said. "More if you haven't eaten or drunk anything with it."

"No time passed," Kari Wang said. "Or not obviously to me."

"Or to us," Helmo said.

"I checked the recordings." Helmo pulled up the recording of his own ship bridge, of the *Wendell* bridge, and the *Eleven*. He played them side by side with a clock underneath, counting seconds in real time. He started where Ean gave Mael the black fire, and stopped when Radko was helping Ean off the floor. There were no noticeable pauses as there had been when Kari Wang had taken them into the void. "I can't tell when you went in or came out of the void. Can you tell from the *Eleven*'s instruments?"

Kari Wang shook her head.

Even Ean couldn't tell, not from a recording. He knew roughly from the singing when he'd gone in, but time didn't flow the same with the lines, so he couldn't say with any certainty.

Wendell sat back, arms crossed. "Watch the captain," he suggested. "She'll do something. Twitch, or look up, or . . . something. What do you do when you enter the void, Marcus?"

"I'm usually watching the boards," Helmo said. "Waiting to see that we've come out the other end without killing everyone."

Wendell grunted what might have been a "me, too." "She'll do something. She'll know."

They started at the black fire again, and watched carefully. It took four rewatches before they agreed that a specific twitch was the actual time of entry into the void.

"Scientific," Rossi said.

"I recollect a certain linesman making disparaging comments about scientists who studied the lines," Wendell said.

Rossi looked at him, opened his mouth to say something, and Ean heard the music of Rossi's lines alter as he changed what he was going to say. "Even I wouldn't base line theory on a single twitch."

"Let's check the time after," Wendell said. "When we all went into the void. See if it's standard."

They forwarded the recordings to when Ean said, "I'll make it fast," and watched until Wendell said, "That was the void."

They watched it three times, and could pick the moment they went into the void from the way the three captains twitched at the exact same time.

Then they watched again while Fergus sang to line seven and Ean took them in and out again. This time only Kari Wang twitched.

"So there you have it," Fergus said, as they all sat back and contemplated the screen. "It's official. Captains twitch on entering the void."

"Or exiting," Helmo said. "Going in is never my worry. It's coming out."

"Mmmh," from Wendell, and Kari Wang nodded.

"I'm sure some enterprising academic could find a paper in it," Helmo said. "I don't, personally, care. I'm more interested in line seven. Do we think we can jump individually if Fergus is on board the *Eleven*? Or better, since he's already on the *Lancastrian Princess*, can he do it from here?"

"Or from the *Wendell*?"

"Such demand," Rossi said to Fergus. "Your ego will be unbearable."

Fergus smiled. "It will be nice to be useful. After all, what's a line without a purpose?"

Fergus didn't have an ego, not like Rossi's.

Rossi's lines surged. "That means Ean and I can also shift individual ships."

It was no secret Jordan Rossi wanted an eleven of his own. If he couldn't get the *Eleven*, he wanted the *Confluence*. It was easy to see his plan. Use line seven to jump the ship he was on. Personally, Ean doubted he'd be strong enough to cope with the *Confluence*, given that Rossi still needed oxygen on a regular basis when he came into contact with line eleven.

Wendell leaned close. "When was the last time you saw lines connecting ships while you were in the void, Rossi?"

"I don't make a habit of singing in the void."

He was going to try it now. Sure as there were lines.

"You'd want to do it under supervision then," Fergus said, "in case you get stuck." Fergus could remind Rossi of things like that, and Rossi would listen.

"Speaking of supervision," Helmo said. "Let's get our plan together. We need to present it to the admirals."

The planning lasted until 04:00 hours. Helmo and Wendell made a ferocious, determined team. Ean suspected Kari Wang might, too, but she didn't have as much invested in the success of this as the other captains did.

Fergus was almost as bad.

"We have a pool of emergency jumps," Helmo said. "We buy them from ships that aren't affiliated with the New Alliance. If we can convince Galenos this is important enough, he'll use one of those."

Jumps were precious. It was a big ask.

"Do we need a Gate Union jump?" Ean asked. "We know where the ships are in this sector. Can't we jump locally?"

All three captains shuddered, and a wave of almost terror swept the lines. "No cold jumps," Helmo said.

Back all those months ago, when the suicide ship had tried to jump into *Gruen* space, the *Eleven* and the *Gruen* had prevented it. "What about the suicide ship Gate Union sent through? We stopped that. Surely we can risk a jump to an area we know is safe."

"No." Wendell was as forceful as Helmo.

They should trust their ships.

"I can't believe the alien ships required gate controllers in every sector." Otherwise, there would be more evidence of aliens.

"Not until blind jumps are proven technology," Helmo said.

How could they prove it if the captains wouldn't let them jump?

"You realize," Kari Wang said. "That none of us knows how to set a jump on the *Eleven*."

That pulled them up short. They all laughed, the sort of laughter you did at 04:00 when you hadn't had any sleep.

"Ean can do it," Helmo said.

Ean didn't even know how to set a normal jump. "Suppose I can't."

"You'll work out a way," Helmo said, and called Abram. "Admiral, we need a jump."

Only Helmo or Michelle would wake Abram at 04:00 hours to ask for that.

"Wish I could do that to some of my admirals," Wendell muttered to Kari Wang, and she nodded.

Abram didn't look as if he'd just been woken. "Right now?"

"It's not that urgent," and Helmo smiled somewhat sheepishly. "I'm used to having you instantly available."

"This jump?"

"As soon as you can would be nice. We want to jump the *Eleven*."

Abram became more alert. "The whole fleet?"

"No. Just the *Eleven*."

He didn't have to say any more. Abram knew what that meant as well as they did. He knew, too, that Helmo wouldn't have woken him for anything trivial.

"I'll see what I can do." From the pause that followed, Ean thought Abram must have been doing some snap thinking of his own. "The *Eleven* is watched closely. People noticed the ship disappeared for five seconds yesterday. I might put it out that we're doing more experiments." He smiled. "Gate Union is getting complacent. It will be good to give them something to worry about."

It made acquiring jumps more dangerous, but Ean could

see why he was doing it. The media had speculated already that yesterday's jump was an experiment gone wrong.

"I'll get you that jump, and I look forward to your report." Abram clicked off.

Now all Ean had to do was convince the *Eleven* to jump to the coordinates Abram gave them. He hoped he could do it.

THIRTY-SEVEN

STELLAN VILHJALMSSON

WHEN STELLAN CAME around, his head ached so much he wondered if he was dead. It took a moment through the haze of pain to see Neela Cotterill sitting by his bed.

She handed him a bottle of water. "I've heard the dehydration headache is debilitating," she said.

He grabbed the water. If it was drugged, he'd know next time, but right now he wanted anything that might stop the headache. As he glugged it down, he realized he was naked. Nudity didn't bother him, but the fact that she knew to strip an assassin so he couldn't get to any of the tools in his clothes was disturbing. So far as he knew, it was a military practice.

"Mendez and Charlemaine have weapons trained on you," his captor said. "I won't tell you where they are, but I have put the fear of the lines into them about you. The danger is that they'll shoot you by mistake. If you want to stay alive, move slowly and telegraph what you plan to do."

Stellan took another long mouthful of water. "Do I know you?"

"I sincerely hope not," she said. "I've gone to a lot of trouble to hide my identity. But I know you, Stellan Vilhjalmsson, and you're going to help me get what I want."

"To kill Lambert?"

"Personally, I would love nothing better, but I wasn't trying to kill him last time. I needed him to get me access to something."

"And you don't need him now?"

"No. I need you, and your plan to get to him."

Which she shouldn't have known about. The water hadn't helped Stellan's headache at all. He couldn't think properly.

"We can help each other," Neela said. "I need to get out to

the *Gruen*, and I have the one part of the plan you don't yet have. Once we get there, I can get us onto the ship."

"How?" And more importantly, how did she know his plans? The only person who knew about them was Markan.

"I worked on the *Gruen*." He couldn't read the raw emotion behind that, but it choked her voice. "I have access if I can get close enough. They would have destroyed the ship if they'd destroyed my accesses."

She had cracked his codes. She might even be able to do it.

There would be a catch. There was always a catch. But if she could get him onto the *Gruen*, he'd sort that out when he came to it. "Suppose I agree. What's in it for you?"

THIRTY-EIGHT

EAN LAMBERT

ABRAM HAD A jump when Ean woke from the two-hour sleep he'd managed to snatch.

"It's later today," Abram told him. "So follow standard procedure for the morning." Which meant line training on the *Gruen*. "You can go straight from the *Gruen* to the *Eleven* when it's time."

The captains were nervous about the jump. So much so that it came strongly through the lines, and infected everyone else on ship with nerves.

Ean wasn't worried about the jump. He trusted the *Eleven* to avoid other ships. Hadn't it helped the *Gruen* avoid them last time. No, his worries were more practical.

"What if I can't jump the ship to a specific location?" Ean asked Radko.

"You'll manage," Radko said. "You don't always do it the way people expect, Ean, but you get there in the end."

There was always a first time to fail. Unless you were Abram or Michelle. Ean was sure fail wasn't even a word they understood.

"Trust the lines, Ean. You and they will work it out."

THE New Alliance refused to put all three top-level linesmen into the experiment. Jordan Rossi was moved off the line ships altogether and taken down to Haladea III.

He refused to go. *"If you destroy* my *eleven,"* he sang to Ean, *"I'll kill you myself."*

Not that Rossi had a specific eleven in mind. He wavered between the two, whichever he thought would be easier to get.

Orsaya must have expected resistance, for she went out to Confluence Station herself to be sure he went down to the planet. Ean heard, through the lines, Orsaya tell her assistant, Captain Willow Auburn, "You know what to do if he refuses to go."

"Yes, ma'am," and Auburn checked the settings on her weapon.

Ean hoped Auburn's blaster was on stun.

Rossi had always had a problem going out of range of line eleven. "There is no reason to go off station. If it's as safe as Lambert claims it to be, I will be fine here."

"We've been through this before, Rossi." Confluence Station was part of the *Eleven*'s fleet.

"What? You don't think your pet wonder boy might botch a simple thing like uncoupling a ship. *Get out of my lines, bastard.* Unbelievable."

"Look at it this way," Willow Auburn said, as she raised her weapon and fired. "If Lambert fails, you get full control of the *Confluence* eleven." She holstered the weapon and caught him as he fell. "We're doing it for his own good. You'd think he'd be grateful."

Orsaya managed a tight laugh. "Jordan Rossi?"

Rossi couldn't even talk to line eleven. Ean wiped his hands down the side of his uniform. Who would talk to them if he failed?

"We won't fail." It was a collective thought, from the lines as a whole. Sometimes they did that, thinking as a single unit rather than as individual lines. *"Why would we?"*

He hadn't yet told the lines what they were to do, for he couldn't get lines to understand the concept of future. Once he explained it, they would expect to act immediately.

He couldn't lie to them and tell them he believed them when he wasn't sure he did. The lines would pick up the dishonesty. So he laughed, a little shakily, instead. *"I wish I had your confidence."*

In return, he got an outpouring of support, boosting his lines, so that he started to believe they could do it.

That kind of reinforcement could be dangerous.

"You okay?" Radko asked.

"The lines are confident." Overconfident, but if he had doubts he shouldn't be thinking of that because he couldn't separate his thoughts from the lines.

EAN was glad to arrive on the *Gruen.*

At least today Song would come to her ship, for Abram had insisted the captain be there for the duration of the experiment.

What if something went wrong, and Song and the ship hadn't bonded?

What if Ean worried so much about it that it caused a problem when it wouldn't have otherwise?

LINE training was good today. There was an air of expectancy among the lines that even the trainees caught. The ship buzzed.

Afterward, as they waited for the shuttle to bring Captain Song out to the ship, Linesman Hernandez came up to Ean.

"We should be part of it," she said.

Song's shuttle would take the trainees back to Haladea III. All nonessential personnel were to go off ship.

"It?" He pretended to not understand.

"This thing that's happening. We are linesmen. We have been trained. We should be part of it."

Radko said, before Ean could reply, "That's why you won't be part of it."

Especially not Linesman Hernandez, who was their best hope after Rossi if anything went wrong with Ean.

"That's not a good enough reason."

"Spacer," Bhaksir said, from behind them both. "Are you disobeying an order?"

"I'm saying that if it's line-related, we should be part of it."

"All nonessential personnel are to return to Haladea III for the duration of the exercise."

"This ship is our base while we're training."

Bhaksir looked at her. Hernandez looked as if she was going to argue some more.

"Would you like Admiral Katida to reinforce your orders?"

Hernandez turned away, muttering, "You wouldn't have a hope," under her breath.

"Anyone else want to argue?" Bhaksir said, and glared at Tai as he looked as if he would speak. "Don't put me in an awkward position, Tai." Because, of course, Tai could have argued that technically he belonged on the *Lancastrian Princess*, and therefore should be allowed to be part of it. "You're on secondment."

It said something for Abram Galenos's people that Tai didn't argue although he wanted to, and his lines—all the way up to six—hummed his unhappiness with the decision.

THIRTY-NINE

SELMA KARI WANG

THE SHUTTLE OUT was crowded, despite the fact they'd kept the numbers on the *Eleven* to a minimum. They'd brought Jem Abascal, because he was a seven. A full seven, but everyone involved in the plan thought that having someone Katida had primed would be smarter than picking a single seven, although Ean Lambert had pointed out that they didn't know if the multilines could do what the single lines could. They'd brought Mael because he was a nine, and because he'd been there from the start. And Tinatin, because it was easier to bring her than to leave her behind.

If Tinatin ever went into covert operations she'd be damned good at it if somewhat unconventional.

They'd brought Fitch and Jon in case something happened that needed medical or psychiatric help. Kari Wang wasn't convinced a psychiatrist would be much help. A doctor might.

Tinatin did most of the talking on the shuttle out to the *Eleven*. Kari Wang tuned her out. How much longer could she go on like this? She shouldn't be captain, but they wouldn't let her change her mind. Not unless she was proven mentally unstable. If she wanted out, she should get out now, to give the *Eleven*'s real captain time to build the crew without Kari Wang's influence.

There was no way out. Nova Tahiti was depending on her. Could she live with herself knowing she had destroyed her world's main chance of being an important cog in the New Alliance? Did she care?

She glanced across at Jon, frowning at the crew. He always frowned at this crew. As if he found them lacking but hadn't quite figured out what the problem was.

Mael nudged Kari Wang with his foot.

She looked up at him. He inclined his head slightly toward Tinatin, and she realized the young spacer had asked a direct question.

"Why don't we?"

"Why don't we what?"

"Use the *Eleven* shuttles? Why do we force it to use shuttles that don't fit?"

In all the time they had traveled between the *Eleven* and Haladea III, they had used human shuttles.

"I don't know why," Kari Wang said.

"Maybe the aliens don't use shuttles," Abascal said. "Have you ever seen one?"

"We saw aliens the other day," Tinatin said. "We went to the hospital, remember."

"Mortuary."

"More like lab," Mael said. "They don't know if they're dead yet."

Maybe, as the admirals had theorized, they were still partially in the void and not wholly in human space. Kari Wang tried not to shiver. When they finally came across aliens, would they think humans were monsters for leaving them in that state?

"I meant a shuttle, duh," Abascal said.

"Abascal," Kari Wang said.

Abascal pressed his lips together. Tinatin pressed hers together, too, in what she didn't realize was an exact imitation.

"Why don't you ask Lambert?" Kari Wang suggested to Tinatin. "Maybe there's a reason they don't use them."

"It's our ship. We should be allowed to use our shuttles."

"Okay getting them onto the *Eleven*," Mael said. "Might not be so good at the other end. Suppose it didn't communicate with human ships at all. It doesn't take much in space, and bang." He smacked his palms together.

"If they're our shuttles, they would listen to us."

"Yeah, but you've got to get the right line so it will listen, don't you? Suppose it needs a ten—or a twelve—to do the talking. What happens if your only ten is flat on the floor unconscious?"

They were adapting well to lines that talked back. "Don't forget," Kari Wang said, as the *Eleven* grabbed onto the shuttle and moved it, "these shuttles don't land themselves. The ships take them in."

"They won't always have ships to do it," Tinatin said. "They will have a way to land."

Sale met them at the shuttle bay. Tinatin started on her. "Why do we always use New Alliance shuttles? Why don't we use the *Eleven*'s shuttles?"

"If you can get the shuttles to work, Tinatin—without killing anyone—we'd love to try them."

Tinatin chewed that one over as they made their way up to the bridge.

"Why doesn't Linesman Lambert ask the ship how they work then?"

"Why don't *you* ask the ship?"

"But Linesman Lambert is a level ten."

"Technically, he's a—" Mael said.

Kari Wang glared him into silence. It might be common knowledge among the Lancian crew, but if they wanted the galaxy to know it, he'd be wearing twelve bars on his shirt.

"You're a linesman, too," Sale told Tinatin.

"But he's—"

"Tinatin, Ean doesn't have five minutes of his own in a day anymore. Where's he going to get the time to do all the little things like sorting out the shuttles?"

"Spacer Tinatin," Kari Wang said. "You've talked yourself into an assignment. Get three other crew to work on it with you and find out how those shuttles work."

Tinatin turned to walk backward, so she could talk to Kari Wang. "I'm only a one."

She was also just out of academy, if that. It was a big ask for someone so inexperienced, but if she was smart, she'd choose her other three team members carefully.

"I want those names on my comms by 21:00 hours tonight. I need to approve them before you start." She saw the way Tinatin's eyes tracked. "And, no, you can't have Mael. He's got other work to do." Knowing Tinatin, she'd end up involving the whole crew anyway.

Tinatin was silent for the rest of the walk to the bridge.

"Are you okay about this?" Sale asked, as Kari Wang misstepped and lurched outside the bridge. Sale probably thought

it was nerves, but it was simply balance. She didn't do it anywhere near as often as she used to, but she still couldn't walk
straight all that way.

"I'm fine."

She could feel the other woman assessing her. Sale was too
good to be a simple group leader defending the royal family.
She should be out fighting battles. It was definitely true that
Emperor Yu of Lancia wasted his best staff defending the
royal family.

Sale nodded.

Kari Wang hoped this venture wouldn't kill them. She
wanted to die, but she didn't want to take anyone with her.

"Ean and Fergus will be over once Captain Song arrives on
the *Gruen*."

Poor Edie Song, who'd thought her captaincy a promotion
when it turned out to be a desk job. Maybe, after this, it
wouldn't be such a demotion, and Song might be sorry she
hadn't spent more time on her ship.

It wasn't Kari Wang's problem.

The *Eleven* was a presence in the back of her mind. Hum-
ming along—not as contented as her own ship had been, but
that was understandable. It had a skeleton crew, and they
couldn't communicate with it properly. Or she couldn't, and
that was unacceptable.

She'd have to learn.

Kari Wang settled into the Captain's Chair. If they wanted
a human captain, they had better improve the chair.

She looked at the rows of flickering lights on the walls that
were also all screens—no wasted wall space here—then at the
smaller human screens in front of the Captain's Chair. "You
three," to Mael, Tinatin, and Abascal. "Translate for me. Tell
me what's happening on that wall, so I can understand it on
my screens here."

FORTY

STELLAN VILHJALMSSON

"WHAT'S YOUR REAL name?" Stellan asked, as he and Neela walked through the busy streets to Stellan's hotel.

Somewhere behind them walked trigger-happy Mendez and Charlemaine. He kept his movements gentle and unthreatening. He'd move when he needed to; but until then, he didn't want to die just because someone was nervous.

The darker blue hair, the skillful makeup around her eyes and down one side of her face, subtly changed her. Anyone looking for the person who had been at the Night Owl would look straight past this woman.

"Nice disguise, incidentally." It was enough to deflect the eye but not enough to be obviously different.

"Thank you. I learned the technique from you."

Stellan thought about that as they walked in silence. She'd either been stalking him a long time—how much did she know about him, then?—or they had worked together on a job.

He worked alone, but he often had support staff behind him. That meant she'd be one of the support staff. This woman had to be former Roscracian military. She said she had worked with Stellan before. And she believed Markan had let her down.

Was this whole thing a setup to destroy Markan?

"You didn't say what I should call you."

"Cotterill. Neela Cotterill." She paused to look at one of the giant vid screens as Abram Galenos's head replaced the news that had been on. "But you know that. Your friend Markan told you that two days ago."

Did he imagine the bitterness behind the word friend?

"Markan is a friend of mine, yes." Just to see what she'd do.

"He looks after his friends." There was definite bitterness

behind that. "Hands out their jobs personally. Most captains don't get their orders direct from admirals."

It was true that Stellan technically reported to Commodore Paynter, and that most of his jobs came through Paynter's office, but, "Markan and I go way back." All the way back to academy, in fact, and in the first ten years after that initial training they had saved each other's lives so often, Stellan had lost count. "He knows he can trust me."

Up on the big screen, Galenos was surrounded by reporters. Whatever he was saying had the reporters animated, which meant juicy news. "I need to listen to this," Stellan said, and found the channel on his comms. He didn't, but it gave him a chance to thumb a quick emergency message to Markan.

Someone is setting you up. Need a list of everyone you have pissed off and who I have also worked with.

He sent the message—coded as well as he could, which wasn't that well—and then had to listen to the rest of the press conference.

"Routine test," Galenos was saying.

It sounded anything but routine from the media frenzy around him.

"Will you be attacking Gate Union?" one of the reporters asked.

"No. These are standard tests. We are moving the ships, testing the limits of the alien ship systems. The first test took place yesterday. The second will be carried out today."

"So you are ready to attack. What happens if Gate Union retaliates? Are they likely to attack Haladea III again?"

"No," Galenos repeated. "These are simple tests, moving the ships around. Nothing to worry about."

You didn't move ships without captains on them, and the *Gruen* was irretrievably mixed in with the other ships. Somehow. And wasn't Lambert training on the *Gruen* at the moment? Surely the linesmen would be part of this.

Even if Cotterill was setting Markan up, this was his chance to get to Lambert.

He didn't know how many people Cotterill had with her, and if they were all as trigger-happy as Mendez had been, escaping from them might prove deadly. Better to pretend to work with her, then find a quiet place to pick them all off when he was ready. He was an assassin, after all.

Just hope she didn't get a chance to carry out her plan—whatever it was—beforehand.

"Are you absolutely sure you can get us onto the *Gruen*?"

"Of course."

"Now?"

"Of course."

He could pick them off one by one on the shuttle if he needed to. Provided he could convince Song to keep quiet about it. "Tell those thugs of yours to meet us at the spaceport. Edie Song will be heading out to the *Gruen*. We're going with her."

AT the spaceport, Stellan pulled the Aratogan uniforms he'd obtained from Markan out of the locker. Cotterill had seven people with her. Eight soldiers and a team leader. A full team. Coincidental? Or deliberate? He handed around uniforms. They didn't have one large enough for the lumbering giant they called Lahti.

"You'll have to stay," Stellan said. If anyone questioned it, he'd excuse it somehow. Say one of their crew had cracked their head at triball the previous night.

Lahti left without a word. Three minutes later, he was back, an Aratogan uniform in his hands.

"I hope you didn't kill someone for that." It didn't take long to set up a manhunt once a dead body was found. If Lahti ruined this, Stellan would kill him personally and leave him lying in his stolen uniform for the guards to find. Lahti was dead anyway if this was a threat against Markan.

Lahti didn't comment. Cotterill didn't either.

"Let's go."

He triggered the orders that would get them onto the shuttle, then handed out the fake IDs. Cotterill looked the most soldierlike of them all.

Now, to see if he could fool a captain. "Follow me," and he led them at a brisk squad run around the barracks, to the gate where Markan's expensive security told him Edie Song was approaching.

"Captain Song," he called, as they jogged up.

She looked over her shoulder, and paused.

First hurdle passed.

"B-team reporting for duty, ma'am."

She nodded, and continued walking.

Their fake IDs got them past the first guardhouse, and Song let them walk with her toward the shuttle.

Second hurdle passed.

Provided none of his companions gave themselves away.

No one questioned their right to be on the shuttle. Stellan strapped himself in next to the pilot but didn't allow himself to relax until the shuttle was in space.

THE shuttle pilot's name was Jarrad. She was a Ruon. One of the advantages to any multiworld organization, Stellan had found, was that there were lots of handovers. A Ruon shuttle piloted an Aratogan crew out to a ship that was ostensibly owned by Aratoga but could equally be said to be under the control of Lancia. There were always cracks to exploit where the handovers happened.

The skin down Jarrad's right side was fresh and unblemished, and pinker than the left side. She'd had regen, and recently. She'd probably been fighting, been injured, and come in to Haladea III to recover. Which meant she'd still respond to an incident like a soldier on duty.

"I haven't shipped you lot out before," she said to Stellan, as the autopilot fired the jets to correct their course away from planet and toward the *Gruen*. "Does this mean they're finally adding new crew?"

She was blatantly fishing.

Stellan shrugged. "Who knows what the powers that be—" He cut his words off and half glanced around as if he didn't want Song to hear them.

In fact, what he wanted was to see what was going on. It was very quiet back there.

Cotterill was glaring at Song with what in a normal soldier

would be construed as insubordination. Her crew looked at each other uneasily.

Stellan was glad he'd chosen the team-leader uniform for himself. "Cotterill." He made it sharp, clicked off his seat belt, and somersaulted out of his seat as if to discipline her. This had better not be the start of her plans. He didn't want to kill her this early. This was the only chance he'd have to get onto the *Gruen*.

His first kick gave him enough momentum to get to Cotterill's seat. He leaned close, and made it soft, so only she could hear. "What the eff do you think you're doing?"

Jarrad had loosed her seat belt, too, and was hanging with her left hand on one of the support straps. Her right hand was close to her weapon. She was battle-ready, all right. Even if she had spent time in the hospital.

Song sat back in her seat and closed her eyes.

For a moment, Stellan thought he'd have to kill Cotterill then and there. Then she sat back, too.

Stellan went back to his own seat. He would have stayed near Cotterill, except Jarrad was the one they needed to calm most. "Exactly how long is this trip?"

Jarrad buckled up again. "Exactly?"

He nodded.

"Another twenty-four minutes and fourteen seconds."

Stellan's comms chimed. Markan's reply, thankfully not DNA-coded. Stellan scrolled through the list. There were a lot of names. How had Markan gotten it together so quickly? Did he keep a tally of how many people he had upset?

The silence from behind made his back itch.

Jarrad asked brightly, "Anyone watch the triball game last night between the *Han* and the *Greater Perseus Catter*?"

Given they were both military ships, and the game would have been at the barracks, that was unlikely.

Lahti broke the awkward silence. "Grubmann cracked his head open. Still in a coma, isn't he?"

"Did you see what happened? Don't you think it was a foul?"

Lahti shrugged. "All's fair in triball," he said.

"What, waylaying someone like that? It's criminal."

"You play to win."

Stellan almost didn't recognize the cultured voice that joined in. "Do that to someone in the street, and you're up for attempted manslaughter." Captain Song, who had an opinion on triball, at least.

He scrolled through Markan's list. It was long. How could he narrow it down?

Behind him they'd gotten off last night's specific triball game and onto triball in general. Others were joining in. They'd all played triball. Former soldiers, all of them, for triball was still a military game. Cotterill, thank the lines, was silent.

If Cotterill was setting Markan up, she'd be on this list. If he could identify who she was, they could prevent whatever she was planning. What did he know about her that could narrow it down?

He filtered the list on people who were or had been Roscracian military, or who had worked directly for Markan. Cotterill had to be in one of those groups.

It halved the list, but it was still too many.

She'd changed her identity. He filtered his new list on people who had since left the military. That whittled the names down to twenty.

Jarrad said, "Triball is a way to prove your crew is fit. That's why captains encourage you to play it. They love to show other ships how good they are."

"It doesn't show fitness." Cotterill's voice jerked Stellan out of his list. "Although that helps. It shows how well your crew work as a team. That's why captains love it. It allows them to find weaknesses in their crew without those psych tests that demoralize everyone."

If Cotterill had changed her identity, she might have dropped out of sight with her old identity. Stellan added another filter. People who hadn't used their accounts in the last month.

Behind him, Cotterill's voice became sharp. "But you wouldn't know that, would you?" and Stellan knew exactly who she was looking at. "Because you haven't spent any time on your ship or any time with your crew."

"That ship should have been destroyed," Edie Song said. "It's a useless piece of junk sitting out there waiting to—"

Stellan dropped his comms. He knew, even as he drew his weapon, that he was too late, for Cotterill had fired.

He did the one thing that would keep them alive. He turned the blaster on Jarrad. "Don't move."

She paused, hands over the boards, which gave him just enough time to follow up the weapon to the side of her head. Hard enough to knock her out.

"You crazy bitch."

Cotterill was shaking. "She had no right to insult the ship like that."

"How in the lines are we going to get on board now? They won't let us land."

"I can get us on board."

Of course she could, where they'd walk right into a barrage of blaster fire. Even if they let them out, what would they do when they saw Song's body?

Unless they were expecting a body.

"Make it look like we're giving her oxygen," he ordered Lahti. "Hide the blaster burn," and waited until they had done so before he hit the comms.

"This is Team Leader Vangellan on the shuttle 73B, approaching the *Gruen*," and prayed that Markan's aliases would pass the quick glance the people on the ship would give them. "Captain Song has collapsed. We're administering CPR. Please have the medicenter ready to receive her." Thank the lines Jarrad had set the autopilot before they'd had to knock her out.

"What appears to be the problem?" The woman at the other end was a team leader. He recognized her. She was one of those who had rescued Lambert the night Mendez was injured. Her name was Bhaksir.

"It looks like a heart attack," Stellan said.

"Heart attack." Bhaksir sounded mystified. "But she's never shown any sign of—"

Another voice near them said, "There *are* other sorts of heart attack, too, remember."

Lambert. Stellan's heart hammered almost as heavily as Song's would have if she had been having a heart attack. He was close.

"Can't stabilize her, sir," Lahti said from behind him.

Bhaksir looked up at something in the corner of her screen. "Put her on a stretcher. We'll be ready for you."

The shuttle chimed for landing.

"Will do," Stellan said, and clicked off.

Cotterill's crew had a stretcher down and were strapping Song's body onto it. Definitely military, and they worked as a team. Had they been a team once?

Stellan moved Jarrad's unconscious body away from the boards so that Cotterill could take over.

"You'd better be able to do this."

"Of course.

Stellan strapped the pilot into a seat at the rear, and swung himself back to his own seat. As he buckled himself in for the landing, he picked up the comms he'd dropped earlier. There was one name left on the list.

Hilda Gruen.

FORTY-ONE

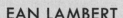

EAN LAMBERT

EAN DIDN'T NEED the lines to tell how the atmosphere on the *Gruen* changed after the emergency call from the shuttle. The air was almost crackling as Bhaksir clicked off her comms. "Anyone heard of Team Leader Vangellan?"

"No." Ru Li didn't add his customary "ma'am." "And no one told us about a change in personnel."

Radko checked her own comms. "It says he's cleared. A whole team."

"Which means we have a security problem somewhere. Ean, we want you." Bhaksir looked around with a frown. "Shuttle bay three," she decided. "In case we need to retreat. Burns, you, too. Radko, Gossamer, Hana, Ru Li. With them."

She looked at the trainees waiting to return on the shuttle. "Hernandez, Klim, Solvej, Chantsmith, Wallace, Tendulkar, Green. You're with me. Weapons on stun. They'll come out attacking, and they won't care who they kill. Ean," for Ean hadn't moved. "Shuttle bay three."

"But you'll have four extra soldiers if we stay here."

Radko grabbed his arm and dragged him away. "The longer we stand here, the less time they'll have to prepare."

He followed reluctantly.

"And the less time we'll have to prepare," she said, once they were down near the third shuttle bay. "We need visuals, Ean."

He sang the visuals for shuttle bay one—where the others were waiting—onto the screen in shuttle three. "What if they are simply who they say they are?"

"Sheesh," Ru Li said. "You've been with us for six months now, and you haven't learned anything."

Radko's look was cold, which warmed Ean. "For that, you

can put the shuttle into warm mode, while Hana and Gossa-mer stand guard."

"I was just saying."

"Sometimes you say too much, Ru Li. Sometimes what you say is uncalled for." She turned to Ean. "They'll be after one of two things. The ship or you. You control the ship, so provided we protect you, we have both covered. Don't try anything heroic. You're welcome to help, but do it the way linesmen do. Through the lines. Don't get in the way of the physical fighting. And when one of us tells you to move, you move."

Ean nodded although he felt a "Yes, ma'am," would be more appropriate.

"Fergus, stick with Ean. Like glue. I don't want to have to hunt for you if we need to run."

Fergus nodded. "I feel I should salute," he whispered to Ean.

Ean did, too. One day, Radko would have her own team, and she'd be the best team leader ever. He would miss her. Much more than he thought he would ever miss anyone. As much as Michelle missed Abram.

FORTY-TWO

SELMA KARI WANG

THE BRIDGE ON the *Eleven* reminded Kari Wang of the bridge on her own ship, when they knew a battle was imminent and were waiting, poised for something to happen but knew it wouldn't for hours yet. Any moment now, she expected Will to turn around and say something in a deadpan voice that would stop the whole crew, then they'd crack up laughing. Will knew how to break the tension.

But Will wasn't here and never would be.

She forced herself to breathe quietly while she listened to the crew match what was on their screens to hers. She'd pulled up the human view of the screens and put an overlay of the alien screens on top. The overlay had the ship names marked—after all, the ships had already been identified—but she hid the names. She wanted to work it out with her crew.

"They're talking to you," Sale explained to the three linesmen. "All you have to do is listen. You recognize them by their song. And their lines."

She might as well have been speaking an unknown language by the way they looked at her. Kari Wang didn't blame them.

Sale indicated the flickering bars on the wall screen. "Which one has a twelve on it?"

They looked blank.

"You're the linesmen," Sale said. She indicated the wall again. "There's only one twelve out there. Pick him out."

Tinatin and Abascal looked to Kari Wang for guidance. Mael simply studied the wall.

Ean Lambert was the only twelve Kari Wang knew of. "Which ship is Lambert on?" she asked.

Their faces cleared.

Tinatin pointed to the brightest flicker. "That one. The lonely ship," and Abascal nodded.

Kari Wang wasn't sure if he was agreeing it was Lambert or agreeing it was a lonely ship. "The *Gruen*?" she asked.

Sale nodded. "You can usually tell the ship Ean's on. It's always bright."

"Loud," Tinatin said.

"You know." Mael put out a hand to touch the flicker. "He really has got twelve lines."

Kari Wang cross-checked the results on her human equipment. The full electromagnetic spectrum, and the comms. Everything confirmed this was the *Gruen*. She linked the *Gruen* on her human view with the overlay of the wall screen, and added a note. "So where's the one with eleven lines?" There were two elevens, and they were sitting in one of them. The other would be the *Confluence*.

Tinatin started to point to another bright flicker, hesitated, and waited for Mael and Abascal to nod before she put her hand close. "That one."

"So the more lines they have, the stronger the display," Kari Wang said.

"No," Sale said. "It's all to do with the crew and seemingly nothing to do with the power of the ship once you get below eleven." She pointed to one of the duller lights on the board. "That's the *Excelsior*."

The *Excelsior* was a massive Alliance fleet carrier, bigger than the *Kari Wang* had been. It was the first ship Kari Wang had come up against on becoming captain. She'd made some mistakes, been lucky to come out of it with her ship intact. Did that mean the *Excelsior* was a poorly run ship? That it was poorly maintained? Or that crew morale was low?

She pinged that one on the human equipment and confirmed it was indeed the *Excelsior*. She marked that on her overlay.

Sale tapped a bright flicker. "That's the *Wendell*"—which was a quarter the size and power of the *Excelsior*, but one of the brightest lights on the board—"and it's been stripped."

Poor Piers Wendell, who'd had a brilliant career in front of him until he'd landed in the wrong place at the wrong time. Kari Wang hoped the *Eleven* shone as brightly as his ship did.

They worked through the ships one by one. The three linesmen couldn't tell her the names of most of the ships, but they could identify them with their own unique song. Kari Wang recorded each song and duly linked and added the records. At least all three had the same song for each ship.

She hoped she could learn the songs enough so that in an emergency, if one of her crew sang the name of the ship to her, she wouldn't waste precious seconds trying to convert it to something she could relate to.

They identified the *Eleven* fleet ships first, then started identifying ships in a radial pattern out from the central flicker that was the ship they were on, moving out in a spiral to collect them all, no matter how far away they were.

Ship by ship. Progress was slow but thorough. The linesmen sang the ship name. Kari Wang recorded it. They identified the ship if they could. Most times they couldn't although Jem Abascal identified a Balian combat ship he had worked on— the *Freedom*—and Mael identified an Aratogan Patrol ship he had worked on—the *Void Cutter*. Kari Wang then checked with the human equipment to confirm the identity of the ship and linked the two. There was a logic to the links, provided you didn't take depth into account on the overlay.

They'd identified some twenty ships when a new flicker appeared on the wall screen between the *Excelsior* and the *Wendell*.

Tinatin clucked with exasperation. "We'll never finish if ships keep jumping in like this."

Mael agreed. "It's probably a million kilometers away."

It had better be a million kilometers away, because Kari Wang didn't like the thought of ships jumping any closer to a fleet, even if it was a stationary fleet. She checked against the human-made equipment to see how far out it was. It wasn't in range.

She fought down sudden panic. She had to see the ship, to identify it. It was irrational, she knew. The ship was simply out of range, but she needed to see it on her screen.

"How far out does the *Eleven* recognize lines?" she asked Sale.

Sale shrugged. "Who knows?" She must have seen something in Kari Wang's face. "I don't know what limits the ships have, but the linesmen themselves have limits. That's two hundred kilometers."

"There's another one," Tinatin said. "They should at least wait until we have them all cataloged."

Sure enough, a second ship was flickering on the wall, moving away from the first one, as if they'd both arrived out of the void close to each other—enough to give one the shivers—and were now moving apart.

Kari Wang checked her own screen. Nothing. She opened her comms to the *Lancastrian Princess*. "Captain Helmo." He could do this faster than she could. "We're registering two ships just arrived in this sector, but here on the *Eleven* we can't work out where they are." She showed him the screen overlay with the two ships. "Can you find out who has arrived, please?"

"I'll let you know."

"Thank you." She clicked off, and tried to still her fast-beating heart. She'd have to get over panicking every time a ship appeared that she couldn't identify. But for the moment, the way to calm herself would be to identify the ships.

Fitch moved close, looking at something registering on his comms. "Your readings have gone off the scale," he murmured quietly. "Do you want me to stop the exercise?"

She shook her head. "Mael, Abascal, Tinatin. I want you to talk to those ships. I want to know everything about them. What you hear, what you see, what you smell. All of you," as they looked at her as if wondering if she was sane. "Go on, start singing."

Tinatin started first. A thin, wavering thread of sound, one eye uncertainly on Kari Wang.

"What's the ship's name?" Kari Wang asked.

Tinatin sang a series of notes. A short series, shorter than the other ships. After a moment Mael picked up the tune, too, then Abascal.

"That's one," Tinatin said. She turned her attention on the other ship. "And the other one is," another series of short notes. "And the other one is," a third series of short notes. "And," a fourth.

Four ships.

"Are you sure?"

Tinatin nodded. "They're together."

"What, together like the *Eleven* fleet?" Sale demanded.

The three linesmen looked at each other.

"No," Mael said, after an interminably long pause, which probably wasn't a pause at all.

Helmo called back. "No ships arrived in the sector in the last hour. Ten ships left."

That was normal. The gate controllers dispatched ships in groups.

"Thank you," Kari Wang said. The pound of blood in her head was the only thing she could hear. Time seemed to slow, like it did in battle.

"So how do you know they are together?" Sale persisted.

"They are," Tinatin said.

Kari Wang opened channels to the *Lancastrian Princess*, the *Wendell*, and the *Gruen*. "We have four unidentified ships showing up on the *Eleven*'s boards. They're not showing up on the human boards."

"Four?" Wendell asked. "What formation?" and she knew he'd picked up the significance.

"We can only see two of them at the moment."

"Three now," Mael said. One of them had moved out from behind the others.

"I want to hear them talking," Sale said to Tinatin.

Tinatin looked blank.

"Positions?" Helmo asked.

Kari Wang sent through the overlay. "No positions yet, just visual on the *Eleven*." Was it a visual? "Aural, rather. Line detected," and felt a surge of satisfaction as she said it. No matter how hard they tried, they couldn't hide from a line ship.

"Whoa," Mael said, nearly losing his feet as the ship echoed her response. Tinatin and Abascal clung to the wall.

"Talking," Sale reminded Tinatin, then snapped her comms open. "Ean."

The override tone cut her off. Bhaksir, through the comms. "Suspected attack on the *Gruen*. Preparing to repel intruders."

"Shit." Sale looked at the comms as if she wanted to throw it at someone, then looked at the three linesmen in front of her. "You," to Abascal. "Line five."

"Seven."

"I don't care if you're line thirteen. Five is the line I want right now. Tell those ships I want to hear them."

Abascal looked as uncomprehending as Tinatin had earlier, but contemptuous, too. "You have no idea how lines work."

"I know they can do this. They've done it before. Tell the *Eleven* you want to hear those comms. Out loud."

"You can't—"

"Just do it, Abascal," Kari Wang said, as her fingers flew over the board, bringing up the visuals on the cameras outside the hull. She knew she wouldn't see anything. They didn't know where the ships were, and the *Kari Wang* cameras hadn't seen anything either. The only way to see a cloaked ship was by comparison against the stars in the background. Unfortunately, you needed someone in a suit in space for that. Not to mention close enough to the ships that they obscured the stars behind them. "Tell the lines you want the communication pushed out on your comms. All of you do it." If anyone was going to make them understand, it would be Tinatin. "You, too," to Sale.

Right now she could have done with one of those linesmen Lambert had been training for months. Or better yet, Lambert himself.

She joined in the request, speaking the words because she didn't know the song. "Ship, channel the ship conversation through the comms." She couldn't identify which ships she meant. She hoped the *Eleven* understood Abascal.

Suddenly, around the bridge a voice poured out in clear, multichannel stereo. It was answered by another.

The second voice was deeper than the first, and Kari Wang didn't understand a word of it, but there was no mistaking the uptrill at the end of each sentence.

Redmond.

FORTY-THREE

EAN LAMBERT

THROUGH THE LINES, Ean could hear and see Bhaksir reporting their situation to Abram. He couldn't see what Abram did, for Abram was on Haladea III, but he heard the alert go through the *Eleven* fleet ships. Except it went through before Abram would have had time, and it was Helmo who sent the alert.

"What's a code yellow?" he asked Radko, as it came through on her comms. On the bridges of the *Lancastrian Princess*, the *Wendell*, and the *Eleven*, all three captains were tense, and as a result the lines were, too.

"Attack warning," she said, but frowned down at her comms. "A warning is normal in a situation like this. But not normally yellow."

"I don't think that's for us."

Sure enough, Abram's alert came through then. It was a situation blue. Behind that, Helmo's calm voice reported that suspected enemy ships were somewhere in the sector, position unknown. Situation yellow.

"At least they won't be here," Ru Li muttered. "With the security we have around the fleet, no one can get closer than a million kilometers."

Ean forebore to point out the enemy in the shuttle.

"Change of plan," Bhaksir said. "We're not letting them off the shuttle. Ean," and Ean was pleased to see that she didn't bother opening the comms to talk to him, "override the shuttle. Don't let it land. You, you," to Hernandez and Solvej, "get up to the bridge and man the weapons boards. You," to Klim, "likewise, on the comms. I want to see where those ships are."

They left at a run.

Ean obediently sang line eight and three. *"No doors. Don't let them on."*

Bhaksir opened her comms. "This is the *Gruen* calling the shuttle. Permission to dock refused."

Ean heard, clear through line one, "We'll see about that," before someone on the shuttle overrode his locks.

Overrode it.

Followed by a joyous song from the ship lines, welcoming the speaker home. *"Ship's back."*

Ean didn't fight it. It wasn't fair to pull the ship between two people like that. "Bhaksir," then grabbed his comms, because he was so flustered he'd forgotten she couldn't hear him if he didn't direct it somewhere. "Bhaksir. I can't stop the shuttle."

"Shuttle has landed," Chantsmith said. "Cycling in air."

"Can you keep the door locked?" Bhaksir asked Ean.

"I'm not sure." Would the *Gruen* think he had betrayed its lines if he did? "I can't, sorry."

"Twenty seconds to all clear on the air lock," Chantsmith said.

At least Bhaksir didn't waste time demanding why he couldn't. "Hernandez, Solvej, Klim. Get back here. We're undermanned." She indicated to the crew she had with her. Her gesture was clear. Under cover.

"They won't get there in time," Radko said. "We'll be outnumbered."

While they sat here hiding.

Radko twitched. They all did.

"Go," Ean said. "Don't stay for us."

At shuttle bay one, Bhaksir and the people around them raised their weapons to the door of the air lock.

"Keep the door closed. Please," Ean sang. *"Lock them in the shuttle."*

"We can't lock Ship out. Ship's part of us."

Ean realized who it had to be.

Gruen.

He sang the comms open as he took off, running, to stop them. "Don't shoot her," to anyone and everyone who had a comms. It came out through the speakers as well. What would a line ship do if its supposed friends destroyed a living part of the ship like that? He didn't want to find out. The ship was likely to go crazy.

Radko overtook him as they reached bay one. "Get back, Ean." But she didn't stop, just kept running and pushed in front of him. She stopped at the entry.

Ean ran into her.

Bhaksir's people had found every bit of cover they could. Their weapons were trained on the people who had exited the shuttle.

Everyone was momentarily frozen.

There were two women. One in front, with dark blue hair tipped blond, and a taller, bulkier woman toward the back, big enough so that the man behind her was blocked. The taller woman moved, and the man behind her moved also, using her body as protection.

Ean tried to push past, but Radko blocked him.

Neither woman looked like Ean's memory of Hilda Gruen, but Gruen had been small. She had to be the one in front. Gruen's weapon moved to center on Radko, and her finger tightened on the trigger.

"Captain Gruen," Ean said, hurriedly. "Don't shoot." Not Radko. He tried to push past again. Radko didn't budge. "We'll give you your ship. *Just please don't shoot.*" The last was through the lines, for if it was Gruen, she'd listen to her ship even if she didn't listen to humans.

FORTY-FOUR

SELMA KARI WANG

"REDMOND." FITCH'S HOARSE whisper broke the quiet on the bridge.

Kari Wang nodded grimly. She should have been surprised, but she wasn't. Who else but the people who'd built the experimental weapons system on the *Kari Wang* would have such a vested interest in destroying it, and anything like it.

Fitch bolted from the bridge.

She couldn't spare a linesman. "Jon, can you see if he's all right." Fitch, being a doctor, had probably never been in battle before.

Jon nodded and followed Fitch out.

The ships spread out. Kari Wang could see three of them, close now to equidistant points apart.

Where was the fourth ship?

Above or below the *Eleven*, the same distance away. They wouldn't have jumped close to the ships, because even though Gate Union knew by now that the alien-fleet ships would avoid other ships, they wouldn't trust that knowledge any more than the New Alliance did. So, it would take time to come in close enough. Not much time, though. Three of the ships looked close to position.

"They'll have to uncloak." She'd thought about it long and hard. They'd only reveal themselves when they had to. "They can't fire cloaked. Once they're uncloaked, whoever is in the center of that tetrahedron has less than three minutes before the Masson field destroys their lines."

She realized she was whispering consolation to her ship. "It's fine. We'll be all right. They're nowhere near us."

She didn't believe it.

The ships were forming a tetrahedron around the *Eleven*.

They'd never escape if the ships loosed their Masson field on them. The *Eleven* would have to jump before the Redmond ships opened the field. It was time to use the jump Galenos had acquired for them. She reached for her comms.

The chatter through the lines was interrupted by another Redmond uptrill.

Kari Wang went cold. This time the voice was familiar.

Fitch.

Not something she could bother about now. Not when their ship was about to be destroyed. Kari Wang called Lambert.

He didn't answer. Damn him.

She called Lambert's comms again. And Bhaksir's. And Radko's. "Override it," she said to the *Eleven*. "Keep calling until they answer."

FORTY-FIVE

EAN LAMBERT

STALEMATE.

"Why should I believe you?"

The blue-haired woman *was* Gruen.

Ean tried to push past the immovable barrier Radko had become. "We know more about the ships now; about how captains interact with them. We won't take that away from you."

Ean's comms signaled. He ignored it.

"*You* took my ship away from me."

"I did." His back was soaked with sweat. What if he couldn't convince Gruen? What if he convinced Gruen, but Abram didn't agree to it? He'd have to. What if someone fired before Ean could talk Gruen round? "I didn't realize what I was doing."

Radko's comms sounded. Bhaksir's, too. Then the ship alert.

Radko didn't move. Bhaksir felt, one-handed, for her comms.

Ean sang the comms open, through the speakers, so everyone could hear, and Bhaksir didn't need to waste a hand.

It was Kari Wang. "I need Lambert. I need to move the *Eleven*."

"We're kind of busy right now," Ean said. He knew the lines would pass it back to her.

"I don't care. Any moment now, four Redmond ships will uncloak, and when they do, they're going to unleash a Masson field on my ship. They'll destroy the lines. I'm moving, with or without you."

Was she aware it was the first time she had called it her ship? She might not be, but the *Eleven* was.

He became aware of the activity on the bridges of the

Lancastrian Princess, the *Wendell*, and the *Eleven*. Tense, preparing for battle.

Gruen said something he didn't hear. The man at the back, the one hiding behind the woman, changed his stance.

"Don't move," Bhaksir said to him. "Or I'll blow you away."

He stopped.

"Ean," Sale said, through the comms and the lines. "We are this close to getting chopped into little pieces."

Ean nodded. "Fergus," because he wanted the lines linked. He started to sing. Fergus's baritone joined him.

Through the lines, Ean heard Wendell's second-in-command, Grayson, say just before Helmo's navigator did, "Four ships uncloaked. Positions," a string of figures. "Surrounding the *Eleven* in a typical regular tetrahedron."

They'd make a Masson field, like they had for the *Kari Wang* and the Ruon university ship. They'd destroy the lines. Ean didn't have time to think where to go. *"Jump,"* he told the Eleven. *"Somewhere safe."*

The *Eleven* jumped.

FORTY-SIX

SELMA KARI WANG

THE SCREENS CHANGED as Kari Wang felt the momentary twitch that signified they had entered the void and exited again.

Through the comms channels, crew on the *Lancastrian Princess* and the *Wendell* finished listing positions of the Redmond ships. Wendell's voice over Grayson's said to someone—presumably on weapons—"Fire at will, and remember you only have six shots, so don't waste them."

Hadn't they moved?

"Safe." It was a whisper in her mind.

Helmo's dispassionate voice cut in over the top of the others. "The *Eleven* has jumped. Gunners, set your targets."

Another voice cut in. Kari Wang couldn't tell whether it was from the *Lancastrian Princess* or the *Wendell*. "Ships identified. GU *Byers*, GU *Haralampiev*, GU *van Andringa*, and GU *Akaki*."

"If that's the *van Andringa*, then I'm a bona fide loyal Lancastrian." Wendell's voice. "Those ships are half the size of the *van Andringa*."

"Redmond ships jumping now," Helmo's navigator said, almost drowned out by a collective whoop from the crew on the *Wendell*. "Got one of the bastards."

Wendell hadn't lost any of the skills that made him and his crew famous.

"Three Redmond ships jumped," the navigator corrected. "Fourth ship damaged."

Kari Wang couldn't see the Redmond ships anywhere, and they weren't flickering on the *Eleven*'s screens. But then, the ships had jumped. Hadn't they?

They'd failed. In another two minutes, the field would surround them, slice through the ship.

"Safe."

In fact, there weren't any ships on the screens at all. Human or alien screen. And Helmo had said the *Eleven* had jumped.

"Where in the lines are we?" Sale demanded.

Kari Wang brought up the image from outside the ship and scrolled through the external cameras so they got a three-dimensional view.

"Holy Jackson and—" Mael cut off the rest. "Wherever we are, I bet we're the first humans who've been here."

There were still unexplored areas of their own galaxy, but even out on the rim you could always find something familiar to take a reading from, even if it was a long way away. This time, Kari Wang knew—even before the puny human screens they had on the *Eleven* told her—that they wouldn't identify anything out here.

They were a long, long way from human-occupied space.

"Mael," Kari Wang said. "Run every test you can. I want to know if there's anyone in this space except us."

The chatter from the other ships continued, clear and in real time. Kari Wang opened her comms. "Piers, Marcus. Can either of you read where I am?"

"Sorry, Selma," Wendell said. "We know that you've moved, but we don't know where. You're still real-time, so you're in the same sector."

There was no way she was in the same sector anymore.

Mael confirmed it then. "We're getting feeds from the *Lancastrian Princess*, the *Wendell*, the *Gruen*, Confluence Station, one Blue Sky Media news ship and one Galactic News ship. Other than that, there are no human signals at all."

"Feeds from ships linked to the *Eleven* only," Sale said.

"Wendell, Lancastrian Princess," Kari Wang said. "Can you confirm your positions please?"

Both ships were exactly where they had been before. Orbiting Haladea III.

Kari Wang looked around the bridge. Her own crew were silent, watching her.

Two of Sale's team arrived back, dragging an unconscious Fitch. Kari Wang had almost forgotten about him. Jon followed, looking somber.

Sale scowled at the alien boards. Most of them were bare

of other ships now, but one board still showed six ships nearby. Since they weren't in the same sector, but were still communicating clearly with the other *Eleven* ships, that had to be the comms board. "You know this is impossible."

"Obviously not," Kari Wang said. Take away the impossible, and you were only left with the possible.

Sale's scowl deepened. "And I swear those ships look different." She turned away. "They look brighter without other ships around them."

She was right. They did seem to glow more.

"They are brighter," Abascal said. "Can't you hear line seven. It's loud."

FORTY-SEVEN

EAN LAMBERT

"KEEP SINGING," EAN said to Fergus. "The *Eleven*'s still with us." That part of the experiment had worked. Would they lose the *Eleven* if Fergus stopped singing?

"You promise me my ship," Gruen said, and Ean had to force himself to remember what they were talking about. "How can you—a linesman—do that?"

Through the lines, he heard Helmo. "Captain Kari Wang. Status report."

"We're fine for the moment." Kari Wang was as clear as if she hadn't moved.

"Good. The Masson field has dissipated."

Ean was the only one who saw her sink down onto the Captain's Chair as if her legs wouldn't hold her anymore, the only one who heard her whisper, "Well done, Ship."

The only one to hear the smug wash of pleasure back from the *Eleven*.

On her stool, Kari Wang smiled.

Maybe not the only one.

"I don't know where we are," Kari Wang said. "Patching through some images. Can you see them?"

Ean heard awe as Helmo and Wendell looked at what came through, while Bhaksir answered Gruen. "If Linesman Lambert offers you captaincy of a ship, then the New Alliance will do what it can to expedite that."

Abram and Michelle would kill him.

"Of course," Bhaksir said, "there will be restrictions. For example, we will choose your crew. And your ship will be made safe."

"Define safe."

"No weapons. Limited access. Much like Captain Wendell has."

Wendell had weapons now. Not many, true, but he had some. He'd just used them.

"You castrated Wendell, and now you want to do the same to me."

Even Ean knew how to answer that. "Then you don't get your ship." Under his breath he sang to the ship lines. *"Don't worry. This is normal bargaining. We won't take Ship away from you."* Ship in this case being the sound he had for the *Gruen*, amended to include the sound that was distinctly Hilda Gruen with it. Gruen would understand the context of his message—not to worry—but not the actual words.

He hoped.

"And you must promise no harm to Lambert," Bhaksir said. "It was you, wasn't it, the other day in the square? And afterward, at the barracks."

"I wasn't planning on killing him. I needed him to get to my ship."

"Your man nearly killed him anyway."

Gruen shrugged.

He became aware that Sale was talking to him. "Are you still around, Ean? You're awfully quiet."

"We're still a little busy here." He opened a comms on the *Eleven* and sang the feed from the *Gruen* shuttle bay to it. He did the same for the *Lancastrian Princess* and the *Wendell*. The other captains might as well know who was joining the fleet.

"*I* promise not to harm Lambert," Gruen said. "For as long as I have my ship, at least."

"You and everyone here on this ship now," Bhaksir said. "You vouch for them all. You guarantee it."

No one could miss Gruen's hesitation.

"I vouch for them all," and she turned her weapon on the man at the back and fired.

One quick movement, less than a second, but he was already moving. He pushed the woman in front of him into the blaster fire. As he moved, he turned his blaster on Radko, who was in front of Ean. His finger tightened. "No." It was an instinctive, protective movement, and six line eights—and probably 130 more if Ean thought about it—moved together to repel the danger.

The stranger was thrown up and away, back into the shuttle bay, where he came to rest with a clang against the exterior of the shuttle. He dropped to the floor. Ean recognized him then. The smooth-talking civilian who'd wanted to "talk" to him although he looked different now.

THE smell of blistered paint and melted plastic filled the area. All the damage was close to the stranger, as if the eights hadn't just repelled the man, they'd repelled the blast as well.

"Anyone hurt?" Bhaksir sounded breathless.

"I forgot you could do that," Radko said. "Thanks, Ean." She sounded a little breathless herself.

"No one else harmed," Gossamer said.

"Good." Bhaksir turned her blaster back to Gruen's people. "Put down your weapons."

They did, with alacrity. Ru Li and Hana moved in to collect them. Gruen didn't notice. She was busy inspecting the damage the blaster had done to *her* ship.

Somewhere in the aftermath, Fergus had stopped singing. Ean had a moment's anxiety. "*Eleven*," before he realized the beat of the *Eleven* was as strong as ever. "Sale?"

"If you're finally done," Sale said. "We'd like to come home. There are no other humans but us for what feels like a billion parsecs."

Ean knew suddenly, instinctively, how to do it. Or had the lines been telling him all along and he simply hadn't realized? He sang, to the *Eleven*'s line seven—to all the sevens, *"Come home."*

"Wait," Radko said. "What about the debris from the Redmond ship?"

It was too late. The *Eleven* was home.

FORTY-EIGHT

✦

EAN LAMBERT

THEY MET IN the large meeting room on the *Lancastrian Princess*, where Helmo and Abram had first presented evidence of the alien ship all those months ago.

The room wasn't full as it had been that day. There were some new faces. Piers Wendell and his second-in-command, Marc Grayson. Kari Wang and her second-in-command, Mael St. Mael. Commodore Jiang Vega. Admirals Jita Orsaya and Marsh MacClennan. Linesmen Fergus Burns and Jordan Rossi.

Plus the people who had been there that first time. Abram, Michelle, Katida, Helmo. Helmo's second, Vanje Solberg, and Michelle's assistant, Lin Anders.

They hadn't invited Hilda Gruen, not that she would have left her ship.

The lines made a choir in Ean's head. The *Eleven* fleet ships were a contented burble of sound. They had captains; the captains were happy. Far happier than you could tell from watching their faces around the table. Watching them you'd have thought the constrained energy they displayed was a sign of impatience.

Underneath all that were the lines of the *Confluence* fleet, niggling a little about their own lack of captains.

Even Abram cracked a smile as he sat back. "Dr. Fitch has confirmed he was working for Redmond. He was to eliminate Captain Kari Wang because of what she knew about the weapons system. He framed Dr. Arnoud so he—Fitch—would be included in Kari Wang's party instead, and he's been trying to kill her ever since."

"His grandparents came from Redmond," McClennan said. "Their whole family spied for them. He'd been indoctrinated in their cause from an early age." He scowled. "Pity. He was a good doctor."

If the music of the lines was anything to go by, both Kari Wang and McClennan were upset about Fitch.

"We also recovered two bodies and the database from the ship Wendell destroyed. We have positively identified both of the dead as Redmond citizens. We're still ascertaining the name of the ship." Abram grimaced at that. "The ship had a dozen different IDs, some of them Gate Union, some New Alliance. Judging from the information in the database about the *Kari Wang* and her crew, we suspect they always intended to destroy the *Kari Wang* once the testing was finished. The whole thing had been planned well before the creation of the New Alliance."

No one looked surprised.

It didn't make sense. "Why would they do it?" Ean asked. "Redmond, I mean. Against their allies."

"They're uneasy allies, at best," Orsaya said. "There have been other incidents where Redmond has gone against Gate Union."

Like an earthquake at Shaolin that destroyed a line factory.

"Maybe they're close to believing they can go it alone. After all, they do control the future supply of lines."

Ean shivered. Even if they solved the problem of getting jumps, ships would wear out. If Redmond controlled supply of the lines, the war would just be put off for a decade. Still, if Redmond was alienating itself from Gate Union, it left Gate Union in the same predicament as the New Alliance.

Except Gate Union still controlled the jumps, and so far as they knew, Redmond didn't have the ability to jump cold.

In ten years, everyone might be able to do it.

Abram blew out his breath in a slow, controlled gust. "Some good has come out of this. Thanks to Captain Wendell, we have the remnants of what appears to be the weapon they used to build the Masson field."

"Unfortunately, they destroyed any evidence of the cloaking device." Helmo said it straight-faced, but Ean could hear the lines singing underneath.

"We can't do *all* your work for you," Wendell said.

Abram let the pause go on just long enough. "It appears Redmond was trying to destroy anyone who might recognize their technology. The Masson field, the honeycomb design on the new ships. The *Kari Wang* had to go, of course. They were testing their weapons."

"It wasn't weapons," Kari Wang said. "It was the weapons system."

Ean looked over at her. She hadn't slept since the battle—he knew that from observing the *Eleven*—but there was a peace about the ship and its lines, as if she had finally come to terms with herself.

"So Redmond has alien technology," Katida said. She was white and drawn, as if she'd stayed awake longer than Kari Wang had, with only depressing thoughts for company. Even her lines were damped. "How many alien ships are out there?"

"So far, no more than those we know about," Abram said. "We think they got their plans from the *Havortian*."

"Surely, we've learned everything we can from the *Havortian* already," Orsaya said. "Gila Havortian took her plans to Redmond, yes, but you can't tell me they've been sitting on this knowledge for five hundred years." Orsaya had studied lines and linesmen with a passion bordering on obsession. She would have known what was publicly available.

Abram tapped his comms to bring something up on the main screen. "May I present to you, Admiral, the schematics of the *Havortian*."

"Damn." They all politely ignored the sudden glitter in Orsaya's eyes and the tremor in her voice. "Where did you get this?"

"From Professor Gerrard's research." Abram smiled over at Ean. "As you yourself said, Orsaya, it was his passion. He discovered where the *Havortian* was found in human space."

"Damn."

Abram tapped his comms. "It was towed to a shipyard and sold as scrap metal. Luckily for us, the shipyard kept records. This is what it looked like." He stopped at an external image of the ship, a series of linked hexagons. "Does this look familiar?"

"The *MacIntyre*," Wendell said.

The *Eleven* was made up of linked hexagons, too, but

Wendell was right. The ship on screen didn't look like the *Eleven*, it looked like the GU *MacIntyre*, whose lines Ean had once mended.

"They broke it apart and sold it." Abram tapped the screen again. On this image the hexagons had been broken into single components. There were three in the picture. "Landing date 82.189," Abram read. "Scrap metal sold to Kai Javed. Composition—" He didn't read out the composition.

Everyone knew the story from there. Javed's son had sold the most famous piece of scrap in the galaxy to trader Havortian, who'd used it to mend his own ship, and whose daughter had talked to the lines. At least, Ean believed Gila Havortian had.

"Gerrard's other passion was dark matter," Abram said. "It's expensive to research. We don't know if Redmond approached him or he approached them. What we do know is that five years ago, someone put up the money for his research, and he never mentioned the *Havortian* again."

Ean said, "He spent five years saying nothing. Why kill him now?"

"According to the University of Ruon, funding was due to run out," Abram said. "Maybe he asked for more money, threatened to take his information elsewhere if they didn't give it to him."

"Or they were done with their planning and research," Orsaya said. "And simply wanted everyone with knowledge about their ships and their weapons gone."

Ean shivered. People were so ready to kill other people to keep secrets.

"More proof, perhaps, that Redmond is ready to split with Gate Union," Orsaya added. "Because they definitely didn't pass that knowledge on to Gate Union. Even though they got them to pay for the tests." Her eyes glittered with a different kind of emotion.

Katida said, "If they're ready, they must think they have five years' knowledge of line ships over us. Enough to win a war. Against us. Against Gate Union."

"But they don't have our linesmen," Orsaya said. "And they don't know yet that they need them."

Orsaya and Katida both grinned. They could have been twins.

FORTY-NINE

STELLAN VILHJALMSSON

MARKAN WAS SITTING by Stellan's bed, scowling as he scrolled through his comms, when Stellan woke.

"How long?"

"Three days." Markan put his comms away. "You look like you got caught in a stampede of mammoths."

"It was a shuttle." Or would you blame the linesman? Stellan moved, and found he was strapped down. He couldn't feel his body. "Am I crippled?" He couldn't stop the surge of panic. It set off an alarm. A medic came over to check him.

"Luckily, no, but you've broken bones, and you're concussed. You're doped to the eyeballs because they don't want you to move yet."

Eyeballs might have been literal. Or maybe only to his neck, because he could talk.

"I hope you don't plan on doing that again," Markan said. "Sending rescuers won't work a third time. It almost didn't work the second."

Stellan tried to nod, couldn't move his head.

"You owe your life to the New Alliance doctor we almost killed getting to you. She could have sounded the alarm. Instead, she made sure they stabilized your head and your back when they carried you out. Our doctors said that if she hadn't, you'd have died."

Markan must have expended a lot of resources to get him out.

"You've fifteen minutes before the drugs they've pumped into you take effect. What can you tell me?"

"I didn't get any information from Lambert."

"A blind man could see that."

"You should have left me there."

"You know too much, Stellan."

There was a solution to that. It usually involved an assassin and a lethal injection or some deadly gas. Or a well-placed poison-tipped projectile.

"You'll be off active duty for months," Markan said. "Which solves our immediate problem of an assassin who can't kill, whose career as a kidnapper tanked before it started. What in the lines happened, Stellan? Give me something out of this fiasco I can use. Otherwise, I'm in as much trouble as you are."

What was fact and what was conjecture? "Hilda Gruen hates you." That was fact.

Markan goggled at him. "What has that got to do with alien spaceships and linesmen? And for the record, I know that. She thinks I should have gotten her ship back for her. I can't do the impossible."

"She's got her ship back now, and she's agreed to work with the New Alliance." Lambert had promised that, backed up by the team leader called Bhaksir. If a team leader and a linesman had any say at all.

"Gruen." Markan pfft'd disbelievingly. "They wouldn't take her."

"They will. On Lambert's say-so." Unless Lambert was the greatest con artist of all time. In which case Gruen was probably rotting in a jail right now.

But if she truly was captain, how could a linesman decree who got to be captain of a line ship? Or was that a stupid question, given his own condition?

"They're learning things from those ships. Useful things. Like this." He tried to indicate his own battered body, could only move his chin.

"They've got a weapon on the ship that did that to you?" Markan looked excited.

Who wouldn't? A weapon like that might justify what he had done.

"I didn't see a weapon. I was going for Lambert's bodyguard. Next thing this"—wave, or force, or noise—"wall of something comes at me and punches me away."

"You couldn't see the actual weapon?"

Stellan tried to shake his head.

"So it's on the alien ship."

"We were on the *Gruen*."

"So they're modifying human ships."

Were they? No, for wouldn't Bhaksir have used the force earlier if she could? Plus, it didn't explain how Lambert could offer Gruen a ship and have a simple team leader back up his promise.

"You were right to go after Lambert." Maybe they were modifying the linesmen. "He learned something from those ships." Maybe that's what the line training was about. "Although next time let's go for someone easier." Like the linesmen they had been training. Or even, "Fergus Burns knew something."

"Linesman Rossi?"

"I didn't see him at all. He was busy fixing ships most of the time, and when he wasn't, he was in a secure area on Confluence Station."

"Burns it is, then." Markan looked disappointed. Stellan shook his head, or tried to, but he was strapped down and couldn't. Even that made everything go black for a moment. He gritted his teeth.

"You also have a security problem in your department."

"I've already worked that out. I know who it will be. Carver Albanesi, who came from the *Gruen*."

The drugs Markan had mentioned earlier were starting to kick in. Stellan forced himself awake. There was one more thing he had to say.

Markan stood up. "I'll talk to you again later."

"Markan."

"It can wait, Stellan."

"Those ships that destroyed the *Kari Wang*."

"The supposed Gate Union ships. What a setup that was."

"It was a setup all right. Setting you up. They were from Redmond, pretending to be Gate Union. We've got a problem, Markan, and it's not the New Alliance. It's our own supposed allies."

The dawning horror on Markan's face was the last thing Stellan saw before unconsciousness overtook him.

FIFTY

EAN LAMBERT

EAN WENT DOWN to Haladea III with Michelle and Fergus to close the deal Rickenback had brokered with Rigel. They'd brought Fergus along to reassure Rickenback, who was still uneasy about the deal.

Captain Gruen had confessed to being behind the two attacks against Ean, so it was considered relatively safe.

"What about Vilhjalmsson?" Vega demanded. Vega was accompanying them, along with Bhaksir's team. "According to Gruen, he was to take Lambert to some quiet place and question him about the lines. He has escaped."

Abram was there, too. It was the first time Ean had seen Michelle and Abram together, and relaxed, in ages. "He's lucky to be alive. He won't bother us for a while."

Ean hadn't meant to nearly kill Vilhjalmsson, but he shouldn't have fired at Radko.

"And he taught us something new," Michelle said. "Line eight deflected the blaster fire as well as Vilhjalmsson. We didn't know it could do that."

She and Abram shared a smile.

"Markan may send someone else, however," Abram said.

Vega's frosty look said she had that under control.

"Is anyone trying to attack Ean likely to succeed?" Fergus asked.

They all laughed. Except Ean. There couldn't be anyone left who wanted to kidnap him, surely.

THE private dining room where they met was twenty blocks and a world away from the Night Owl. It was part of the Lancian ambassador's residence, built into the side of the mountain, with stone balconies from which you could see the city and all the way down to the sea.

The ambassador met them with a low bow. "Your Royal Highness. Such an honor."

He made it sound like an unexpected event, yet Ean knew that Michelle had dined with him three times in the last two weeks, discussing political issues.

"Ambassador Xun," Michelle said, gracious and royal. "Thank you for extending your residence to us for this meeting."

Wasn't that what an ambassador's residence was for? As a de facto extension of the royal house of Lancia, wasn't this really Michelle's house? Or her father's, anyway.

The ambassador turned to Radko next. "My Lady Dominique." His bow wasn't as low.

"Ambassador," Radko said, inclining her head.

It proved one thing. Radko *was* related to Michelle.

"Dominique?" Ean asked quietly, as the ambassador turned to Abram.

"Use that name, Ean, and it'll be line eight all over again."

He put his hands up in mock surrender, the way Rossi did when Radko looked at him after Rossi had said something insulting to Ean, then put his hands behind his back as the ambassador looked at him. He tried to make it look like Abram's "at ease" stance.

"The Lancastrian linesman," Michelle said. "Ean Lambert."

Ean got a small bow. "Delighted, I am sure," Ambassador Xun said.

Ean nodded in return.

Fergus got a bow, too.

Xun provided drinks—chilled Lancian wine—and fresh Gippian shellfish, a delicacy from Lancia. The shellfish darkened the longer they were out of the water. These were a delicate pale mauve. Ean had heard of them, but he'd never eaten them before.

"Caught this morning," Xun assured him.

Michelle came up to take one and slide it out of the shell, into her mouth, and down her throat in a single swallow.

"They're exceptionally fresh," she said. "I'm surprised you can get them so quickly."

Xun laughed complacently. "I have my sources." He turned

away as an aide came in to tell him the cartel masters had arrived, so he didn't see the glance that passed between Abram and Michelle.

Ean knew what it was for. Those sources wouldn't be New Alliance because New Alliance ships wouldn't be able to guarantee same-day delivery from another world. He turned to the table, trying not to think about the next few minutes.

Gippian shellfish, he decided, were an acquired taste.

"I haven't tasted these in months," Fergus said, and ate two with obvious enjoyment.

Ean washed the taste out of his mouth with good Lancian wine and turned to greet Rigel and Rickenback. Kaelea tagged along, looking almost as glamorous as Rebekah Grimes had the first night Ean had met Rebekah.

Rigel bowed over Michelle's hand. "Delighted, Your Royal Highness," and shook Abram's and Vega's hands heartily, as if he'd known them a long time.

"My Lady Dominique," Xun introduced next.

Rickenback looked at her. "Radko?" and got a dimpled smile in return.

"And you know the Lancastrian linesmen Fergus Burns and Ean Lambert," Xun said.

"We do," Rickenback agreed. His handshake for Ean was warm. Fergus got the same half hug he'd gotten last time.

Then Ean was face-to-face with Rigel.

"You're looking well." Rigel was more formal, more correct than Rickenback.

"I could say the same for you." Although it was a lie. Rigel obviously hadn't slept much recently.

Rigel smiled, and his smile said he knew it was a lie.

Michelle rescued Ean. "Cartel Master, you must try some Gippian shellfish. It's fresh today."

"Thank you," and Rigel ate while he and Michelle chatted about how his cartel house was coping during this time of change.

Kaelea stopped in front of Ean.

"Hello, Kaelea," Ean said, conscious of Radko stiff and disapproving beside him.

"You're making a mistake, Ean," Kaelea said. "Linesmen belong in the cartel houses."

"Not me, Kaelea." He belonged with the line ships.

She stepped forward, and said softly, "I'll save you, Ean. I'll get you out of here. Somehow."

The words were so unexpected, he had to translate them in his head to be sure he'd heard her correctly.

Radko stepped forward. Ean waved her back. "Thank you, Kaelea." He took both her hands in his, and kissed them. "But I don't need rescuing."

He was aware of both Michelle and Radko watching.

"I'm happy here."

She gripped his fingers tightly. "I know what will happen if you try to go home." It was still soft. "I'll get you out of here. Somehow."

"Kaelea."

She moved away, over to where Ambassador Xun was helping himself to another Gippian shellfish, and was soon talking to the ambassador.

Fergus, Abram, and Vega talked to Rickenback.

Ean watched her for a while, then turned his own attention to the conversation nearby. Michelle and Rigel.

"And your linesmen," Michelle asked. "Are you building up to the higher lines again? One of your apprentices is an eight, isn't he? Or is it she?"

Ean had told her once that Rigel had an eight as an apprentice. He wasn't sure Rigel knew that yet.

"I . . . I'm thinking about it," Rigel admitted. He faked a jovial laugh. "After all, I have some money at present. I may try for one of the tens at the lesser houses."

"Why don't you try for one of the higher houses?" Michelle suggested. "I hear some of them are struggling."

Rickenback must have been listening, for Ean saw his expression glaze. Based on what Rossi had said, that ten might even come from House of Rickenback, for according to Rossi, being Grand Master was sending Leo Rickenback broke. Fergus hadn't confirmed it when Rossi said it, but he didn't deny it, either.

Ean left them talking and wandered out onto the balcony. Halfway up the cliff like this, the wind was strong. He enjoyed the feel. This was the third time he'd been on world since Michelle had obtained his contract. He missed the open spaces, and the breeze, and the way you could see all the way to the horizon. But he wouldn't exchange the line ships for it.

"Six months ago, this was a different world," Rigel said, from behind him.

Ean glanced around. They were alone. Which meant that everyone had decided they should have time to talk. He smiled faintly at that. Even private conversations were orchestrated this high on the tree. One day, it might bother him. Today, he accepted it.

"I never got a chance to thank you. For training me. For protecting me from the other linesmen. For giving me a chance to certify."

"You always knew what you were, Ean." Rigel leaned on the balcony beside him. "I knew what you were by then, too." He smiled, and it was the first real smile Ean had ever seen from him. "And it was nice to shove it in Paretsky's face when we got you certified." He turned away from the view, to lean back against the railings. "It wasn't bad doing it this time, either, although that wouldn't have happened if it hadn't been for Leo Rickenback. I'm still not sure it was the wisest thing."

"So why did you do it?"

Rigel laughed. "Money, pure and simple." He turned back to the view. "And future proofing. Once this war is over, Lancia will be a power again."

"Many people don't think that." Most people thought Lancia would be a defeated nobody.

"Families like the Yus. Worlds like Lancia. They don't stay down long."

That was a different attitude.

"And I have an in now."

"I'm not sure—"

"Not you, Ean. Lady Lyan. She paid a lot of money for your contract."

Ean hadn't asked how much Michelle had agreed to pay. He wasn't sure he wanted to know.

"She knows how good you are. I'm the cartel master who sold her your contract. She'll acknowledge me now."

She would, too, for Michelle was like that when she wanted to be.

"Give me ten years, Ean, and I'm in a good place. Provided I survive internal line politics."

Ean was glad. "I'm in a good place, too, Rigel. Can you tell Kaelea that, please? Make sure she understands." He didn't want Kaelea trying to help when he didn't need it. "Please."

"Of course I will," Rigel said, then looked up as Michelle came out to join them.

"Ambassador Xun is serving dinner."

They went in together.